The Fugitive Mind

Brian Jones

Published by

An Imprint of Melrose Press Limited
St Thomas Place, Ely
Cambridgeshire
CB7 4GG, UK
www.melrosebooks.com

FIRST EDITION

Cover designed by Jeremy Kay

ISBN 978 1 906561 81 9

Printed and bound in Great Britain by:
CPI Antony Rowe. Chippenham, Wiltshire

I'd like to dedicate this book to Julian

Contents

Chapter 1
The Reverend Magnus Robertson

Tom Merrington thought he was an average twelve-year old. He certainly had no reason to believe that he was gifted in any way. At school, he was quite good at some subjects and not so good at others, although some of his teachers, and his parents, thought he could do a lot better if he tried harder. He enjoyed having fun with his friends, and he frequently got into trouble, like most boys of his age. But soon, unknown to him or his family, his life would change dramatically. He would unwillingly develop a talent that would get him into more trouble than he could imagine; in fact, he would have to risk his life. But for the moment, he was safe.

Tom lived in the old Vicarage, next to the churchyard of St. Peter's Church, Drumbridge. He was in the churchyard one evening with his friend, Frank McGinty, when they saw old Mrs Bratherstone tottering towards them, flourishing her walking stick in an attempt to hurry her old frame towards the boys.

Frank saw her coming. 'Oh, here we go again – another lecture from Mrs Bratherstone on its way. What's she going to tell us off for now?'

'Why do you boys spend so much time in the graveyard? Shouldn't you be doing something healthy like playing football?'

'We do play football, Mrs Bratherstone, but we're doing a project at school on the people who used to live around here years ago. Our teacher said it was a good idea to look at all the graves, so here we are. My great-great-great-great-great-grandfather is buried over there – he was the vicar of this church over a hundred years ago.' As Tom related this gem of information, he counted the "greats" on his fingers.

'Yes, I know about your great-whatever-grandfather. He was a fine man by all accounts. Did a lot of good work to educate the poor children around these parts. Of course, in those days Drumbridge didn't have big houses for stockbrokers and bankers and such like.' She pointed with her stick to a block of luxury flats on the other side of the road. 'Just across the road where that block of flats is, there was a row of terraced houses where the mill workers lived, and they were poor, very poor indeed. I remember when they knocked those houses down. Such a shame. They were sturdy little houses.'

Mrs Bratherstone, who was once a teacher at the local school before she retired, was not convinced that a school project required the boys to spend so much time in the graveyard. It seemed that most times when she was there in the early evening, she found Tom and Frank wandering among the graves or sitting on Tom's ancestor's tombstone. She gave the boys a disbelieving stare and raised her walking stick in warning. 'Just you take care – there are some strange characters who wander around here. Oh – and one other thing – let me know if you need any help with your project.' And with that, she turned and hobbled away on her arthritic legs towards the gate.

'Thank you Mrs Bratherstone,' Tom and Frank called in unison. Mrs Bratherstone raised her stick in acknowledgement.

'Phew – that wasn't so bad,' said Tom. 'At least she didn't rant on for long this time.'

'Oh, she's not a bad old sort. Sometimes she's got something interesting to say.'

It was true that there were some strange people who visited the graveyard, but Tom and Frank knew most of them. Old Jacob Willoughby was definitely strange. He was known as "Mr Jake" and was once a well-to-do farmer but now he was avoided by most people because of his eccentric ways. He was exceptionally tall and thin, walked with a stoop and always wore a creased old blue suit and a flat cap. He came to visit his wife's grave occasionally. He just stood over it and looked at it for several minutes. He didn't tidy it or put any flowers on it – it was just as overgrown as his garden. He always brought his old black and white sheepdog Bessie, who was once a working dog but was now too old to chase sheep. Both of them looked as though they could do with a good scrub. Even so, Mr Jake knew a lot about the people who lived in the area many years ago, because he had lived there all his life, and he was said to be at least ninety years old. He had given Tom and Frank a lot of useful information for their school project, but when they talked to him, they were careful not to get downwind because of the awful smell that hung around him. They weren't sure whether it was him or Bessie, or both. They avoided stroking Bessie – she had sticky, matted fur that they suspected was full of fleas. They were a strange-looking group when they were chatting: old Mr Jake, with Bessie sitting obediently at his feet, would be raving on about the old times while the two boys stood together with at least one grave between them and Mr Jake, but listening intently. Tom was the smaller of the two, about average height for his age but rather skinny, with cropped blond hair and bright blue eyes. When not in school uniform, he liked to wear jeans and loose tee-shirts or sweatshirts that made him look a bit broader than he really was. Frank was much taller and heavier than Tom. In fact, he was the biggest boy in their class at school. He had black spiky hair and small oval spectacles that magnified his large, staring, brown eyes. At school, he had a reputation for being a bit scary, but only among those who didn't know him. Tom knew that he was as gentle as a lamb, except when he got really angry. Then, he could be frightening. He was the kind of boy who gave the impression that he didn't care what he looked like. He was always scruffy, no matter what he wore, even his school uniform.

On the other side of the churchyard was Tom's great-great-great-great-great-grandfather's grave. He was Magnus Robertson, vicar of the church from 1843 to 1875. As Mrs Bratherstone had said, Magnus Robertson was known for the work he did to educate poor children in the area, but he had also done a great deal to help poor communities in Scotland, where he was born. He spent the first thirty-eight years of his life in Scotland and then came south to Drumbridge with his wife and five children, where he lived in the Vicarage. The Merringtons bought the Vicarage about ten years ago, when the church decided to sell it to raise funds. Tom's parents jumped at the chance to bring it back into the family, but it cost them more than they could afford and for the first few years they had barely enough money to live on. Tom was two years old at that time and his sister Amy was not even born. They loved the house; it was big and rambling. It had a large garden, but Tom rarely spent any time in it; he preferred to go straight to the bottom and through the rickety gate into the graveyard.

Since Tom's mother had shown him Magnus Robertson's grave, he had spent a lot of time pulling out the ivy and the other weeds around the grave and making sure it always had fresh flowers. The grave stood in the shade of an old yew tree that had almost certainly been there in Magnus Robertson's time. Tom found that the stone base of the grave was high enough so that he could sit on it comfortably. Sometimes he would lean back on the large impressive headstone, knowing somehow that Magnus did not regard his casual posture as a sign of disrespect. It was when Tom was weeding one day that he discovered something special. He decided to take a break, so he sat on the grave, rested his head between his hands and closed his eyes. It was a peaceful summer day, sunny but not too hot, with a gentle breeze and only wispy clouds in the sky. The air was fresh and he could smell the mint that was growing wild nearby. The soft rustling of the leaves in the trees made him feel sleepy. He wasn't sure whether he had fallen asleep or not, but he began to imagine the time when his famous ancestor was alive, almost as though he was there. It began with Magnus Robertson appearing in front of him with an arm outstretched. Tom took his hand and the two of them walked through a narrow alley between the houses into a street. Tom saw people driving horse-drawn carts along a muddy road and others on foot carrying wicker baskets and going into quaint shops. He saw the blacksmith outside his forge fitting a shoe to the hoof of a large shire horse while the farmer waited with his cart. Tom watched until the horse was back securely between the shafts of the cart and the farmer had driven him off down the main road and into a side-road. As the horse and cart disappeared from sight, Tom's dream, if that's what it was, ended abruptly and he found himself looking up at Frank and feeling bewildered.

'Did you fall asleep?'

'Er – I think I must have done.'

'It's such a nice day; I thought I'd find you here. I wondered if you'd finished your history homework.'

Tom looked at his watch. He meant to go back and finish his homework half an hour ago. 'Oh, no. Thanks for reminding me.'

'I brought mine in case you wanted some help.'

'Thanks, you're a pal. I need some help.'

'Next time we get maths homework, I'll expect some help from you.'

'If I can.' Tom knew that Frank's weakest subject was maths, but he was exceptionally good at history. They hurried off back through the rickety gate and into the Vicarage. Tom shouted to his mother that he had Frank with him and they were going up to his bedroom to finish their homework. She and Frank exchanged shouted greetings to each other between kitchen and stairs.

A few days later, Tom had a similar experience in the churchyard, and then again a few days after that. He soon realized that the dreams occurred most times that he sat on the grave and closed his eyes. They didn't come every time, but one thing Tom was sure about was that he had to be either next to or on the grave for them to happen at all. He tried to do the same thing in his bedroom: if he sat on his bed, or anywhere else in his bedroom, nothing happened. If he sat in a position where he could see the grave through the window, nothing happened. He was sure now that the vivid pictures were more than just his imagination; he really believed that Magnus Robertson was showing him those scenes. Tom decided to confide in Frank about his daydreams. After all, he was his best friend and he trusted him. He also hoped that Frank would have some ideas to help him understand what was going on.

Chapter 2
The Portrait

TOM AND FRANK WERE IN THE CHURCHYARD again, exploring the names on the gravestones, when Tom broached the subject of his daydreams.

'Frank – you remember that day you found me asleep on Magnus Robertson's grave?'

'Yes. So what?'

'Well, I had a kind of dream.'

'What do you mean, a kind of dream? Was it a dream or wasn't it?'

'I'm not sure.'

Frank looked exasperated. 'Give me a clue. What was the dream about?'

'I saw Magnus Robertson and he showed me what it was like when he was alive. I saw old Drumbridge, with tracks instead of roads and horses instead of cars.'

'Don't you think that's reasonable as you were sitting on Magnus Robertson's grave? You must have been thinking about him before you went to sleep.'

'But it was so vivid – I don't think I could dream all that detail; it was more like looking into the past.'

'Don't be daft. How could that happen?'

'I don't know, but it's happened several times now.'

'And is it always the same dream?'

'No, it's different every time, but it's always old Drumbridge.'

Frank looked puzzled. 'How do you know it's old Drumbridge?'

'I recognized the names of some of the roads and some of the houses are still in existence. The Vicarage, for instance.'

'Well, that's obviously familiar to you.'

'Yes, but it didn't have the extension on the back then.' Tom could see that Frank was not sure whether to believe him or not.

'Let me try.' He went over to Magnus Robertson's grave, sat on it and closed his eyes. After concentrating hard for a few minutes and then trying to doze off, he gave up. 'It doesn't seem to happen to me.'

'Perhaps that's because you're not a descendant of Magnus Robertson.'

Frank looked hard at Tom. 'Don't think I don't believe you, Tom, but it is a bit far-fetched, you must admit.'

'I know, but I can't think of any other explanation.' Tom was beginning to wish he hadn't said anything.

'Do you have a photograph of Magnus Robertson?'

'No.'

'But you're still certain it's him you see in your dreams?'

'Yes, he's told me who he is.'

'There's got to be a way of matching up what you see with the facts – like old photographs of Drumbridge. I'll go down to the library to see what they've got and let you know how I get on.' Tom was grateful that Frank was at least trying to help and he felt a little better.

After school the next day, Frank went to the local library. He knew his way around the old records because searching for historical information on Drumbridge was one of his favourite pastimes. Unlike most of the students in his class, Frank thought the project on Drumbridge was a lot of fun, not a chore. Most of the other students thought that Frank was a bit of a bore because he could always come up with another gem of local history when asked. They were also a little jealous of Frank because he was always very determined whatever he did and it usually meant he achieved more. But his search for old photographs of Drumbridge proved fruitless. It wasn't as though Drumbridge was a place that was likely to appear on postcards – it wasn't a tourist attraction or a place of much importance. He decided to change his strategy and look for information on Magnus Robertson. Much to his surprise, he found a lot of information, because it seemed that Magnus Robertson had been an important figure in Drumbridge. He had held several official posts and had a lot of influence on the affairs of the town. It was while Frank was reading some boring details about town council meetings that he hit upon a note that made him jump up and silently punch the air. He wanted to shout but it was a library, after all. He discovered that a portrait of Magnus Robertson had been painted by a well-known local artist and was now kept in the museum at Walchester, the nearest big town to Drumbridge. This was the answer! Tom would recognize him if he really had seen Magnus

Robertson in his dreams. Frank couldn't concentrate any longer. He took his school books home and then telephoned Tom to ask if he could come round to the Vicarage straight away. He rushed round and showed Tom what he had found.

'This is just what we need. If you recognize him, I'll believe you. Have you told your parents about your dreams?'

'No, of course not.'

'So I'm the only one who knows?'

'Yes.'

'You realize, if this really is something supernatural, you'll have to tell your parents.'

Tom looked apprehensive. 'I suppose so.'

'Promise.'

'I promise,' said Tom reluctantly.

Frank showed Tom's mother the copy that he had made of the paragraph in the book describing the portrait.

'Well done, Frank. I didn't know about this. We'll have to go and see it.'

'Can we go and see it now?' Tom was twitching with excitement.

Mum looked at the clock. 'Yes, I think we can make it in time.'

Tom suddenly became nervous. He looked thoughtful and he could not stop a worried look spreading across his face. The reality had hit him - he was going to see what Magnus Robertson really looked like, and if he was the same as the Magnus Robertson of his daydreams, what would it mean? He looked up at Mum and managed a weak smile. Mum looked a little puzzled.

'Amy, come on, we're going to Walchester,' called Mum to her young daughter. Mum was just as excited about it because, of course, Magnus Robertson was her great-great-great-great grandfather.

Soon they were all bundling into the car.

'Why are we going to Walchester?' asked Amy.

'You'll see,' Tom answered.

'No, explain it to her, please.'

Frank explained to Amy what he had found, but she wasn't particularly excited about seeing a portrait of someone who really meant very little to her, even if he was a special ancestor.

When they got to the museum, Mum immediately went to ask the steward where the portrait was. He directed them to a large gallery upstairs that contained many portraits of local figures. There was nobody else in the gallery and the only sound was the hum of a fan. The floor was made of old oak boards and as they walked around, the sound of Amy's footsteps echoed around the gallery, so she tried walking on tiptoe, stifling a giggle.

Tom and Frank quickly scanned the labels of the pictures. There were a lot more portraits there than they had expected and it took some time before they found what they were looking for.

'Here it is,' called Frank in a trembling voice.

He was standing in front of one of the bigger paintings with a heavy gold frame. The face of Magnus Robertson looked down on them through round spectacles. He had a square, friendly face, thick grey hair and side whiskers. It was hard to tell from the portrait, but it looked as though he had the same bright blue sparkling eyes that both Tom and his mother had inherited. Mum was overjoyed to see what he looked like, but Tom was shivering with a mixture of fright and amazement – this was exactly as he had seen Magnus Robertson in his dreams! It was then that he knew for sure that the daydreams by the grave were not just his imagination – he was really seeing into the past!

'You look as though you've seen a ghost,' Mum whispered in Tom's ear.

Tom struggled to speak. He didn't know whether to say what he was thinking. When he finally spoke, he said: 'He's just like I imagined him,' which of course was the truth. Just as he said that, he imagined that the face in the painting became real and smiled at him! He stifled a yell, then took a breath and tried to relax. He had seen Magnus smile benevolently at him in his daydreams, so he was sure that was why he imagined it. After a few minutes, he gained his composure and felt more at ease in front of the portrait. Mum was a little puzzled at Tom's immediate reaction, but decided to confront him about it when they got back home.

Frank sidled up to Tom as casually as he could. 'So it's him, then?' he whispered. 'I could tell from your expression.'

'Yes, no doubt about it. What do I do now?'

'Tell your Mum when you get home, of course. She can tell by your face that something is bothering you, anyway.'

They drove home with Frank and Amy talking non-stop about the portrait, while Mum and Tom were silent.

'I think he looked like Grandpa, don't you think so, Mum?'

'Yes, I suppose he did. But Grandpa doesn't have so much hair!' Amy laughed.

They dropped Frank off at his house and when they got back home, Mum cornered Tom in his room and started to cross-examine him.

'Tom, what's going on? Why did you look so shocked when you saw the portrait and yet you said he looked just like you imagined?'

Of course, Tom knew this was coming and he had already decided to be absolutely straight with Mum and tell her about the visions at the grave, even though he didn't expect her to believe him. She was staring at him with her bright blue eyes, a wisp of her blonde hair hanging across one of them. She was too focused on Tom to worry about pulling it back.

'It's because I've seen him in my daydreams and he looked just like that.'

'You mean you just created a picture of him in your imagination and he looked like the portrait?'

'Not exactly. I have to sit next to his grave in the churchyard, and then I can imagine what it was like when he was alive. He has spoken to me.'

Mum swallowed hard and looked at Tom with her piercing "I want to know all the details" look. Then she drew back, realizing that Tom was as puzzled as she was and asked the simple questions: 'What did he say to you? What was his voice like?'

'He hasn't said much. He just asked me whether I was well and how I was getting on at school. Nothing very exciting. He spoke with a Scottish accent and he had a gentle voice, quite deep but clear and soft and kind of comforting.'

Mum thought that might be just what someone who has given lots of sermons would sound like. 'What else have you seen in these dreams?'

'I've seen Drumbridge in Victorian times when the high street was just a muddy track and there were only a few shops. The Reverend Robertson always leads me into the road. I've spoken to some of the people there and they are all friendly to me – except that they all call me "Ben". I just feel like I'm living in their time.' Tom looked at the clock. 'Frank promised to be back here in about half an hour because we want to clear a few of the old graves. He just went home to tell his parents – he should be here soon.'

'OK, let's talk again tomorrow.'

Frank arrived on time and they went to see some of the graves in the oldest and most overgrown part of the churchyard.

'Well, did you tell her?'

'Yes.'

'Did she believe you?'

'I think so, but she wants to talk about it some more.'

'I'm not surprised. It's not every day your son tells you he can see into the past.'

'So do you believe me now?'

'Yes, of course I do. I didn't doubt you for one moment.'

'That's a lie.'

'Not really. I was hoping all along it would turn out like this. It's exciting! I'm looking forward to hearing about your next dream. Or perhaps we should call them "visions". Yes, I think that's the right word.'

'But what does it all mean, that's what I'd like to know? Why is it happening to me?'

'The best thing to do is go along with it and see what happens. I'm sure it will all become clear eventually.'

'Perhaps you're right. Let's get on with the graves.'

They intended to clear off the weeds and brambles from the graves and had come armed with garden shears, secateurs, and a hoe. There were three big headstones that they were hoping to clear. Tom had a feeling that they were important graves and it wasn't just that they were big. He had been drawn towards them several times and now the urge to find out who was buried there had become too strong to resist.

It was a lot more difficult than they had expected. The ivy was clinging steadfastly to the headstones and it was hard work pulling it off. After an hour, they had cleared most of the weeds and brambles from around the graves and had got the ivy off one of the headstones. They had created quite a pile on the compost heap in the corner of the churchyard.

The sun was getting low behind the trees and it was nearly time to return home. Tom only had to go through the gate to his back garden but Frank had a five-minute walk to his house. They decided to take a closer look at the headstone they had uncovered.

'How do you think we might clean it up so that we can read the inscription?'

'Perhaps we could give it a good scrub with a stiff brush.'

'Don't know, I think we could damage the stone – it looks a bit flaky.'

'Look – we can read some of it, so why don't we start by writing down what we can and leave spaces for the letters we can't read – you know, like one of those puzzles where you have to fill in the missing letters?'

'That's a good idea, but there's not enough light to do it now – let's do it tomorrow.'

'Tom, Frank, it's getting late.' Mum was calling from the gate.

'OK, I'll see you down here tomorrow after school,' Tom said, as the two began walking towards the path. Frank hurried out through the main gate and Tom squeezed through the narrow gap in the gateway to his back garden – the gate always stuck when it was only partially open and it needed a big heave to open it fully. Tom's dad had been meaning to fix the gate for months but there always seemed to be something more important to do.

Amy was helping Mum get the dinner ready by setting the table. Dad was not in yet, but he had called to say he was on his way. He was Professor James Merrington, Head of the Computer Sciences department at Walchester University, which was about eight miles away. Today was one of his cycling days. He always tried to cycle to work at least twice a week to help him keep fit and to save on fuel.

'See you tomorrow, Jim,' shouted a voice from the road. Dad often cycled back with Mike Brennan, one of his research team from the University who lived in the next village three miles further on. A squealing of brakes outside announced Dad's arrival

'Mum, Dad's here,' Amy shouted.

'Yes, I can hear,' said Mum with a chuckle.

Dad came into the kitchen to greet everyone, struggling with the strap on his cycling helmet. He pulled it off and nearly took his spectacles with it. Amy laughed to see Dad with his glasses perched on one ear and the other end tangled in his hair. He playfully bent down to pull a face at her with his glasses still awry and his dark, wavy hair hanging down over them. Amy giggled, straightened out his spectacles and then put her arms round his neck. While their heads were touching, it was clear that they had almost the same colour hair. And unlike Tom and Mum, they both had brown eyes.

'Go and get ready for dinner,' Amy demanded.

'At once, boss.'

Within fifteen minutes, they were all tucking into a delicious meal of roast chicken, followed by apple pie and ice cream. The Merringtons did not watch much television and after dinner on weekdays, they often sat down in the lounge and talked about all sorts of things. Tonight, Amy spoke first and told Dad about the portrait in Walchester.

'That's quite a find – Frank's a smart lad,' said Dad. 'I'll have to take a look at it myself.'

Mum and Tom looked at each other, and somehow seemed to reach a silent understanding that they would not bring up the subject of Tom's daydreams in the churchyard until they had talked about it tomorrow.

Tom broke the silence.

'Mum, what's the best way to read an inscription on an old grave when it's nearly worn away?'

'If you took an interest in our family history, you might know that.' Mum had been researching the family history for about a year now and had collected a lot of interesting information, or at least she thought so.

'First, you would normally find out if the local family history society had already done a survey of the churchyard – that would save you doing it yourself.' Then she smiled and said: 'But I know they haven't because I'm supposed to be doing it later this summer. You could help me if you like.'

'Er, yes, I think I'd like to, but there's one that Frank and I want to do tomorrow.'

'What's special about it?'

'There's just something different about it; it's a feeling we get. It's a very big stone, so we think it could be someone important.'

Mum smiled knowingly. She understood exactly what Tom meant when he said he had a feeling it was special; sometimes she had feelings like that herself. 'I can show you how it's done tomorrow. How about that?'

'That would be great. Thanks Mum.'

'What about you, Dad? Did anything exciting happen to you today?' asked Amy.

'As a matter of fact something strange did happen today. We are getting some odd messages coming up on our computer, as though someone is tampering with it.'

'Do you mean that someone is getting into the lab and interfering with it?' asked Mum.

'That's possible, but we don't think so. We're wondering if it's a hacker.'

'What's a hacker?' asked Amy.

'I know that,' said Tom. 'It's someone who uses another computer to find out all the secrets you have in your computer.'

'Is that right, Dad?' asked Amy.

'That's about it,' Dad replied. 'Anyway, we've got our own hacker expert on the case now, so we should get to the bottom of it soon.'

'Who's that?' asked Mum.

'Jerry Tomlins, you remember him, don't you? Short, scruffy, black hair, beard.'

'Yes, I remember, but I can't imagine him being an expert at anything,' said Mum.

Tom remembered him too. He often went to Dad's lab during the school holidays, so he knew Mike and Kala, who worked in the lab. Jerry had a lab just along the corridor, but he often came in to talk about their experiments. Tom liked him because he was like an overgrown schoolboy – always making silly jokes. That was probably why Mum couldn't believe he'd be good at anything.

'Jerry and I want to make an early start tomorrow, so I'll be leaving at about seven o'clock. And I'll probably have to go in on Saturday morning.'

'Oh, no,' Amy and Tom exclaimed in unison. They enjoyed their family weekends so much.

'Never mind,' Mum said, 'I was planning to go to an antiques' auction on Saturday. How would you two like to come with me?'

Amy and Tom were not enthusiastic, but they hadn't been to an auction before. Amy asked: 'What happens at an antique auction?'

'Well, in the morning we look at all the items in the auction to see if there is anything we fancy. Then in the afternoon, we can bid for them – that means the person who offers the most money buys the item. This auction is mostly furniture. I'm looking for an old oak chest.'

Mum did a bit of buying and selling of antiques and was thinking of setting up her own shop. She was becoming quite an expert in furniture, although her speciality was art. She had studied art history at university and that's where she had met Dad. Then, she was nineteen-year old Julia Robertson, daughter of Archibald Robertson, antique dealer, who of course was the great-great-great grandson of the Reverend Magnus Robertson.

'Can I ask Frank if he wants to come? He likes old things.'

'Of course.'

In case he forgot, Tom made a note to ask Frank tomorrow.

Tom thought that Dad looked worried. Perhaps this hacker business was serious. Tom was good at computer studies at school and he was interested to find out what was happening to Dad's computer. He didn't want to get in the way, but he wondered if he could go to the lab to see what Jerry was doing. But he knew that when Dad was preoccupied with something, he didn't take kindly to being distracted, so Tom decided not to bother him just at the moment.

Chapter 3

The Old Oak Chest

THE NEXT DAY, AFTER SCHOOL, TOM AND Mum had a longer talk about Tom's daydreams. She listened intently as Tom described more about how Magnus Robertson seemed to guide him through his daydreams. He explained how he just had to close his eyes and he was transported to another world, but it only worked when he was near the grave. It was definitely Drumbridge he saw because he recognized some of the roads and the buildings, but it was in the nineteenth century. At first, Tom had thought it was just his imagination, but after seeing the portrait, he knew he really was in contact with Magnus Robertson. Tom was relieved that Mum believed him and seemed to be sympathetic.

'You said that the people in old Drumbridge called you "Ben". Do you know why?'

'No, but it didn't happen at first. People just smiled at me and didn't say much; they just spoke to Reverend Robertson because I was with him then. More recently, I've walked around the town on my own and that's when people started to call me "Ben". It's almost as though I've grown up a little since the start.'

'Perhaps Ben was a real person who lived in the past.'

'Do you think so?'

'Maybe.'

'Mum, I'm surprised you believe I'm seeing into the past. Has it ever happened to you?'

'Not exactly, but I've been in contact with someone from the past.'

'Really? When?'

'Several times, some quite recently. I haven't seen anyone, but I've had advice from one of my ancestors.'

'What sort of advice?'

'Telling me to be careful of certain people who can't be trusted. It's as though she is trying to protect me.'

'She? Do you know who she is?'

'Not for certain, but her name is Margaret, so I wonder if it's Magnus Robertson's wife. I know her name was Margaret because I've got a copy of their marriage certificate.'

'How does she contact you? She's not a ghost, is she?'

'No. Mostly, she appears in dreams but sometimes I just get thoughts popping into my head at odd times.'

'But how do you know that it's not just your imagination?'

Mum smiled. 'It seems you probably understand that in the same way that I do. I just know.'

Tom felt as though he was sharing something special with Mum. Suddenly she seemed more vulnerable, less like a mother, more his equal. He put his arms round her and hugged her. She gave him a gentle kiss on the cheek.

'From now on, tell me about your daydreams, don't keep them to yourself. I'll explain it all to your father this evening, so no doubt he'll want to talk to you about it.'

'It's not really Dad's thing, is it?'

'What do you mean?'

'Well, he doesn't believe in this sort of stuff, does he?'

Mum smiled. 'You're right. He doesn't believe in the supernatural, so I'll have to persuade him otherwise. Leave it to me. I suppose Frank knows all about your daydreams?'

'Oh, yes, he wants to know every little detail.' Tom realized he had just confessed to telling Frank first and he felt ashamed.

'Don't look so guilty. I would have expected you to confide in Frank first. It's only natural.'

'Is it?'

'Of course. That's probably Frank at the door now. Go and let him in.'

It was indeed Frank ringing the doorbell. It was time to start their investigation of the big grave.

'I'll be out in a minute,' called Mum.

Tom and Frank went straight through into the garden, picked up their gardening tools and pushed through the rickety gate into the churchyard.

When Mum came out, she was carrying a bucket.

'I told you it needed a good scrub,' said Frank.

But the bucket didn't contain any water at all. There was a white powder and an old paintbrush at the bottom.

'What's that, Mum?' asked Tom.

'Flour.'

'Flour?'

'You'll see.'

Mum pulled out a large clean paintbrush from her pocket and brushed off the dust from the surface of the headstone. Then she dipped the other brush in the flour and softly brushed it over the surface. As if by magic, the letters began to appear. The flour filled up the carvings so that they showed up white. Even so, some of the letters were so badly worn away by the weather that they could not be read.

'That's really clever,' exclaimed Frank.

'Looks like we'll be able to read about half of it, the rest we'll have to guess at,' said Mum.

She took a notebook and pencil from her pocket and asked the boys to try to read the inscription.

Frank started at the top. 'I think it begins with "In Loving Memory of'", like a lot of the other graves.'

'Yes, I think you're right,' said Tom.

The next bit was a name. It began with an "E", they all agreed, and it had six letters.

'That looks like "th" in the middle and I think it's followed by an "e" – what do you think?' asked Tom.

'The second letter looks like "s". I know – it's "Esther",' exclaimed Frank.

Mum squinted at it from several angles and then agreed that Frank was right.

'OK, next word.'

'That's "wife"',' said Tom and Frank almost together. They had seen this sequence before on other graves.

'Esther, wife of somebody with a name beginning with "S"',' said Tom.

'It's "Samuel"',' declared Frank, confidently. He had seen the tall "l" at the end and then quickly picked out the other letters.

The surname was going to be difficult. They could see it began with an "L", but the rest was badly worn.

'Let's try a bit more flour,' said Mum, and carefully brushed a little more into the letters.

'It's got tall letters in the middle and at the end and I think the second letter is an "a" or "o"',' she suggested.

Frank was switching from the letters above that were quite clear, back to the worn surname, hoping to find some similarities. He was getting the hang of this.

'I think that letter is a "v",' he declared, pointing to what appeared to be the third letter. 'It's the same as the one in "Loving".'

'Yes, I think you are right,' agreed Mum. 'In fact, I'd say the first three letters are the same. So what name begins with "Lov", has a tall letter in the middle and at the end and is, let's see, eight or nine letters long?'

Tom had the same look on his face as he had in the portrait gallery. 'I know, it's "Lovelock",' he declared in a flat voice.

Mum and Frank turned to face Tom. Mum's eyes were boring into him to read his expression. 'Is this another person you've met in your daydreams?'

'Not exactly, but I've seen his name above the forge. He was the local blacksmith.'

Frank was excited. 'We can check that,' he said, 'I'll do it next time I go to the library.'

'I think the library opens at nine thirty tomorrow morning – we can check it before we go to the auction,' said Mum.

'OK.'

'Shall we continue to decipher the inscription?'

They discovered that Esther Lovelock died aged forty-five but Samuel lived on until he was seventy-three or seventy-eight – the dates were difficult to read. Even so, it seemed that he would have lived at the same time as Magnus Robertson. When Magnus came to Drumbridge, aged thirty-eight, Samuel Lovelock would have been sixty or sixty-five, so they could have known each other.

The next day, the three of them were with Amy outside the library waiting for it to open. Frank nearly knocked the assistant over when he burst in as she opened the door at precisely nine thirty.

'Oops, sorry,' apologized Frank.

'That's all right,' said the assistant. 'It's good to see such enthusiasm for books in a young man.'

Frank was not sure he was a young man yet, but he smiled apologetically and hurried over to the local records. He retrieved the microfilm of the 1841 census and soon had it loaded in a reader. After a few minutes of winding his way through it, he found what he was looking for.

'Here it is. In 1841, Samuel Lovelock, blacksmith and widower, aged fifty-five, lived at The Forge in Market Street with his son Sidney, aged twenty.'

'Those ages are rounded down to the nearest five, so from what we worked out from the gravestone, he was probably fifty-eight rather than fifty-five,' said Mum.

Tom just shrugged his shoulders – he knew Frank would confirm what he had said at the grave. Mum was thoughtful, but she expected it too.

'Well done Frank, that didn't take long. Let's be on our way,' said Mum.

She ushered Amy in front of her and out through the door with Tom and Frank following behind. They walked round behind the library to the car park where they had left the car. Soon they were on the road to Walchester.

The furniture auction was being held in a large hall near the railway station. The furniture filled most of the hall and did not seem to be arranged in any order. There was not much space between the items, so it was difficult to squeeze between them. There were many old chests but they were all over the place. Mum examined each one in turn and made notes in her little notebook.

Frank was fascinated by some of the furniture and wondered why anyone would want to buy furniture that was so scratched and dented or full of woodworm holes. He was getting left behind because he kept stopping to peer inside cupboards and drawers and then when he looked up, the others were out of sight. Mum suggested that Frank and Tom could go round at their own pace and she would stay with Amy.

'See that big grandfather clock in the central area? Make sure you are there at twelve o'clock,' she said.

Tom didn't have the same fascination with old furniture that Frank had, probably because there was plenty of antique furniture in his house and he had got used to it. Frank's parents had mostly modern furniture.

'Look at this,' he exclaimed to Tom, 'the wood is so worn away here – it must be all the hands that have lifted the lid over so many years.' He was looking at an old chest with the edge of the lid worn so smooth that it felt like glass. Frank just couldn't get enough of old things. He was stroking the chest as though it was a pet. He gently lifted the lid and paused before he peered inside, almost as though he expected a genie to come out. It was pitch black inside and he dared not open it fully in case he was spotted. It smelt musty. He closed it silently and then read the label. 'Lot 175. Oak panelled chest, original ironwork, ca 1660.'

'This is nearly three hundred and fifty years old no wonder it's so worn! It would be great if your mum bought this one. Do you think she might?'

Tom shrugged. 'Maybe.'

He was not as excited about it as Frank was. In fact, he was getting a little bored and checked his watch. Another fifteen minutes before it was time to meet at the grandfather clock.

Frank was now looking at a large table with carved legs. He was fascinated by the carving and he got down under the table, running his fingers over the wood, trying to imagine how the craftsman had done it. He knew quite a lot about woodwork, because his father was a carpenter. He had helped his father in his workshop and had even done some woodcarving, so he had a good idea how the table legs might have been carved. His father also had a collection of antique tools, so Frank knew what the carpenter would have used. The carpenter must have been so proud of this table. He thought of him standing back to admire it when he had finished it. But when was that? He looked at the label – ca 1820. The carpenter would have been so pleased that his table was still being used nearly two hundred years after he made it. Frank's mind began to wander off as he thought of the skill that would be needed to make such a magnificent piece of furniture. He was under the table at the time, so he couldn't be seen from above.

Tom was walking around aimlessly when he realized that Frank was nowhere to be seen. He looked at his watch and realized that it was only a few minutes to twelve o'clock.

'Frank?' he whispered, but there was no response. He looked all around him, but there was no sign of Frank anywhere. There were lots of tall pieces of furniture that Frank could be lurking behind. He looked across to the grandfather clock in the middle of the hall and could see Mum and Amy heading towards it. He decided to go and meet them. They could then decide what to do to find Frank.

'Mum, I've lost Frank. One moment he was there, then I looked around and he was gone.'

Mum was annoyed and a bit distressed. It was one thing to lose one of her own children but it was quite different to lose someone else's.

'Where were you when you last saw him? Take us there.'

Tom headed towards the big table where he had last seen Frank. They wandered around without any success until Amy saw a pair of feet sticking out from under the table. She looked down and there was Frank, with his leg trapped under the cross-rail of the table.

'I've found him,' shouted Amy.

Mum and Tom rushed over to find Amy giggling while she shook Frank's legs. Frank was struggling to get out, and banged his head on the underside of the table.

'Ouch,' he yelled.

Mum took his shoe off so that he could free his leg and soon he was crawling awkwardly out from under the table.

'Sorry, I didn't mean to get stuck. I didn't want to shout for help in this place, so I was hoping you would come back.'

Mum laughed. She was happy now that they had found Frank. 'Come on; let's find somewhere to have some lunch before the auction this afternoon.'

They went into a self-service restaurant just across the road from the auction room. Tom and Frank loaded up their trays with food and drinks while Mum helped Amy choose what she wanted. Frank dug deep into his pocket to pull out the money his mother had given him to pay for his food.

'I'll pay for all of us – you don't need that, Frank,' called out Mum.

'Oh, thanks very much, Mrs Merrington.' He looked guiltily at his tray, wondering whether he should put something back. It did look rather a lot, but when he looked at Tom's tray, it had even more on it, so he didn't feel so bad.

They found a table on the far side of the restaurant, by a window. After a while, Tom noticed a man sitting alone at a table a short distance away. He glanced up, saw that Tom was looking at him, gave Tom an unpleasant glare, and continued with his meal. Tom was puzzled. Who was he? He was a big, well-built man with a round face and thick, unruly grey hair. His jacket was hanging over the back of the chair and he was wearing a short-sleeved shirt. Tom noticed that he had a tattoo on his muscular right arm.

'Tom, stop dreaming and get on with your meal,' interrupted Mum.

'Mrs Merrington, have you decided which chest you are going to buy?' asked Frank.

'I've noted four that I like and I've put them in order of preference. But of course it depends on whether I can afford any of them. I'm sure the best one will be too expensive.'

When they got back to the auction hall, Mum asked them to remain quietly at the back to let her concentrate on bidding for the chests. The first one to come up was the one she liked the best and sure enough, it was sold for a lot more than she could afford. The next one was the one she liked the least and she was only prepared to buy it if it was cheap. She stopped bidding for it when the bids went too high. The third one was the one with the worn lid that Frank had admired so much. This was also Mum's second favourite. Tom and Frank could see what was going on and they saw Mum bidding for it. When the auctioneer banged his gavel on the table to announce the sale, he pointed to Mum to say that she had bought it!

'She's bought it,' whispered Frank to Tom.

'Good, perhaps we can go now,' said Tom, wearily. He thought they had been waiting long enough. Then he noticed a man near Mum turn around and look at them menacingly. It was the same man he had seen in the restaurant.

Mum paid for the chest and then came to the back of the hall.

'Let's go to the car and drive round to the loading bay at the back. The porters said they would bring the chest round there for us to pick it up.'

They hurried across to the car park and got into the car. Mum drove around the building and through another entrance to a pair of large sliding doors. She jumped out and opened the tailgate of the car. Almost immediately, one of the large doors slid open and a tall man in a brown overall stepped out. He surveyed the car to check that the chest would go in and then went back into the warehouse. Mum's car was a multi-purpose vehicle with three rows of seats. She had folded down the back row before they left. The porter was soon out again, this time with a shorter man, also in brown overalls, who was helping him carry the chest. They placed it carefully in the back of the car.

'Do you want a few bits of foam to protect it, madam?' asked the taller man.

'No, that's OK; I've got some straps to hold it down and a blanket to cover it.' Mum often carried pieces of furniture in the back of the car, so she was well-prepared.

'Fine, we'll leave you to it then. Have a safe journey.'

'Thanks, 'bye!'

The two men trundled off into the building and the door slid back into place noisily. Mum placed an old blanket over the chest and then fixed the straps over it and secured them to the floor of the car.

'That looks safe enough,' she declared, and closed the tailgate. She jumped back into the car and started off back to Drumbridge. Amy and the boys were chattering away.

When they had gone a little way, Tom said, 'Mum, did you see that big man standing close to you in the auction?'

'What did he look like?'

'Tall and broad, grey hair and I think he was wearing a blue jacket when he was in the auction.'

'Yes, I did. Why do you ask?'

'He turned round and looked at us when you bought the chest. He was in the restaurant too and he looked at me then. He looked angry.'

Mum looked worried. 'That's Mr Grimley, an antique dealer from Walchester. Let me know if you see him again, won't you?'

'Yes.'

They were approaching the Vicarage now and Mum carefully eased the car through the drive and parked near the back door.

'Who's going to help me carry the chest in?'

'I will,' said Frank.

Mum opened the back door and went into the house to clear a passage for them to bring the chest in. She went back to the car, unclipped the straps and took off the blanket.

'OK, Frank, you take that end and we'll get it out of the car first. Place it on the ground carefully.' Frank was careful not to bang the chest on the side of the car as he and Mum carefully lifted it out and placed it on the ground.

'Right, now get your hands under the base and lift it. I'll lead the way.'

They carried the chest carefully through into the lounge, lowered it gently into place and then stood back to see how it looked.

'I think that looks splendid,' said Mum.

'So do I,' said Frank. He gave the chest a welcoming stroke on the smooth patch and then looked at the clock. 'I think I'll have to go home now; it's getting late.'

'Hmmm, yes it is. OK. We'll see you soon then.'

Tom and Frank hurried out with Amy scampering behind. Tom opened the gate to let Frank out. 'See you tomorrow.'

When Frank had gone, Mum grabbed Tom and pulled him into the kitchen.

'I meant what I said when I asked you to let me know if you see that Mr Grimley again. He's a nasty piece of work.'

'How do you know?'

'I tried to do a deal with him once and he did all he could to cheat me. For some reason that I don't understand, he seemed to take an instant dislike to me. Perhaps he thought that because I'm a woman, I didn't know much about antiques. Fortunately, I saw through his little game. I've kept out of his way since. And another thing – Margaret told me not to trust him.'

'Oh, I see. I'll be careful and I'll let you know if I see him again.'

'Make sure that you do. He's got a shop in Walchester, so steer clear of it.'

That night, as Tom was lying in bed, he thought about Mr Grimley. Why should he dislike Mum without even knowing her? Anyone who did not like Mum was definitely Tom's enemy. The incidents in the restaurant and the auction room had upset him and he had a nagging feeling that he had not seen the last of Mr Grimley.

Chapter 4

Computer Mystery

JIM MERRINGTON HAD BEEN WORKING WITH JERRY Tomlins in his lab on Saturday while the others had been at the auction. They were trying to understand who or what was interfering with their computer.

Jim and his team of two scientists, Mike and Kala, had been working for about five years trying to make their computer behave like a human brain, or at least part of a human brain. They had made a lot of progress in the last year and there was a lot of interest in their work from scientists all over the world. The reason they were doing it was because they believed if they could create a computer model of the brain, they might be able to understand what happens when the human brain goes wrong in mental diseases. They had a collaboration going with one of the big mental hospitals in London so that they could obtain advice from some of the best psychiatrists in the country. Their greatest hope was that their research would help people with mental diseases like depression and schizophrenia.

Only Jim, Mike and Kala were able to program the computer. Kala had set the security so that nobody else could interfere with it, or so she thought. But it seemed that someone else was feeding data into the computer that made the computer respond. This is what Jerry Tomlins was brought in to investigate. He was an expert on computer hacking, having been an avid hacker himself in his younger days! Jim suspected that he still did a bit of hacking in his spare time, but he claimed he was merely keeping up with the latest techniques. Kala had given Jerry access to the computer security system so that he could work out what was going on.

'I've been through this pretty carefully and I'd say that Kala has done an excellent job on the security. I've studied the log and it seems that the hacker has somehow been able to use this computer directly to get in. Most of the entries have been at night.'

'That's the conclusion I came to, but it seemed a bit far-fetched,' said Kala.

'You mean an intruder has been getting into the lab?' asked Jim.

'That's what it seems like. I'd prefer not to stay up all night to keep a watch on the computer, so let's start with a simple experiment. I'll set it up to print out all inputs and make each user enter his or her name, date of birth, place of work and job title every time they make a new entry.'

'OK, that's a start, but I can't see someone who is obviously very smart telling us his or her name!'

'Maybe, but let's just take it in easy stages. All clues are useful,' replied Jerry.

It took Jerry about an hour to complete the programming. There was nothing more they could do, so they locked up and set off to go home. On the way out, Jim spoke to the security guard and told him to keep a special watch on their lab. There was a closed-circuit television camera in the corridor outside the lab, so the guard could see if anyone entered the lab through the door.

On Monday, Mike and Kala were in early to study Jerry's log. It showed more inputs on Sunday, but the camera had not picked up any intruders. But surprise, surprise! The author of the entries signed in as Joshua Robertson, date of birth 23 May '29, Walchester University, Professor of History!

When Mike and Kala saw this, they immediately thought it was a hoax – there was no history department in the University any more. And besides, he would be over seventy years old. Jerry came in, looked at the print-outs and responded in the same way at first. Then he said 'Why would he use a name like "Joshua Robertson"? If he was kidding, he would have entered something like "Joe Bloggs".'

Jim had intended to get in early but he forgot that he had promised Julia she could use the car, so he had to cycle. When he arrived, hot and sweaty, he charged straight across the lab to where the others were clustered over the print-outs.

'Ever heard of Joshua Robertson?' asked Jerry.

'No.' Jim paused. 'But Robertson was Julia's maiden name. She doesn't have a relative called Joshua that I can remember. I'll ask her tonight, but I can't see that it can be more than a coincidence.'

'So, Jerry, what do we do next?' asked Kala.

'Depends on whether you want to block this Joshua Robertson from interfering, or whether you want to find out who he is.'

'Whoever he is, he's done some pretty clever things and he's got some interesting data out of the computer. What's more, he seems to be following a logical series of experiments,' remarked Mike. 'I'd like to see what his experiments turn up.'

'Hang on Mike; we can't just let a completely unknown character use our facilities for his private study! Besides, if he's getting into the lab out of hours, we've got to stop him. Who knows what else he might meddle with?'

'I guess you're right, Jim. OK, I'll volunteer to stay in the lab overnight to try to catch this Joshua Robertson.'

'It's against the safety rules to stay in the lab at night on your own – I'll join you,' said Jerry. 'It's not exactly a high-tech solution, but I think it's the next sensible thing to do. How about tonight?'

'Suits me,' replied Mike. 'I'll call home to explain what's happening.'

That evening, Jerry went out to buy a couple of pizzas for Mike and himself. Kala and Jim were still in the lab while Mike and Jerry were eating their pizzas in the common room before beginning their all-night vigil. Kala was checking the computer settings before leaving to go home. When she was satisfied, she logged off, packed up her bag and headed towards the door.

'Goodnight, Jim.'

'See you tomorrow. I'll wait here until Mike and Jerry get back.'

Kala stopped by at the common room to tell Mike and Jerry she was leaving and that Jim was still in the lab.

'Thanks, Kala. Will you be in early tomorrow?'

'Yes, probably about seven thirty. Do you want me to bring in some breakfast for you? The refectory's not open that early but I could make you something at home and bring it in'. She lived only two minutes' walk away from the University.

'That would be fantastic!' exclaimed Jerry. 'You're a gem!'

Kala smiled. 'See you tomorrow.'

Jim was packed up and ready to leave when Jerry and Mike got back to the lab.

'I'll leave you two to have fun tonight then. Hope you've got plenty to do. I'll remind the security guard what we're doing as I leave. Goodnight.

'Thanks, goodnight.'

'Any suggestions how we handle this?' Jerry asked Mike.

'I suppose one of us could sleep while the other keeps watch and we could take turns.'

'That's too risky – we could both fall asleep. Remember we haven't prepared for this. We'll both be tired.'

'Well, I was planning on finishing the paper I've been trying to write for the last two weeks. That should keep me awake,' he said, doubtfully.

'I'll listen to some music, then. I won't disturb you – I'll use my personal stereo.' Jerry went down to his lab and got his personal stereo and a selection of CDs. When he got back, Mike was at his desk, already busily typing away on his computer. The monitor on the main computer was facing away from Mike's desk, so Jerry turned it round. The lab was extremely untidy: it contained a lot of additional computer equipment and the benches were littered with electronic gadgets and piles of books, journals and papers. The large windows did not have any blinds and the street lights outside gave an annoying yellowish glow. The fluorescent lighting inside the lab created a stark white light and all the tall equipment in the lab generated deep shadows.

Jerry was lounging in Kala's chair facing the computer monitor and listening to his music. He was on his third CD and unfortunately, even his heavy metal music was lulling him to sleep rather than keeping him awake. His eyelids drooped and then one of his arms slipped off the arm of the chair. He woke with a start and a snort that made Mike leap from his chair. As if it had taken that as a cue, the computer monitor filled with text. The two of them stared, unbelieving.

'But nobody's touching the computer,' exclaimed Jerry.

They looked at the text and sure enough, it was Joshua Robertson who had signed in again. He was putting in new data and it was appearing on the screen at a rate much too fast for anyone to be typing it in.

'This is fascinating,' Mike whispered. 'He's definitely continuing the same series of experiments. It's almost as though he's studying a real patient.'

This was not Jerry's field, so he didn't understand what Mike was talking about, but he could see by Mike's face that whatever Joshua Robertson was doing, he was no novice. About two screenfuls of data appeared on the screen in about thirty seconds, and then it took the computer about as long to process the data before it churned out the results. As Jerry had set it up to print everything, the printer whirred into action and began spewing out both inputs and outputs. Then it all went quiet.

Mike and Jerry looked at each other in the silence, wondering what was going to happen next. Perhaps some stranger would come into the lab to check the results. Was there anyone else in the lab? Thoughts of ghosts came into their minds and they scanned the darkest corners of the lab to look for movements. The shadows seemed to move, but only in their imaginations. The only sound was the gentle humming of the fan in the computer. They waited expectantly, but all was still.

The phone rang and they both leapt in alarm.

Mike, panting for breath, staggered over to the phone.

'Hello.'

'Mike, it's Jim. I spoke to Julia about Joshua Robertson. It was a bit late by the time we were able to check, but she had an ancestor called Joshua Robertson who was a professor at Walchester University! Can you check the date of birth he entered into the computer?'

Mike shuddered. 'OK. It's Jim,' he remarked to Jerry as he went over, ashen-faced, to the printer to check. Jerry looked at him with a puzzled expression. Mike brought back the page where Joshua Robertson had signed in. '23rd May '29.'

'That's it exactly – 23rd May 1829!'

'1829?' Mike went even paler and sat down with a thump on the nearest chair. Jerry grabbed the phone from him and shouted down the phone at Jim. 'Jim, what's going on? Mike looks as though he's gone into shock!'

Jim explained it to Jerry, whose turn it was to look shocked. Then Jerry reported the events of the night to Jim.

'I suggest you two go home and get some sleep. Don't come in tomorrow until you've had a good rest.'

They didn't need persuading to leave the lab, but neither of them felt tired any more – the adrenaline was rushing through their bodies and they were as tense as piano wires. They both grunted to the security guard as he let them out of the building. As the security guard was returning to his little office, he shook his head, wondering what went through the minds of these academics and how they could be polite one minute and rude the next.

Needless to say, neither Mike nor Jerry slept well that night and they were both in early as usual, much to Jim's annoyance. Kala had made some bacon sandwiches for them. As it turned out, both Mike and Jerry were ravenous as they hadn't even thought of breakfast in their urgency to get into the lab to talk to the others about last night's exploits. They all went into the common room while Mike and Jerry tucked into their breakfasts.

'Did Julia have any more information on Joshua Robertson?' asked Kala.

'Well, apparently he wrote a couple of books that Julia said she would try to track down. One was a fairly standard history textbook, but the other was a set of short biographies on historical personalities – and here's the bit that's fascinating – he concentrated on famous historical figures that had mental diseases!'

Mike was just about to swallow a mouthful of sandwich. He choked and gasped for breath. Jerry thumped him on the back and Kala passed him a glass of water. Jim waited for Mike to recover before continuing.

'I've told Julia to try to get that one first.'

When Mike had regained the power of speech, he started surmising. 'I wonder – the experiment that Joshua Robertson is doing might be based on one of those characters. We absolutely must get hold of that book.'

'I wouldn't be too hopeful. I don't expect it was a best-seller, so there may not be any copies in existence. Anyway, I suggest we get on with our normal work for the rest of the day. I don't think it's worth doing any more investigations on how Joshua Robertson interferes with our computer. I suggest we just let it run its course.'

'But this is crazy!' said Jerry. 'How can a dead person be entering data into the computer? It makes no sense at all. Perhaps we should tell the police.'

'I don't think it's worth bothering the police. It's not really their scene and besides, we'd be hard pushed to make a proper complaint. I'd appreciate it if you didn't talk to others about what we've found. They'll think we're all nuts.'

'I agree with that,' said Mike. 'I've told my wife because she loves all this mystical stuff. I expect she's talking to Julia about it right now. But of course, Jerry's right. It doesn't make sense. Even so, I'm keeping an open mind.'

'It doesn't sound like it to me,' said Jerry. 'You seem convinced that we've got a computer-wise ghost.'

Jim jumped in to avert an argument. 'Let's just see what happens, shall we? There appears to be very little we can do about it and as far as we can tell, it doesn't appear to be causing us any trouble.' Everyone nodded in assent.

Julia had indeed been talking to Mike's wife on the telephone about Joshua Robertson that morning. Since then, she had been re-checking her sources of information in case she had missed anything vital. Joshua was Magnus Robertson's eldest son. He had left Drumbridge to study at Oxford University but then returned to take a job in the History Department at Walchester University. He was only about thirty years of age when he became Professor of History, so presumably he was an outstanding academic. Joshua married and had two sons of his own, Benjamin and Arthur. Unfortunately, Joshua's wife died of tuberculosis while the children were very young. Julia did not have any records of the deaths of Joshua, Benjamin or Arthur. She had not seen their graves in Drumbridge or Walchester.

Julia was descended from one of Magnus Robertson's younger sons, so she had not spent a lot of time researching Joshua. She thought that there could be some more information on Joshua's work in the University archives, but she knew that the nineteenth century documents at the University were kept in bundles in date order, so it would probably be like looking for a needle in a haystack. She thought that she needed some more clues on what to look for before plunging into the archives. She decided to check the local records to find out more on Joshua and his two sons.

The following day, Julia headed for the library early. She discovered after scouring the census records that in 1861 Joshua was living in Roseberry Lane, Walchester, with his two sons, but in 1871 there was no record of them that she could find. Perhaps they had moved out of the area, or even died. Joshua would have been forty-two years old in 1871. She decided to look at the records of deaths between 1861 and 1871. Much to her surprise, she found that Joshua had died in 1869, but what was more surprising, both Benjamin and Arthur had died in the same year. What could have happened to them? Perhaps they all caught a fatal disease, or died together in an accident. She decided to order copies of the death certificates – they would give the causes of death. It would take a week or so for them to come in the post, so she had to be patient.

Chapter 5

Benjamin Robertson

As Mum had predicted, a few days later Dad queried Tom about his visions at Magnus Robertson's grave. Much to Tom's surprise, Dad was very understanding. Mum had obviously prepared him well. His biggest concern was that it was upsetting Tom and could affect his school work.

'I don't want to stop you from sitting at Magnus's grave, but I am worried that you are bound to have these visions on your mind when you are at school and it will distract you from your lessons.'

'I understand, Dad, but I don't think I can do anything about the visions. It seems like something drives me to go to the grave when it's time for the next vision. It's as though I've been chosen to see the visions.' Dad pondered a moment, his chin in his hand.

'It does seem that way, I must admit.'

'I'll try harder at school, I promise.'

'You are capable of more at school, you know, Tom. Your mother and I have been telling you that for some time.'

'I hope you're right, Dad. Perhaps I need something like this to wake me up.'

'Your friend Frank is a good example to follow. He's a bright lad and he works hard.'

'Yes, I know. I'll try to keep up with him.'

'OK, well let's see how things go, shall we?' He then went on to explain his own mysterious problem with the computer.

'We've also had a strange experience in the lab. You remember I told you about a hacker we thought was getting into our computer? Well, I don't know quite how to put this, but the "hacker" purports to be one of our ancestors.'

'Tom was shaken. 'Who?'

'Joshua Robertson, Magnus Robertson's eldest son.'

'But that can't be true. It's impossible.'

'I agree, but it's happening. If it's a hoax, the hoaxer is extremely clever. Not only has he researched our family history thoroughly; he understands how our computer program works and he has an insight into mental disorders. I find it hard to believe that anyone could be that brilliant. Anyway, you leave us to sort it out and don't worry about it. Your mother has collected some information on Joshua Robertson, so you might be interested in that, purely from the family history point of view of course.'

'Do you think it might be connected to my visions?'

'I suppose it's possible, but I don't think so. Just give us time – I'm sure we'll have a simple explanation soon.' He wasn't convincing.

The following day, Mum explained to Tom what she had discovered about Joshua Robertson. She expected the death certificates to arrive any day.

'It's odd, isn't it,' said Tom, 'that both Dad and I should be having experiences with Robertsons of the past? I wonder if there's a link? Dad doesn't think so.'

'I was wondering that myself but I really don't know. Oh, there's the post, could you check if there is anything for me, please Tom? I'm expecting the death certificates for Joshua and his two sons.'

Tom ran to the front door and picked up the post. Yes, Mum had several letters. He took them to her and she hurriedly scanned them and picked out one that she thought was what she was looking for.

'Good – this is it. Joshua Robertson died on November the 12th 1869 from – burns! Arthur also died of burns on the same day and Benjamin died of burns on November the 14th. So it looks as though they must have all been in a fire together. Perhaps their house burned down.'

'That's awful,' said Tom.

'I've got their address from the census records, so I think I might check whether the house is still there,' said Mum. 'Tom, you had better be getting along to school. Amy, are you ready yet?'

'Coming, Mum.'

Amy came crashing into the room swinging her school bag behind her.

'Do you have everything?'

'Yes, Mum.'

'Are you doing games today and do you have your kit?'

'Yes, Mum.'

'OK, let's get going.'

After school, Tom knew he had to go to Magnus Robertson's grave. He went into the graveyard, sat on the grave and waited with his eyes closed. Soon, Magnus Robertson came into his mind and held out his hand to take Tom on another trip through Victorian Drumbridge.

'Tom, try to understand what you are seeing this time,' Magnus said. He gave Tom a look of encouragement that seemed to signify it was time for Tom to move on to the next stage.

With that, Tom was left alone in Drumbridge, outside the Vicarage. Magnus Robertson was walking away towards the house, waving goodbye to Tom. It was then that Tom realized he was sitting on a broad-backed chestnut horse. He waved to Magnus, turned the horse and headed towards the village centre.

'Come on Hector, we need to take you to get that shoe seen to before we set off.' The horse walked slowly, one of its shoes making a clipping sound on the cobbles. They reached Market Street, where they headed for the blacksmith – Samuel Lovelock and Son. Samuel had been dead for many years and his son Sidney ran the business.

'Hello, Master Ben. What's the problem? Oh, wait – I can see for myself. He's got a loose shoe.' Sidney Lovelock was standing outside the smithy straightening his broad back and wiping his brow with a filthy rag.

'Could you fix it for me please, Sid?'

'Of course I can. I'll have it done in a jiffy.'

'Thanks very much. You seem to be busy.' He noticed Sid's son and an apprentice working furiously at the back of the smithy.

'Oh, yes, but still got time to fix this for you.' He checked the shoe and then announced that he would have to make a new one. Ben watched Sid's display of skill and strength as he manipulated and hammered the new shoe on the anvil. He tried the hot shoe against Hector's hoof, returned to the anvil to make the final adjustments and then nailed the shoe in place. After clipping off the ends of the nails and filing the sharp ends, Hector was ready for the road once again.

'There you are, Master Ben.'

Ben paid Sid and mounted Hector. 'Thank you, Sid.'

'Safe journey, Master Ben.'

Waving goodbye to Sid, he turned Hector towards the road out of Drumbridge towards Walchester. The road was just a rough track but it looked familiar. It had hawthorn hedges on both sides, but he could see over the hedges into the fields where the cattle and sheep were grazing. The leaves on the trees were turning a golden-brown and were starting to drop to the ground around the animals.

Tom was controlling the horse competently, but he had never ridden a horse before. He saw his hands. They were not his. Now that he knew it wasn't a dream, he tried to move a hand. Nothing happened. He wasn't in control of his body. His clothes were made of coarse material and his legs were longer than normal. Perhaps this was what Magnus was talking about. He was looking through Ben's eyes, not his own. Whoever Ben was, Magnus wanted Tom to experience his life. Why? Tom just had to wait and see.

They arrived on the edge of Walchester. It was much smaller than the Walchester he knew. They came to a neat thatched house near the University. Ben got off the horse and led it round behind the house. He took off the saddle and bridle and let the horse roam free in the paddock. He went in through the back door of the house.

'Is that you, Ben?' called a voice from inside the house.

'Yes, Millie.'

A middle-aged lady dressed in working clothes came into the room. Tom assumed that as he had called her by her first name, she was not his mother.

'And how is your grandfather?' she asked.

'He's very well, thank you Millie. I had a good day's fishing with him and I've brought home a brace of trout for our supper.' He pulled out two good-sized trout from his bag.

'Thank you, Ben. Your father is out with Arthur at the moment but they should be in soon. Your supper will be ready as soon as they're in.'

Arthur? That rings a bell, thought Tom. What did Mum say? Arthur and Benjamin were the sons of Joshua Robertson. Of course, that's why they call me Ben – I must be Benjamin Robertson! And Millie said that Magnus was Ben's grandfather. It all fits. When did Mum say they all died? I can't remember. Perhaps it's today!

About fifteen minutes later, Joshua and Arthur came in looking pleased to be home. Arthur was a small, lively boy with bright blue eyes. He looked several years younger than Ben. Joshua had similar features to Magnus, but his face was long rather than square and he was considerably thinner than Magnus. Like Magnus, he wore spectacles. He had a serious look on his face as though he never smiled.

'Good evening, Ben, I trust you had a good time at Drumbridge.'

'Good evening, Father. Yes, Grandfather and I had an enjoyable day fishing. I brought home two nice trout for our supper.'

'Splendid. That will do nicely.'

Tom thought their behaviour was rather formal for father and son, but he supposed that's what it was like in Victorian times.

'Ben, I'm getting in a bit of a muddle with all the information I've collected for the book I'm writing. I wondered if you might give me a hand sorting it out when Arthur has gone to bed.'

'I'd love to, Father,' said Ben excitedly.

Supper consisted of a rather thin soup, followed by the trout with bread, washed down with a dark liquid that Millie served from a jug. They ate in silence. Joshua was still eating the last of the trout after the boys had finished.

'That was excellent trout, Ben. Now, Arthur, get ready for bed, please.'

Arthur obediently left the table and went to his room to prepare for bed. Millie cleared up the dishes and left to return to her home.

Joshua and Ben went into a small room full of books and papers. Below the window was an oak chest that looked very similar to the one that Mum bought at the auction. Could it be the same one? Tom wished Ben would look at the chest. Then Joshua went over to it and opened it. It was definitely the same one! He pulled out a large, leather-bound notebook and a pile of papers and placed them on his desk.

'Let me explain what I'm doing, Ben, so that you can understand what I want from you. You see, I'm writing a book on the mental health of several famous people. I've noticed that genius often goes hand-in-hand with mental instability and a lot of great people had quite serious mental disorders. I've collected a lot of information, but it's got completely out of hand. I need all these papers – my notes for the book – sorted into files for each of the individuals. It's not so easy because some pages have more than one subject on them. I suggest you cut those up with scissors. I've actually nearly finished the book, but I need to be able to refer to all my notes to be certain that I've not missed anything.'

'I understand, Father. Can you give me a list of all the people in your book, please?'

'Of course. Each chapter is on a different person – here is the list of chapters. The last one is on Michelangelo. I've still got a little bit to do on him, so I'll keep his pile on my desk. You can take all the others into the drawing room if you like to give yourself some more space.'

Then he began musing about Michelangelo. 'You know, Michelangelo was a very interesting subject. He suffered badly from melancholia, but he must have had confidence in his own ability to tackle such challenging projects as his great statue of David. He would have needed to generate a lot of energy to accomplish such a project. In my opinion, he was the greatest sculptor that ever lived, but I wonder if he really believed he was so good? Perhaps in his better moments, he appreciated what he had achieved. Ah well, I suppose we'll never know.'

'What's melancholia, Father?'

'Oh, sorry, I should have explained. Sadness, depressed mood, sometimes so severe that the person cannot find the energy to do simple things like dressing himself. And Michelangelo was known not to change his clothes for weeks, so perhaps that was because he was so miserable.'

'I see. I'd like to read your chapter on Michelangelo if I may, Father.'

'Of course, when I've finished it. In the meantime, you might want to look at that book on the shelf over there. It's about the works of Michelangelo – shows what a great artist he was. Of course, as well as being a great sculptor, he was also a great painter.'

He pointed to a large volume on the shelf behind Ben. Ben turned round and took the book from the shelf and opened a few pages.

'Thanks, Father. I'll look at it tomorrow. I'll get started on your notes now.'

He gathered together the large pile of notes and took them into the drawing room.

'If you come across any notes on Michelangelo, bring them in here, won't you?'

'Of course, Father.'

'You won't get it all done tonight, but if you complete it in the next few days, that will be satisfactory.'

'I'll do my best, Father.'

At that point, Tom's vision broke off and he found himself back in the churchyard. He was still puzzling over why Magnus wanted him to experience the life of Benjamin Robertson when his mother appeared in front of him.

'Had another daydream?'

'Yes, but now I know that I'm seeing through the eyes of Benjamin Robertson. I just don't understand why.'

'Benjamin Robertson? How do you know?'

'Because I saw his father, who looks like a thinner version of Magnus, and his younger brother, Arthur. They lived in a thatched cottage in Walchester.'

'Did you get a chance to ask Joshua why he's meddling with Dad's computer?'

Tom laughed. 'I can't ask anything because I'm only seeing through Ben's eyes. Oh, I've got a surprise for you. That old chest you bought at the auction – it belonged to Joshua Robertson. I saw it in his study.'

'Really? What an amazing coincidence.' Then she seemed to reconsider what she had said. 'Or maybe it's not a coincidence.'

'You mean we were meant to have it?'

'Perhaps. No, not really, just a silly thought.'

'Anyway, he keeps all the notes for his book in it.'

'Did you see any of the notes?'

'No, but Joshua has asked Ben to help him sort them out, so I may get to see them next time.'

'You realize that Ben died when he was only fifteen, don't you?'

'Yes, I think he must be about that age in my vision. Do you think I'll experience his death?'

'Perhaps, but you know it's only a vision, so there's no point in worrying about it. Come in and have some dinner.'

Tom got up and followed his mother through the rickety gate into the Vicarage.

The next day, during their morning break at school, Tom and Frank were deep in conversation about Tom's most recent vision.

'I think it's a puzzle why you are having these visions at all, not just why you are re-living Benjamin Robertson's life,' said Frank. 'Perhaps you've been selected for something special.'

'I've been wondering that – but what could it be?'

'How should I know?'

'But why should Benjamin Robertson's life have anything to do with me?'

'Perhaps you should wait and see what happens next. What about when you get to his death? Perhaps you'll become someone else.'

'I think his death might come soon. He seems to be about fifteen in my vision, and that's when he died.'

'What was the weather like last time? What time of year do you think it was?'

Tom thought carefully. 'It was quite cool and breezy, and the leaves were falling off the trees – probably October or November. He died in November, so it could happen soon.'

'Are you keeping a record of everything you see in these visions?'

'Well, no, but I can remember all of it.'

'Perhaps you can now, but it's going to get more difficult to remember all the detail.'

'I suppose you're right.'

'I'll do it for you if you like. You just tell me everything and I'll write it down and make it sound interesting. Besides, I'm better at writing than you are.'

Dad's words came back to Tom and he had to admit that Frank did nearly always get better marks in his essays than he did. 'Yes, I suppose you are. OK, thanks. Let's start this evening after school.'

'Fine by me. Do you want to come round to my place for a change?'

'OK.'

The bell went for the end of break.

That evening, Frank and Tom met at the McGintys' house and went through all the daydreams Tom had experienced, even though the first few seemed to be little more than trial runs. Frank wrote copious notes and promised to write the full account at the weekend.

'Do you think there might be some special relationship between you and Benjamin Robertson?' asked Frank. 'Obviously, he's distantly related, but there might be something more than that.'

'Like having something in common, you mean?'

'Perhaps. Magnus Robertson must have the answer. After all, he's the one who's made it all work. He must want you to do something and that's got to be a family thing. Could it be something that Ben didn't finish before he died and he wants you to complete it?'

'But why me?'

'Why don't you ask him?'

'I'm not sure that I can. He has called me "Tom", but when he leaves me alone, I'm Ben and I have no control over anything. If I can speak to him next time, I will, but I don't hold out much hope.'

'Do you know when that will be?'

'Not yet, but I'll know when it's time.'

'How do you know?'

'I just get an urge to go to the grave. I suppose it must be Magnus making it happen. If I just go and sit next to the grave when I don't have the urge, nothing happens. I don't have to go as soon as I get the urge. Sometimes I get it during the day at school, but it seems OK to wait until I get home to go to the grave.'

Frank couldn't help making fun of Tom's choice of words. 'So it's not like having an urge to go to the toilet, then.'

Tom laughed. 'Hardly. It's more like knowing that your favourite programme is going to be on the television that evening.'

'So it's always something you look forward to.'

'Yes, so far, but I'm not looking forward to Ben's death. That could be the next one.'

'It's only a vision. You're not going to die.'

'That's more or less what Mum said.'

'Changing the subject, why don't we have a go at clearing those other two big graves? Now that we know how to read the inscriptions, we could tackle them tomorrow. Do you want to?'

'Yes, I think we should. It will help Mum with her survey as well.'

'Good, that's settled then.'

'I think I'd better be getting back. Mum will have the dinner ready soon.'

Tom opened the door of Frank's room and went downstairs with Frank following behind.

'Hello, Tom, how are you?'

'Fine, Mr McGinty, thank you very much.'

'I heard your mum bought a fine old oak chest the other day. Do you think she'll mind if I pop round to have a look?'

'I'm sure she'd be very pleased to show it to you, Mr McGinty. I'll tell her you'll be calling round sometime.'

'Thank you, Tom. I'll give your mum a call before I come round.' A broad grin spread across Mr McGinty's tanned face. He was a very big man, like a larger version of Frank. He put one of his huge hands on Tom's shoulder and gently ushered him through the front door. As Tom waved to Frank and his dad from the front gate, he thought how lucky he was to have such a good friend as Frank.

As he strolled home, he wondered again what his visions could mean. Perhaps Frank was right and Magnus wanted him to complete something for the family that Ben had started but couldn't finish because he died so young. If that were the case, Tom would need to know before Ben died, so it would have to be soon.

For the first time in his life, Tom was captivated by something. Throughout his school days, he had drifted along, doing just enough to be average, when in fact he was capable of a lot more, as some of his teachers, and of course his parents, knew. Perhaps it was because his parents had both achieved a lot academically that he did not believe he could match their standards: his father had a distinguished academic career and his mother had obtained a first-class honours' degree in art history. Perhaps things would change now that he had a focus that was uniquely his. In fact, he was determined that they would.

The following evening, Tom met Frank in the graveyard and they began to clean up the other two big headstones that were still overgrown with ivy and brambles. They made good progress and were soon ready to try the flour trick again. Tom went into the Vicarage to get Mum's bucket and brush and a little flour. It worked just as well as before, and the grave next to Samuel and Esther Lovelock's was another Lovelock, Peter, who was possibly Samuel's brother. The other one had a lot of names on it from a family called Sturgess. They had not come across this name before. They were a little disappointed that their efforts had not revealed anything exciting, but they had the information for their school project anyway. They gave Tom's mum their copies of the inscriptions for her survey.

'We might as well try to decipher that little gravestone in the corner as we've still got time. It's not readable without flour,' suggested Frank.

'OK, let's give it a go.'

This grave was tucked away in a corner as though the people who buried the occupant did not want it to be noticed. The inscription was badly worn, but with a bit of flour, the words became visible.

'Sebastian…something like Shinley, no, that's a "G" – Grimley!' They looked at each other knowing that they had discovered something important.

'And it says at the bottom that he was from Walchester,' added Frank. 'That's strange. Why would someone from Walchester be buried here? There are at least three churches in Walchester.'

'He was buried in 1871, so Magnus would have buried him. Presumably he was an ancestor of old Grimley the antique dealer, and if he was as nasty as him, it's not surprising they tucked him away in a corner. I haven't come across him in my daydreams, not yet, anyway.'

'That's something else you could ask Magnus – why he buried Grimley in Drumbridge.'

'I've got more important things than that to ask him. Come on, it's time we went home.' It was a fitting time to end their search, so they packed up their tools and walked back to the gate.

Chapter 6

The Fire

JULIA HAD TRIED TO TRACK DOWN COPIES of Joshua Robertson's books but without success so far. She had tried all the obvious sources, including a search on the internet. One specialist in medical books had promised to try to find a copy, but so far he had not come up with anything. At the moment, the University archives looked like the best bet. They were unlikely to have the books, but they might have Joshua's notes for his books. Kala had tried to find them in the archives covering the two years after his death, but had failed to come up with anything. She concluded that Joshua probably kept all his notes for his books at home and they were probably destroyed in the fire.

Tom had his own thoughts on the subject. He knew what Joshua Robertson's notebook looked like. If he saw it again he would recognize it instantly. If it survived the fire, who would it have been returned to? Joshua's wife was already dead. Of course, Magnus! He would have looked after Joshua's books and notes. Would he have given them to the University archives? Probably, but he would have needed time to sort them out, and think how he would feel – it would have been a painful job, so he may have left it until he felt he could face it. It could have been years later, so Mum and Kala's strategy of looking at all the documents in the archives just after Joshua's death would not work; they had to look in the later archives. That was a lot of work, so he decided not to suggest it to Kala and Mum for now.

Now that Tom had thought a lot more about the fire that killed Joshua and his sons, he was no longer afraid to experience it. He was not exactly looking forward to it, but he wanted desperately to know what happened. He knew that the following day would bring the next vision and wondered whether it would be the one he was waiting for.

He decided to go to the graveyard early in the morning before school, so he set his alarm clock and was out in the early morning mist. This time, he did not meet Magnus first. Within seconds of sitting down by the grave, he found himself back with Ben, who was at home with Arthur and Millie. Joshua was out, presumably at the University. Arthur was doing some school homework and Ben was continuing to sort out his father's notes. Several times, he found notes on Michelangelo, so he placed them on Joshua's desk in the library. Tom could read the notes and he could see that Ben was reading a lot more than was necessary to sort the notes into chapters; he was obviously finding his father's work interesting. Tom got the impression that Ben must have been very intelligent.

'Time for tea, boys.' Millie had brought in some tea and cakes on a tray. 'Your father will be in a little later this evening because he's gone for a ride.'

Both Ben and Arthur immediately stopped what they were doing and tucked into the cakes.

'What are you doing, Ben?'

'Sorting out some of Father's notes for him. He's too busy to do it himself. Have you finished your homework?'

'Nearly.'

'When you've finished, would you like me to read you another chapter of "Great Expectations"?'

'Oh, yes please.' Arthur looked overjoyed and he stuffed his cake into his mouth to finish it quickly.

Ben laughed at him. 'No need to rush, we've still got plenty of time before Father gets home.'

When Joshua did get home, he looked angry. 'That fool of a man Grimley accused me of killing his wretched dog. The stupid thing barked at Major and made him rear up. Shame for the dog, it was under Major's hooves when they came down again – killed it outright. Grimley gave me a string of abuse. He wouldn't listen to reason. All he cared about was his wretched dog. Folks say he's a bit soft in the head and I think they're right. Oh, well, we have to tolerate fools I suppose. I'm starving – is supper nearly ready, Millie?'

'Coming up in about five minutes, sir.'

'Excellent. Just time for me to wash. Boys – how have you been today?'

'Fine, Father,' said Arthur. 'Ben read me another chapter of "Great Expectations".'

'Excellent. Fine yarn, that. Wonderful author, Dickens.' He seemed to have forgotten about the incident with the dog and was ready to enjoy his family. He bustled off to wash for supper.

During supper, Joshua asked Ben how he was getting on with his notes.

'I've got through over half of them. I should finish sorting them tomorrow.'

'Excellent. Did you find any notes on Michelangelo?'

'Yes, I put them on your desk'

'Ah, good. I made a couple of pages of notes on the time he was in Florence when it was invaded. I'd like to have those tonight.'

'I think I found those. They are on your desk.'

'Excellent. That will save me searching for them in the pile. Well done, Ben.'

After supper, Joshua sat down for a while with Arthur and Ben and listened to Ben reading some more from "Great Expectations".

'You read well, Ben.'

'Thank you, Father.'

'Now I must be getting on with my book. Arthur: come into the library to see me before you go to bed.'

'Of course, Father.'

'When Arthur had gone to bed, Ben continued sorting his father's notes. He found another note on Michelangelo and took it into the library.

'Thank you, Ben. I'll check the remaining notes when you have sorted them, but I think I can say that the book is just about finished.'

'You must be very proud, Father.'

'As a matter of fact I am. It's been hard work and I think it's fair to say that nobody has attempted anything like it before. The publishers will have it in the next few days. They've been pestering me for a while now.'

'Father, I'd like to be able to do something to be proud of like writing a book when I am older. Do you think I'll be able to do that?'

'Of course. You're a very bright boy. But you must choose the right career. I'm not sure I chose the right career even though I have been rather successful. I wish I had studied medicine now. It's a fascinating subject, and there are still lots of mysteries to solve. Take the brain for instance – almost a complete mystery but the most important organ in the body. What a challenge!'

'I think I'd like to study medicine, Father.'

'Then you shall, my boy, you shall! I'll do all I can to help you find the right place at university. I have some good friends who are physicians and they will be only too pleased to guide us, I'm sure.'

'Thank you very much for your encouragement, Father. I think I'll go to bed now. I'll have all your notes sorted for you when you get back from work tomorrow.'

'Yes, of course, Ben. Goodnight.'

Goodnight, Father.'

Ben's bedroom was at the other end of the house from the library. As he went past Arthur's bedroom, he peered around the door to check that Arthur was asleep. He heard Arthur's gentle, regular breathing. He was fast asleep.

Ben was exhausted and he went to sleep almost as soon as he had drawn the blankets over him.

This was a strange sensation for Tom. His vision went blank as Ben fell asleep. Then he started to experience Ben's dream. He was in a baker's shop, selling bread to customers. The shop was full of customers and they needed more bread for the shelves. He went to the back of the shop where they were baking the bread. Two men were sweating as they moved loaves in and out of the oven. One of the men motioned to Ben to put some more logs into the oven fire. The oven was so hot. Ben lifted the cover and the heat was intense; flames licked up to the ceiling.

'Ben! Ben! Wake up! The house is on fire!'

Ben awoke with a start to find his room full of smoke and his father struggling to open the window. He jumped out of bed and staggered to the window, but he was choking on the smoke. The instant he got to the window, his father slumped to the ground. He bent down to help, but it was no good. He was coughing and gasping but more smoke filled his lungs. He was feeling weaker and weaker; he had no energy left. There were shouts from outside...breaking glass…can't breathe…can't breathe! It all went black again, then there was a blinding light, and everything was spinning. Who is calling me? Where am I? The voices were getting more and more distant, and then they were replaced by gentle, comforting sounds like a group of people chanting. They were welcoming him. No! I won't give up! I must go back…go back…go back.

Tom was relieved to find himself sitting in the graveyard, but he was sweating profusely and shaking all over. To his surprise, it was cold, not hot. So that was it! The house did burn down, but why? Was it an accident or was it arson? Seeing it all through the eyes of Ben had its problems. He could not answer any of those questions. Reluctantly, he stumbled back into the Vicarage where he met his mother in the kitchen.

'Where have you been? I thought you were still in bed. What's happened to you? You look terrible.'

'I couldn't wait. I know about the fire now. It was Joshua's house that burned down and both Joshua and Ben died in the fire. It was horrible.' Tom was still trembling and his face was ghostly white.

Mum drew Tom to her and held him tightly. 'At least you know now. You were brave to face up to it.'

'It wasn't me who was brave. Joshua tried to save Ben but they were both overcome by smoke. They just choked to death. I heard people shouting outside, so I think someone must have tried to save them, but they were too late.'

'I'll see if I can track down a copy of the local paper to see if there was a report on the fire. Come on, I'll make you some breakfast and then you'll have to get ready for school.'

That day, Julia checked on the listings for the "Walchester Chronicle" in the Newspaper Library. Much to her surprise, it was listed, and it covered the year 1869! There was a note stating that some issues were missing, but it did not say which ones. She thought she just about had time to get there and back before the children came in from school. Just in case, she left a note at the school for Tom and Amy to say where she had gone and that she might be a bit late.

The "Walchester Chronicle" was a weekly paper, published every Friday. When Julia checked the detailed listings, she found that the issue she wanted was there, so she ordered it plus the two following weeks just in case there were further reports. It took a while before they were delivered to her desk. When they arrived, she scanned the pages as carefully as she could but her heart was pounding with excitement.

There it was! "University Professor Dies in Fire" was the headline on the third page. She devoured the words with wide eyes. It seemed that the fire only affected the rear half of the building because rescuers were able to stop it spreading to the front. Joshua, Ben and Arthur were dragged from the blaze, but both Joshua and Arthur died before they could get to hospital. Ben was still alive but in a critical state in hospital and was not expected to live. So far, this tallied with Tom's experience. Then she came to the interesting bit: it said that police suspected this was the result of an arson attack and they were questioning a local man. It did not give the name of the man.

Julia then hurriedly went to the next week's edition. She found a brief article about the fire. Ben had died as expected a few days after the incident. The "local man" had now been charged with arson. His name was Sebastian Grimley. It stated that he had an argument with Joshua on the day of the fire over the death of his dog and the police claimed he burned the house in an act of revenge. Sebastian Grimley! It was his grave that Tom and Frank had cleaned up in the churchyard. It was even more strange that Magnus buried him in Drumbridge when not only was he a Walchester man, but also it seemed he killed Magnus's son.

Julia checked the following week's issue but there were no further reports, so she obtained copies of the two articles and then hurried back home. As it happened, she was a few minutes late. Almost as soon as she got in, the phone rang. It was Frank. Tom and Amy were at his house, but they would come home now that they knew she was in. Julia thanked him and waited for Tom and Amy to get home. She watched out of the window and then went to the door when she saw them arrive at the front gate.

'Hi, Mum. Did you find anything at the Newspaper Library?'

'Yes, come and see.'

Tom read through the reports. 'So Ben survived a few days after the fire. It must have been awful for him. Only half of the house burned, so perhaps Joshua's notes survived. But of course they did! How could we be so stupid?'

'Why are you so certain?'

'Two reasons: he only finished the book that night, so someone must have given his draft to the publishers after his death, otherwise the book would never have been published; the second reason is we know his chest survived because we've got it! He kept it in the library with his notes inside it, although I suppose they could still have been on his desk during the fire.'

'Yes, of course – all the more reason to continue to look for them.'

Tom was getting excited now and eagerly began reading the second newspaper report. 'Sebastian Grimley! So the man Joshua called a fool is the same Grimley who's buried in the churchyard. Why would Magnus have buried him in Drumbridge when he killed his son? Magnus must have been an incredibly forgiving man. I wonder how Grimley died? It wasn't long after the fire. Do you think he was an ancestor of Mr Grimley, the antique dealer?'

'I think that's very likely.'

Although Mum had warned Tom to be wary of Mr Grimley, Tom decided he would confront Mr Grimley to find out whether he could tell him anything about Sebastian. He did not like to do anything against Mum's wishes, but he was not afraid of Mr Grimley. He would work out a plan with Frank. He called Frank on the telephone and explained what Mum had found out about the fire and Sebastian Grimley. Just in case Mum could hear, he did not mention his idea of going to see Mr Grimley.

While the Merringtons were enjoying their dinner that evening, a United Airlines flight from Washington touched down at Heathrow Airport. On board, in the first-class cabin, was a tall, well-dressed man with angular features disguised expertly in a wig and tinted spectacles. He had the air of a celebrity. He was also carrying one of his many false passports. He went through passport control and customs without anyone recognizing him. In the arrivals reception area, a driver of a black Mercedes was waiting to take him to his destination. The man was wanted by police the world over and, although he didn't know it himself, he was going to change Tom's life.

Chapter 7

Mr Grimley's Grudge

Tom and Frank had a chance to talk during a break at school the next day.

'Are you serious about going to see old Grimley?' asked Frank.

'Of course. Why? You're not afraid of him, are you?'

'No.' Frank was not convincing.

'I think you are.'

'Why are you so confident he'll talk to you? It's not like you to be so confident.'

'I'm not, but I think it's worth a try. What can he do anyway? He's not going to bite our heads off. He can only chase us out of his shop.'

'OK. I just hope your mum doesn't find out. She'll roast you alive after specifically telling you to keep out of his way.'

'Well, as long as you don't tell her, she won't find out, will she?'

'I won't tell her.'

'Good. Then let's wait for an opportunity to go into Walchester and visit Mr Grimley.'

It was the day before Tom and Frank had agreed to help Mum and Kala search the University archives that Mum's car developed a problem and she had to take it to the garage for repair the next day. She suggested that Tom and Frank should catch the bus into Walchester and go without her to the University. Tom told Frank and they agreed to catch the early bus and go to Mr Grimley's shop before meeting Kala.

It was only a five-minute walk to Mr Grimley's shop from the bus stop. When they got there, they peered into the window. The shop was dark and dingy and Mr Grimley was sitting in the back looking as miserable as ever.

'Come on, we can't put it off for ever, let's go in.'

They pushed the heavy door open and a huge bell started clanging. Either Mr Grimley was deaf or he was paranoid about missing customers coming through the door, Tom thought to himself. At the sound of the bell, Grimley looked up and glared at the two boys. They walked directly towards him, ignoring the antiques surrounding them.

'What do you want? You've not come here to buy anything, I'll wager.'

'That's right, Mr Grimley, we've come to ask for your help.'

'Help? Why should I help you? You're the Robertson kid aren't you?'

'Well, my mother was a Robertson, but my name's Tom Merrington.'

'Same difference. Clear off – I can't help you.' He was glaring at them with malice just as he did at the auction.

Tom was shaking, but he was determined this time. 'But Mr Grimley, I wanted to ask you about one of your ancestors, Sebastian Grimley.'

At the mention of the name, Grimley started to go purple and looked as though he was about to explode. Tom and Frank were scared but stood their ground. Grimley glared ferociously as though he was about to pounce and bite their heads off after all.

'What do you know about Sebastian Grimley?' he snarled.

'Not enough,' answered Frank. His words were now falling over each other. 'That's why we've come to you. You see, we're doing a project at school about people who lived here in Victorian times. We know that Sebastian Grimley lived in Walchester, but we wondered why he was buried in Drumbridge.' He had planned to use this approach if the going got tough. His intervention seemed to catch Grimley off guard and the snarl softened to a growl with mutterings.

'You two at school together?'

'Yes, we're working on the same project. The other thing we know about Sebastian Grimley was that he was arrested for arson.'

'Ah, so you know that do you?' Grimley snapped at them, suddenly paying attention to what they were saying. 'Yes, Sebastian was arrested, but he wasn't convicted. He was innocent, that's why. They found out who did it six months later. But the locals took the law into their own hands – strung him up, they did. All because of a damned Robertson.'

'You mean the argument over his dog with Joshua Robertson.'

Grimley was surprised. 'So you know that as well. That's right. And you can see now why the Grimleys have hated the Robertsons ever since. Sebastian was none too clever, but he wasn't a murderer.'

'Do you know if any of the Robertsons were involved in hanging Sebastian?'

'They didn't have to be. That Professor Robertson was treated like a king by the locals, being so clever, while poor Sebastian was the opposite.'

'So if there was so much hatred between the Grimleys and the Robertsons, why did Magnus Robertson bury Sebastian in Drumbridge?'

Grimley's tone had changed considerably. He squirmed in his chair, but he was becoming almost co-operative. 'That was unfortunate. The locals in Walchester terrorised the vicar so that he was too scared to bury him in Walchester. The Rev Robertson said he had not been convicted, so he would bury him. Terrible thing – a Robertson doing the Grimleys a favour and the Grimleys in no mind to pay it back.'

Tom seized his opportunity; he could sense that Grimley was softening. 'It's never too late. Why not pay it back now, Mr Grimley, by making peace with the Robertsons?' Tom asked.

Grimley looked puzzled, as though he was turning over the thought in his mind, knowing it shouldn't be there. All his prejudice, handed down by his embittered father and his grandfather before him, was like a huge boulder standing in his way. He knew in his heart that Tom was right and there was no sense in maintaining the grudge. Then he looked at Tom's fresh, young face, free of all malice.

'I suppose it was a long time ago. Times have changed. You seem to be a nice enough lad and I can't say it's been hard to talk to you. Perhaps it would be better not to hold grudges, but, lad, it's not so easy for me.' He seemed almost apologetic.

'I understand Mr Grimley. You've been very helpful and we don't want to take up any more of your time, so we'll be off now.'

As they went out they could see disappointment on Grimley's face. He wanted them to stay longer. As they reached the door he called out: 'Don't be afraid to come in and see me again if you want any more help. Oh, one other thing, lad: what's your mother's first name?'

'Julia. And thanks again Mr Grimley.'

'Thank you.' And he wrote "Julia Robertson" in a heavy scrawl on a pad on his desk. Then he crossed out "Robertson" and wrote "Merrington".

As soon as Tom and Frank were out of the shop, they started talking furiously.

'Gosh, what a result! It was so good I think I can confess to Mum that I went to see Mr Grimley. That was great information he gave us. And I think he's even thinking of chatting up Mum sometime!'

'He seemed as though he wanted to get rid of the burden he's been carrying all his life. Perhaps we should go and see him again sometime. I think he'd be pleased to see us.'

'I think you're right.'

Frank gave Tom a pat on the back. 'You gave a great performance there,

Tom. I'm proud of you!'

'You're proud of me?'

'Yes, you reduced that ogre to a snivelling wretch. He was eating out of your hand.'

'You think so?'

'Of course.'

'Shame about poor old Sebastian Grimley. I bet Magnus buried him because he believed he was innocent. I wonder how the local vigilantes felt when the real criminal was discovered?'

They arrived at the University on time and Kala was waiting in the foyer. They went straight down to the archives in the basement.

'Where's your mother today, Tom?' Her big brown eyes seemed to bore into his brain and he felt more guilty than he should have done.

'She couldn't come. The car's broken down, but we can manage without her.'

'I'm sure we can.'

They shared out the boxes and ploughed through them. After an hour, they had drawn a blank and had covered 1880 to 1884. Then Frank discovered something in the September 1879 box. It was a collection of pieces of paper of different sizes with notes on historical personalities and it had been deposited by Rev M Robertson. 'I think I've found something,' he called in a rather loud whisper.

Tom and Kala hurried over and stood behind him, peering anxiously over his shoulder.

'Yes, you've got something there. I've seen some of those before. But there were more than that.'

'Perhaps there are more in this box.' Frank quickly went through the rest of the documents in the box and found another folder submitted by Magnus. It was another bunch of similar notes.

'We need copies of these. I'll ask the archivist whether we can copy them.' Kala went over to the archivist who was soon explaining animatedly what could be done. Kala returned.

'They can get them copied for us, but they will have to be done photographically, not with a photocopier, and it will take some time. She said we can borrow them for a couple of days as long as they stay in the University, so I think we'll borrow them first and then get them copied. Mike and Jim will be anxious to see these.'

They continued their search and had gone back to 1876 by the time the archives closed. They took them upstairs to the lab where Mike and Jim greeted them noisily when they saw that Kala was clutching the folders.

'Aha, what have you got for us there?'

'I thought you'd be pleased.'

As Mike began to scan the notes, Tom explained that there might be more of Joshua's notes in the archives. 'If we had the list of contents of Joshua's book we would know whether we had all the notes. Each chapter was about a different personality and Ben had sorted them into chapters apart from a relatively small bunch of notes.'

'Did you get an idea of how many notes Joshua made?' Mike asked.

'Yes, I saw the pile of unsorted notes and it was big – that's why I think we haven't got them all yet.'

'Well, we've only got 1870 to 1876 to go through. I think we can do that in one more session,' said Kala. 'Bring your mother next time, Tom.'

'I'll try.'

Tom and Frank went home on the bus. Frank said he wanted to come round to see Tom's mum's face when he told her about Mr Grimley, so Tom said he wouldn't say anything to her until Frank got there.

'Hi, Mum. Get the car fixed?'

'Yes, but it took them most of the day to sort it out. How about you – did you find anything in the archives?'

'Sure did,' with a smug look on his face. 'We found three folders of Joshua's notes that had been deposited by Magnus.'

'Oh, I'm so pleased. So you were right about Magnus having Joshua's notes.'

'Yes, but I don't think we've got them all yet. I remember the pile at Joshua's house being bigger than the pile we've collected, but we've still got plenty of boxes to go through, so we're not finished yet.'

There was a ring at the door. 'That'll be Frank.' Tom rushed to open the door.

'Hi Frank. How are you?'

'Fine, thank you, Mrs Merrington.'

'Mum, you'll never guess who we went to see before we went to the archives.'

'You're right, I'll never guess. Who?'

'Mr Grimley.'

Her eyes widened and she took in a deep breath. 'You went to see that evil man Grimley? I thought I told you never to go near him.'

'Well, you didn't exactly say that, Mum. And besides, we survived unharmed. He even invited us back.'

'What? You must never see that man again. Do you hear me?' She was getting very agitated by now.

'But Mum, he's not half as bad as you think. He's been harbouring a grudge against the Robertsons all his life, but I think we persuaded him it was time to give it up.'

'Oh, yes? Explain yourself,' she said with her most disbelieving look.

'Well, we went to ask him if he could give us any information on Sebastian Grimley. At first he was rude and told us to clear off, but when we asked him about the arson attack and why Sebastian was buried in Drumbridge, he gave in and explained it all to us. Apparently Sebastian did not burn down Joshua's house – they found the culprit six months later. Although the police arrested Sebastian, he wasn't convicted. The locals thought he was guilty because of the argument he had with Joshua over the dog and they hanged him. That's why the Grimleys hated the Robertsons and have done so to this very day. The vicar in Walchester was too scared of the local vigilantes to bury Sebastian in Walchester, so Magnus agreed to bury him in Drumbridge, probably because he thought he was innocent. That was seen as a favour from a Robertson by the Grimleys and it's been eating away at them ever since. I suggested to Mr Grimley that he might repay the debt by dropping the grudge.'

'And what did he say to that?'

'Well, I think he was almost ready to give in, but he wouldn't commit himself. As we were leaving, he told us we could come back again if we wanted. He also asked me what your first name was.'

'You didn't tell him, I hope.'

'Of course I did. Come on Mum, now you're the one who's being prejudiced. You need to give him a chance.'

'Look, there's more to Mr Grimley than you've seen. Did you notice he drives a Bentley and yet he seems to do very little business? With his attitude, he probably frightens all the customers away. No, I'll wager he's got an income from some shady dealings.'

'What do you mean? Criminal activities?'

'Quite likely. I'll have to consult Margaret over this one. She warned me of him in the first place.' Frank looked puzzled. 'Sorry, Frank – she's a ghost friend of mine.'

'Of course, I should have known,' he said to himself. 'Nothing unusual for the Merrington household.'

The following day, Julia went into Walchester to see whether Joshua Robertson's house was still standing. Roseberry Lane was certainly still on the modern map of Walchester, but no doubt it had changed since Victorian times. In the 1871 census, there were six houses in Roseberry Lane. Julia arrived at the end with the high numbers – there were now fifty-two houses in the road. She walked along the road looking for older houses but they were all relatively modern. When she got to the far end, there was one old house, but it was a two-storey Victorian house with a slate roof. So Joshua's house must have been knocked down. It didn't surprise her at all, but it was a shame nevertheless.

Roseberry Lane was a short walk from Mr Grimley's shop and as much as she detested the man, Julia decided to pass by and see if he was there, although she had no intention of going in to see him. She walked up to the shop window as casually as she could and stopped to look at a Georgian desk that Grimley had in the window. She could see him sitting at his desk in the shop looking as miserable as ever, talking on the telephone. She cringed at the thought that he might soon be contacting her.

Chapter 8

Close to Death

TOM WAS FRUSTRATED. HE THOUGHT HIS VISIONS must have ended now that Ben was dead and he could not understand why he had experienced them. He also didn't have the urge to sit by Magnus's grave, so he knew there would be no new visions in the next day or so. Two weeks went by and he was convinced it was all over, but then one day he woke at about five o'clock and knew he had to go down to the grave. He quickly got dressed and hurried downstairs and out into the churchyard. It was cool and a little misty, but Tom didn't even notice the weather.

This time, he emerged into the vision with no idea where he was because it was completely dark. He had a desperate feeling of fighting against a force that was dragging him forward. He struggled with all his might until it seemed he would have to succumb as the last of his strength was draining from him. But somehow he summoned up one last effort, and the force finally released him. There was a surge of pain and he went tumbling backwards, then down and down until he came to a gentle stop in something soft and warm. It was not like a pillow, it was something that was all around him. It was comforting and he felt no pain. Was that light? Yes, it was definitely getting lighter. Gradually, the light filled his eyes but that's all it was – light. There were no shapes; nothing was in focus. There was no sound but then, suddenly, there was a voice in the distance. It came closer and shapes were appearing.

'Give it time, young man. You should be able to see clearly in a few minutes.'

Sure enough, the room began to come into focus. It was bright – a white room, with white cupboards and a white table. There was a middle-aged gentleman standing in front of him, staring into his eyes. He had a large moustache and a bald head, apart from frizzy grey hair that stuck out at the sides, making him look rather comical.

'How do you feel?'

'I don't know really. I can't feel anything.'

'Ah, that's understandable, but you'll get better.'

'Get better? What's wrong with me? Where am I?'

'I'll explain in a moment, but first, do you remember who you are?'

'Of course, I'm Ben Robertson.'

'Do you remember what happened to you? Do you remember the fire in your house?'

'The fire! Oh, yes. Am I dead?'

'No, you're not dead.'

'Father and Arthur – are they here as well?'

'Alas, no – they both died in the fire. I'm sorry.'

Tom could see the scene go misty as the tears welled up in Ben's eyes. Then he seemed to grasp the situation quickly and started the questioning once again.

'How did I survive?'

'Rescuers broke in through the windows and dragged you out. You were in a terrible state but you were the only one of your family still alive when you got to the hospital. The doctors there said there was no hope and you would not last more than a few days, but I had other ideas. I stole you from the hospital.'

'You stole me?'

'Yes, it wasn't difficult. I replaced you with a bandaged dummy and when the doctors discovered what had happened, they were so embarrassed that they covered up by issuing your death certificate. So you're officially dead!' The gentleman was clearly excited about his exploits.

'But how did you save me?'

'With a lot of special care and attention. You see, I have developed my own way of dealing with burns. You are suspended in a bath of special oils that allow the wounds to heal without drying out. As far as I know, I'm the only doctor practising this technique. To tell you the truth, I've been banned from practising it, but that's only because one of my patients was unfortunate enough to drown in the oil. It was just a technical problem and we've sorted it out.'

'I'm glad to hear it. How much longer will I be in this bath?'

'Oh, we'll get you out today. That's why we've brought you back to consciousness.'

'How long have I been in here?'

'Just over three weeks.'

'Goodness me.'

'By the way, my name's Isaac Protheroe. I studied medicine at Edinburgh twenty-five years ago and I've been practising here in Bragford for the last twelve years.'

'Bragford? But isn't that a long way from Walchester?'

'Yes, indeed. It took us five hours to get here and I feared you might not survive the journey, but you did and here you are.'

'I'm extremely grateful, Dr Protheroe. But why did you want to save me and how did you hear about my plight?'

'Ah, the reason I wanted to save you is that I knew I could with my technique. I have spies in hospitals looking out for cases such as yours because as I said, I'm not supposed to be using my technique. One of my spies contacted me quickly when he knew you had survived the fire. He even arranged an accomplice in the hospital to help me get you out. All it needed was a little bribe. You see, I have to use these devious procedures so that I can document enough cases to get my method re-instated and accepted by the medical profession.'

'What will happen to me now? Can I go back to stay with my grandfather?'

'I'm afraid your grandfather believes you are dead. He conducted the funeral. In any case, you must stay here for at least another four weeks. I suggest we discuss your future as soon as you are strong enough. In the meantime, I don't think it would be a good idea to tell your grandfather that you are alive.'

'Well, I owe you my life so I won't argue, but I'd dearly love to see my grandfather again.'

'Of course, I understand, but we must plan your future carefully and that would compromise any plan.'

'Then can we discuss my future soon?'

'You need a few more days to build up your strength. I'll call the nurse and we'll get you out of this contraption and into a comfortable bed. When you are back to a regular sleeping pattern, we'll talk about it again.'

It went dark again and then Tom was back in the churchyard. He sat there gasping for a few moments. What an incredible twist! So Ben didn't die after all! I must tell Mum and Dad! He rushed off back to the house. It was still early and only his father was up, munching a piece of toast, still looking as though he was asleep. He was startled when Tom burst in through the door, but he guessed immediately where Tom had been.

'Dad, Ben didn't die after all! He was saved by a doctor who stole him from the hospital!'

'Good gracious! Stole him from the hospital? That's incredible. Julia, come down!'

'What's up? What's up?' Mum came stumbling down the stairs.

'Tom's just had another vision and it seems that Ben survived after all. I haven't heard Tom's explanation yet, but Ben was stolen from the hospital and saved by a doctor.'

'But how could that have happened? I've got his death certificate.'

'That's right. The doctors at the hospital issued it because they didn't want anyone to know that they'd lost a patient. They thought he was as good as dead anyway. Magnus buried a dummy. By the way, Mum, where are their graves?'

'I don't know. I've never been able to track them down. They're not in Drumbridge or any of the graveyards in Walchester – but that's not important now. If Ben survived, what happened to him? Did he go back to live with Magnus?'

'I don't know yet. Dr Protheroe has promised to discuss Ben's future with him as soon as he's well enough. It's going to be a bit tricky as he's officially dead.'

'Well, that should be interesting,' said Dad. 'This Protheroe chap sounds like a bit of a maverick. Man after my own heart.'

Mum was pleased that Tom was excited about the latest developments and in reality, so was she. 'I'm dying to see what happens next.' She gave Tom a hug. 'Do you want some breakfast?'

'Yes, please, I'm starving.'

Tom was ecstatic about this latest revelation. He had been in the doldrums thinking that his visions had been a complete waste of time, but now he felt a renewed sense of purpose. Perhaps at last he was going to find out what was expected of him. The experience of going through Ben's terrible ordeal had shaken Tom badly. Was that what it was like before you died and what were those voices? Did Ben somehow cheat death with his willpower? Tom knew that Ben was very close to giving in to death, but he survived against the odds and now he was ready to start a new life. Tom was ready to follow him into it.

Chapter 9

William Protheroe

Tom had noticed that Magnus was no longer present in his latest visions. It seemed that the hand-holding wasn't necessary any more. In one way, it was probably good because Magnus must think he didn't need the reassurance, but it also meant that Tom didn't get the chance to challenge him over why he was having the visions. He wondered if he was ever going to be able to speak to Magnus. Frank had been pestering Tom to ask Magnus a long list of questions but of course it had proved impossible.

It was only two days after the last dramatic vision that Tom had the next one. It was an evening after school and he was with Frank. This time Ben was sitting in a comfortable chair in a cosily-furnished room. He was next to a large fireplace. Hanging above the fireplace was a portrait of a distinguished-looking gentleman in a dark blue velvet robe holding a large book in his hands. On the other side of the fireplace, sitting opposite Ben on the sofa, were Isaac and an elegant lady dressed in a full-length, pale green dress made of a shiny material. Her grey hair was pulled away from her face and tied up at the back so that it draped over one shoulder. She had a long face with a pointed chin and a small mouth. Her large eyes seemed out of proportion, but they gave her a kindly appearance. Tom guessed she must be Isaac's wife. The log fire was burning strongly and the flickering light was reflecting off the side of her face.

Isaac spoke first: 'Now Ben, I appreciate that the thing you want most of all is to return to your grandfather. There are several problems to doing this. First, as you know, you are supposed to be dead and that is what your grandfather believes. He has been hurt by losing you already, so we can't make that worse. Admittedly, he would be overjoyed to have you back, but it would also give him a shock. There would be many questions asked and I would be in a lot of trouble for stealing you. Your grandfather is also old and it would be a burden on him to be your guardian. He may not have many years to live and when he dies you would be on your own.'

'I'm sure one of my aunts or uncles would look after me.'

'Perhaps, but can you be sure?'

'I did get on very well with one of my aunts but not her husband or her son, so perhaps it would be a bit risky.'

'Ben, the last thing I want to do is to put you into a family that may not look after you properly. Celia and I have become very fond of you and we would not want to put your future in jeopardy. We have an alternative plan if you are ready to listen to it.'

'Please, go ahead.'

'In a nutshell, that you stay here and live with us as our son.' Tom could sense the puzzlement within Ben. This was a possibility he had not even thought of.

'This is a surprise. I don't know what to think.'

'Let me explain a little more. Celia and I have not been able to have children of our own and we would be deeply honoured if you would let us adopt you. I think I can arrange all the paperwork, although it may take a bribe or two. We are quite wealthy and we can promise you a good education.'

'You want to adopt me? How will you overcome the fact that I'm Ben Robertson, certified dead?'

'Ah, well, I've thought about that one. You are an orphan of course, so I don't have to lie about that, but I think we'll have to change your name – may have to pretend that you came from a workhouse. I think I can arrange that.'

'Yes, I think I understand. What will you call me?'

'Celia and I have always liked the name "William". It was Celia's father's name. What do you think of that? We would call you "Will".'

'Yes, I think that would be fine.' But Tom could sense that Ben was far from convinced and he could see that Mrs Protheroe was getting anxious.

'Fine, it's settled then. I'll start the proceedings and let you know when it's all settled. In the meantime, we should stop calling you "Ben" and call you Will" instead.'

'I'm still a little shocked. I haven't taken it all in. I do like you a lot and I'm sure I'll be happy here, but it's a big step to become your son.'

'Of course it is my dear,' interposed Mrs Protheroe, 'you need a little more time to think about what it means to you. Why not talk about it again tomorrow? Isaac, please don't do anything rash just yet.'

'Yes, please, Mrs Protheroe. I'd like some time to think about it on my own.'

'Please feel free to walk in the garden or find somewhere private in the house. I find the library a very good place to sit and contemplate.'

'Thank you, Mrs Protheroe.'

Ben went out into the garden and sat on a bench by the ornamental pond. His mind was racing; he tried to focus on the decision he had to make, but it seemed so difficult to weigh up the pros and cons. He tried to clear his mind and start his train of thought again as he watched the fish swim smoothly and effortlessly among the lily pads. What a simple life it was being a fish! If only his life could be as simple. But it was not and he had to make a decision that would affect the rest of his life. If it wasn't for Dr Protheroe, he would be dead, so a part of him already wanted to accept the offer to show his gratitude. He had so many happy memories of his grandfather that he desperately wanted to see him again. It pained him to know that his grandfather was grieving over his death when here he was, alive and almost well again. But it was true what Dr Protheroe said – it would be a big burden for his grandfather to be his guardian and he was getting old. If only he could live with the Protheroes and visit his grandfather occasionally – that would be perfect. But it wasn't practical. Much as it upset him, perhaps it would be better to let his grandfather remain in ignorance of his survival and he would start a new life as William Protheroe. Yes, it was obvious really; the sensible decision was to accept their kind offer. He decided not to wait until tomorrow; he would tell them this evening.

Ben went into the library and looked around. He ran his fingers over the books on the shelves and came across a copy of "Great Expectations" among several volumes of Dickens's works. At once he thought of his father and Arthur, and of his father's book. Was it destroyed in the fire? If it survived, who would get it published? He could not remember who the publishers were that his father said were waiting for the draft. Could Dr Protheroe help? He decided to ask him that evening.

Tom's vision changed back to the sitting room and Ben was in the armchair once again with the Protheroes sitting on the sofa opposite him.

'Well, Ben, have you made up your mind already?'

'Yes, I'd like to accept your kind offer.'

Dr Protheroe was so overjoyed he bounced up and down on the sofa while somehow remaining in a sitting position. 'That's splendid!'

Mrs Protheroe could not hold back her tears and threw her arms around Ben. She hugged him until he felt he would choke. When she finally let him go, she gave him a gentle kiss on the cheek and then said: 'Now, Ben, you must start to call us "Mother" and "Father" and we shall call you "Will".'

Ben smiled. He was happy that they had responded so enthusiastically. He knew that he had made the right decision. 'Yes, Mother. From now on,

I'm happy to be Will.'

Dr Protheroe gathered himself together and resumed a stable sitting position on the sofa. 'I presume, my dear, you are happy for me to proceed with the legal arrangements?'

'Of course, Isaac.'

Ben, alias Will, thought "legal arrangements" was perhaps not an accurate statement since they seemed more likely to be illegal. Even so, he knew Dr Protheroe only had his future in mind.

'Father, I wonder if you could help me with a problem I have.'

'Of course, if I can.'

'My father, I mean my previous father, Joshua Robertson, had just finished writing an important book on the night of his death and I wondered if his draft survived the fire.'

'Did he have the draft in the library?'

'Yes.'

'Then it almost certainly survived. Only about half of the house burned down. I believe the bedrooms were at one end and the living rooms at the other and it was the bedroom end that burned down. That was the way your house was arranged, wasn't it?'

'Yes. So if the draft survived, do you know what happened to it and whether anyone sent it to the publishers?'

'That I don't know, but I can ask my spy to find out for you.'

'I'd be extremely grateful if you could.'

'That's no trouble at all. I'll see to it tomorrow.' Tom's vision ended at that point.

'So, what happened?' Frank was peering down at Tom, who was still sitting on the ground next to the tomb.

'Come indoors and I'll tell Mum at the same time.'

Frank and Mum listened intently to Tom's account of his vision. They didn't interrupt until he had finished.

'Well, it gets more and more fascinating,' declared Mum. 'Isaac Protheroe sounds like a kindly rogue – he obviously has good intentions but he doesn't worry much about breaking the law. But of course there was a lot of bribery and corruption in Victorian times.'

'But, Mum, he's such a kind man. You should have seen how pleased he was when Ben accepted his offer.'

'Ah yes, the talk of bribery and corruption reminded me – Mr Grimley rang me today, as you predicted.'

'What did he have to say?'

'He said he had something that belonged to my family that he wanted to return to me. He wouldn't say what it was but he said he wanted to come round in person to explain it all to me. I'm not quite sure what he means but he sounded genuine enough so he's coming round on Thursday.'

'I told you he wanted to make it up to you.'

'I still don't trust him, but we'll see.'

On Wednesday, Mum, Tom, Frank and Kala went through the remainder of the documents in the University archives and came up with two more folders of Joshua's notes. Tom was happy that they probably had the complete set. Mike and Jim went through the notes in fine detail.

'Well, Jim, now that we seem to have got all the notes, I think I can help the mystery scientist with his experiments. Comparing the data he entered on the computer with Joshua's notes makes it quite clear that the subject was Michelangelo. I suspected that some time ago, so I've been doing some research of my own. There is quite a lot of literature on the mental state of Michelangelo and not all of it was available to Joshua. It will be interesting to see whether our mystery scientist takes any notice of the additional data I put in. It should be great fun collaborating with a ghost!'

Jim grinned. 'I suppose we should be grateful to our ghost scientist. He's done some good work for us and we don't have to pay him.'

Later, Jim had a call from Julia. She explained that the bookseller who thought he would be able to track down Joshua's book had said that he had been unable to find a copy so far. He was still trying, but he was running out of options.

'Mike, that was Julia. It's looking more and more unlikely that we'll find a copy of Joshua's book. Still, we've probably got all we need in his notes, but it would be nice to confirm it.'

'It would still be very valuable to have the book. I don't think we could reconstruct the book from the notes. Joshua may have put some more of his own interpretations in the book that weren't in the notes.'

'Yes, of course it would be better if we had the book. I'm just warning you that we may have to live without it.'

'Oh, we'll get by without it but I would dearly love to get my hands on a copy.'

'Yes, I know what you mean.'

Chapter 10

A Gift from Mr Grimley

As he promised, Mr Grimley arrived at the Vicarage promptly at two o'clock in the afternoon on Thursday. Through the window Julia saw him arrive and waited for him to knock. She answered the door cautiously. He looked apprehensive, standing in the doorway clutching a small parcel.

'Hello, Mr Grimley, please come in.'

'Thank you.' He drew his bulky frame through the doorway. Although his size made him intimidating, he looked a lot smarter than Julia remembered. His normally shaggy hair had been cut neatly and he wore a crisp white shirt, a green tie and a grey suit. She always thought of him as close to retirement age, but now he looked much younger; he was possibly not more than fifty. Julia guided him to the lounge where she had laid a tray with coffee and biscuits. She gestured to one of the armchairs and he sat in it obligingly. Julia sat in the other armchair and offered him coffee.

'Black or white?'

'Oh, black please.'

Mr Grimley was clearly anxious to say something. He seemed to be summoning the courage to start his speech.

'Mrs Merrington: as I said on the telephone, I have something here that I'd like to give to you because it really belongs with your family, but first I need to explain the background. As you probably know, the Grimleys and the Robertsons hated each other in Victorian times and in our case, I'm ashamed to admit, the hatred continued until the present day. Your son Tom made me realize the folly of this and I'd like to offer my friendship. I'm sorry if I've been unpleasant to you in the past and I promise that I won't repeat that kind of behaviour.'

Julia was taken aback and struggled to reply. She did not expect an offer of friendship in the first few seconds. Sensing her problem, Mr Grimley continued his monologue.

'An ancestor of mine, Sebastian Grimley, had an argument with one of your ancestors, Joshua Robertson. Because of that, Sebastian was falsely accused of burning down the Robertsons' house and was hanged by local vigilantes. It was discovered several months later that he was innocent. Ever since, the Grimleys have hated the Robertsons.'

'Yes, I know about that – Tom explained it to me.' Julia had found her voice again. 'But were there any Robertsons among the vigilantes?'

'The police didn't find out who they were, but Sebastian's family believed that the Robertsons were behind the hanging. At least, that's the story that's been passed down through the generations. Anyway, Sebastian had a younger brother who, let's say, didn't have much respect for the law and he was determined to avenge Sebastian's murder. He was finally hanged for killing two of the people he believed were in the vigilante gang. They weren't Robertsons, by the way. He was also convicted of burgling Magnus Robertson's house. The police retrieved most of the stolen goods but there was one item that he managed to hide and that has been passed down through the generations as a kind of symbol of the hatred of the Robertsons. I think it's time it was returned to the Robertsons. Here you are.' He handed the parcel over to Julia.

Julia carefully unwrapped the parcel, which had the shape and feel of a book. Sure enough, it was a leather-bound book in immaculate condition. Julia looked at the gold lettering on the spine, glanced quickly at Mr Grimley, and then opened the book to the title page. It was entitled "Madness and Genius: A Study of the Mental States of Some Famous Artists, by Joshua Robertson, MD". To think that she had been searching for this book for weeks and it was now in her hands, a gift from a man she thought to be an outright villain.

'I think you will find that's the only copy of that quality in existence. It was specially bound by the publishers for Magnus Robertson.' Mr Grimley was still looking apologetic.

For the first time, Julia was able to smile at Mr Grimley. This was the best present she could have had. Tears came to her eyes as she said: 'Thank you, thank you, Mr Grimley. I understand now how difficult it must have been to part with this. It would be wonderful if we could break down the old barriers and be friends. Why don't we have something a little stronger than coffee to celebrate?'

'Sounds good to me,' Mr Grimley said. He was obviously greatly relieved that Julia's response to his apology had been so positive, but he was not to know that she had been searching desperately for a copy of the book. 'Perhaps you could be so kind as to call me George. I know your first name is Julia because I asked your son. I'd like to call you by your first name if I may.'

'Of course.' Julia now had a huge smile on her face. 'Tom told me you had asked about my name. Well then, George, what will it be? I don't have champagne, but I have whisky, gin, brandy or vodka. I prefer wine myself, so I'll be opening a bottle of red wine.'

'In that case, I'll join you if I may.'

Julia went to the wine rack and pulled out a bottle of Chilean red wine with a garish label.

'Julia, please, allow me.' Mr Grimley took the bottle and the corkscrew from her and deftly pulled the cork, then placed the two glasses on the table and filled them without spilling a drop. He gave the impression of having been trained as a waiter. He examined the label on the bottle. 'I must say I enjoy South American wines. I have quite a few in my cellar at home.'

'Oh, so you are a wine lover.'

'Indeed I am. I've been collecting fine wines for several years. I sell some, but I can't resist drinking most of them. You know how it is.'

Julia smiled understandingly.

'Perhaps you and your husband would come over to dinner some time. My wife is a fine cook and I can guarantee the wine will be excellent.'

Julia had never imagined George Grimley with a wife and at once wondered what she might be like. 'That sounds wonderful. My husband never misses the chance of good food and wine, so I'm sure he'll be pleased to come.'

'Good, I'll give you a call to settle a date. I must consult my wife first of course.'

The two settled down to an animated discussion about antiques, fine wines and their families. They had a tour of the house to admire the antiques and Grimley was intrigued when Julia explained that the old chest had belonged to Joshua Robertson. Finally, reluctant though he was, he declared that he must leave.

As he was leaving, he thanked Julia. 'Thank you very much for being so understanding. I've got a great weight off my mind at last. I look forward to seeing you and your husband at my place.'

'It's been a pleasure. I'll wait for your call. See you soon.'

When he had left, Julia sat down and contemplated what had just happened. She found it hard to believe that Tom had managed to change Grimley's attitude to the Robertsons so easily. Unless, of course, Grimley was considering it before and Tom had just given him the excuse to do something about it. And he was such a pleasant man – nothing like the ogre she had tried to do business with years ago. He even looked different. There was no doubt she liked the new friendly, polite George Grimley and having spent a few hours with him, she was sure he was genuine. Then why did she have this nagging concern that something strange was going on? Perhaps when she got to meet Mrs Grimley she might understand more. She couldn't wait for dinner at the Grimleys.

Julia rang Jim at the University to tell him what Grimley had given her.

'I'll try to get away early – I'm dying to see it. I don't suppose there is anything in it that we haven't seen already, but it will be nice to see what was actually published.'

When the children came home from school, Julia told them that Mr Grimley had given her a copy of Joshua's book, but she did not show it to them because she wanted Jim to see it first. When he did come home, the first thing he said was: 'Well, where is it?'

Julia opened a drawer, took out the book and handed it to him. He held it as though it was a new-born baby. 'What a beautiful book.' He caressed the cover and then gently opened it randomly. He scanned through several pages and checked the contents' page. 'It's in perfect condition. From first glance, I'd say that you were right, Tom. We probably do have a complete set of Joshua's notes.' He passed the book to Tom.

When Tom looked through the pages, the book began to feel like an old friend. So much of its content was already familiar to him. But this was a high-quality, published book, not a set of notes. He felt strangely proud, almost as though he had helped in its creation. Ben would have been proud if he had seen it. Perhaps as Will Protheroe, he did. That's something Tom hoped to discover.

'Could I have a look?' asked Amy. Tom gave her the book. 'Is it very old? It looks quite new.'

'Yes, it's well over a hundred years old,' said Dad. Turning to Mum, he said: 'I wonder why the Grimleys took such care of it when it was just a symbol of hatred to them?'

'I think they must have kept it locked away until it was time to be passed down to the next generation. After all, it is stolen property. No doubt they told their children the story of Sebastian's murder, so I expect that was enough to fuel the hatred.'

'Does George Grimley have any children?'

'Yes, three boys, two at university and one working as a civil engineer. He said that they were not interested in the feud with the Robertsons, so he doesn't think he'll have to convince them that it was right to put an end to it. It's his father and his sister he's most concerned about. He expects to have a difficult time with them.'

'So he didn't tell them before he acted.'

'No.'

'Mum, if it was such a big thing with the Grimleys, why did Mr Grimley give in so easily when I asked him to end the feud?' asked Tom.

'That still puzzles me. You must have been very persuasive.'

'But I didn't really say anything special to convince him.'

'Well, he told me that it was your influence that changed his mind. And he says he feels a lot better for it, too. You're obviously better at persuading people than you think.'

'I wish I could persuade the teachers to give me better marks for my homework.'

Mum laughed. 'I think that's a bit different. You'll just have to try harder if you want better marks.'

The following day at school, Tom was anxious to ask Frank what he thought about Mr Grimley giving in so easily to his persuasion. He waited until the break after an art lesson, where they had all been huddled on one side of the room because the boy sitting next to Frank had spilled paint on the floor. The teacher had insisted on carrying on with the lesson and had arranged for the caretaker to clear up the mess during the break. Frank had to sit next to the mess while the culprit moved to the other side of the room. As soon as they were out of the lesson, Tom grabbed Frank and put the question to him.

Frank thought for a while and then said: 'You remember the time that Mr Watson the maths teacher wanted to give me a detention for accidentally breaking his ruler? You persuaded him not to and he was in a rage at the time. When you spoke to him, he calmed down straight away.'

'Yes, I remember that, but I only convinced him that it was an accident, which it was.'

'I know, but you didn't have to say much. You seemed to have some kind of influence over him.'

'Don't be daft. If I had, he'd give me better marks for my homework.'

'Not if you don't deserve better marks. It probably only works if you are in the right.'

Tom stared hard at Frank. 'Do you really believe I have some kind of special power over people?'

'Could be. You seem to be the chosen one for looking into the past.'

Just then, Terry Paterson, a prefect, came up to them. 'You're Frank McGinty aren't you?' he said.

'Yes.'

'I've been told by someone in your class that you spilt the paint that's on the floor in the art room. The caretaker wants you to help clear it up.'

'No, it wasn't me.' He was reluctant to say who it was.

'That's not what I've been told. Come with me.' He grabbed Frank by the collar.

'He's speaking the truth, I was with him,' interrupted Tom.

Terry turned on Tom as though he was about to collar him as well. 'And what's your name?'

'Tom Merrington.'

Terry stared hard at Tom and then he gradually released his grip on Frank's collar. 'OK, I'll see what my informant has to say.' He walked away.

'I wonder who the lying so-and-so is who tried to get you into trouble?' said Tom.

But Frank was looking at Tom with a wide grin on his face. 'I don't care. Don't you see? You did it again!'

'But I didn't do anything. I just told him the truth.'

'He didn't believe me when I told the truth.'

Tom was puzzled. He did not believe he had any special persuasive powers. 'Do you really think I persuaded Terry by casting a kind of spell over him?'

Frank laughed. 'I wouldn't put it like that, but I think you do have more persuasive power than anyone else I know.'

'How do I do it then?'

'Don't ask me, I'm just making an observation. Most people would be pleased about it. Why are you so negative about it?'

'I don't want to be a freak, that's why.'

'You're not a freak. As far as I can see, you've only got one head and it's got the regulation eyes, nose, mouth and ears.'

'But if I have visions into the past and I can persuade people I'm right without doing anything, I must be a bit odd, mustn't I?'

'Perhaps.'

'Thanks.' Tom was getting himself upset.

'Look, this is the sort of advice my Dad would give. If you've got a special talent, make the most of it, don't hide it.'

'OK. You're right I suppose. I really do appreciate your advice.'

'Well, you can be a bit of a wimp at times.'

Tom gave Frank a weak grin and then became serious again. 'I'll try to be a bit tougher.'

'Good for you.'

Chapter 11

Will at School

TOM WENT DOWN TO THE GRAVEYARD THE next evening knowing that he would have his next vision. He was anxious to find out what happened to Ben in his new life as Will Protheroe. He saw Mrs Bratherstone busily weeding round her husband's grave on the other side of the graveyard. He sat down by Magnus's grave and closed his eyes. As before, there was no introduction from Magnus; he found himself in the garden by the pond again. Will was on his own, reading a book. Isaac came bustling along the path, gesticulating and shouting to Will.

'Good news, Will! Two pieces of good news in fact. First, I've got you a place at Fettersham School, the best in the district. How about that?'

'That's wonderful, Father, thank you very much. When do I start?'

'Next Monday. Just gives us time to get you kitted out.'

'So soon. I must admit I'm a bit apprehensive after such a long spell off school.'

'Don't worry, dear boy, I've thought of that. Mr Phillips, one of the teachers at the school and a fine one at that, has offered to be your personal tutor if you need help to catch up with the class. I can give you a bit of help as well during the holidays if you need it.'

'Thank you, Father – that's comforting. And the other news?'

'Oh yes. I discovered that your grandfather sent Joshua's manuscript for his book to the publishers and I have ordered a copy for you. Apparently, it will be published in April.'

'Oh, thank you. It's a great relief to know that all his work won't be wasted.'

'I thought you'd be pleased about that. My spy in Walchester was able to speak to your grandfather in person. Apparently he is still very upset at the loss of his son and his two grandsons, but he continues to work as hard as ever.'

'Poor Grandfather. Does your spy know about me? He won't have told Grandfather that I'm still alive will he?'

'He doesn't know that, but don't worry, he can be trusted. He's the same person who told me about you in the first place, so he does know that you were still alive when we took you from the hospital, but he doesn't know that you survived. He doesn't ask because he prefers not to know. And only Celia and I know that Will Protheroe was once Ben Robertson.'

'So it's probably best that I don't meet your spy. I think I'll take his approach and I'll ask you never to tell me who he is.'

'Very sensible – I promise never to tell you.'

'Father, could you please tell me a little more about Fettersham School? Did you go there?'

'No, I wasn't brought up in this area, but I happen to know some excellent doctors who were pupils there. It has a remarkably good success record for sending boys to medical school. Would medicine interest you Will?'

'My father, Joshua that is, wanted me to study medicine. He said he would have studied medicine if he knew he was going to develop such an interest in mental disorders. He convinced me that it would be the best career for me. I presume you would also like me to study medicine?'

'I would love to see you take a medical course. As a medical man myself, I can say that it's the finest career any man can follow. It hasn't always been the case, but with improvements in medicine, we are gaining in status. As a doctor, you are a valued and respected member of the community, and you also have a tremendous responsibility. You must be strong enough to take on that responsibility. You must also be ready to learn new things throughout your career – medicine is advancing all the time. Do you think you could face that, Will?'

'With you to guide me, I believe I could.'

'Well said, my boy. Just one point I noted in our conversation – could you bring yourself to refer to your father as "Joshua" in future? I think it would avoid any slip of the tongue in conversation.'

'You are right, Father. It could be embarrassing if I let that slip.'

'Good. Now the Headmaster of Fettersham gave me a list of all the things you need for school, so tomorrow we'll take a coach into town and get it all for you.'

'That will be fun. I hope it's not too expensive.'

'Don't worry about that my boy. It's money well-spent as far as I am concerned. Now let's go in for dinner.'

Tom awoke to find Mrs Bratherstone peering down at him. 'Are you all right?' she said.

'Yes, thank you, Mrs Bratherstone.'

'Not a very comfortable place to have a nap is it?'

'Oh, I often doze off here. I try to imagine what it was like when Magnus Robertson was alive and then I fall asleep,' which was almost the truth.

'I hope you won't be doing that when the weather gets cold; you could catch your death out here when that north wind blows.'

'Oh, I expect I'll be out here in the middle of winter. Don't you worry about me – I'll just wear a warm coat.' He grinned at Mrs Bratherstone mischievously. She gave him the kind of teacher's stare she would have used on pupils just before putting them in detention. Then she changed it to a look of resignation and sighed loudly.

'You be careful. I don't want to find you out here frozen solid.'

'You won't, Mrs Bratherstone. I'll be OK.'

As she stumbled away to leave the graveyard, Tom felt an urge to close his eyes again. He sat back, relaxed and closed his eyes. This time, Will was in a dormitory with several other boys but he was seated on his own bed, opening a parcel. Inside were a letter and a book. He read the letter first:

"Dear Will,

I've enclosed the copy of Joshua's book that I promised you. It arrived this morning, so I dispatched it straight away. I hope you enjoy it.

By the way, I was fascinated to read your account of how you seemed to be able to anticipate that the school bullies were going to attack you and your friend. We must discuss that when you come back for the holidays. If you can read people's minds, then you really must become a psychiatrist!

Your Loving Father."

Will picked up the book. It was similar to the one that George Grimley had given Mum, but not so luxuriously bound. He turned the pages. When he saw that Joshua had dedicated the book to him and Arthur, tears came to his eyes. After wiping his eyes on his sleeve, he turned to the Introduction and began reading. He settled into a more comfortable position on the bed and it seemed to Tom that he was preparing to read it from cover to cover. He was a fast reader and Tom was getting annoyed that he was turning the pages too quickly for him to keep up. Then one of the boys in the dormitory came up to Will and asked him what he was reading.

'It's a book my …er… uncle wrote and it's just been published.'

'What's it about?'

Will explained as simply as he could what the book was about, but he could tell that the other boy did not really understand.

The boy went away and Will continued to read the book. After a while, he put it down on the bed after having placed Isaac's letter in it as a bookmark and went to the bathroom to get washed before bed. As soon as he got into bed, he started reading again. Eventually a voice called 'Lights out!' Will placed the book in his bedside cupboard and settled down in his bed. A few seconds later, the room was in darkness and Tom's vision ended.

Tom thought about what he had just seen. Obviously, Will was now at Fettersham School and it must be April because Joshua's book had just been published. That would have been April 1870. But what was the bit about reading people's minds in Isaac's letter? Tom wondered whether Will had looked into the mind of the boy who was asking about the book. Was that why he had seen so clearly that the boy had not understood Will's explanation?

He wondered if Mum knew how to find out whether there were any records of the pupils at Fettersham School from that time. His visions were only giving him snapshots and it would be great if there were some records to fill in the gaps. He wandered back to the Vicarage deep in thought. The struggle with the rickety gate broke his concentration. He kicked it angrily. 'I wish Dad would fix this gate! It's getting worse!'

Mum was coming down the path.

'I was just coming to get you.' She put her arm round his shoulders and walked back into the house with him.

'Mum, Will went to Fettersham School. Do you think there will be any records of how he got on at school?'

'I'm sure there must be. It's a well-known school so they should have records of their pupils' achievements. Let's hope that Will did something that was worth a mention in the school records. I think the best thing to do is to write to the Headmaster. I'll do that this evening. What else have you got to tell me?'

'Oh, Isaac sent Will a copy of Joshua's book and it seems that Will can read the minds of some of the other boys.'

Mum was puzzled. 'How do you know?'

'Because Isaac mentions it in his letter. Will must have told him in the last letter that he sent home – he knew some bullies were planning to attack them before they did. And I think I saw Will look into another boy's mind as well.'

'Really?' Mum was not convinced, but she tried not to show it.

That evening, Mum sat down with Tom and they drafted a letter to send off to the Headmaster at Fettersham. Tom posted it on his way to school the following morning.

They received a reply from the Headmaster almost by return of post. It was more exciting than they had expected. Will had been Head Boy in 1873 and had excelled as a pupil both academically and as a sportsman. He went on to study medicine at Edinburgh University, just as Isaac had done. The Headmaster said he had quite a lot of information on William, as he referred to him, and he suggested that they should call him to arrange a visit to the school so that they could see the records for themselves. Tom wondered if the Headmaster would be willing to see them at half-term so that he could go. It would be something like a three-hour drive to Fettersham.

Mum called the Headmaster that day. He sounded very enthusiastic about meeting them and agreed to a visit at half-term. Mum explained that she would be bringing Tom.

The drive was tedious and took half an hour longer than Mum had predicted, but she had allowed plenty of time – they just had less time for lunch than they had planned. The school was very grand. It had large cast-iron gates and a long drive to an imposing building. They parked the car and went into the entrance hall. There was a wide oak staircase leading up to a landing with a window containing the school emblem in stained glass. The sun shone through the window and cast a coloured image on the oak floor where they were standing. Tom noticed a large wooden panel on the wall with a list of names in gold lettering. He went closer and saw that it was a list of the Head Boys at the school since 1820.

'Look, Mum, there's Will.' He pointed to "1873: William Protheroe".

'Oh, yes, that's impressive.'

Mum saw the sign to the school office and walked across the hallway to find it. The heavy oak door was open, so she peered into the room. A middle-aged woman with rimless glasses and hair pulled tightly back in a bun was poring over some papers. She seemed to be just about to commit her thoughts to her word processor.

'Excuse me; I've come to see the Headmaster – Mrs Merrington.'

The secretary lowered her glasses and waited for her eyes to focus on Mum. 'Ah, yes. He can see you now if you would like to go up. His office is on the first floor. When you get to the top of the stairs, turn right and it's facing you. I'll call to tell him you've arrived.'

They went up the wide staircase to the first floor where the Headmaster, Mr Swinburne, was already waiting outside his office to greet them. He was a short man with a ruddy complexion, small but bright eyes and bushy brown hair. He gave them a welcoming smile. When he spoke, his voice was unexpectedly powerful. 'Welcome to Fettersham School, Mrs Merrington. And you must be Tom. Please come into my office.'

'Thank you very much for seeing us, Mr Swinburne. We're very grateful.'

'Not at all, it's a pleasure. Please sit down. Would you like some tea or coffee?'

'A cup of tea would be most welcome, please.'

'And how about you Tom?'

'Could I have a glass of water, please Mr Swinburne?'

'Of course, I'll ask Winifred to bring some up.' He called his secretary on the phone and asked her to bring the drinks.

'Now, let me show you what I've got for you. First, you may have noticed the list of Head Boys on the panel in the foyer.'

'Yes, we did. And we saw Will's name up there.'

Mr Swinburne looked a little puzzled that Mum should refer to him as "Will". How could she be so familiar with someone who lived in Victorian times?

'Do you know that he was known as "Will"?'

Mum thought quickly. 'Yes, we have seen a letter from his father where he referred to him as "Will".' She thought she must be careful not to let anything like that slip again.

'Ah, I see. Letters give us a very personal insight into the past. Well then, let's refer to him as "Will". Of course, you won't have had a chance to see our trophy cabinets in the main corridor. I can take you there later. Will was a fine sportsman, you know. He was captain of the rugby team when we won the National Schools Championship. He was also an exceptional athlete. We have some of his medals in the display cabinet. He must have been generous enough to give them to the school when he left. We still encourage the boys to do that if they perform particularly well.'

There was a knock on the door and the secretary came in with a tray of drinks and placed it on the Headmaster's desk.

'Thank you very much, Winifred.'

The secretary gave Tom a generous smile and walked smoothly out of the office. She was upright and slim. Mum thought she must have been trained in deportment as a young girl, or perhaps she had been a ballet dancer.

The Headmaster poured the tea. He placed two coasters with the school emblem on them in front of Tom and Mum and put their drinks on them.

'Now, let me show you some of the notes we have on Will. I should explain that, ever since this school was founded in 1820, the Headmasters have been encouraged to record achievements of Old Boys; that is of course, pupils who have left the school. To a large extent, they are dependent on the boys keeping in contact with the school, but it seems that Will sent several letters to his Headmaster. We don't have the letters, but we do have the notes that the Headmaster made on the information Will gave us. As you know, I think, Will went to Edinburgh University to study Medicine. He later specialized in psychiatry and became one of the foremost psychiatrists in Britain. If you want to know more about his medical achievements, I suggest you speak to Professor Robert MacDonald at Rothbank University Medical School. He has researched Will's life quite extensively. I know that because Professor MacDonald contacted us to find out what information we had on Will. I can give you his address and telephone number if you wish. I suggest you write to him first – tell him you have spoken to me.'

'Yes, please let us have his address. I didn't realize Will was such an important man.'

'Oh, yes indeed. Professor MacDonald told us that he was quite a controversial figure too. He had his own way of dealing with psychiatric patients that did not meet with the approval of all of his peers. I don't understand enough of it to explain it to you, but Professor MacDonald can.'

'Sounds intriguing.'

'Yes. What I can say is that Will believed that to treat psychiatric patients, it was necessary to see into their minds. Make of that what you will.' Tom looked at Mum wide-eyed. Mr Swinburne noticed but decided not to comment.

Mum broke the spell. 'It seems we must speak to Professor MacDonald!'

'You'll find him a pleasant man – not at all like the eccentric professor stereotype.'

Mum was eagerly looking at the small pile of documents that Mr Swinburne had in front of him. As though he sensed her eagerness, he lifted the first one from the pile and handed it to Mum. 'You can browse through these documents and let me know if you want photocopies of any of them. Actually, why don't we put them on the table over there so that you've got some space to sort them out?' He picked up the pile and placed it on the table at the side of his office. He shifted some documents that were already on the table. There were about twenty sheets of paper in the pile and most of them were handwritten notes on letters received by the Headmaster from Will. There were a few based on conversations with Jeffrey Protheroe.

'Mr Swinburne, who was Jeffrey Protheroe?' asked Tom.

'He was Will's son. He also attended Fettersham.'

'Oh, I didn't know he had a son,' said Mum.

'Yes, I believe he had some daughters too.'

'We must look into that.' Mum felt a little embarrassed – that was something she could have discovered from the public records.

The last note was the saddest. It was based on a letter from Jeffrey telling the Headmaster that his father had died at the age of fifty-five. He didn't give the cause of death, just that he had died in "mysterious circumstances" and the police were investigating.

'Mr Swinburne, do you know what the "mysterious circumstances" of Will's death were?' Tom asked.

'I'm afraid not. It's possible that Professor MacDonald has discovered how he died, but when I spoke to him, he did not know.'

'Actually, Mr Swinburne, we'd like copies of all of these if that's possible,' said Mum.

'Of course, I'll get Winifred to copy them for you. I suggest we take them down to her office and I'll show you the trophies while she does the copying. Here is Professor MacDonald's address and telephone number.' He handed Mum a slip of paper.

'Thank you very much. You have been very kind.'

Mr Swinburne gave a satisfied smile and led them out of his office and down the stairs. He took the papers into the secretary's office and was out again in a few seconds. 'This way.' They went behind the staircase and along a wide corridor. The wall was lined on one side with display cabinets and the other side had full-length windows looking out on to an inner quadrangle with many colourful shrubs and flower beds. About two-thirds of the way down the corridor, Mr Swinburne stopped. 'Here we are. Most of the trophies from that era are in these cabinets. Here is the cup that the rugby team won – it's only a replica – the real one had to be given back. The team members are listed underneath and there's Will's name at the top – captain. And here are some of Will's medals for athletics.' He pointed to an array of seven medals. The largest one showed that Will had been the National Schools Champion at four-forty yards – the equivalent of the modern four hundred metres.

'He was quite an achiever,' remarked Mum.

'Indeed. And I believe he gained more honours at university. Now – would you like a brief tour of the school so that you can see what it was like for Will to study here?'

'That's very kind of you. Yes, please.'

'It hasn't changed much since Will's day. We've just had one additional building constructed but quite honestly, the original buildings serve us well enough.' They reached a pair of large oak doors. Mr Swinburne pushed one of them open and held it for Mum and Tom to enter. 'Now here's the main hall.' They found themselves in a grand hall with a high ceiling and oak panelled walls on which were hung about fifty paintings of people who had been associated with the school. 'They are mostly major sponsors of the school.' Mum cast her expert eye over them and noted that some of them were clearly done by accomplished artists and must be very valuable.

They left the hall by a side entrance and entered another corridor. Mr Swinburne took them through a door with a glass panel at the top. 'This is a typical science laboratory. As you can see, the inside has been modernised.'

Although it was an old room, the benches and the equipment were all modern.

'We also have several computer rooms – here is one of them. We do try to keep up with modern technological advances. I think it's essential in today's environment.'

'It certainly is,' agreed Mum, thinking of how difficult she found it keeping up with the advances in home computers.

Mr Swinburne took them to see typical classrooms, an art room, the gym, a domestic science room and a technology room. 'How does it compare with your school, Tom?'

'It's very different. You have a lot more space and a lot more equipment, and the rooms are so much nicer. I love those big windows – they let in a lot of light.'

'Well, when this was built, the craftsmen took a great pride in their work, and they didn't charge so much for their services. The old oak panels have withstood the ravages of thousands of pupils. Do you get a feel for what it must have been like for Will?'

The question caught Tom in a reverie. He could imagine exactly what it had been like for Will to be at Fettersham. 'Yes, yes, I really can feel what it was like for Will. Thank you very much for letting us see the school, Mr Swinburne.'

The Headmaster seemed a little puzzled at Tom's response but then Mum spoke to him and he turned to her.

'You've been extremely helpful, Mr Swinburne. You've given us much more information than we dared hope for. I'll certainly contact Professor MacDonald and if we find out how Will died, I'll let you know.'

'Please do. Winifred will have finished your copying by now. Let's go along to her office.'

Sure enough, the photocopies were waiting for them when they went back to the office. Mum picked them up and thanked the secretary. Mr Swinburne led them to the main entrance.

'Thank you once again, Mr Swinburne. We'll be in touch.'

'And give me a call if you need any more information.'

'Thank you, Mr Swinburne,' said Tom as he shook Mr Swinburne's hand.

As Mum and Tom drove back home, they discussed what they had seen.

'What a fabulous place to go to school! Isaac Protheroe must have been really wealthy to send Will there.'

'Yes, I think the fees are quite high.'

'What about the comment that Mr Swinburne made about Will believing it was necessary to see into patients' minds to treat them? I said Will could see into the minds of other boys at school.'

'Yes, you did. Well, perhaps he could.'

'Can we contact Professor MacDonald soon, Mum?'

'Yes, I'll write to him as soon as we get back.'

'I wonder how Will died?'

'We've got the date when he died, so I'll order his death certificate. It may be a while before we get to see Professor MacDonald.'

'Will we have to go to Rothbank?'

'I expect so. We could go by train. I don't fancy driving all that way.'

The return drive was much easier than the outward journey and they made good time. As they turned into the drive at home, Dad and Amy came out to meet them.

'Mum, the police want to see you!' shouted Amy.

'What? Why?'

'Come inside and I'll explain,' said Dad. He looked serious.

Chapter 12

Tragedy at the Grimleys'

'So, what's it all about?'

Dad pointed to the armchair. 'Sit down. The police came with some bad news: George Grimley has been murdered.'

Mum was badly shaken. She thought again of the big, gentle man who had sat in this very armchair only a couple of days ago. 'Murdered? How?'

'He was found in his antique shop stabbed with one of his own swords.'

'How awful. His poor wife – she must be feeling so distraught. And we were going to have dinner with them.'

'The police said they'd call back tomorrow at ten am. They want to talk to you about the conversation you had with Mr Grimley when he came here.'

'I can't see how I can help, but I'll tell them what I can.'

That night, they all slept rather fitfully. In the morning, Tom and Amy were up early and took breakfast to Mum and Dad in their bedroom. Mum looked particularly tired. As it was half-term, Tom had promised Frank he would go fishing with him and Amy was expecting one of her friends to come round later. Dad was planning to go to the University after the police had been.

The police arrived just before ten o'clock. There were two of them: one was a tall, slim man dressed in casual plain clothes who looked to be in his mid-thirties and the other a policewoman in uniform who was almost as tall as the man and probably of a similar age. They rang the front doorbell and Jim let them in.

'Good morning, Professor Merrington. Is your wife in today?' said the policeman.

'Yes, she's waiting for you in the lounge. Come through.' They filed through into the lounge where Julia was pacing up and down in front of the fireplace looking agitated.

'Hello, Mrs Merrington. This is PC Singleton and I'm Detective Inspector Reynolds. May we sit down?'

'Of course.' She pointed to the sofa.

'We need to ask you a few questions about George Grimley. You know of course that he was found dead at his shop, probably murdered.'

'Yes, Jim told me last night.'

'How well did you know Mr Grimley?'

'I used to know him on a professional basis, but recently he came here to give me a book that belonged to our family and we spent a few hours together. He explained that he wanted to end the feud that had existed between our families since Victorian times.'

'And what was the nature of the feud?'

'Well, to be honest, it had been long forgotten as far as we, the Robertsons, were concerned – that was my maiden name by the way. It was only the Grimleys who still held the grudge. Mr Grimley had been rather unpleasant to me in the past, but he apologized for that.'

'In what way was he unpleasant?'

'He tried to swindle me over a deal with an antique chest of drawers. When I saw through it and called the deal off, he got angry.'

'Did he harm you in any way?'

'No, he just shouted and swore at me.'

'In what way was he trying to swindle you?'

'He told me the chest was in original condition, but I found traces of restoration and the feet were not original, so it wasn't worth as much as he was asking.'

'So did he offer to reduce the price?'

'Yes, but I said I didn't want to deal with him after that. That's when he got angry.'

'I see. Do you know why he decided to apologize to you and end the feud?'

'Well, that's still a bit of a puzzle to me, but he claimed it was my son Tom who convinced him. You see, Tom and his friend Frank went to see him in his shop to get some information on one of his ancestors. Apparently, after being objectionable at first, Mr Grimley softened and gave them the information they wanted. He must have liked Tom because he agreed it was time to end the feud. Soon after that, he called me on the telephone and arranged to come here.'

'You said he gave you a book. What was it?'

'It was a special copy of a book written by one of my ancestors. Apparently one of his ancestors stole it and it's been kept in their family ever since. Mr Grimley decided it was time to give it back.'

'You said that the feud meant very little to your family. Was that true of all your family members?'

'I think so. My brother had a few altercations with Grimleys at school, but that was all in the past. He moved out of the area when he went to university and he now lives in Australia.'

'Sorry if it seems that I'm looking for a suspect in your family, but obviously we have to investigate when we learn that there has been a family feud.'

'Of course, I understand.' She still looked worried.

'Did you know Mrs Grimley?'

'Not at all. Mr Grimley had invited Jim and me to dinner, so we were hoping to meet her soon.'

'And when was your dinner date?'

'I was waiting for Mr Grimley to give me a call to set the date.'

'Did Mr Grimley say anything about how his family would react to the news that he had ended the feud?'

'Yes. He said that his father and sister would be difficult to convince, but his three sons couldn't care less about the feud anyway.'

'So he must have taken a unilateral decision – he hadn't consulted them before he came to you.'

'That's the impression he gave me.'

'Did he mention his religious beliefs to you?'

'No. Why? Is that relevant?'

'Possibly. I can't really say any more at this stage. Did you discuss anything else that might be relevant to our inquiries? Did he mention any of his business associates for instance?'

'No. He didn't talk about his business at all, although we did discuss antiques. We also talked quite a lot about wine, but I can't see how that can help you.'

'You're probably right, but if there is anything else you think of that could be relevant, please give me a call. Here's my telephone number.' He handed Julia his card. 'After what you told me about your son's visit to Mr Grimley's shop, I think I should speak to him if I may. Is he around?'

'No, he's gone fishing. He's up at Thompson's Lake with his friend,' said Jim.

'I know where that is. I'll go and have a word with him if you don't mind. How old is he?'

'Twelve.'

'In that case, I'd be grateful if you or Mrs Merrington could come along so that a parent is present when we interview him.'

'I'm going that way in any case,' said Jim. 'I'll come with you.'

'Thank you, Professor and thank you, Mrs Merrington, you've been very helpful. Depending on how we get on with our inquiries, we may have to come back another time.'

All three went out together. Jim drove out first and the police followed.

Tom and Frank usually fished at Thompson's Lake. It was an old gravel pit surrounded by trees. There was a small car park at the entrance and just one footpath all the way round the lake. On the far side, behind the fence, was an industrial estate. During the week, it could be quite noisy on that side of the lake. Tom and Frank had several favourite places to fish and today they were about half-way between the car park and the industrial estate.

They had different approaches to fishing. Tom liked to catch plenty of fish and was happy to catch small fish as long as he kept catching them, whereas Frank was more patient and preferred to go for the big fish. Today, Frank had already caught a couple of good bream and Tom had caught a lot of small roach and perch.

'Fancy a swap for an hour?' Frank asked Tom. They often did that just to add to the fun, although Tom always found it difficult to be patient and wait for the big one.

'OK, one more cast and then you can have a go.' He had just re-baited his hook with a couple of maggots. He cast his line out and waited for the float to settle down until there was just the orange tip sticking out of the water. He had been getting bites every few minutes but this time nothing seemed to be happening. Tom usually re-cast if he didn't get a bite in five minutes. He was bringing it in when Frank got a bite. His electronic bite alarm gave a few bleeps at first. Frank watched the line intently, ready to lift the rod and strike. Suddenly, the line went taut and the bleeps became a continuous screech. He lifted the rod to set the hook and then started reeling in, but the fish kept pulling the line out against the clutch on the reel.

'Wow, this feels big!' exclaimed Frank as they both watched the line criss-cross the lake.

'Don't let it get in the reeds!' shouted Tom as the line headed towards the left bank. Frank expertly pulled the rod to the right, coaxing the fish away from the reeds. It came back rapidly, giving Frank the chance to reel in some line. The fish was still deep but it was slowing down. He reeled in a little more. It was getting closer. Then a bronze-coloured flank broke the surface and it dived again, pulling more line out. 'Looks like a big tench!' Tom had got the landing net in the water ready for Frank to bring it in for the final moment. But the fish wasn't ready yet. It broke the surface again and dived immediately, pulling out more line, but it was getting tired and the next time it dived, it only took out a small amount of line. Frank was able to reel it in carefully until it was almost at the net. When it broke the surface this time, it allowed Frank to steer it over the net. As soon as it saw the net, it struggled again, but it was too late, Tom had safely netted it. He heaved it out of the water and gently lowered it on to the waiting unhooking mat.

'That's the biggest tench I've ever seen!' Tom was full of admiration for Frank's achievement. Frank had a satisfied grin on his face. He bent down and gently turned the fish round so that he could take out the hook. The hook looked so small in the large mouth. Frank took it out easily with a pair of forceps then stood and admired the fish. It was a beautiful bronze colour with bright orange eyes.

'Let's have a photo!' Tom had got his camera out ready. Frank bent down on one knee and lifted the tench gently in front of him.

'Smile! Frank – I mean you, not the fish! That's a good one. I'll just take a couple more.'

They weighed the tench before Frank lovingly lifted it back to the edge of the lake and lowered it into the water. He held it until it gently swam away.

'That was the biggest tench I've ever caught. Don't you think that was better than catching tiddlers?'

'Well, I guess so,' said Tom grudgingly. 'But it's your turn to catch tiddlers now. We were just about to swap, remember?'

'Yes, OK. I'll leave you to bait up.'

Tom and Frank switched positions. Frank quickly baited his hook and cast out while Tom was still attaching a large worm to his hook. Just as he cast out and had set the rod down in the rests, Frank said: 'Isn't that your dad over there? He's with a couple of people. One looks like a policewoman.'

Tom looked across to the other side of the lake to the car park where Frank was pointing. Sure enough, it was Dad. He waved. Tom and Frank waved back. Dad was leading the police along the path that skirted the lake. It would take them a few minutes to reach Tom and Frank.

'I wonder why they're coming to see us? Do you think they want to talk to us about Mr Grimley?'

'I should think so. They've probably finished talking to your mum and she must have told them about the time we went to Mr Grimley's shop.' His float tip dipped and he pulled his rod tip up. 'A bite! Feels like a tiddler though.' He reeled in a small roach. Just as he cast out again, Dad and the police came rustling through the shrubbery behind them.

'Hi Tom, Frank – this is PC Singleton and this is Detective Inspector Reynolds. They want to ask you a few questions about Mr Grimley.'

Detective Inspector Reynolds addressed both boys: 'This won't take long, lads. We just want to ask you about the time you went to see Mr Grimley. First, why did you go to see him?'

Tom spoke first. 'It was my idea. We wanted to find out about Sebastian Grimley, one of Mr Grimley's ancestors. I thought the easiest way was to ask Mr Grimley directly. We knew he was a bit of an ogre, and Mum had told us to avoid him, but we weren't scared of him, not much anyway. He was rude to us at first and told us to clear off, but as soon as we mentioned Sebastian Grimley, he started to listen and in the end, he gave us more information than we dared to hope for.'

'Tell us more about Sebastian Grimley. Why were you interested in him?' asked Inspector Reynolds.

Tom was conscious of finding a way of telling Inspector Reynolds about the argument between Sebastian and Joshua without mentioning his vision. He explained that they had found Sebastian's grave in Drumbridge and wanted to know why he wasn't buried in Walchester like the other Grimleys. He gave Inspector Reynolds the impression that Mr Grimley had explained the argument about the dog.

'Thanks – that's helpful. Now can you explain how you persuaded Mr Grimley to abandon the feud between the Grimleys and the Robertsons?'

'He said that the Reverend Magnus Robertson, my great-great-great-great-great grandfather, had done the Grimleys a favour by burying Sebastian Grimley when the vicar in Walchester refused to do it. I said to Mr Grimley that the favour would be repaid if he agreed to abandon his grudge. I didn't really expect him to give in so easily, but he did. It was almost as though he had been waiting for the opportunity.'

'Did he say he was going to see your mother?'

'Not exactly, but he asked me what her first name was, so we thought he must want to speak to her.'

At that moment, Frank's bite alarm went off and Tom turned quickly to grab the rod and strike. He felt a big fish pulling powerfully on the line. 'Sorry, Inspector.'

'That's all right, Tom. You enjoy your fishing. We've finished now anyway. If I need to speak to you again, I'll call at your house. Thanks for your help.'

'You know how to get back to your car, don't you? I'll wait to see what Tom's caught,' said Dad.

'Yes, no problem,' said Inspector Reynolds. He led PC Singleton back through the undergrowth to the path.

Tom was playing the fish well, with Frank giving advice. 'Don't try to pull too hard. Give it line if it needs it.'

The fish put up a good fight but Tom succeeded in bringing it safely into the net that Frank was holding for him. 'Not as big as yours, but not bad.'

'Did you catch a bigger one, Frank?' asked Dad.

'Yes, just before the police arrived.'

'I wish I'd been here to see it. I'll have to leave you now because I've got to get to the University. I'll see you later. Enjoy the rest of the day.'

'Thanks, Dad. See you later.'

'Bye, Professor Merrington.'

Tom and Frank settled down again to their fishing. They had brought sandwiches for lunch. Frank was looking thoughtful. 'Tom, did the police say how Mr Grimley was killed?'

'Dad knew that he had been stabbed with one of his own antique swords. I suppose the police must have told him.'

'It seems an odd way to commit a murder. If the murderer had come with the intention of killing Mr Grimley, he would have brought his own weapon. Perhaps it was a burglar and Mr Grimley found him in his shop. The burglar grabbed the nearest weapon, panicked and stabbed Mr Grimley. There were certainly plenty of swords in the place. Do you remember them?'

'Yes, he had all sorts of weapons, but I thought they were locked in cabinets.'

'Yes, I think you're right. So they wouldn't have been to hand. Perhaps the burglar had come to steal the swords and had already broken into a cabinet.'

'I hope you're right, that it was a burglar I mean. I'd hate to think he was killed because he was too soft on the Robertsons and ended the feud.' They looked at each other, each with fear in his eyes.

Chapter 13

Two Swords

THE CHILDREN HAD GONE BACK TO SCHOOL after the half-term holiday and Julia had been trying to pluck up the courage to telephone Mrs Grimley. She desperately wanted to know whether she was coping in the aftermath of her husband's death, but on the other hand, she did not want to interfere if Mrs Grimley preferred to be left alone. Eventually, she decided to take the plunge. She picked up the telephone and dialled the number that Mr Grimley had given her. A female voice answered.

'Hello, is that Mrs Grimley?'

'No, this is her sister. Who's calling, please?'

'It's Julia Merrington. My husband and I were due to come round for dinner before this tragic event happened. I was wondering if Mrs Grimley needed any help.'

'I'm looking after her at the moment. You will understand she doesn't want to see many people just now, but I'll ask her if she wants to speak to you.' There was a clatter as she placed the telephone on a hard surface. Julia could just hear a conversation going on in the distance. Soon a voice said: 'Mrs Merrington, this is Theresa Grimley. It's very kind of you to think of me. I'd like to speak to you – could you come round to my house?'

'Of course. I could come now if it's convenient.'

'Yes, please. Do you know where the house is?'

'No, I don't.'

'You know the shop?'

'Yes.' She shuddered at the thought of the body of Mr Grimley murdered in the shop.

'Well, it's just up the hill from the shop, in the same road – number twelve.'

'Oh, that's easy. I'll be there shortly. See you then.'

'I look forward to it.'

She hurriedly got herself ready to go out, grabbed the car keys and set off. She knew she would approach the road from the bottom of the hill, so she would have to pass the shop on the way to the house. As she passed, she noticed it was still cordoned off and there was a policeman standing in the doorway. She continued driving until she reached number twelve. It had a wide drive, so she drove in and parked the car in front of the house. She noticed how tastefully the front garden had been planted. There was a lot of colour created by plants growing at the base of the walls and the walls were covered with purple, pink and white varieties of clematis. It was particularly welcoming, not at all what she had expected. She rang the doorbell. There were voices from inside, then footsteps along the passage followed by a moment's pause as the person behind the door checked through the peep-hole to see who the visitor was. The door opened. 'Hello, Mrs Merrington. I'm Theresa Grimley.' She was not in the least like Julia had envisaged. She had expected a plump, plain woman, but Theresa Grimley was tall and elegant, at least ten years younger than her late husband. She could have been Italian with her short dark hair, deep brown eyes and stylish clothes.

When Julia had gathered her composure, she managed to stammer: 'Pleased to meet you.'

Theresa Grimley was remarkably calm considering her circumstances. She led Julia into the interior of the house. They went into a large comfortably-furnished room where her sister had just prepared a tray for tea. 'This is my sister Isabel – Mrs Merrington. Isabel is a nurse, so she's well-equipped to look after me.'

'Pleased to meet you, and please call me "Julia",' she said. Isabel was also tall and dark, but not as striking in appearance as her sister.

As soon as they were all seated, Theresa started the conversation. 'Sorry to drag you out here, but I was anxious to talk to you. I'll come straight to the point – I think my husband's death has something to do with the old family feud between the Grimleys and the Robertsons.'

'You don't think a Robertson killed him?'

'Oh, no! Sorry if I gave you that impression. Definitely not. In fact, it's hard to see how any normal human being could have killed him.'

'What do you mean?'

'I was the one who found him in the shop. If you can stomach the gory details, I'll tell you the state he was in.'

'Please go on.'

'You probably know that he was stabbed with his own swords.'

'Swords – plural?'

'Yes. He was pinned to one of the oak pillars in the shop with one sword through his neck and the other through his chest. He was suspended well above the ground, so whoever killed him would have to be superhuman to lift him off the ground and pin him to the pillar. Not only that, the swords were so deeply embedded in the wood that the police couldn't pull them out by hand – they had to get a winch.'

'Oh, that's awful!' exclaimed Julia. She felt sick but she managed to pull herself together well enough that the two sisters didn't notice.

'So you see why I don't believe he was killed by any normal human being.'

'Yes, but what could have done that?' Julia had visions of creatures like Frankenstein's monster in her mind.

'I don't know, but the Grimleys have always been riddled with evil and I know some of them have dabbled in weird stuff like devil-worship. I'm sure something evil and supernatural is involved.'

Julia was shocked, not just at the thought of a demon killing George Grimley, but that Theresa should condemn her husband's family so openly. 'Why did you marry George if you knew all this?' Julia was getting into the spirit of coming straight to the point.

'Oh, I understood the risk I was taking by marrying into the Grimleys, but George was a good man. He was a perfect father and husband and he protected us from all the evil in his family. Admittedly, he was objectionable to people outside his family, but that was because he was brought up not to trust anybody, least of all the Robertsons. George's father is evil. He probably knows why George was killed, but I'm not going to ask him. He might even know how he was killed. I told the police they should question him, but to be honest, this is not something they can handle.'

Julia's brain was racing. 'I'm sorry, Theresa, but I've never believed in demons and the like, so I find it hard to accept that there's some supernatural force at work here. There must be a more rational explanation.'

'Perhaps, but you must admit it's hard to explain how George could be killed in such a way by natural forces. What concerns me most is, we don't know whether the killer will strike again. If he does, we could be next!'

'Why do you think that?' Julia looked terrified.

'We were part of the family feud whether we wanted to be or not. I certainly don't feel safe and I thought it was only fair to warn you. I hope that killing George was the end of it, but who can tell?'

'So what can we do to protect ourselves?'

'I don't think we can do anything, but at least we can stick together.

George broke the barrier between us and we should take advantage of that. We're in this together and I think we should support each other as much as we can.'

Isabel interrupted the conversation: 'I understand how you feel, Julia. I don't believe in any of this mumbo-jumbo either, but Theresa is right – until we know how and why George died, you should be careful.'

Julia found it hard to accept that she was linked to George Grimley's murder because of what was for her a long-forgotten family feud. And the thought that some unseen evil force could be out to get her filled her with horror. She felt herself shaking. She tried to tell herself that such things don't exist, but then she kept thinking of George Grimley suspended by two swords deeply embedded in a wooden pillar. But surely the police would find an explanation, wouldn't they?

'Well, thank you both for putting me in the picture. It's a bit of a shock and I feel a bit shaky.'

'Please rest a while, Julia and I'll make a fresh pot of tea,' said Isabel.

'Thank you, that would be welcome.'

'Sorry if I was a bit blunt; I'm afraid that's just me,' said Theresa. 'Of course, I could be completely wrong about this whole thing, but I know the Grimleys and several of them have come to violent ends. I just hoped that it wouldn't happen to George.' For the first time, she looked upset and a tear rolled down her cheek. She wiped it away quickly as though she did not want to show any weakness.

But Julia noticed. 'Did you know that George had helped my son with his project at school?'

'Yes. George came home that day and said what a nice boy he was and it was time to abandon the feud with the Robertsons. I was very proud of him because he was breaking away from the past. He said he was going to give you an old book that belonged to you as well. He didn't tell me what it was.'

'It was written by one of my ancestors but stolen by the Grimleys in Victorian times. I think the Grimleys had kept it as a symbol of the hatred that they had for the Robertsons.'

'Then I'm very pleased that he did that before he died.'

Isabel came in with the fresh tea and poured it out. 'Here you are Julia. Are you feeling better?'

'Yes, thank you.' Julia had another cup of tea and Theresa showed her some of the antique furniture in the house as a diversion from the subject that was foremost in their minds. They agreed that they would keep in regular contact from now on. When Julia left, her mind was still in turmoil, but she had stopped shaking and she felt well enough to drive the car.

On the way home, Julia thought about her experience with Theresa and her sister. She had expected to have to console Theresa, but it turned out to be the other way round. Theresa was clearly an unusually strong woman, and even the little tear she shed was only a brief sign of distress. Perhaps when you are married to a man who has such a terrible family, you accept that something awful might happen one day. She churned these thoughts over in her mind all the way home and then when she got home, she continued to think about demons and evil forces and the danger she might be in. What about Jim and Tom and Amy? Were they at risk? She told herself that these things didn't exist and there was really no risk at all. But what could have killed George Grimley in that horrific way? The thought kept recurring.

When Tom and Amy came home from school, Julia tried to be her normal self, but Tom noticed that something was wrong. 'You all right Mum?'

'Yes, I'll be all right, thank you Tom. I saw Mrs Grimley today and it was a bit upsetting.' She had decided she would not tell them about Theresa's revelations unless she had to, but she would talk to Jim first when he came home that evening.

'Is she OK?'

'Yes, she's coping remarkably well. She's got her sister staying with her and she's a nurse, so she'll be well looked after.' Tom thought he wouldn't pry any more because Mum still looked upset. He went off to do his homework. He did not have much homework to do and when he finished it, he knew he must go down to the grave.

Chapter 14
A Special Skill

Tom went into the churchyard and sat down next to the grave. It was windy, but the headstone sheltered him. He closed his eyes and was transported to a room he had never seen before. Will seemed to be sitting behind a desk in what appeared to be a sparsely-furnished office. He was writing notes on a sheet of paper, but Tom could not understand them. They seemed to be medical notes.

There was a knock on the door. Will shouted: 'Come in.'

A young nurse walked in through the door. 'Dr Protheroe, we are having trouble with Mr Molloy. Could you come to see him please? He's very distressed.'

'Of course.' Will got up out of his chair and went out of his office with the nurse, closing the door behind him.

As they walked briskly along the corridor, Tom noticed that he was looking down on the nurse. Obviously, Will was now adult and qualified as a doctor. This was presumably a hospital – but what kind of hospital? They turned the corner of the corridor and walked into a huge ward with rows and rows of beds occupied by men. The walls were a dirty grey colour and the windows were tiny and barred, so they did not let in much light. At the far end of the ward, a commotion was going on and the sound was echoing around the walls. A nurse was shouting at one of the patients but he was just wailing continuously. Will and the nurse were heading that way. When Will got to the patient, he put his hands on each side of the patient's face and looked closely at him. This was presumably Mr Molloy. He looked awful. His eyes were bloodshot and his skin was blotchy, but most of all, he looked desperately sad. Tom felt the intensity of the sadness as Will held his head and talked to him gently. It was as though he was at the bottom of a pit with no way out, no light above and nothing but hopelessness all around. Then gradually, some light came into Mr Molloy's mind and the sadness subsided. At the same time, Mr Molloy began to relax. Will moved his hands from the man's face to his shoulders and began to guide him back to bed. He meekly got back into bed and the nurses took over from Will.

'Thank you Dr Protheroe,' said the nurse who had alerted him in the first place.

'Keep an eye on him, nurse and call me again if he has another episode like that. I'm sure it will happen again.'

'Yes, but I don't like to keep bothering you Dr Protheroe.'

'It's no bother at all. It's my job. I don't expect you to be able to manage all the patients all of the time. If you need help, don't be afraid to ask.'

'Thank you Dr Protheroe.' The nurse gave Will an admiring look.

Will walked back to his office, casting glances at all the other patients as he went. The place had an air of despair about it. These patients were mentally ill and the amount of care they were getting was minimal; the two nurses seemed to be the only ones looking after the whole ward.

When Will got back to his office, he finished the notes that he had been making before the interruption and then he picked up a letter that was lying at the side of his desk. He must have opened it previously and wanted to read it again. It was on headed notepaper from the "University of New Mallington Medical School, May 14th, 1892". This is what it said:

"My Dear Will,

As you know, I have been trying to improve my skills at probing the minds of my patients under the guidance of Max Weissman. He has been a great help to me and we have made excellent progress, but we have one patient who is completely resistant to the technique. Even Max has failed to make any impact on him. On the last occasion when Max tried, the patient seemed not only to resist him, but reversed the process. Poor Max was in a bit of a state and I had to drag him bodily out of the ward. When he had recovered, he said: 'That man's mind is pure evil.' I have had no success with him at all. Max thinks you are probably the only person who has a chance of succeeding with him. I beg you to come here and see for yourself. We do not want to put you in any danger, but if you can get through to him, you would be doing us a great service.

I should give you some information on the patient. His name is Marmaduke Constable, aged forty-eight. He was once a successful and wealthy businessman, having made a fortune in the steel industry in Sheffield. Apparently he was always something of a tyrant with his employees, but when he started to use a club to beat them, they revolted against him and almost killed him. His son had him committed to our institution and took over the business himself. According to his son, the change came over his father rather suddenly. He had always been tyrannical and vocal, but never out of control or violent. Then he developed uncontrollable rages and that is when he took the club to his employees. His son described it as 'being possessed' and 'not the father I knew'. We have certainly experienced his uncontrollable rages and have had to put him in a strait-jacket several times. You know my views on that and you will appreciate that I will only use the strait-jacket under exceptional circumstances. He is so troublesome that we are desperate to find a solution. That is why I am begging you to help us. Please let us know your decision at your earliest convenience. As always, you are welcome to stay in my house.

Your Friend and Colleague,

Bernard Simmonds"

Will put the letter down on the desk in front of him, took a sheet of writing paper and wrote a reply. It was brief and said simply:

"My Dear Bernard,

I shall catch the late train on Wednesday, so you can expect me at about nine pm.

Your Friend and Colleague

Will Protheroe"

Tom was puzzled by what he had seen. It made sense that Will had become a psychiatrist because of his previous interest in mental disorders, but he had also developed his technique of looking into the minds of mental patients. That was obviously what he was doing with Mr Molloy. Tom had felt the deep, deep unhappiness in Mr Molloy's mind, and then the relief as Will had replaced those unhappy thoughts with happier ones. Tom also felt what Will had expressed: that Mr Molloy would not get better. All Will could do to help him was to bring him out of his deep depression temporarily. Tom felt the experience had improved his own mind.

There had been a huge jump in time since the last vision, when Will was still at school. Why was that? Tom thought about what he had learned from Mr Swinburne: he knew that Will had progressed from Fettersham to Edinburgh and then became a psychiatrist. Perhaps there was nothing else of significance to know about Will's life of that period, so it wasn't necessary to have the visions. But if that were the case, somebody who knew about his visit to Fettersham was engineering his visions! Tom shuddered.

The next day, Mum received a letter from Professor MacDonald, inviting her and Tom to visit him and talk about Will Protheroe. She telephoned him that day and arranged the visit.

'Tom, as you don't have any school on Monday, I've arranged our visit to see Professor MacDonald.'

'Oh, Frank had asked me if I wanted to go with him and his dad to the football match in the evening. Walchester are playing in the FA Cup. It doesn't matter, I can tell him I can't go.'

'Are you sure? I can see Professor MacDonald on my own.'

'Oh, no, I want to meet him. I've got a lot of questions for him.'

'OK. Make sure you write all your questions down. Let me see your list before we go.' They had to set off early on Monday morning to catch the train to Rothbank. From the station, they were able to walk to Professor MacDonald's department. They went through the grand old entrance among a throng of students. Professor MacDonald had given Mum clear instructions on how to find his office, so they went up to the second floor and followed the signs to his department. His office had his name on the door, so they knocked and went in. There was a secretarial area in front of his office, so Mum told the secretary who she was. The secretary escorted them across the room to Professor MacDonald's office.

'Professor – Mrs Merrington and her son to see you.'

'Thank you very much, Angela. Pleased to meet you Mrs Merrington. And you must be Tom.' He indicated to them to take two chairs on the other side of his desk. It was a small office, so there was little room for furniture other than bookcases, which were filled to overflowing with books and journals. He was a middle-aged man of average height and build, dressed casually but smartly in a blue tweed jacket, open-necked blue and white checked shirt and grey trousers. He had short, curly ginger hair and a freckled face. He was one of those people with whom you felt at ease immediately. He had an informal, friendly manner and his voice was steady, calm and cultured, with a gentle Scottish accent.

He got straight to the point. 'First of all, let me tell you what I've been doing and my motive for doing it. I discovered some time ago that William Protheroe had a special gift for probing the minds of mental patients. According to the records, he was remarkably successful at correcting some mental disturbances, permanently in a lot of cases. Of course, at that time he did not have the drugs we have available to us today, so the cures were purely the result of his particular skill. As far as I can tell, there were hardly any psychiatrists who had this skill and today, there are none. Whatever it was that William Protheroe learned to do, the skill has been lost. I have dug up all the records I can on his achievements and his life to try to give me some clues on how we might regain that skill. That is my objective. Now, can you explain to me exactly what your interest in William Protheroe is?'

Mum looked at Tom and then began to explain. 'First of all, William Protheroe was one of my ancestors. We have discovered a lot about him by tracing records and visiting his old school, but most of our information has come from my son Tom here. You see, he also has a special gift – he has been seeing into the past through the eyes of William Protheroe.'

Professor MacDonald looked incredulous. His first thought was that he had been lumbered with a pair of time-wasters, but then he thought about William Protheroe's unfathomable skill, so he opened his mind to considering another special skill from the same family. Then the analytical side of his brain kicked in – he wanted to hear the evidence. 'So, Tom, can you tell me some of the things you have learned about William Protheroe?'

Tom started at the beginning. 'First, William Protheroe wasn't his real name. He was born Benjamin Robertson and his father was Joshua Robertson, Professor of History at Walchester University.'

'Just a moment, Tom – do you mean the Joshua Robertson who wrote the treatise on mental disorders in great artists?'

'Yes.'

'That makes a lot of sense. Fascinating – please go on.' Professor MacDonald had absorbed the first shock and now he was ready for more. He put his head between his hands, his elbows on his desk, like a child listening intently to a fairy story.

'Joshua and his youngest son died in a house fire, but Ben survived and was adopted by a doctor, Isaac Protheroe, who gave him the name "William", although he always called him "Will". Will went to Fettersham School and then Edinburgh University to study medicine. He could already probe the minds of people when he was at school, so when he became a psychiatrist he used his talent on his patients. I know he had two colleagues at the University of New Mallington Medical School: Max Weissman and Bernard Simmonds.'

'That's incredible! You know about Max Weissman and Bernard Simmonds! As far as I can tell, they were the only other two people who had the mind-probing capability. Now you said that Will survived a fire. Was he badly injured?'

'Yes, he almost died. Isaac Protheroe took him from the hospital and used his own special technique to keep him alive.'

'That's very interesting. The reason I say that is that people who have survived near-death experiences have been known to come out of the ordeal with special insights into various things. Perhaps in Will's case, it was the insight into people's minds. Tom – you don't know if Max Weissman and Bernard Simmonds also had near-death experiences, do you?'

'No, I haven't actually met them yet. I've only seen a letter that Bernard wrote to Will, asking for his help with a patient.'

'Did he give the name of the patient?'

'Yes – Marmaduke Constable.'

'That's helpful – I might be able to track down what they did with him. They wouldn't have given his name but they might have referred to him as "MC". Max Weissman wrote a book on their experiences with patients at New Mallington, so he could be referred to in there. I know he wrote about his collaborations with Will.'

'Professor, do you know if Will carried on with Joshua Robertson's work?' Tom asked.

'Now you mention it, I suppose in a way, he did. Several of his patients were important people, among them some artists, musicians and authors. He wrote an essay on creativity and insanity, and raised a few eyebrows in the process. He claimed that being on the edge of sanity was necessary for some of the most creative people to be creative. In other words, if he cured them of their mental disorders, they would lose their creativity. He also said that if they went completely mad, they also lost their creativity. This was all based on his experience with these people. There were only a few, of course, so these days his work would probably be dismissed because he didn't have enough patients to prove his theory.'

'Do you have a copy of that essay, Professor?' Mum asked.

'I can certainly make you one. It's quite long, so I'll send it to you in the post.'

'Thank you very much.' She was sure that Jim, Mike and Kala would want to see it.

'So, Tom, to go back to your question – it makes a lot of sense to me now that Will was the son of Joshua Robertson. That's quite a revelation to me. I don't suppose there's any documentary evidence that Will Protheroe was once Ben Robertson?'

'I don't think so,' said Tom. 'Isaac Protheroe did all he could to hide that. When he adopted Will he claimed he was an orphan who came from the workhouse.'

Mum interrupted. 'I've even got a death certificate for Ben Robertson. He formally died of burns sustained in the fire that killed his father and brother.' The professor looked puzzled.

Tom continued: 'Isaac stole Ben from the hospital and left a dummy. The doctors were so embarrassed that they issued a death certificate for Ben. So at the funeral they buried a dummy.'

'Why should Isaac Protheroe want to steal a patient from the hospital?'

'Because he had a special way of treating burns and he thought he could save Ben. It was better than letting him die.'

'But why wouldn't the doctors at the hospital let Isaac treat him anyway?'

'He was forbidden to use his technique because one of his patients had drowned in the oil bath he used.'

Professor MacDonald laughed. 'That sounds typically Victorian. Well, I suppose the important thing is Will survived. As far as I'm concerned, it doesn't really matter that he changed his identity. I am interested in following up the idea that the near-death experience gave him his powers, though. I'll try to find out whether the same thing happened to Max Weissman and Bernard Simmonds. If that's the link, there could be some people out there today who have similar talents.' He became detached and deep in thought. Mum interrupted and he snapped back to reality.

'Tom, I think you had another question to ask Professor MacDonald.' The professor turned his face towards Tom.

'Yes. Professor, do you know how Will died?'

'Yes, I do. He was murdered – stabbed to death. The killer was never found, so I understand. I haven't looked into that in any great detail because it would be a bit of a diversion for me. I can give you the date if you like.' He rummaged through his papers.

Mum interrupted him: 'It's OK, I've got the date; but I'm still waiting for the death certificate.'

'You might find this interesting though.' Professor MacDonald showed Mum an obituary of Will Protheroe copied from a scientific journal. It specifically stated that he was stabbed to death by persons unknown. From the comments on his professional abilities in the obituary, he was obviously highly respected in the medical profession.

'Do you think his murder would have been reported in the national press?' Mum asked.

'Very likely – he was an important figure.'

'Then I'll take another trip to the newspaper library and see what I can find.'

'If you find anything interesting, please let me know, won't you? I can't really justify doing the search myself because it's not key to my objective; at least I've assumed it's not.'

'Yes, of course.'

'And I'll put together a package of what I've got for you. I've written up most of the work in a paper and I've got a list of all Will's publications at the end.'

'That's very kind of you. You've been most helpful.'

'Not at all; I've probably learned more from you. But just before you go, Tom, I'd like to ask you a few questions.' He then proceeded to cross-examine

Tom on how the visions occurred, whether he had experienced anything like it before, whether he lost consciousness during the visions, and then on seemingly irrelevant topics such as his favourite subjects at school, the books he read, what television programmes he watched and what he liked to do with his friends. Tom was relieved when he finally said: 'Thank you, Tom, that was very helpful. Thank you both for coming to see me and please keep in touch. Tom: if you learn any more about Will from your visions, I'd like to hear from you about it.'

Tom felt important. He had helped the Professor in his work and the Professor was treating him as a friend and equal. 'Yes, I will. Thank you, Professor.'

'I'll show you the way out. Do you want a cup of tea before you go? Sorry, I got so involved in our discussions, I completely forgot about offering you a drink.'

'No, we'll be fine, thank you.' They said their farewells and Mum and Tom emerged into the street.

Professor MacDonald went back to his office, dropped into his chair, folded his arms and exhaled loudly. His mind was racing with what he had just heard. Perhaps this was the opportunity to take a major step in his research. Many of his colleagues thought he was wasting his time trying to understand William Protheroe's amazing skill, but he would show them! He regretted not making more definite plans to keep in touch with the Merringtons and wrung his hands anxiously. He was determined to put that right. He would give them a call tomorrow to make sure that Tom gave him every last detail of his visions.

Tom and Mum headed straight for the station and arrived in plenty of time.

'We've got some time to kill – let's go into the café and get a drink before we catch the train,' suggested Mum.

They sat down with their drinks and started talking. Mum had been thinking all the way to the station about Will's murder. The fact that he was stabbed aroused the memories of Mr Grimley's murder. She decided it would be a good time to tell Tom how Mr Grimley had been murdered.

'Tom, you know Dad said that Mr Grimley was stabbed?'

'Yes.'

'Well, it was a bit more complicated than that. Mrs Grimley told me that he was pinned to one of the wooden pillars in his shop with two swords – one through his neck and the other through his chest.' She watched Tom's face carefully in case she was upsetting him. 'But it gets worse – he was suspended off the ground. So it's hard to imagine how a normal human being could have done it. Mrs Grimley believes there is some evil force involved.'

Tom's eyes were wide and staring. 'What kind of evil force?'

'I don't know – it's probably just Mrs Grimley being over-dramatic. I didn't want to scare you but I thought you should know about it.'

'It is scary for sure. Have the police got any idea how it was done?'

'I don't think so.'

'Do you mind if I tell Frank? He'll have some ideas.'

'As long as you don't spread it any further. The police haven't given any details to the press, just that he was stabbed.'

'We can keep a secret.'

Chapter 15

Sebastian's Sister

DISTRESSING THOUGH IT WAS, TOM COULDN'T WAIT to tell Frank how Mr Grimley had died. He told him at the first opportunity they had at school. Much to Tom's disappointment, Frank didn't have any ideas. That evening, they met in the graveyard and discussed it. They were deep in conversation when old Mr Jake and Bessie came up to them.

'How are you two then?' And then without waiting for a reply: 'Did you hear about old George Grimley?'

'Yes, we did. We were just wondering whether the police had made any progress.'

'Oh, I don't think so. They won't find a murderer who's not of this world.'

Tom and Frank pretended to look puzzled. 'What do you mean by that, Mr Jake?' asked Frank.

'Well, apparently, he was pinned up to a pillar in his own shop with two swords, as though someone had used him as a dartboard. The swords were so far embedded in the wood that they needed a winch to pull them out. There's no human being who could do that. I think it's all to do with the Grimleys meddling in black magic.'

'Black magic?'

'Aye, the Grimleys have always been a queer lot. They had all sorts of villains in their family over the years and some of them were supposed to worship the Devil. When I was a youngster, I knew a couple of the Grimleys. Nasty kids they were, always in trouble and always ready to steal anything from other kids. I heard their father used to practise voodoo and the like. He'd been a sailor and had travelled to lots of places in the world where he picked up a few tricks on how to raise demons and other nasty things.'

'Do you believe in all that stuff then, Mr Jake?' Tom asked.

'Well, now, I don't know about demons and the like, but I do believe in ghosts – seen one myself in this very churchyard! It was one evening when I saw an odd-looking woman standing over a grave in the corner over there.' He pointed to the corner of the graveyard where Sebastian Grimley was buried. 'She had a bonnet on her head and a dark cloak that went right down to the ground. She looked a bit distressed, so I thought I'd go over to see if she might like a tot of brandy – always keep a bit for emergencies in my hip flask you know. Anyway, when I got near, she turned round and I saw her face. White as a sheet it was and she had tears rolling down her cheeks. She didn't seem to notice me and she walked away, straight for that big tree. When she got there, she just went through the tree and vanished. I looked all around but couldn't see her anywhere. I pinched myself to check that I wasn't dreaming, so I reckon I saw a ghost all right!'

'Could you show us exactly where she was, please, Mr Jake?' asked Frank.

'Come along.' With Bessie trotting obediently behind, he took them to the corner of the graveyard and stood right in front of Sebastian Grimley's grave. 'She stood here looking at that grave.'

'Mr Jake, I know it's hard to read, but that's Sebastian Grimley's grave – he was an ancestor of George Grimley.'

'Well I'll be blowed! Told you they were a queer lot didn't I?' And then as if he had suddenly thought the woman might come back, he moved a couple of paces away.

'Have you only seen her once, Mr Jake?' asked Frank.

'Yes, thank goodness.'

'I don't suppose anyone else has seen her?'

'Not to my knowledge. Perhaps old Maggie Bratherstone knows something about it. She's over there – let's go and ask her.'

Tom and Frank had not noticed Mrs Bratherstone tending her husband's grave. They knew she thought that Mr Jake was a bit strange, so they were wondering how this confrontation was going to develop. Much to their surprise, Mrs Bratherstone smiled at Mr Jake when he approached her.

'Hello you old rogue, have you been filling these boys' heads with your tall stories?'

'Now, now Maggie, you know I wouldn't do a thing like that. We wanted to ask you about a ghost.'

'Ghost? Are you mad? Who's seen a ghost, anyway?'

'I have.'

'Where?'

'Over there, in the corner of the graveyard. These boys tell me it's right in front of the grave of one of George Grimley's ancestors.'

Mrs Bratherstone looked serious. 'What did she look like?'

'She had a long cloak on and a very pale face. Crying she was.'

Frank interrupted: 'Mrs Bratherstone, how did you know it was a woman?'

'I've heard tales of a woman in a cloak who is supposed to visit her brother's grave in this graveyard whenever anyone in her family dies before their time. I've also heard it was a woman whose brother was hanged for a crime he didn't commit.'

'That's right. Sebastian Grimley was hanged for a crime he didn't commit,' said Tom. 'Mr Jake, did you see her on the day that George Grimley was murdered?'

Mr Jake searched his memory. 'It could have been. Let's think – no, my memory's not good enough to be sure, but it could well have been.'

Mrs Bratherstone tried to stimulate his memory: 'I saw you here the day he was murdered. Do you remember I put some flowers on your wife's grave for you? It was the evening and you were still here when I left.'

'Ah, yes, I remember. Bessie and I sat down for a while after you left and it was when we got up ready to go that I saw the ghost. So it was when George Grimley died! It all fits, like you said, Maggie.'

'Well, I must say I've never believed those stories, but now we know they were true all the time,' said Mrs Bratherstone.

Tom looked at his watch and realized he said he'd be home half an hour ago. 'I'm afraid we'll have to be going now; we're already late. It's been nice talking to you.' They said goodbye to Mrs Bratherstone and Mr Jake and went back through the gate to the Vicarage.

When they got indoors, Tom said: 'Mum, have you ever seen the ghost in the graveyard?'

Mum laughed. 'Who's been telling you about ghosts in the graveyard? I'll bet it's old Jake, isn't it?'

'Well, yes, but it's true. He's seen it.'

'I'll bet. He sees all sorts of things.'

'But Mrs Bratherstone said it was true as well.'

Mum at last took notice. She had a lot of respect for Mrs Bratherstone. 'So what does she say?'

'She said that there was a tale that a woman came to visit her brother's grave every time one of the family died before their time. What she didn't know was that the family was the Grimleys.'

'How do you know that?'

'Because Mr Jake saw her visiting Sebastian Grimley's grave. She appeared when George Grimley died.'

Mum's brow was thoroughly knitted by now. She sighed. 'Well, then, I suppose it must be true. I've got the names of Sebastian's brothers and sisters – just let me get it up on the computer.'

They went to the small room at the rear of the house where Mum kept all her family history information. She started up the computer and was soon searching the records she had entered on the Grimleys. 'I don't know why I kept information on the Grimleys. I just thought it might come in useful one day. Here we are – he had three sisters and two brothers. Sebastian was the youngest son, but only one of his sisters was older than him. I should think she cared for him. I believe he was mentally retarded. Isn't that what George Grimley said?'

'More or less,' said Tom.

'Her name was Marian. I suspect she's your ghost.'

'Thanks, Mum.'

Mum decided she would talk to Mrs Bratherstone about the ghost at the earliest opportunity. Old Jake's stories were always coloured by his imagination, but she had to admit that this one did seem to fit together even though it was bizarre.

Chapter 16
St. Caithrin

TOM WAS EAGERLY AWAITING HIS NEXT VISION but it was several days before he felt the urge to go down to the grave. Frank had intended to be there, but he had got a detention for forgetting his geography homework. Tom settled down by the grave and closed his eyes. Will was entering a large building with heavy wooden doors at the entrance. He was walking alongside a short man who was obviously quite agitated.

'I do hope we're not putting you in danger, Will,' said the man.

'Don't worry, I can look after myself.'

They reached an office door and the man peered through the glass panel. 'Max is in his office.' He banged on the door and they both walked in.

'Hello, Max. It's good to see you again,' said Will.

'I'm so pleased you have come, Will.' An older man with a large moustache and bushy grey hair stood up from his desk and shook hands with Will. Tom thought he looked like the pictures he had seen of Einstein. He presumed that the short man was Bernard Simmonds. He was still agitated. Below his furrowed brow, he wore round spectacles that kept slipping down his nose, which was not really big enough to support spectacles. Max looked controlled, but he seemed to be that sort of person who remains calm in the worst situations. 'Before we go in to see Mr Constable, I think I should explain what happened to me the last time I tried to see into his mind.'

Will sat down and waited expectantly for Max to begin. 'Please, give me the details.'

'I had tried about three times to make contact with his mind, but there seemed to be an impregnable barrier that was blocking my efforts. Then, on the fourth occasion, I felt that I was making some progress. I had penetrated to some degree and I detected some evil thoughts in his mind – thoughts of war and mass killings. Then, suddenly, he turned his mind against me and I felt the pressure of his evil thoughts. It was all I could do to resist them. Bernard shouted at him and pinned him down on his bed. Fortunately, it broke the link and he just lay gasping on his bed. I felt drained and Bernard had to help me out of the room.'

'Do you have him isolated?'

'Yes, he was also in a strait-jacket at the time – we couldn't take any risks.'

'That probably angered him even more. If we are to get through to him, he must not be restrained.'

'That will be risky – he's very violent.'

'I'll take my chance. I'd like to see him now if I may.'

'This way.' Bernard led them along a dismal corridor until they reached a locked door at the end. He took out a large key and unlocked the door. Inside, the room was pervaded by a suffocating feeling of evil. It had the minimum furniture. Seated on a plain wooden chair by the side of the bed was a heavily-built man with thinning grey hair and a wispy beard. From the look on his face, it was clear he was full of hatred. He was not restrained, but he stayed firmly seated in his chair. Bernard locked them all in the room.

'Hello, Mr Constable, I'm Dr Protheroe. I've come to see if I can help you.' No response, just a fixed glare. 'Would you like to get out of here and go back to your family, Mr Constable?' Again, no response. Will continued to talk to him while trying to probe his mind. All the time, Mr Constable was glaring at him. Tom could see some strange images in his mind. There was a lot of red, like blood and a feeling of terror. He could see a hand feebly reaching out from a pool of blood. After only a short while, Will decided to end the session. 'I'll come back to see you another time, Mr Constable.' Still there was no response.

The three doctors left the room and went back to Max's office. 'Well, did you see anything, Will?'

'Yes. I saw enough to know that there are two separate forces at work in his mind. One is very weak and almost extinguished – I think that's his original mind. The other has almost taken over completely and is pure evil, as you suggested, Max.'

'But how can that be?' asked Bernard.

'I don't know. I've never seen it before, but it seems to me that Mr Constable is inhabited by a mind that is not his own.'

'You mean he's possessed?'

'That's one way of putting it.'

'Can you do anything about it?'

'It will be difficult, but I hope I can chase it out of him by displacing the evil thoughts. My fear is that Mr Constable's own mind is so weak that he will probably die if I succeed. If we wait much longer he will certainly die.'

'And if you don't succeed, you could end up with the demon, or whatever it is, transferring into your mind,' said Max.

'Yes, but I have to take that risk.'

'No you don't. We can just keep Mr Constable restrained here until he dies.'

'But Max, this is a great opportunity to achieve something special. How many other cases like this are there?'

'Probably none, so it's not worth taking the risk.'

'We don't know that. We could be on the verge of discovering what drives serial killers and psychopaths. This "other mind" could have been manufactured inside Mr Constable's own mind – it doesn't have to be a "demon" that came from outside.'

'I suppose that's true, but goodness knows how such a process could occur.'

'I don't pretend to understand that, but however it occurred, I believe we should try to get rid of this evil influence in Mr Constable's mind.'

'Very well, if you insist on being foolhardy, I'll support you. How about you, Bernard?'

Bernard looked extremely reluctant. 'If you're prepared to support him Max, I'll do so too.'

'Thanks, both of you. I suggest we do it right now. Mr Constable will not be expecting us to return today, so we could catch him off guard.'

Both Max and Bernard looked even more alarmed. Then with a resigned look on his face, Max said: 'Oh, very well, let's get on with it.'

Will marched purposefully back to Mr Constable's room with the others hurrying behind him. Bernard unlocked the door.

'Hello again, Mr Constable. I thought we might continue our talk.' This time, Mr Constable looked surprised for a moment, and then resumed his normal scowl. Will then asked Mr Constable about his business at the steel works, without getting a response. Tom could see the images building up in his mind while Will changed the subject to Mr Constable's family. Will had managed to retrieve images of children from Mr Constable's mind and Tom could see happy scenes of parents playing with children. Then, suddenly, these images were completely overcome by scenes of destruction, with corpses lying on the ground. Will again replaced the scene with a picture of a beautiful smiling young woman holding a baby with a happy young man behind her. They disappeared, to be replaced by a huge army of soldiers rampaging through a crowd of people, slashing at them with swords and trampling over the helpless bodies. At the same time, a tray from beside the bed flew up and headed towards Will. He ducked just in time and it smashed against the wall. This alternation of happy and frightening scenes continued until the switching became so frequent that Will's mind was a blur.

Other objects flew towards him but he managed to avoid most of them. A cup hit him on the arm with such force it shattered into tiny pieces on his arm. But even under this terrifying pressure, Will somehow managed to keep attacking Mr Constable's mind. Tom could feel him weakening, but so was Mr Constable. Just as it seemed that Will's brain would burst, Mr Constable let out a fearsome scream and his head fell forward. It was over. Max went to stop Will from falling over while Bernard attended to Mr Constable.

'How is he?' Will was gasping and struggled to say the words. Sweat was running down his face.

'He's still alive – just. His pulse is very weak.'

After taking several deep breaths, Will responded: 'He won't be any trouble any more, but he'll need a lot of care if he is to survive.'

'I'll get a nurse to help me to make him comfortable.' Bernard had managed to get Mr Constable on to the bed. He went out to fetch a nurse.

Will and Max went back to Max's office where Max made them both a hot drink. 'You were splendid, Will. You showed such strength. I feared he might overcome you at one point.'

'So did I.'

'Will, you don't look happy with the outcome. You should be overjoyed.'

'It's not all over, Max. That evil parasite has gone elsewhere. It's probably already found another being to inhabit.'

'How can you be sure?'

'It left completely – it must have come from outside Mr Constable's mind in the first place, so I'm sure it's capable of doing it again.'

'Well, let's hope we never have to meet it again.'

'That's what bothers me – it's got a score to settle with me now, so it won't surprise me if it comes to find me.'

'I hope you are mistaken, Will.'

'So do I.'

'What did you make of the flying objects?' Then, without waiting for an answer: 'Oh yes – let me look at your arm.' Max carefully took off Will's jacket and rolled up his sleeve. After a few prods he said: 'It's not broken, just badly bruised. It's going to be painful for some time.'

'To answer your question, I don't know. I've heard of this sort of thing happening before, but it's very frightening when it happens to you. That cup hit me with some force. It was fortunate that there was very little in the room to hurl at me.'

'Not fortunate, Will – we deliberately kept the contents of the room to a minimum because he was so violent.'

Bernard came puffing back into the room. 'Will, I think you should see this.' It was a pillow-case with some writing on it that looked as though it had been written in blood. 'I noticed it soon after you left the room.'

Will took the pillow case and laid it on Max's desk. On it were the words: "You cannot stop me. Thank you. St Caithrin."

'See, Max, I told you.'

'Who the hell is St Caithrin?'

'I think you used the right expression there, Max. It's certainly not a saint. I'd guess the name is some kind of joke.'

'Is it written in blood, Bernard?' said Max.

'Yes, it's Mr Constable's blood. It oozed from his ear and formed the words on his pillow.'

'How is he?'

'Very weak. I don't think he's going to survive. I'll send a message to his son to tell him that he is gravely ill.'

'What will you tell his son and what will you say is the cause of death if he dies?'

'Will, don't worry about that. He's our patient and we'll deal with it. You've done all you can.'

'But you can't tell his son the truth – he won't believe it. If only we could save Mr Constable.'

'We'll do our best, Will, but I doubt that it will be good enough.'

If Tom needed convincing that Will could probe the minds of his patients, this was an amazing proof. Tom had seen clearly how Will retrieved happy memories from Mr Constable's mind to displace the evil ones that had been implanted by St Caithrin. But Tom was most impressed by Will's strength in maintaining the pressure and finally driving out St Caithrin. He felt exhausted just being a witness to the event.

When Tom came round from his vision, Frank was waiting. 'I came as soon as I could. What did you see this time?'

Tom looked at Frank with drooping eyelids. He struggled to speak. 'Have you ever heard of St Caithrin?'

'St Catherine?'

'No, C-a-i-t-h-r-i-n.'

'Sorry, can't help you there. Why?'

'It's some kind of demon.'

'Not much of a saint then.'

'No, that's what's puzzling. Anyway, Will managed to get rid of it from a patient's mind.'

'You mean an exorcism?'

'In a way.'

'Do you want to give me the details and I'll write it out?'

'OK, let's go back to the house.'

Chapter 17

Tom's Power

Tom was having trouble concentrating in his lessons at school. His mind was wandering back to the experience with Mr Constable. He wondered whether he had survived and who or what St Caithrin could be. He thought he should contact Professor MacDonald again to explain what he had seen.

'Tom Merrington! Can you tell us what I have just been describing to you?' Tom's mind had wandered and he had not been listening to Mrs Parkin, the geography teacher. He looked at her in bewilderment at first and then after a long pause and a large gulp said: 'Yes, you were telling us how the attractive force of the moon creates tides.'

'Go on.'

'The spring tide is highest because that's when both the moon and the sun are in line and their forces add together.'

'Anything else?'

'The neap tides are lowest because the forces of the moon and sun are then at right angles to each other.'

Mrs Parkin was clearly shaken by the accuracy of Tom's description. How could the boy know it when his mind had been miles away? 'Thank you,' she said. 'I am glad to see that you must have been paying attention even though you were making a very good impression of not doing so.'

The truth was that Tom had seen it in her mind, but he didn't have a clue how he had done it. Mrs Parkin had cornered him and he hadn't been paying attention. He was desperate and somehow he managed to draw on a power he didn't know he had. It seemed quite easy and natural to focus on her mind, but he wasn't sure he could do it again. Was this the purpose of the visions? Were the experiences with Will a kind of training? He thought of Will's amazing ability to probe minds and wondered whether he would be able to do that if the visions continued. But why? What was he being trained to achieve? There must be an objective. He decided to confide in Frank at the break.

'Frank, I saw into Mrs Parkin's mind in the geography lesson.'

Frank's expression of surprise changed slowly to one of interest as he thought of Tom's visions. 'How do you know?'

'She asked me what she had been telling the class and I hadn't been listening, so I didn't have a clue until I saw it in her mind.'

'So you are becoming more like Will. It's the visions. They are showing you how to do it. You can put thoughts into people's minds as well. I said you were too good to be true at persuading people.'

'But I don't know how I did it. I think it may only happen when I'm under some kind of pressure.'

'That's fair enough. You can only do it when you need it. It would be a pain if you could see into people's minds all the time. You wouldn't have to talk to them.'

'But why me? Am I some kind of freak?'

'You're not a freak. I think you've been chosen for some kind of mission.'

'You said that once before.'

'I know. All these experiences with Will – they must be leading up to something. It's not as though you've experienced all of his life; you've just seen the bits that matter. And it seems that what you see rubs off on you – you can do what Will does.'

'I'm sure I can't drive a demon out of someone's mind like Will did.'

'You don't know that. If you were faced with it, you might be able to do it. That's a thought – I wonder if that's what you are going to have to do?'

Tom looked terrified. 'Oh no, I hope not!'

'What about this "St Caithrin"? It was still at large in your last vision. Perhaps it's still at large now.'

'You're doing your best to terrify me, aren't you?' Tom was getting extremely anxious thinking about the terrifying ordeal that Will went through with St Caithrin. 'Let's just wait and see, shall we? I'm sure I'll get more visions. I wonder if I'll experience Will's death? All I know is he was stabbed and he died in mysterious circumstances. Do you think St Caithrin had anything to do with his death?'

'Quite likely.' The bell went for the end of break. 'I'll see you at lunchtime.'

'Yes, see you.'

During the lunch break they talked again about Tom's powers. Tom tried probing Frank's mind but it didn't work. He didn't know how to do it without some kind of provocation. Mr Garrett, the chemistry teacher, was patrolling the playground. He strutted rather than walked, turning abruptly at the corners of the playground and scowling at any boy who dared to look at him. His conceit was not merited by his appearance; he had longish mousey-coloured hair that looked as though it had been cut with a knife and fork and a mangy little goatee beard. His clothes were creased and his trousers were too short. He always wore safety glasses, even when he was out of school. He came towards Tom and Frank. 'You two look a bit furtive. Are you plotting something?'

'No, Sir,' said Tom.

'Then don't hide away in a corner looking as though you are. Get some exercise. Let me see you walking around.'

Tom and Frank had to end their little experiment, so they obediently walked away into the crowd of pupils playing games and chasing each other. Mr Garrett continued to stare at them.

'I don't like him. He's weird,' said Frank. 'Fancies himself too, even though he's as ugly as sin.'

'I know what you mean. He treats all the pupils like dirt, except for the sixth form girls, of course.'

'I've heard that the other teachers don't like him. He came into detention the other day when Miss Halsey was taking it. He was muttering something to her and she got annoyed. I bet he was trying to chat her up. I got the impression that she detests him.'

'I don't blame her.'

'I think he's married anyway, with children.'

'His wife must have been desperate to marry him. And fancy having a father like that! Poor kids.'

'Anyway, let's not worry about him. When do you think you'll have your next vision?'

'I don't know; not tonight for sure. I hope it's soon.'

Tom had to wait several days for the next vision. In the meantime, he and Mum telephoned Professor MacDonald to relate Tom's most recent visions to him. Professor MacDonald had found some information of interest to them. Mum put him on the speakerphone.

'I think I've found the account of Marmaduke Constable's case. Max Weissman did not give any clue to his name in the report, but I'm pretty sure it must be him. They described him as showing considerable aggression and frequently having fits of uncontrollable rages, requiring restraint. His death was caused by a stroke following a fit. He died the day after the stroke. Before becoming ill, he was a successful but ruthless businessman. Does that sound like him?'

'Yes, that's him all right,' said Tom. 'Would that be the kind of description they would have given of his death if he died after the incident with Will?'

'Oh, yes, I would think so.'

'So Will must have felt guilty about that, even though he knew it was likely to happen.'

'We all feel guilty when one of our patients dies although we're taught not to get involved emotionally. He did what he thought was right in his professional judgement. He thought that the invasion of Mr Constable's mind was probably too far gone for his original mind to survive, but he knew that if he left it any longer, there was no hope. He didn't have much choice.'

'Professor MacDonald, did you discover any more about Max Weissman and Bernard Simmonds? You were wondering whether they had near-death experiences, like Will.'

'No, I'm afraid I've drawn a blank there. The only clue I've got is that Bernard Simmonds was an army medical officer and he was wounded in the first Boer War in 1880. It was serious enough for him to be sent home, but whether it was a near-death experience, I can't tell.'

'But I haven't had a near-death experience and I can see into people's minds,' said Tom.

'You can?'

'Yes, I discovered that in a geography lesson when I saw into the teacher's mind.'

'Really, well I think I can understand that. The visions are a way for you to share Will's mind. In a way, Will has taught you how to do it. What puzzles me is why it is happening to you. I wonder if you are destined for some kind of mission.'

'That's what my friend Frank keeps telling me. He even suggested I might have to fight St Caithrin again, like Will did.'

'Well, I must admit, that thought occurred to me as well. It might be a good idea to prepare for it.'

'How do I do that?'

'I can help you there. I've had a lot of experience with criminals and I've been able to teach myself to block the evil thoughts that emanate from them. Talking to some of the really nasty characters can have unpleasant effects on your own mind if you are not careful. If you can strengthen your defence against evil thoughts, it should help you to block out an attack by St Caithrin. Of course, you have to attack as well, but I can't help you there – I can't do what Will did. You will be able to do it when the time comes, I'm sure, but it won't work if you have to put all your energy into defence – that will have to be second nature, hence the need for training.'

'How long will it take?' Tom asked.

'Oh, I think a week will be enough. But then of course you will have to practise daily. I'm afraid you will have to come here because I'll need to expose you to some of the criminals I have access to. Could we arrange something for your next school holidays?'

Mum interjected: 'Could I give you a call when we've checked the calendar?'

'Of course. I'll do my best to fit into your diary. This is important enough to take top priority in my diary. Tom, I'd appreciate it if you could keep me up-to-date with any new visions you have.'

'Yes, of course.'

'Was there any more information for me from either of you?'

'I tried to search the newspapers to find out more on Will's death, but there wasn't really anything more than we know already. One writer suggested it might be a ritual killing, but he didn't explain why he thought that.'

'He must have known more about the nature of the murder than he could print.'

'I suppose so. By the way, there was an apparent ritual killing near here recently.'

'Really? Please tell me more'

Mum recounted the murder of Mr Grimley to Professor MacDonald. When she had finished, there was a long pause before Professor MacDonald spoke. 'That sounds rather too much of a coincidence to me. Tom, we need to get together as soon as possible, in case St Caithrin was responsible for this killing.'

Mum took a sharp breath after that remark. 'I'll get back to you as soon as I can,' she said.

'OK. I don't think there is much more we can do over the phone. I'll be in touch shortly.'

They said their goodbyes and then Tom said to Mum: 'Do you really think I've got to face St Caithrin?'

'I certainly hope not, but if Professor MacDonald can help you to prepare for it in case it does happen, then that can only be good, can't it?'

'I suppose so. I wonder what his lessons will be like? A bit different from school, I'll bet.'

Mum chuckled nervously and thought how calmly Tom was taking all this. 'I'm sure they'll be very different.'

When Tom was lying in bed that night, the thought of facing St Caithrin was buzzing around in his mind. The more he thought about it, the more terrified he became. How could he possibly cope as well as Will did? Will was an experienced psychiatrist, not a twelve year old schoolboy. And he needed a lot of energy to stave off the attack from St Caithrin. Even Bernard and Max failed, so how could he possibly succeed? If the visions were a kind of training, he had a long way to go before he had any hope of surviving a challenge from St Caithrin. The call from Professor MacDonald had eased his mind a little, knowing that he had his support and a promise of some practical help. He tossed and turned in bed until he fell into a restless sleep.

Chapter 18

The New Mallington Murders

It was several days after Tom had spoken to Professor MacDonald that he had his next vision. Will was back in his own hospital going round the ward with a nurse. The dreary atmosphere of the place was still evident, but Will was doing his best to keep everyone cheerful. Unfortunately, few of the patients were remotely cheerful. He spoke again to Mr Molloy, who was looking awful as usual. After a few minutes with Will, Mr Molloy appeared to be more relaxed, but there seemed little hope for any lasting recovery. He had no happiness in his life at all. Tom could understand why some people as depressed as Mr Molloy committed suicide.

Another nurse marched up to Will. 'Dr Weissman has arrived, Dr Protheroe. I've left him in your office.'

'Thanks, nurse, I'll see him in a few minutes when I've finished here.'

Will completed his rounds and then strode back to his office. Max Weissman was waiting for him. 'Hello, Max. Good to see you again. What news do you have?'

'I've brought some of the cuttings from the local papers for you to look at. I've spoken to the police and said that you might be able to help. I did say that I must speak to you first of course.'

'I should hope so. There's no guarantee that I'll be able to help.'

Will looked at the newspaper cuttings. They referred to murders that had occurred in the New Mallington area. There had been three and each one had been in or near a church that had been desecrated on the inside. Two other churches had been desecrated without associated murders. The murders were particularly brutal – each victim had been bludgeoned to death with a heavy blunt instrument.

'I see that the first incident occurred two days after I chased St Caithrin from Mr Constable's mind. I think I agree with you – it looks as though it could be the work of St Caithrin. It has taken over someone else who is probably unwittingly committing these crimes, although I suspect that St Caithrin is attracted to minds that already contain an evil streak.'

'Do you think we can do anything?'

'I can't see how we can help the police catch the criminal. We don't have any way of tracking down St Caithrin, although I think I could detect it if I were in the same room as it.'

'I think I could too, but I've no doubt you are the most sensitive of the three of us.'

'Have the police obtained any clues?'

'From the damage in the churches and the states of the victims, they think the weapon is a long-handled sledgehammer. Presumably, the criminal must be quite strong to be able to wield such a tool. That fits with the description given by a witness who saw a man leaving one of the desecrated churches soon after the attack – a tall, heavily-built man wearing a long dark overcoat. He destroys the most sacred parts of the churches – the altar, icons and any other sacred objects, so the police think he is running a vendetta against the Christian Church. They believe that the murders are incidental – his victims were people who have been unfortunate enough to get in his way. Two of the churches were Roman Catholic and three were Anglican, so he is not choosy. One of the victims had some of the murderer's hair gripped in his hand and the police say it's hair from a beard, so we are probably looking for a big man with a black beard.'

'What have I done Max? You were right; we should have left Mr Constable to die. Instead, I've created a much worse monster and I'm responsible for three deaths.'

'Don't blame yourself, Will; you didn't know what you were up against. You did a brave thing believing that you might save Mr Constable. I'm sure St Caithrin would have left Mr Constable when he died and inhabited a new being in any case.'

'Yes, but at least we wouldn't be having the murders now. We must find a way of stopping this evil thing for good. But I don't have a clue how to do it.'

'If the police catch the murderer, he'll probably be hanged and then St Caithrin will find some other unfortunate being. If we could somehow persuade them to keep the murderer alive, we could at least postpone St Caithrin's transfer.'

'What makes you think St Caithrin can't transfer at will?'

'I don't know; it's just a feeling I got that it was trapped in Mr Constable.

And there was the message on the pillow – you remember it said "Thank you"?'

'You're right, Max. I released it and it was grateful.' Will paced up and down, deep in thought. 'I wonder what St Caithrin's range is?'

'You mean how far it can travel to find another body?'

'Yes. These murders are local to the hospital, so let's assume it has a short range. Were there any people near to Mr Constable who were good candidates?'

'We haven't lost any patients, if that's what you mean. I can check who was discharged in those two days.'

'Yes, please, Max. And what about out-patients?'

'They would have been seen in a ward in the next block, so that's quite close to Mr Constable.'

'It might be helpful if you can make a list and let the police see it. They might spot a known criminal. You may find it hard to explain to them what you are trying to achieve, though.'

'Don't worry, I'll find a way.'

'Remember we are looking for people who were around at the time I released St Caithrin. One thought: if we are right and St Caithrin has a short range, then a solution might be to exile the murderer to a remote uninhabited place where it couldn't find another mind to infect.'

'Good idea, but it wouldn't be easy to convince a judge.'

'Point taken.' Will accepted the voice of reason from Max. 'I feel so guilty about this and I wish I could help, but unless you think otherwise, there doesn't seem to be a good reason for me to come to New Mallington just yet. If you make any progress, let me know, won't you?'

'Of course. And please, Will, don't blame yourself for this.'

Tom emerged from his vision feeling as though he had learned a great deal more about St Caithrin. He decided he would call Professor MacDonald the next day to give him the latest information. First, he went back to the Vicarage and told Mum what he had seen. Then he called Frank so that he could write his usual account of the vision.

When he got back from school the next day, he called Professor MacDonald and gave him a detailed account of his last vision.

'So it looks as though Will is going to try to avoid having another battle with St Caithrin this time.'

'Yes, but what if St Caithrin attacks him?'

'Then I think Will will do the sensible thing and keep up his defences without trying to drive St Caithrin out.'

'Do you think it's likely that St Caithrin killed Will in the end?'

'The thought did cross my mind. But Will died at fifty-five; he's still a relatively young man in your visions isn't he?'

'Yes, the date on the letter from Bernard Simmonds was May 14th, 1892, so that puts Will at thirty seven.'

'Then we can assume he survives this time, if indeed there is a confrontation. You'll probably see the outcome in your next vision. Let me know, won't you, Tom?'

'Yes, of course.'

Sure enough, in Tom's next vision, Will was back at New Mallington with Max and Bernard. Presumably something had happened to prompt Will's visit. Max was showing Will a document. 'This is our prime suspect: Bartholomew Green, petty thief and vagrant. The police know him well but he hasn't been spotted for several weeks. We have seen him in the hospital several times in the past; he was once an in-patient but he comes in occasionally to try to get food and drink out of us, pretending he is ill. He was in the out-patient room when you released St Caithrin from Mr Constable. The distance is about twenty yards.'

'What does he look like?'

'He fits the description perfectly. He's a burly man and usually wears a heavy black overcoat. He never shaves or gets his hair cut, so he has a long black beard.'

'Any history of violence?'

'None at all. He was very mild when he was an in-patient. His main problem was drink, but even that didn't make him violent. He's never threatened anyone; his thefts have been from shops and market stalls. He has been seen begging, but as far as we know, he's never tried any physical form of persuasion.'

'So if he's our man, it fits perfectly that he has been taken over by St Caithrin. We must find him. Do we know his favourite haunts?'

'Yes, the police are familiar with them and they have been watching out for him. But I suspect he's trying to avoid those places.'

'You could be right. Can we help?'

'Well, he did frequent several of the worst pubs in town, so he might have tried some different pubs now he knows that the police are on the lookout for him. He likes his beer.'

'But with his appearance, he would be noticed immediately if he went into an unfamiliar pub.'

'Perhaps he's cleaned himself up. I don't suppose the police would spot him if he shaved and cut his hair.'

'No, but we would if we came within range of him. Anyone fancy a pub crawl?'

Bernard shrugged his shoulders. 'I'm game.'

'And so am I,' Max said. 'Here, let me plan a route.' He pulled a map from his drawer and started to write a list. 'There are quite a few, so it could take more than one evening.'

They put on their roughest clothes so that they did not look too conspicuous and strode out into the chill evening air.

'I think it would be wise to go in his regular pubs as well,' suggested Will.

'Yes, we can do that. I've picked the areas where his regular pubs are in any case.'

They must have gone into a dozen pubs without a glimmer of hope. They avoided drinking in most of them by pretending they were looking for a friend and thought he must have gone to the wrong pub. Then there was one that gave them some cause for hope. Will and Max sensed an evil presence, but Bernard could not pick up anything. They bought drinks and sat down. Will wandered around to try to find the source. It got weaker wherever he went and he concluded that it was an unsavoury-looking character a few feet away from them at the bar.

'He might be evil, but he's not in the same league as St Caithrin. This is not him. Let's move on.'

They tried several more pubs without any luck. The next one was one of Green's regulars – the "Sow and Pigs". As they walked in, they felt it at once; even Bernard had no doubt this time. Will walked around and again he felt the energy weaken as he walked away from the bar. He came back to where Max and Bernard were waiting for the barman to pour their drinks and noticed Max twitching his head to signal something to Will. He was indicating that it was the barman! Sure enough, Will felt the strongest energy when the barman was right in front of them. But he didn't look a bit like Bartholomew Green! He was tall, slightly built, clean-shaven and had thinning sandy-coloured hair. But here was St Caithrin – there was no doubt about it in their minds. They took their drinks to a table.

'Have you seen him before, Max?'

'No.'

'Bernard?'

'No.'

'Do we agree it's him?'

'It's St Caithrin all right, but he's not in Bartholomew Green. Our theory has to be wrong,' said Bernard. 'I'll ask the barman if he's seen Bartholomew Green.'

'Take care, Bernard. Don't arouse any suspicions that we know about him.'

Bernard went up to the bar, waited until the barman had served two customers and then confronted him. 'Excuse me, but I'm looking for Bartholomew Green. Has he been in here?'

'You the police?'

'No, I'm actually his doctor. I'm a bit worried that he seems to have gone missing.'

'Not seen old Bart for at least a week. Told the police that too.'

'Thanks.' Bernard went back to the table. 'He says he hasn't seen him for a week, but I'm sure he's lying.'

'You think he's hiding something?'

'Yes, he knows something.'

'There has to be a good explanation for this. I don't know about you, but I'm too tired to think about it any more. Shall we sleep on it?'

'Good idea. Let's get back.' They walked slowly back to the hospital. The chill air invigorated them again and they discussed the possible reasons for this new revelation, but they didn't have much energy left and they had drunk too much beer for their minds to be active enough to solve the problem. They were weary when they got back and were all ready for bed.

'Good evening, gentlemen.' The voice came from the shadows by the entrance to the hospital and out stepped a tall man with a trilby hat and heavy overcoat.

'Ah, Inspector Bates, what brings you here at this hour?' said Max. 'This is Dr Protheroe – I mentioned him to you.'

'Yes, indeed. Pleased to meet you, Dr Protheroe.' They shook hands. 'Could we find somewhere to talk in private?'

'Of course, let's go to my office.'

The inspector strode firmly behind the three weary physicians. They were all thinking the same thing – why did the inspector have to arrive just now when they were desperate to get some sleep? When they arrived in Max's office, they all slumped into chairs while the inspector carefully removed his hat, sat on the remaining chair with precision and placed his hat on his lap. He spotted a small fleck on the brim of his hat and smartly brushed it off with the side of his hand.

'Now then, this case has taken an unexpected turn. We've found Bartholomew Green in St. Joseph's church – dead. The doctor saw his body at about nine o'clock and thought he'd been dead about three hours. He'd had a taste of his own medicine by the look of it – battered with a blunt instrument. It seemed he was in the act of destroying the interior of the church when he was attacked – probably from behind. There was a trail of destruction from the entrance to where we found his body. He still had the sledgehammer in his hand. I wondered if any of you had any ideas.'

Will, Max and Bernard all looked at each other as if they were all saying "So that's why St Caithrin was in someone else" and they were all thinking how they were going to explain it to Inspector Bates. Max spoke first. 'Inspector, we went around some of Bartholomew Green's old haunts this evening to try to find clues to his whereabouts. The only observation we made was that the barman in the "Sow and Pigs" seemed to be hiding something when we asked him if he'd seen Green recently.'

Bernard interrupted: 'I spoke to him, Inspector. It's hard to put a finger on it, but I thought he was lying. In our business, we get used to patients lying to us and we learn to recognize it. I think it might be worth your while talking to him.'

'Do you mean Patrick Farrell – tall, slight chap with sandy hair?'

'Yes, that's him.'

'We've already questioned him, but that was before Bartholomew Green's murder. We'll have another try. If there's anything else you can think of, let me know, won't you?' He looked threatening as if he was about to tell them that withholding information from the police was an offence deserving of capital punishment.

'Of course, Inspector. And thanks for letting us know about Bartholomew Green.'

'All part of the job. Goodnight.'

'Goodnight, Inspector.'

When Inspector Bates had gone, they huddled over Max's desk. Will spoke first: 'So it's likely that this Farrell chap – the barman – killed Green and St Caithrin jumped into him.'

'I think that's the most likely explanation. But why should Farrell kill him and why was he there? Do you think he was following Green?'

'Could be, but I don't think we're going to solve that tonight. Let's just see what Inspector Bates comes up with. I'm going to bed.'

Tom's vision broke off when they all moved out of the office. He sat for a while wondering what could happen next. He thought about St Caithrin. Why did it need to get to a nearby host when its present host died? Perhaps a more realistic question was how could it jump from host to host anyway? It seemed likely that it had to find a host almost instantly. So perhaps it wasn't the distance as much as the time – it couldn't survive for long outside a human body. Yes, he thought that was the most likely explanation. He knew that any knowledge of St Caithrin's weaknesses would help him if he had to face it one day and he was gradually building up a knowledge base.

Chapter 19

Professor MacDonald's Lessons

THE TIME HAD COME FOR TOM TO travel back to Rothbank to learn from Professor MacDonald how to ward off evil. Mum was to go with him, but she would have to occupy herself at Rothbank while Tom had his lessons. Professor MacDonald had invited them to stay for the week in his house just outside Rothbank. As before, they took the train. It was a Sunday and Professor MacDonald said he would meet them at the station when they arrived.

The last time they had been to Rothbank, the weather had been dull and miserable, but this time it was a bright sunny day. Tom felt cheerful as he watched the countryside flash past the windows. He could not help wondering what Professor MacDonald had in store for him. He was a little worried but excited too. He had seen how Will had kept St Caithrin at bay and wondered if he could do it as well. After all, he could do things that he hadn't thought possible, like looking into a teacher's mind. If only he knew how he did it. It seemed that he could do it when he was desperate, but how could he be sure that he was capable of defending himself against St Caithrin? After experiencing the battle that Will had with St Caithrin, he did not feel at all confident that he could do it, but he told himself that his lessons with Professor MacDonald were going to make a difference.

As the train sped smoothly through fields and villages, Tom drifted off into a light sleep. He dreamed of the countryside and a gently-flowing river. He was fishing with Frank and they were alone apart from the cows grazing in the fields and the birds singing in the trees. A blackbird flew down to steal a worm from Tom's bait tray. It was a perfect scene. Then Frank got a bite and tried to reel in the fish. But it was too powerful and it was pulling Frank's line up and down the river. Then the line raced towards them and with a huge surge of water, a hideous creature with an enormous mouth and fearsome teeth leapt out at Tom. He yelled in fright as he held up his hands to defend himself, but the creature was upon him. It was dragging him back into the river as he shouted to Frank to help him, but there was nothing Frank could do. Tom tried to yell again but his head was in the water. It was hopeless – he was going to die.

'Tom, what's the matter?' Mum was shaking him.

Tom was trembling and feeling cold. 'Oh, thank goodness it was only a dream. I was attacked by a terrible monster and it dragged me under water. It was horrible. There was nothing I could do to defend myself.'

'Well, it was only a dream, so there's nothing to worry about. We don't have far to go now. We should be arriving in about fifteen minutes.' Mum offered Tom a sweet from a bag that she pulled out of her pocket. He took one and chewed it, but he was still thinking about the dream. It made him think how vulnerable he was.

The train began to slow down. Outside, there were streets, factories, shops and houses passing by. The wheels of the train squealed as they approached the station. There were many people waiting on the platform to get on to the train; their upright figures sped past the windows, then slower until the train came gently to a halt. It was a few seconds before the doors were released and the first passengers jumped down on to the platform. Mum and Tom waited until most of the passengers had left, then they picked up their cases and stepped out of the train and headed towards the ticket barrier. Mum spotted Professor MacDonald waiting for them and led Tom towards him.

'Hello, pleased to see you again. Let me take that case from you. It's only a short walk to the car.' Professor MacDonald led the way out of the station to the car park where they stopped at a large four-wheel drive vehicle. He placed the bags in the back and opened the back doors for Tom and Mum. They stretched up to gain entry into the high vehicle.

'I live on a farm so I need a vehicle like this.' He had noted that they were scanning the spacious interior of the vehicle. 'I also have four children, so that's another excuse.'

'Do you keep animals on your farm, Professor MacDonald?' asked Tom.

'Yes, we keep some Highland cattle, but that's more of a hobby than a business. Most of the land is let to other farmers. By the way, if you don't mind, I'd like to drop the formalities now; I'd feel more comfortable if you both called me Robert. Is that OK?'

'Yes, of course, please call me Julia,' said Mum.

'OK by you Tom?'

'Er – sure.' Tom was not on first name terms with many adults, so he was a little uncomfortable but felt more grown-up.

They drove out of the town through some hilly countryside for about five miles, and then they came to a small village with a church that looked big enough to hold the population three times over. There was a little shop with an ice-cream sign outside. A young mother was struggling to put a baby into its pushchair while its older brother was doing all he could to make life difficult for his mother. It was a scene that could occur anywhere.

'This is our nearest village. We're just a mile further on.' They crested the brow of a hill and took a narrow lane that forked off the main road. It gradually deteriorated into a track with tufts of grass and weeds down the middle.

'Here we are.' They had reached a large old stone house with an extensive garden at the front. Tom thought the dark stone looked rather forbidding, but he kept his thoughts to himself. Mrs MacDonald was waiting for them as they stepped out of the car. She was a small woman with an elf-like face and a large mouth. She grinned at them, showing a perfect set of white teeth.

'This is my wife Elizabeth – Julia and Tom Merrington.' They all shook hands and spoke politely to each other.

'The children are all at their aunt's place at the moment. That's my sister – she lives about twenty miles away. They should be back soon,' said Elizabeth. 'Please come inside and have a cup of tea.' She ushered Tom and Mum through the front door. When they got inside, Tom was pleasantly surprised. The forbidding exterior was forgotten in an instant – the room was welcoming and friendly. It was decorated in light colours and the windows facing the sun were letting in bright shafts of light. In the middle of the room was a large sofa that looked soft and comfortable. When Elizabeth asked them to sit down, Tom headed straight for the sofa. It was just as he expected. He sank into the soft cushions and leaned back against the padded back with a satisfied smile on his face. Elizabeth had noted his reaction.

'So you like our sofa too then Tom? I must warn you that there is a penalty for sitting there. It's nothing unpleasant, so you need not worry. Oh – it looks as though you are about to see what I mean.' She looked across to a side door that was partly open. A black cat with a white patch on its head came through the door, strolled across to the sofa and jumped on to Tom's lap. Tom was a little startled but quite happy to have the cat as a companion. He stroked it, but it seemed not to be interested. It curled up and went to sleep.

Elizabeth explained: 'That's Monty; we don't allow him to sit on the sofa, so this is his way of getting as close to breaking the rule as he can. If it gets uncomfortable, just throw him off.'

'It's OK, I don't mind,' said Tom.

Elizabeth served them drinks and they talked about their families for a while. Then there was a commotion outside as a car drew up and children shouted, making a dog bark. 'The children are back,' Elizabeth informed them, stating the obvious. She went outside to greet them and to thank her sister for bringing them back. Robert sat back in an armchair waiting for the onslaught. It was preceded by the sound of running footsteps on the cobbled path, and then a small girl burst in through the door, followed by two older girls and finally a boy, who looked about the same age as the small girl, ambled in. They all came up to their father to greet him.

'Now, you lot, come here and let me introduce you to our visitors.' They all stood obediently by Robert's chair. 'This is Jane, our eldest daughter. She's eleven. Next down we have Lucy, who is eight, then the twins, Fiona and Angus, who are six. Say hello to our visitors: Julia Merrington and her son Tom.' They all did as they were told as politely as they could and then made a beeline for the sofa to sit next to Tom. Angus grabbed the cat and put it on the floor. When it tried to get back on Tom's lap, Angus shooed it away. Sulkily, it went out through the door.

They all looked at Tom as though he was a prize exhibit, then Jane spoke to him. She was a pretty girl with mousey-coloured hair pulled back into a pony-tail. Her mouth was large and active, like her mother's. 'My dad told me about you. He said he was going to give you some lessons in protecting yourself from danger. Is that right?'

'Yes, that's right.'

'Are you going to the prison to meet some of those horrible men that Dad knows?'

'I think so.'

'We're not allowed to go to see them. Children are not allowed, so you must be special.'

Tom felt a little embarrassed. 'I don't think I'm special, it's just that your dad thinks I might be in danger. You're not in danger.'

'I suppose not. Some of those men in the prison have done some terrible things. One of them killed his own father. Can you believe that?'

Robert butted in: 'Don't scare Tom before we've even started. The man who murdered his father has some good in him, although he has plenty of his father's evil in him too. The father was a drunkard and he beat his son senseless many times. The son grew up hating his father, so you can understand why he killed him, even if we can't forgive him for it. As it happens, Tom, he'll be one of the prisoners you'll meet. He's not the worst, I can assure you; there are some very nasty characters in there.'

'Will Tom meet the really bad ones?' asked Jane.

'Oh, yes. We'll build up steadily to the worst villain of all.'

'Who's that?'

'His name is Matthew Montgomery. He's a well-educated man but has no sense of right and wrong. He admitted to killing eight people, but the police suspected he killed a lot more. He said he enjoyed killing and wasn't at all sorry about what he did. He claimed that the people he killed were all deficient in some way and that he did the world a favour by getting rid of them. He's what we call a psychopath.'

That term rang a bell with Tom. He had heard Will mention it when he was dealing with St Caithrin. He understood what it meant now. Although he was apprehensive about meeting a real psychopath, he wanted to get on with it. 'When are we going to start?' he asked.

'Tomorrow morning, you can start your training. In the afternoon, we'll meet the first of the criminals. Every day, we'll do the same: training and practice in the morning, facing a criminal in the afternoon. I've got five convicted murderers lined up in order of evil intensity, from mild to extreme. So you'll see Matthew Montgomery on Friday.'

'What sort of training will I have to do?'

'Very simple, really. I'll expose you to various representations of evil: pictures, recorded voices, video clips and the like. You will have to learn to displace the evil thoughts in your mind with good or pleasant thoughts. I'll be able to check whether or not you are succeeding by monitoring your pulse. I've done it with students and it seems to work pretty well.'

'Can I try that as well, Daddy?' asked Jane.

'Do you want to try now to see how good you are? I've got some pictures we can use, but I won't be able to check your pulse.'

'Yes, please.' The other children then pleaded to try.

'No, not yet, just watch how Jane and Tom get on.' He went out of the room and soon came back with what looked like a photograph album. In it were all sorts of pictures that conjured up thoughts of evil. He opened it at a page with a particularly hideous representation of the devil. The predominant colour was blood red. 'Now, look hard at this picture for a few moments.' Tom and Jane stared at the picture. Jane looked particularly disgusted by it. 'OK, now try to change the picture in your mind to something pleasant, but keep looking at the picture.' Robert was watching the expressions on their faces. They were both frowning deeply. Then Tom's expression relaxed until he had a large grin on his face. Robert didn't interrupt. Jane's expression began to change a little, and then the frown returned. Once again, she relaxed and almost smiled. This time the smile developed into a broad grin.

'I did it!'

'Well, done, both of you. Now tell us what pictures you created to block this out.'

'I changed the devil into you, Daddy!'

'Oh, that's good to know that you can use me to displace the devil.' He gave Jane a gentle hug. 'And what about you, Tom?'

'I turned the devil into a silly clown.'

'Ah, that's interesting. So not only did you block him out, you humiliated him. Did you think of it that way?'

'I don't know. Perhaps I did.'

'That's a very promising start. Now the rest of you – let me get some different pictures that you can play with. These are all rather unpleasant.' He went out of the room and came back with another album. 'Now, these are all sad pictures. See if you can change them into happy pictures. Tom and Jane, can I leave you to help them, please? You've got about an hour before dinner.' He went and sat with Mum and started chatting. Tom and Jane eagerly took up their roles as teachers to the younger children. Over the next hour, there were periods of silence interrupted by excited shouts and arguments, but the children all seemed to have a great time. When dinner was served, they were reluctant to stop their game. Dinner was a noisy affair, with the children still arguing about who was best at changing the pictures and Robert and Elizabeth trying vainly to tell them to get on with their meal. As a result, dinner took a lot longer than it should have done, bath-times were delayed and the children went to bed later than normal.

Both Tom and Mum were pleased with their day – they were comfortable in Robert and Elizabeth's house and they enjoyed the company of the children. Tom was at ease with Robert and as he was lying in bed contemplating the day ahead, somehow he knew that he would learn a lot from his new teacher.

It was pouring with rain when Tom got up in the morning and looked out of his bedroom window. He was hungry and was looking forward to breakfast. Mum had already told him that breakfast would be ready in five minutes, so he dressed and hurried downstairs. Only Angus and Fiona were already down; Elizabeth was shouting up the stairs to Jane and Lucy that breakfast was ready. Within seconds, Lucy appeared on the stairs and almost fell down them. Tom could see the stairs from where he was sitting at the table. He saw Jane's feet appear at the top with her left foot hovering ready to take the next step. When that one finally made it, her right foot hovered. She was obviously doing something that occupied her concentration while she was negotiating the stairs. When she finally came into full view, Tom could see that she had been brushing her hair and was just tying up her pony-tail. She dropped her brush at the foot of the stairs and hurried across to the table. Elizabeth scolded her: 'How many more times do I have to tell you not to do things like brushing your hair while you are coming down the stairs? One day you'll fall and break your neck. Finish getting ready in your bedroom.'

'Sorry, Mummy, I'll try to remember.'

After breakfast, Robert and Tom drove off to the University. Tom remembered the big stone surround to the entrance and the wide staircase. They went up to Robert's office and into an adjoining laboratory, where Robert opened the door of a small cubicle and asked Tom to go inside. He sat Tom at a table in front of a television screen.

'I'm going to give you the exercise that I developed for my students. You will have to wear these headphones and this strap around your wrist so that I can monitor your pulse. All your instructions will come through the headphones and all the pictures or video clips will be shown on the screen. If you want to pause the recording to give yourself more time, just press this black button. Pressing it again starts the recording from where it left off. If you are ready to move on to the next exercise before the time it gives you is up, press the green button. If you decide you've had enough and you want to abandon the recording, press the red button. That's about all you need to know. If you don't press the green or black buttons, the recording lasts for about half an hour. Any questions?'

'Yes, can I go to the toilet before I start?'

Robert laughed. 'Of course. Turn right outside my office, second door on the left. I'll wait here for you.'

Tom felt a little embarrassed that he had not thought of going to the toilet first, but he knew that Robert didn't mind. He went out hurriedly and was soon back, ready to start the exercise. He donned the headphones and Robert fixed the pulse monitor to Tom's wrist. He went out to start the recording.

After the game the previous evening, Tom found the first part of the exercise quite easy because it was all based on still pictures. Then it switched to silent video clips. He needed to pause the recording for the first two, but then he got the hang of it and soon felt confident at handling them. The next block of video clips had sound as well. Tom found this a little more difficult because of the added intensity the sound gave. But the most difficult was the last session, where the screen went blank and Tom was left with just sound. He found it almost impossible at first, but then he began to create pictures to go with the sound and it seemed more promising. Even so, he still found it much too difficult. He decided he needed some help, so he pressed the red button. Robert opened the door of the cubicle and went in.

'I need you to help me with the last session,' pleaded Tom.

'That's what I'm here for. The reason you had so much difficulty with the sound-only clips is that you need something visual. You have to create images in your mind that go with the sound.'

'I tried that but it didn't help much.'

'I'm not surprised. It's very difficult. Some people cope with the sound better than the images – it depends on the way your brain perceives outside stimuli. But let me tell you something: you achieved more in your first session than any other person who has done this exercise.'

'Really?'

'Yes, really. I'm not surprised because in a way you've already had some training by going through Will's experiences, but I think there's more to it than that. You seem to have an inherent ability to do this kind of thing and all that's needed is some way of arousing it. I think the reason you are experiencing Will's life in your visions is to awaken those abilities. Perhaps Will would not have been much good at the sound-only exercise either.'

Tom was thoughtful. 'So do you believe I could chase St Caithrin out of someone's mind like Will did?'

Robert gave a wry smile and turned around inside the little cubicle with his hand clasping his chin. 'It's a little early to answer that one. Can you ask me again at the end of the week?'

'I won't forget.'

'Neither shall I. Now, let's take a break and then I'll show you some techniques to help you with the sound-only exercise.'

Robert took Tom back to his office where he made drinks. After the break he explained to Tom how he could create an image in his mind from sounds and then displace it with different images and sounds. They tried a few techniques until Tom found one that suited him. Eventually he declared that he was ready to try the exercise again.

'You don't have to do it now. You can leave it until tomorrow if you want.'

'No, I want to try it now.'

'Very well.'

They went back to the cubicle and Tom set himself up again as before. Robert went outside to control the recording. It started at the final sound-only session. This time, Tom was much more confident that he could cope with it and sure enough, he sailed through it with remarkable ease. He was satisfied now that he had completed that final session. It reminded him of completing a difficult task on a computer game. Robert opened the door.

'Well, there you are. You've done it. You should be very pleased with yourself.'

'I am.' Tom had a big smile on his face.

'OK. We'll get some lunch here before we drive to the prison. It only takes about twenty minutes to get there if the traffic is light.'

During the drive to the prison, Robert gave Tom a brief description of the murderer whom they were going to meet that afternoon: 'His name is Edward Docherty and he's probably about seventy years old now. He's been in prison for about twenty years. He was a member of a gang that broke into the house of a wealthy man and stole most of his valuables. Unfortunately, some members of the household tried to put up a fight and they were shot by the gang. Docherty was found guilty of killing the owner's nineteen-year old son. You'll see when we talk to him that he still has a crystal-clear recollection of the murder. This wasn't his only crime; he'd been in prison before for other robberies, but he only committed one murder.'

As they approached the gates of the prison, Tom thought it was a frightening place and would have been perfect in a horror film. It was an enormous building made of huge grey stone blocks and it had hardly any windows. It had four turrets that made it look like a fortress. It was, of course; no prisoner had escaped from it since about 1930, according to Robert. At the gate, they were met by a security guard who obviously knew Robert. The guard had been told to expect Tom, so after a brief introduction, they were allowed to drive into the prison grounds. Inside the main gate, there was another security post where both Tom and Robert were searched before they were allowed to sign in. From that point, they were accompanied by a security guard who kept someone at the other end of his hand-held radio informed of all their movements. He led Robert and Tom to a side entrance in one of the main buildings. They walked along a short corridor until they came to a series of doors. The guard selected one, opened it with a key and told Robert and Tom to go in. He followed behind them and locked the door from the inside. Tom could see another room of a similar size through an opening in the wall protected by a heavy steel mesh. It was like the zoo. He could imagine monkeys clambering about on tree branches in the other room. The security guard sat them down behind a table that was between them and the opening. He remained standing and informed someone on the radio that they were ready. After a few minutes, the sound of a key in the lock of the door in the other room could be heard. It opened and in walked a small, bespectacled, thin man with a stoop. He looked older than Robert's estimate of seventy. His face was almost skeletal, the wrinkled skin seeming to be barely thick enough to cover the whiteness of his skull. He was handcuffed to the security guard, who towered over him. They both sat down in chairs facing the mesh opening.

'Hello, Eddie, how are you?'

'I'll be a lot better when I get out of here.' His voice was much stronger than Tom had expected.

'Is that soon?'

'Forty-seven days to go.'

'That's if he behaves himself,' interrupted the guard. He seemed to treat Docherty like a child. Tom felt sorry for Docherty. He seemed like a broken man looking forward to spending his remaining years in the open world again.

'Eddie, this is Tom Merrington. He's come visiting with me today.'

'Pleased to meet you,' said Tom.

'I'm sure you are.' Docherty grinned, showing a large gap in the front of his teeth.

Robert asked Docherty a few trivial questions, and then he got him on to the subject of the murder. He asked Docherty, for Tom's sake, to describe it in detail. Tom was ready for this. Docherty looked directly at Tom and related the incident in detail. 'We were about ready to leave. We'd disconnected the phones and herded the family into one room. Bill wanted a painting from the room the family were in, so I went in with him to get it. When he took it down, the young lad shouted "No" and rushed at us. I pushed him away but he clung to my leg like a limpet. I told Bill to get out with the painting and I'd follow. The kid grabbed my ankles and pulled me down. I shouted at him to let go or I'd shoot. He didn't think I would, but I did. I had to. The others were all in the cars waiting for us. I shot him in the head. I left him with blood running across the floor and the rest of the family screaming at me while I locked the door behind me. I was shaking like a leaf. I didn't want to do it but he made me. I was sick in the car. We got away and lived well for six months or so in Spain. Then the police caught us. It was a relief. I told them it was me who'd killed the kid. There wasn't much point in trying to hide it. So here I am, nearly finished paying off my debt to society as they say.'

'Thanks, Eddie,' said Robert. 'That's all we need.'

Tom had been enthralled by the account. He had seen it all in detail in Eddie's mind: the colours of the walls, the carpets on the floors, the family cowering in the room and the young man rushing foolishly at the villains. He saw the face of the young man as he defiantly challenged Eddie to kill him and the look of horror when he knew that Eddie was going to do it out of desperation. Now, Eddie had no evil left in him. He lost it all the day he killed the boy.

The guard took Eddie away and then Tom and Robert went in the opposite direction with their guard. When they got back to the car and were out of the prison grounds, Robert asked Tom what he had learned.

'Eddie has no evil left in him.'

'That's my conclusion, but it's taken me a long time to get to it. How can you be so sure?'

'I saw it in his mind. He regretted his whole life when he killed that boy. He wanted to be caught. He wanted to go to prison and be punished. Now that it's nearly over, he just wants to be free again. He won't hurt a fly.'

'That's impressive. I'll be interested to see what you make of the next of our criminals. He's completely different. I'll tell you about him tomorrow.'

Chapter 20

The Minds of Murderers

The morning's training consisted of running some more exercises similar to the ones the day before. It became a matter of how fast Tom could operate. He could do it quickly now, but he remembered how quickly the scenes in Mr Constable's mind kept changing, so he knew he had to be able to respond even quicker. Robert had told him that he would give him more difficult exercises the next day.

In the afternoon, as they drove to the prison, Robert described the next prisoner. 'Now, don't be afraid when you see him. He's very big, but not as fearsome as he looks. His name is John Redman; not surprisingly, he's known as "Little John". He was a bodyguard to a well-known film star who was a drug addict. Redman got into a fight to protect his boss from some drug dealers who were demanding money and apparently killed two of them with his bare hands. His boss was convicted of possessing drugs and Redman for murder. To be honest, he seems to be quite a gentle man most of the time, but apparently if he loses his temper, he can be ferocious. I've never witnessed it and I don't think I want to.'

They went through the same procedure as before except that they used a different room, but inside it was identical to the other one. When John Redman came through the doorway, Tom was startled. He was the biggest man he had ever seen. He had to bend down to get through the doorway and when he stood to his full height in the room it seemed he nearly touched the ceiling. His head was shaved, his neck seemed wider than his head and his body was bulging with muscle. His hands were huge and Tom understood how easy it would be for him to kill an average man with his hands. He was flanked by two guards, each handcuffed to him. He looked across at Tom and roared: 'What's a kid doing here?'

'John, this is Tom Merrington. He's here at my invitation.'

'Why?'

'Let's just say it's work experience.'

Redman burst into peals of laughter that shook the room. 'Work experience?' he shrieked amid his laughter. 'That's funny. I haven't heard anything that funny for ages. OK, that's fine by me. Work experience!' And he collapsed with laughter again. This time Tom started laughing, then one of the guards did and finally they were all helpless with laughter. It was only when Redman calmed down that they had any hope of getting on with their work.

'John, are you OK now?' asked Robert.

'Yes,' as he wiped the tears from his face with his huge hand.

Robert asked him a few questions to settle him down and when he was sure that Redman was being serious, he asked him to describe the killings. He didn't say it was for Tom in case it started the laughter all over again. Tom studied Redman carefully.

'My master was addicted to heroin and he needed more drugs. These guys came to the house with the heroin, but they wanted more money than we had agreed. My master got angry with them and told them to leave. They pushed him around so I stepped in to protect him. One of them pulled a gun and pointed it at me. I told him to get out, but they demanded more money again from my master. When I saw my chance, I wrenched the gun from the dealer's hand. I punched him in the face and he went down. There were two others. I hit them both. I was so angry. My master was screaming at me to kill them. He made me even angrier and I kept hitting them. I put them out in the street and shut the gates. Later, the police came and said two of the men were dead. I said it was self-defence, but in court they said it was murder.'

'Thank you, John. That was very clear.'

It certainly was. Tom had seen more than John had described. He saw the hatred. John hated the drug dealers, not because they were attacking his beloved master, but because they were destroying his life by supplying him with the drugs that fuelled his addiction. He hated them and he wanted them dead; he was disappointed that the third had survived. When he was angry, he was ferocious and deadly.

As Tom and Robert drove away, Tom explained what he had seen.

'Well, I have to say that was not my opinion, but it is only opinion, not insight. You have the advantage over me Tom and I believe what you see is the truth. That's very enlightening for me.'

'But what you said about him was true; he's a gentle person until he gets angry, then he becomes an uncontrollable monster. That's the way he is.'

'Yes, I see that now.'

They drove home with similar thoughts racing around their brains. What a crazy scene that was! First, everyone was infected by John Redman's laughter and then they were plunged into the deeply depressing memories of a double murder. Both Tom and Robert felt drained. They needed a good night's rest before the next session.

Robert was relentless in driving Tom through the training sessions in the mornings. He had developed some more difficult tasks where the video clips changed unexpectedly from harmless to threatening and Tom learned to be on his guard and be prepared for a sudden attack. They were half-way through the week and Tom had made excellent progress. In the afternoon, they would meet Duncan Johnstone, the prisoner who had killed his father.

'Tom, we'll have to probe a bit deeper into Duncan Johnstone's life; it won't be adequate to recreate the murder scene. It's important for you to understand what drove him to kill his father, so we might have to spend a bit more time with him than we did with the others.'

'Was his father a criminal?'

'Well, he was always in brawls and he was convicted of assault a few times, but he didn't commit a serious crime as far as I'm aware. Duncan was a car thief. He was convicted twice, but he got away with a lot more. That was his main source of income. The family lived on a farm and Duncan and his two older brothers worked the farm while their father drank the profits.'

'Were Duncan's brothers involved in the car theft?'

'They knew it was going on, but I don't think they were involved. They still run the farm. No, Duncan partnered up with another local villain. That's how he learned how to steal cars.'

'So if Duncan's brothers still work on the farm, they couldn't have been involved in their father's murder.'

'That's right. They didn't know that Duncan had murdered him and buried his body in one of their fields. Duncan's mother was involved though. She helped him plan the murder. She's also in prison.'

'So the murder was planned, then.'

'Oh, yes. Duncan had already dug his father's grave and was waiting for him when he came back from the pub. He knocked him out with a rock, dumped him in the grave and then drove a fork through his chest a few times. The next morning, he was up early to plough the field and conceal the traces of his digging. His mother reported that her husband had not come home from the pub. The local police investigated the case and were very thorough. It was Duncan's greed that gave him away. The police found his father's watch and wallet in his room. His mother was furious with Duncan and she eventually confessed to the police and took them to where the body was buried.'

Robert and Tom went through the usual procedures at the prison before being led to a room to await Duncan Johnstone. He came through the door at a pace that made a sloth seem positively speedy. His cold blue eyes fixed on Tom as soon as he saw him. This was different; Tom felt the evil in him. Johnstone averted his eyes to sit in the chair. He was about average build with fair hair and sharp features. His mouth was small. It seemed to Tom that few words were likely to issue from it. Sure enough, when Robert introduced Tom to him, he just grunted. This was going to be a tedious process. While Robert asked him questions, he kept his eyes fixed on Tom. Even though his answers to Robert's questions were mostly just a few words, Tom could see the images in his mind. Then Robert asked him about his father.

'How did your father treat you when you were a child?'

'He beat me.'

'Did you ever have any happy times with your father?'

'No.' Tom could see that wasn't true. He could see the two of them walking through the fields holding hands and playing.

'How old were you when he started his heavy drinking?'

'About eight or nine.'

'Did he beat you before then?'

'Can't remember.'

'Did he beat your brothers?'

'No.'

'Why was that?'

'They were bigger than him.'

'How often did he beat you?'

'Every day if he could.'

'How old were you when you decided you were going to kill him?'

'Eighteen.'

'What was it that made you decide to kill him?'

'He stole my savings and spent it on booze.'

'How old were you when you started stealing cars?'

'About sixteen.'

'Did your father know you stole cars?'

'No.' Tom didn't think this was true.

'Did your mother know?'

'Yes.'

'Did she try to stop you?'

'No.'

'Did your brothers know?'

'Yes.'

'Did they try to stop you?'

'Yes.'

'What did you do with the money you made stealing cars?'

'Saved it. Gave some to Mum.'

'Did your father find any of it?'

'No.' He was lying. Tom saw that the "savings" that his father had stolen and spent on drink were the proceeds of car theft. After that, he hid the money.

'Have you still got some of the money?'

'No.' Tom could see this was a lie. He glanced to Robert who realized Tom wanted Johnstone to keep thinking about the money.

'Are you sure?'

'Yes.' Robert paused and Tom managed to see in Johnstone's mind that he had two boxes of money buried on the farm.

Robert looked across at Tom to signal that he was going to ask about the murder. Tom nodded to show that he was happy to move on.

'Duncan, I want you to think back to the time just before you killed your father. Did you plan it with your mother?'

'Yes.' Much to Tom's surprise, that appeared to be a lie. His mother didn't seem to get involved until after the murder.

'How old were you?'

'Twenty.'

'Can you tell me how you did it?'

Johnstone looked uncomfortable. He didn't want to get involved in long descriptions, but at last he started mumbling the tale. 'Waited for him when he came out of the pub…followed him home…when he got on the farm hit him from behind…tipped him in the hole…stabbed him with the fork…covered him up…ploughed the field the next day.' It was just like Robert had told Tom, and it seemed to be true up to a point. But he didn't hit his father from behind; he argued with him and told him he was going to kill him because he was drinking away all his profits from the car thefts. His father pleaded with him and promised to stop drinking, but it was too late – Duncan's mind was made up and he battered his father with the handle of the fork. From then on, it was as he had told it, except that it seemed his mother was enraged when he told her he had killed his father, but finally she decided to do what she could to protect her son.

Tom had felt some attempt by Johnstone to transmit evil thoughts into his mind, but he could not do it in spite of his constant staring. So far, Robert's criminals had not given him much of a challenge. There was no doubt in

Tom's mind that Duncan Johnstone was not the downtrodden son that he tried to make people believe. His father may have beaten him, but not to the degree that he claimed. At the end, the father was no match for his twenty-year old son.

As Robert and Tom went home, Robert apologized for Johnstone. 'Sorry he was so unhelpful. It was like getting blood out of a stone.'

'No, that was all right. It gave me time to see what he was really thinking.' And he explained to Robert what he had seen. 'So it seems that his mother was really quite innocent – her only crime was to protect her son from the police. But the other thing he lied about was not having any money left. He's got two boxes buried on the farm.'

'Really? We should tell the police. Do you think you will be able to find them?'

'No. I didn't see that much detail.'

'That's tricky then. The police won't start a search on a bit of mind-reading. There is one detective I can talk to and he might believe me, but I don't know what he can do. I'll speak to him in the morning.'

When they arrived back at the house, Tom slumped on to the plush sofa, feeling desperately tired. Monty jumped on to him but he ignored him. The session with Duncan Johnstone had taken him into areas he did not know he could go. Not only had he seen into Johnstone's mind, but he had been able to drag thoughts from his memory and see a lot more than Johnstone was willing to admit to. It seemed to come naturally, even though he had never done it before.

'You look tired, Tom,' said Elizabeth. 'You must be hungry as well. Are you ready for dinner?'

Tom realized he was ravenous. 'I certainly am.'

Chapter 21

Face-to-Face with Matthew Montgomery

ROBERT SPOKE TO THE POLICE ABOUT THE hoard of money that Duncan Johnstone had buried on the farm. It transpired that they already suspected as much. They were planning to keep an eye on his mother when she was released from prison in two years. They were convinced she knew where it was.

The fourth murderer was a multiple killer: Michael Kolowski, an ex-soldier who decided to make money in civilian life by killing people. He was an expert with a rifle and at gaining access to the most difficult terrain. He found jobs all over the world and he was always on the run, but he was caught near his childhood home in Scotland when a bomb he was making exploded accidentally and nearly killed him. He was identified by police while he was recovering in hospital. The bomb blast left him with one arm and a damaged leg.

When he appeared through the door and walked into the room to face Robert and Tom, he limped slightly but walked upright. His face had obviously survived the bomb blast because it had no scars at all. His right arm was severed at the elbow. He was probably about fifty years old. He smiled at Robert and Tom with no hint of malice at all. Robert introduced Tom and Kolowski gave Tom a nod and said politely: 'Pleased to meet you.'

Robert quizzed Kolowski about his life in the army. He had been on active service and had served as a mercenary in civil wars in third-world countries. He boasted how he picked off enemy soldiers at long distance with his rifle. He was an expert in guerrilla warfare and could survive in the toughest terrain. He could make bombs and set up all sorts of booby traps. What was alarming was that he thought it was perfectly logical to use his warfare skills in civilian life. The truth was, he was not capable of doing anything else; he craved the excitement that it brought and he got depressed if he was not either killing or torturing people.

'How do you cope with prison life?' asked Robert.

'Badly. I'm on drugs all the time to keep me sane. I don't have much contact with the other prisoners because I'm a danger to them.'

'Are you?'

'Probably. I still yearn to feel a rifle in my hand, although I wouldn't be much use with half of my best arm gone.'

'What do you do to pass the time?'

'I write poetry. Not what you would expect, I'll bet, but the poems are all about war. I've taken a correspondence course and I've had a few poems published.' Then he laughed. 'I'll tell you a funny thing: I was invited by a poetry society to go to one of their meetings and read my poems! I thanked them for their invitation and then explained that I would be staying in that evening.'

'Tell me what you enjoyed about killing.'

'I'll give you an example. I was a mercenary in the jungle, fighting for government forces against insurgents. I was on my own because the rest of my group had been wiped out. I came across a small enemy camp with about thirty troops. I watched them for most of the day. I saw which tent the leader was in and I waited for my opportunity to place a bomb behind it. I got back to a position where I could see the whole camp and got my gun set up. I detonated the explosive. It caused pandemonium and the troops were all over the place. They had no discipline. I shot all of them in about two minutes. That made me feel so good – a real feast.'

Tom had been concentrating on Kolowski's mind images and he could see the mixture of fear and lust that drove him to kill. The excitement was intense and he was addicted to it. Human life meant nothing to him; he was prepared to lose his own life in his quest for the thrill of a mass killing. He was insane, and a formidable adversary.

'Were you ever close to being caught?'

'Oh, yes, many times. There was the time when two of us in a Jeep attacked a large battalion of soldiers on a beach. The driver went at them at speed while I swept them with gunfire. When we got on the road to escape, they were already after us. We drove up into the mountains until we got to a sharp bend over a big drop. We jumped out and let the Jeep go over the edge. When the soldiers saw the Jeep in flames below them, they assumed we'd perished. But we were hiding behind the rocks.'

Again, Tom could see the killing lust in Kolowski's mind as he strafed the soldiers with gunfire and watched them drop in large numbers. The intensity of the excitement as they made their escape was almost unbearable. It was a crazy thing to do and their chances of getting out alive must have been close to zero, but that's what Kolowski craved.

'And what about your contract killings?'

'Oh, that was just a job to keep me in pocket money. I didn't get paid much as a mercenary.'

'But it meant that you were a wanted man.'

'Oh, yes, but I'd been a wanted man for most of my life. The police couldn't catch me – it was my stupid mistake that gave me away.'

'Did you enjoy the contract killings?'

'Yes, because they all involved a fair amount of risk. And I got paid well.'

Tom had found it quite easy to see the images in Kolowski's mind, but there was something that he found a bit of a puzzle. Kolowski didn't have any emotions other than the surges of elation he got from killing and taking risks. There was nothing in his brain about personal relationships with other people, not even his parents. There did not seem to be any childhood memories, either. Tom probed harder and harder, but he could find nothing. He decided to try an experiment. He knew, if he had inherited Will's abilities, he should be able to put thoughts into Kolowski's mind, but he didn't know how to do it. He just hoped it would come to him. He focused on Kolowski's thoughts, and then thought about young children playing in a garden. Whether it worked, or it was just coincidence, Kolowski thought about his childhood and an image of him with a toy rifle appeared and then disappeared in an instant. Somehow, Kolowski was able to hide these thoughts. Tom had not been concentrating on what Robert was asking Kolowski, so he was startled when Kolowski stood up to leave. Robert had concluded the conversation.

'Thanks very much for your help,' said Robert.

'It's been a pleasure talking to you.'

Tom and Robert got into conversation about Kolowski as soon as they could. 'Robert, I wasn't concentrating on what you were asking him for the last few minutes. Did you ask him about his childhood?'

'No, but he said that he was interested in guns as a child.'

'It's just that he didn't seem to have any memories of childhood, but when I tried to put a childhood thought into his mind, I immediately saw him as a child with a rifle.'

'Hey! Did you say you put a thought into his mind?'

'Well, I tried but I don't know if I succeeded or whether it was just a coincidence that he thought of childhood. I don't think so because he seemed to be able to suppress those thoughts at will. I couldn't get at them.'

'That makes sense. He was such a skilful killer that he was able to focus all his energies on the one task and could block out all other thoughts.'

'He didn't seem to have any memories of personal relationships either. He didn't seem to have any emotions.'

'Ah, I'm sure that's another trick to focus the mind. Emotions get in the way if you're a professional killer.'

'One other thing I've noticed – I seem to be able to look into the minds of these people without any problem. Before, I had to be in a desperate situation for it to happen.'

'I suspect you won't be able to do it with everyone, though. These men are rather unusual and you have a good reason to see into their minds. Even so, you're developing your skills at an impressive rate. So far, the prisoners haven't been able to attack your mind, but that's just as well. Tomorrow you could be under attack from Matthew Montgomery.'

'Has he threatened you?'

'Yes, the first few times I spoke to him I struggled. He was lying most of the time and basically playing games with me. If I tried to talk to him about anything personal he became aggressive. Gradually, he came to trust me and now he's happy to discuss most things with me. That doesn't stop him having his little games at my expense. He could be more difficult when he sees you though. Be ready for an unpleasant reception. I did warn him that you would be coming and he didn't object.'

The day had arrived – Tom would come face-to-face with a psychopathic serial killer that afternoon. The morning was spent with the final session of training at the University. By now, Tom could cope with anything that Robert threw at him.

'I really don't think I can offer you any more exercises that are going to improve on what you've achieved. In a week, you've reached a higher level than anyone else I've known by a very long way. There's no doubt in my mind that you have Will's gift.'

'Thanks for making it possible. The exercises were brilliant and they helped me a lot.'

'Well, you're as ready as you can be for facing Matthew Montgomery. Let's get some lunch and then be on our way.'

Robert had already given Tom a detailed account of Matthew Montgomery's murders. They were all quite grisly. He didn't just kill them; he beheaded them and stuck their heads on poles in the manner of ancient warriors. He left the heads and bodies in places where they would be found, as though he intended them to be warnings. Tom found it hard to understand how anyone in our civilized society could do such a thing. But he expected to find out soon.

Matthew Montgomery came strutting through the prison doorway, dragging his guard behind him on his handcuffs. He exuded arrogance. He was taller than average, athletically-built and handsome. His shoulder-length hair fell over his face and he ran the fingers of his free hand through it to draw it back.

'Well now, Robert. Is this your little protégé? Aren't you going to introduce me?' Tom knew Montgomery was well-educated, but even so, the resonant upper-class accent surprised him. It gave Montgomery an air of superiority.

'Yes, of course. Matthew, this is Tom Merrington.'

'Ah, now young Tom, what are you here to learn?'

This was the first time that one of the prisoners had asked him anything. He wasn't prepared for it and he blurted out the truth: 'I'm here to find out how your mind works.'

Montgomery laughed out loud. 'Thank you for being honest. I've had a lot of people, including Robert here, who have wanted the same thing. They have all failed and you're the youngest by far, so what hope have you? Nil, I'd say.'

Tom felt inclined to challenge him, but he didn't want to annoy Montgomery right at the start, so instead he said: 'I can but try, can't I?'

'Of course you can. Now, what do you both want to talk about?'

Robert started with: 'Could you tell us what drove you to kill the first time?'

'Do you mean human or any killing?'

Robert was thinking of the murders, but he thought it would be interesting to hear what Montgomery had to say about other killings. 'Oh, any killing.'

'Well, now. I must have been about six or seven I suppose. We had a pet cat that slept most of the day and only woke up to be fed. I looked at it one day and thought: "What a useless creature you are. Why are we stupid enough to look after you?" So I strangled it and threw it in the river. After that, I killed a few more cats. I would hit them on the head with a piece of wood and then leave them in the road so that the owners would think they had been run over by cars.'

'And what about your first murder?'

'It was a young boy I saw shoplifting. I followed him when he left the store. He walked through the park and when he got to a quiet place, he examined the contents of his pockets. I went up to him and told him that I had just watched him steal them. He denied it, so I hit him. He tried to run away, so I grabbed him round the neck and dragged him into the woods. He begged for mercy, but I gave none. I wrote on his forehead "Shoplifter" and sat his body up against a tree.'

'So you didn't behead him.'

'No, I didn't think of that until the third one.'

Tom felt uncomfortable watching the images in Montgomery's mind. Montgomery was extremely calm, sitting in front of them relating his exploits, totally different from the raging creature that Tom saw in his mind. When he committed the murder, he was completely out of control, stabbing his victim numerous times and then collapsing on the ground from his exertions. Tom was sickened that anyone could be like this. He wasn't like Kolowski, who was a thrill-seeker; he got intense pleasure from killing in the most violent way. As he related another of his murders to Robert, Tom decided that was enough – he was going to attack. An image of Montgomery wrestling a young girl came into his mind. He lifted his knife to stab her, but Tom changed the image: the girl grew huge fangs and leapt up to bite Montgomery's throat. He rolled back, terrified, dropping the knife. He ran, but the girl was much faster. She leapt on him from behind and sunk her fangs deep into his neck.

'What's wrong?' asked Robert.

Montgomery was trembling all over, shaking his head uncontrollably. 'What are you doing?' he shouted at Robert. Robert looked puzzled. Then he turned his head to Tom. 'It's you!' he screamed. And a look of determination came over his face. He was going to fight back!

Tom was startled at the intensity of Montgomery's attack. Tom had obviously caught him off guard, but now he was putting all his effort into attack. Tom could not stop the images of Montgomery attacking him with a huge sword, but he was able to avoid the wild swings. First, he changed the scene from what looked like a dingy cellar to an open field. He could see better now, but he didn't have anything to defend himself. Montgomery was getting bigger. He was swinging his sword wildly at a faster and faster pace. Tom was desperate. He gained some respite by putting a big hat on Montgomery's head. It was so big that it fell over his eyes and while he was struggling with the hat, Tom armed himself, but he wasn't thinking clearly enough and he found himself with an ancient pitchfork in his hand. The sword swung towards him and he held up the pitchfork to defend himself. The shock as it hit the fork was intense but Tom had just enough strength to divert the sword away from him. It thudded into the ground, shattering the pitchfork into splinters and throwing Tom on to his back. Montgomery lifted the mighty sword again and swung it with all his might. Tom could see the rage on his face; he was determined to slice Tom in two. But Tom rolled over and just evaded the sword as it sunk deeply into the ground beside him. In the moments it took Montgomery to heave his sword out of the ground, Tom leapt up and ran towards a bridge over the river. He was gasping for breath.

Montgomery was still getting bigger, and so was his sword. Tom ran over the bridge. It was rickety and rotten. Montgomery followed behind, his rage driving him over the bridge with one thought in mind – to kill Tom. But he was so heavy that the bridge collapsed under his weight, just as Tom had planned. He fell screaming into the river below. He was so big, the river wasn't deep enough to drown him, so Tom changed it to a roaring torrent that carried him away, thrashing and screaming, into the distance. Tom noticed Montgomery's sword had stuck in the bank. He lifted the huge weapon and held it aloft in victory.

Tom had won; his guile had beaten Montgomery's fury. Montgomery was slumped in his chair, no longer the calm, arrogant, handsome man that had entered the room. 'I think you had better take him away,' said Tom to the guard. The puzzled guard lifted him out of his chair and dragged him out of the room.

'What on earth did you do to him?' asked Robert.

'I guess you could say we had a mind-fight, and I won!'

'Tell me more on the way home. Let's get away from here.'

They got back in the car and drove out through the gates of the prison for the last time. At least, it was the last time for Tom. Whether Matthew Montgomery would ever speak to Robert again was highly doubtful.

'Now, explain to me how it started.'

'Well, I couldn't take any more of Montgomery's boasting about his disgusting murders, so I decided to give him a fright. I made one of his victims fight back and wound him instead.'

'Oh, so that's when he went into a trembling fit.'

'Yes, and when he realized it was me who was attacking his mind, he fought back. We literally had a fight in our minds. He armed himself with a sword and he just grew and grew. I escaped from him and led him over a rotting bridge where he fell to his doom. I don't suppose it's done any good, but at least he's had a taste of his own medicine, even if it is imaginary.'

'Well, what an end to the week! We must have a celebration tonight. You've done so much better than I could have hoped. And before you ask the question, yes, I believe you are ready to face St Caithrin.'

Tom looked at Robert and a huge grin spread over his face. 'Thanks. I was hoping you would say that. I've improved so much this week that I can hardly believe it myself.'

'Does your mum allow you to drink champagne? I've got a bottle at home that I was saving for a celebration like this.'

'Mum has let me drink wine at home before, but we've never had champagne. I'm sure she'd let me try it.'

'I'm sure she will. Especially when I tell her what you've accomplished.'

When they arrived back at the farm, Mum was waiting to greet Tom. She knew it could have been a terrifying experience for him and she was anxious to see that he was all right. When she saw the big smile on his face, she was relieved and she asked for a full account of what had happened.

'Julia, you should be proud of this boy. He's come through the most difficult of tests with flying colours.'

'Well done, Tom. I've been desperately worried and I'm so relieved that you're safe.'

Jane came rushing up. 'What was Matthew Montgomery like? Did he frighten you? Does he really have horns?'

Tom laughed. 'No, he doesn't have horns, but he's a very nasty man. I don't think I've ever met anyone as nasty as him before.'

'Were you scared of him?'

'Yes, at first, but then I got very angry with him because he was boasting about all the horrible things he had done.'

'So did you shout at him for boasting?'

'Not exactly, but I did pay him back.'

Fortunately, Elizabeth called all the children into the lounge at that moment and Tom didn't have to give Jane any more details. Robert had opened the champagne and there was lemonade for all the children, apart from Tom and Jane, who were allowed a little champagne.

'It's a shame you have to go back tomorrow,' said Elizabeth. 'It's been a pleasure to have you and of course you are welcome to come back at any time.'

'Thank you very much, Elizabeth,' said Mum. 'You've been wonderful hosts. And thank you, Robert, for giving Tom so much help.'

'Julia, I'll let you into a little secret: I think Tom has taught me more than I taught him. I told him that if he ever has to face St Caithrin, he's ready for it.'

'Oh, I'm so relieved to hear you say that. I've been worried sick that it might happen. At least I know now that Tom is well-prepared if it does happen.'

Tom was sitting on the sofa and Monty cat came and sat on his lap again. He thought what that terrible man Matthew Montgomery would have done with this harmless creature. It was going to be difficult to get him out of his mind.

Elizabeth had made a special dinner as it was the last night for Tom and Mum. Tom discovered that he was ravenous again and he ate large portions of everything. He went to bed a little uncomfortable and wished he had eaten less. When he thought about the events of the week, he felt a mixture of happiness and fear. He was overjoyed with the progress he had made, but frightened because he was entering a world that he had not known before – a world that was occupied by forces like St Caithrin and characters like Matthew Montgomery. He thought about Matthew Montgomery, but then blocked him out so that he could get to sleep. Unfortunately, he couldn't stop himself dreaming about him.

The next morning, Tom and Mum had to leave early to catch their train. They said goodbye to Elizabeth and the children, and then Robert took them to the station. As the train left the station and they waved to Robert, they were both sad to leave the place behind. But Tom knew he could call on Robert at any time if he needed him. That was a great comfort.

Chapter 22

Where is St Caithrin?

TOM HAD HIS NEXT VISION A FEW days after he got back from Rothbank. Will was with Max, Bernard and Inspector Bates again at New Mallington.

'I went to the "Sow and Pigs" to question Farrell, but the landlord told me he had left and gone back to Ireland. I'm not inclined to follow him there because I've only got your opinion that he's worth interviewing; I don't have any hard facts. However, the landlord did tell me that Farrell was incensed by the church desecrations, particularly when it happened to the church he attended. He was apparently a devout Roman Catholic.'

'Did the landlord say whether Farrell had any idea who was damaging the churches?'

'I asked him that, but he didn't know.'

'So does that mean the case is closed, Inspector?'

'Oh, no. We still have to investigate Bartholomew Green's murder, but it's not going to be my highest priority.'

'Have you finished with our services then, Inspector?'

'Yes, thank you. You've been very helpful. Perhaps we'll get the chance to collaborate again another time. Good day to you all.'

'Good day, Inspector.'

When Inspector Bates had gone, Bernard stated the obvious: 'So it looks as though St Caithrin has evaded us.'

'Yes, and I don't see much point in chasing after Farrell. I don't suppose any one of us has the time, anyway,' said Max.

Will agreed, reluctantly. 'I should be getting back to my patients. Thanks for looking after me, Bernard. I'll catch the early train tomorrow.'

'Shouldn't we try to keep up with the news from Ireland? If St Caithrin goes on the rampage again, there could be more murders.'

'Perhaps, but Farrell did not seem like an evil man. The Inspector implied he was a regular church-goer. I suspect that St Caithrin jumped into him because he was the nearest body. It may take some time before St Caithrin takes over his mind.'

'But then he'll end up just a shell, like Marmaduke Constable.'

'I'm afraid so.'

'I'll find out from the landlord at the "Sow and Pigs" whether anyone is keeping in touch with Farrell. Unlikely, but it's worth a try,' said Bernard.

That closed Tom's vision and he wondered whether he would get any more for a while. Will was obviously not prepared to chase St Caithrin, so another confrontation was unlikely. Did Will ever meet St Caithrin again? Tom was sure he would find out.

At school, Frank and Tom had heard some gossip that Mr Garrett had been in trouble with the police. Apparently, he was involved in an anti-government demonstration that turned into a riot. He was taken away by the police but released the following day without charge. But Tom had a feeling that he was up to no good.

'Just look at him now. He accused us of looking furtive, but he does furtive much better than we could,' said Frank.

'Yes, he does seem to be behaving strangely. Look, he's going into the sports store. He does that at every afternoon break. What do you think he's up to?'

'I don't know, but why don't we hide in there tomorrow at afternoon break and find out?'

'Yes, that would be a laugh! There's plenty of stuff in there to hide behind. And the door's never locked. If we're caught, it's a certain detention, though.'

'At least.'

The next afternoon, they hurried out at break. The door of the sports store was a bit exposed, so Frank stood at the doorway while Tom slipped in. As soon as he thought nobody was looking, he crept in himself. As Tom had said, there was plenty of equipment to hide behind. They settled down to wait for Mr Garrett. They didn't have to wait long. The door opened and in he came, looking as furtive as ever. He pulled out his mobile phone and quickly dialled a number. Tom and Frank could hear every word he said.

'Hello, G6 here. Yes, I am coming tonight. Look, I'm worried about D7; he's been talking about his son and getting revenge for what he thinks you did. I suspect we'll have trouble tonight. No, I don't think he gave away anything to the police – they're still as baffled as ever, but he's a risk. What?

Are you serious? Well, you know best. I'll see you tonight. I'll get there early, at about seven.'

Mr Garrett stuffed his phone in his pocket and hurriedly went outside. Tom and Frank were left wondering what his conversation was about, but they were sure it was something illegal. 'What do you think all this "G6" and "D7" stuff is about?' said Tom.

'Seems like they have to avoid stating their names on the phone. Perhaps it's some kind of secret society.'

'We need to get out of here. I'll go first and I'll knock when it's OK for you to come out.' Tom opened the door slightly and peeped through the crack. He waited until he saw a prefect go past, and then he crept out. When he thought it was safe for Frank to come out, he knocked on the door. Frank came out and shut the door quietly behind him.

'And what were you doing in there?' A prefect seemed to have come from nowhere and now stood menacingly in front of them.

'Er, we thought we saw a rat go under the door,' Frank lied.

'Nonsense.' He opened the door and strolled around the sports store, sniffing. 'You've not been smoking in here, so what have you been doing? You haven't got any drugs have you? Empty your pockets.' Tom and Frank did as they were told but they didn't have anything incriminating in their pockets. 'OK, you're both in Prefects' Detention this Friday. Names?'

'Tom Merrington and Frank McGinty.'

He wrote their names in his notebook. 'See you on Friday at four o'clock in room twelve, then.' He turned around and strode away briskly like an army sergeant-major.

'Prefects' Detention – the worst detention of all!'

'It could have been worse – Garrett might have seen us.'

'I suppose so. What are we going to do about Garrett? Do you think we should follow him tonight to find out what he's up to?'

'Could be risky, but I think we should. Do you know where he lives?'

'No, but I know Amanda Smithers lives near him. I'll ask her.'

'Be careful with Amanda – she fancies you!'

Frank went bright red. 'Of course she doesn't.'

'I'm sure she does. I've noticed how she goes all dreamy when she sees you.'

Frank went even redder and decided he must change the subject. 'What will you tell your parents?'

'About what?'

'About where we're going tonight, of course.'

'You say you're going out with Amanda. I'll say I'm coming round to your place.'

Frank gritted his teeth and ignored Tom's remark. 'What if Garrett goes to this meeting by car? How will we keep up? And what if it's a long way?'

'We'll have to take that chance. Let's take our bikes. At least we can keep up with him if he gets stuck in traffic.'

'OK. I'll meet you outside the gates after school.'

As the bell went for the end of the school day, Tom and Frank both hurried from their classrooms and met at the gates. 'Amanda told me where Garrett lives – it's at the far end of Greenfield Road. We can get there in about fifteen minutes from your place. I'll meet you in the road outside your house at six o'clock.'

'OK, see you then.' Tom hurried home because he knew the tyres on his bike needed pumping up. He hated lying to Mum but he knew she wouldn't let him out if she knew what he was going to do. He donned his cycling helmet and went out to meet Frank.

They cycled to Greenfield Road and found Mr Garrett's house at the far end. They went into the entrance to the park at the end of the road and stood behind some bushes where they could see Mr Garrett's front door. They tried to look casual.

'Hello Frank, hello Tom. I thought I saw you cycling past.' It was Amanda. 'Why are you spying on Mr Garrett?'

'Amanda, please don't interfere,' said Frank. This was the last thing they wanted.

'I'm not interfering; I just want to know what you are doing. I might be able to help.'

'I doubt it.'

'You can see his front door easier from my bedroom window. You can park your bikes in the front garden if you like and I'll look out for you from my bedroom and tell you when he comes out.'

Tom and Frank looked at each other. It was a bit awkward where they were standing. 'And I suppose in exchange you want the whole story,' said Frank.

'Of course.'

'Oh, all right, but you must promise not to say a word of this to anyone.' And Frank gave her an account of the telephone conversation they had overheard in the sports store.

'How exciting! You will tell me tomorrow how you got on, won't you? I promise I won't tell anyone.'

They took their bikes to Amanda's front garden. She went up to her room, opened the window and called down to them. 'No sign of him yet.'

They waited until about fifteen minutes to seven, and then Amanda called: 'He's coming! He's walking. He's gone into the park – hurry!'

They jumped on their bikes and cycled back down to the end of the road and into the park. Cycling was not allowed, but they could see Mr Garrett crossing to the far entrance of the park, so they jumped off their bikes and pushed them. When Mr Garrett got to the other entrance, he turned left. When they got to the entrance and looked to the left, they just caught sight of him on the other side of the road, turning right into Dean Avenue. It was difficult to keep him in view without getting too close. They jumped on their bikes and cycled over to the road on the right. When they got there, he had gone! They pedalled faster, looking all around to try to find him. They were really exposed now. Then Frank gesticulated to Tom. There he was, waiting in a doorway. He was facing away from them as if waiting for the door to open. Frank and Tom sped past and then turned around when they had reached a safe distance.

'Do you remember which house it was?' asked Tom.

'Yes, it was the one with the blue gate.'

It was a large, detached house with a garage at the side. There was a side entrance between the garage and the house, presumably leading to the back garden, but the blue gate was the only way into the property from the road. The front garden was surrounded on all sides by a tall hedge.

'Where can we put our bikes?'

'The house next door looks empty. Let's put our bikes in the garden.' They crept into the front garden of the big, empty house and stood their bikes behind the rambling hedge. 'Nobody will see them there.'

'Somebody's coming!' They peered through the hedge to see another arrival at the house. A short man in a smart suit stepped out of a BMW and walked up the path to the house. He rang the bell. The door opened and he walked in; there were no words of greeting from either side.

'You remember that Garrett said he would be early – perhaps the meeting doesn't start until half-past. It's now twelve minutes past seven. Let's wait and see if anyone we know turns up.'

Sure enough, four more people arrived just before seven-thirty. Only one of them looked familiar. He reminded Tom of Mr Grimley – much older, shorter, and he walked with a slight stoop.

'Let's see if we can get a peep at what they are up to,' suggested Tom. 'The lights are on in the back of the house, so that's bound to be where the meeting is.'

'OK. Let's go through the side entrance.'

They went through the front gate and crept silently to the side entrance. The gate opened easily and they were able to steal into the back garden with hardly a sound. They crouched down and worked their way to the back of the house and carefully peered into the first room they came to with a light on. It was the kitchen. There was a room with a large bay window that they guessed would be the meeting room. The curtains were closed, but right in the middle, there was a small gap between the curtains. Frank looked in. 'I can only see one person. He must have been here from the start because I didn't see him arrive.'

'Let me have a look.' Tom edged up to the window and looked through the gap. He stared and stared as though he was trying to bore a hole in the window.

'What is it?'

'It's him. I can feel it.'

'Who?'

'St Caithrin.'

'What! Are you sure?'

'Come on, Frank, let's go home. I've seen enough.'

They crept around to the side entrance and out into the front garden. Tom was so agitated he tripped over a loose paving slab and fell headlong into the dustbin, sending it crashing across the garden. Frank grabbed Tom by his coat and hauled him into the garden next door where they hid behind some shrubs. Unfortunately, their bikes were in the garden on the other side. The door of the house flew open and Mr Garrett came out shouting 'Who's there?' He looked at the fallen dustbin and replaced it. He walked to the front gate and looked around. Tom and Frank were trying to keep as still as they could. Just as Mr Garrett started walking back into the house, the door of the house next door opened and an old lady carrying an umbrella stood framed in the doorway. Fortunately, Mr Garrett had no wish to speak to her so he slipped back inside as quickly as he could. The lady came out into the garden and prodded Frank with her umbrella. 'Get out of my garden at once!'

Frank and Tom did not need any more persuasion. They raced round to retrieve their bikes and cycled with all their might back to the Vicarage. Frank was bombarding Tom with questions but Tom wouldn't say anything. He was sure now. There was no way out of it. Sooner or later, he would have to face St Caithrin.

Chapter 23

Marian Grimley Walks Again

TOM HAD BEEN FEELING DOWNCAST AFTER SEEING and feeling the evil of St Caithrin, but he was beginning to see everything more clearly now. St Caithrin was in a man he had never seen before. Tom did not know how tall he was, because he was sitting down when he saw him through the gap in the curtain. But he had a very distinctive face. His eyes were small and close together; his nose was long and pointed. His mouth was wide and straight like a slit and his lips were thin. It was hard to see the colour of his hair, but it was dark and neat, parted on the right. There was no doubt in Tom's mind – he would recognize him when he saw him again.

It was Friday and time for Prefects' Detention. Tom and Frank went forlornly to the detention room where two prefects were waiting for them. One was Simon Drew, who had caught them in the sports store, and the other was Terry Paterson. There were six other unfortunate pupils in detention. When they were settled, Terry Paterson spoke: 'You will each write an essay of a minimum of one thousand words on the subject you are given. You can only leave when we are satisfied that your essay is of adequate standard and you cannot leave before five o'clock. We are prepared to stay as long as it takes. Any questions?'

It was all perfectly clear, so there were no questions. The two prefects went around the group handing out sheets. At the top of Tom's first sheet was the title of his essay: "Why I was hiding in the sports store." So they were expecting a full confession. Tom looked across at Frank. From his expression, it seemed he had got the same title. Tom scrawled in big letters in pencil on his sheet: "I'M GOING TO TELL THE TRUTH" and held it up for Frank to read. Frank nodded in agreement. They didn't care who knew about Mr Garrett now. If he were involved with St Caithrin, then he must be involved in evil. They both set about their essays with determination. It was easy to tell the truth, much easier than making up a story.

'By the way,' interrupted Terry. 'Count your own words and put one hundred-word markers in.'

Tom was nearly finished. He counted his words and the essay was only about a hundred words short. He had plenty more he could say, so he soon finished off. He took his essay up to the prefects. Simon began to read it. He gave Tom some menacing looks at various points, and then he whispered to Terry and passed the essay over to him. Frank took up his essay and handed it to Simon. This time Simon did not look up. He read it intently and then passed it on to Terry. Terry read through it, whispered to Simon and then pointed at Tom and Frank and indicated he wanted them both to go out into the corridor with him.

'You two can get yourselves into serious trouble writing stuff like this. Did you know you were going to get this essay and did you agree to write all this nonsense?'

Frank spoke: 'We didn't know what the essay was going to be about, but when we saw the subject, we agreed to tell the truth. It's not nonsense either. Mr Garrett is up to no good.'

'And what sort of "no good" is he up to?'

'We don't know yet, but when we find out, we're going to tell the police.'

'Why don't you tell the police now?'

'Because they probably wouldn't believe us without any evidence.'

'Exactly. Now look here, this is what I'm going to do: I'm going to tear these essays into a million pieces and we'll forget they ever existed. You can go back into the detention room and read until five o'clock.'

Frank and Tom went back and read for the remaining five minutes. When five o'clock came, Terry indicated to them that they could leave. The others were still writing.

'Terry's a good sort, really. I think he believed us,' said Frank.

'He did. It was hard for him not to believe it when we wrote the same account. You didn't mention St Caithrin did you?'

'No, I thought that was going a bit too far.'

'Good. Neither did I.'

Tom got home earlier than expected, having told Mum that Prefects' Detention could go on a long time. He explained to Mum that he and Frank had written truthful accounts of what happened and Terry decided to destroy the essays. What he hadn't yet told Mum was that he had seen St Caithrin. He decided he must tell her.

'Mum, you know on Tuesday I said I went round to Frank's?'

'Yes.'

'Well, I didn't. We thought that Mr Garrett was doing something illegal and we knew he was going to a meeting of some kind of secret society, so we followed him.'

Mum was shocked. 'Why on earth did you do such a stupid thing?' She was about to give Tom a good telling-off when Tom interrupted her.

'Mum, let me give you the whole story. We followed him to a house in Dean Avenue. We saw other people arrive for the meeting and then we went round to the back garden to see if we could see anything through the windows. We did. There was a crack in the curtains and I could see a man sitting at the head of a table. I'd never seen him before but I won't forget him because…because I felt St Caithrin. He's St Caithrin's host and he's here.'

Mum looked horrified. She jumped out of her chair and paced up and down, biting her nails. Then she grabbed Tom and clutched him to her. They were interrupted by the phone ringing. Reluctantly, Mum released Tom and went to answer the phone. It was Theresa Grimley.

'Julia, I'd like to come round if I may. I've got some more bad news. Can I come round now?'

'Of course. See you soon.' Mum had kept in touch with Theresa Grimley since their first meeting. They shared their anxieties and it helped both of them. 'Tom, Mrs Grimley is coming round. She should be here in about twenty minutes. Let's talk again when she's gone.'

'OK.' Tom decided to go for a stroll around the churchyard. When he went through the gate, the churchyard was empty. He walked over to Sebastian Grimley's grave and casually pulled a few weeds out. He was crouched by the small headstone, pulling out ivy, when he felt a sudden chill. He felt as though someone was watching him. He looked up and saw a woman in a long dress who appeared to be looking at him. She was crying and tears were running down her cheeks. She took out a handkerchief and dried her tears. Tom stood up but the woman continued to look towards the grave.

'Are you all right? Can I help?' The woman ignored him. Then she turned and walked away. Tom went after her. She was heading straight for the big oak tree. 'Watch out for the tree!' But she walked through it and was gone. Tom then realized that he had seen Marian Grimley. There had been another Grimley death. That was what Mrs Grimley had come to tell Mum. He ran back into the house where Mum and Mrs Grimley were talking.

'Mrs Grimley, sorry to interrupt, but please tell me who has died.'

Mrs Grimley looked shocked. 'George's father. But how did you know?'

'I've just seen Marian Grimley's ghost in the churchyard. She only shows up when a Grimley dies before their time. Can you tell me how he died, please?'

'He was hit by falling masonry at his house.'

'Was it an accident?'

Theresa looked at Mum. 'That's what we've been discussing. The police are not sure, but I am – it was murder.'

'Do you have a photo of Mr Grimley?'

'Yes, but why do you ask?'

'I may have seen him the other evening.'

Theresa took out a photo from her handbag. 'That's George with his father. It was taken about six months ago.'

'That's him. Yes, it all fits now. St Caithrin killed both of them.'

'Who?'

'I'll explain later,' said Mum. 'Let Tom go on.'

'I think Mr Garrett, our maths teacher, must have been talking to St Caithrin in the telephone conversation I overheard. He mentioned a man who wanted revenge because of "what he thought you did to his son". That must have been Mr Grimley Senior, because I saw him go to the same meeting that Garrett went to. The leader of the group was St Caithrin.'

'OK, Tom. Let me explain about St Caithrin to Mrs Grimley.' Mum gave Theresa a detailed description of Tom's visions, how Will had faced St Caithrin and the expectation that Tom would one day have to face St Caithrin. Meanwhile, Tom was on the phone to Frank, explaining his theory to him.

'We're going to have to get some evidence so that we can tell the police who the murderer is,' said Frank.

'Any ideas how we do that?'

'We need to keep watch on the house in Dean Avenue and find out what St Caithrin and his cronies are plotting.'

'That's easier said than done. We haven't got time to watch the house every day.'

'That's true. We'll have to think of something a bit smarter than that. We can't listen in to Garrett's conversations any more. If we're caught a second time in the sports store, we'll really be in trouble.'

'If you have any bright ideas, give me a call.'

'OK.'

Tom went back into the lounge, where Mum was still talking to Theresa Grimley. 'Tom, Mrs Grimley thinks that Mr Grimley Senior was involved in some kind of criminal gang.'

Mrs Grimley continued: 'Yes, my husband believed that his father was part of a gang involved in smuggling weapons. He thought they were selling weapons and explosives to terrorists. Don't ask me why he suspected that.

He wouldn't tell me.'

'That might explain why your husband was killed. He discovered too much and he was a risk to the gang. I'm sure St Caithrin thought Mr Grimley Senior was becoming a risk when he spoke about getting revenge for killing your husband.'

'You could be right. So the suggestion that my husband was killed because he got soft and ended the family feud with the Robertsons was probably wrong.'

'I don't think the family feud would have interested St Caithrin.'

'I see. Well, shouldn't we go to the police?'

Mum said: 'Did you tell the police about your husband's suspicions that his father was involved in this gang?'

'No, because I didn't think it was relevant to George's murder, but I shall now. Unfortunately, he wouldn't tell me what evidence he had. He said he didn't want me to know too much because it would put me at risk.'

'If you're going to tell that to the police, then I think we should tell them about the house in Dean Avenue, Tom. Putting the two bits of evidence together might persuade the police to keep an eye on the house. I'll call them now and find out who is in charge of the case.' She went to call the number that Inspector Reynolds had given her. She came back in a few minutes.

'I spoke to Detective Inspector Reynolds. He's coming round now. I hope that's OK with you Theresa.'

'Yes, I'm not in a hurry to get back.'

Inspector Reynolds came alone this time. He carefully took down all the information that Tom and Mrs Grimley gave him, asked a few probing questions and then said to Tom: 'Tom, please don't take any more risks with these people; they could be very dangerous. We'll keep watch on the house, so you don't have to do any more detective work. Do you understand what I'm saying?'

'Yes.'

'Good, then I'll leave you now. If any more information comes to light, please call me.'

Inspector Reynolds was doing his best to keep Tom out of harm, but Tom knew that the police would not be able to handle St Caithrin. Even worse, they could let it loose by killing the man who was acting as its host, and then the search would be back at the start all over again. Tom knew if St Caithrin was to be stopped, a smarter plan was needed. But was it possible?

Chapter 24

Terry Learns the Truth

Tom and Frank were watching Mr Garrett sneak into the sports store again. He could be speaking to St Caithrin about selling arms to terrorists for all they knew. Terry Paterson came up behind them without making a sound. 'Still watching Mr Garrett are you?' They turned round in surprise. This time, Terry had a grin on his face. 'Don't worry, I'm not going to put you in detention. Come and see me tonight after school outside the Prefects' Common Room – I've got something I want to show you.' He walked away.

'He looks smug. I wonder what he's got?'

'Don't know, but I've got a feeling it's going to be interesting.'

When the bell went for the end of school, Tom and Frank met up to go together to the Prefects' Common Room. They waited outside for about five minutes before Terry arrived. 'Just wait a moment longer; I just have to get something from my locker.' He went inside the Common Room and within a few minutes, he was out again clutching something in his hand. 'Come in here.' He took them to an unoccupied classroom. They sat round a table and Terry showed them that he was holding a miniature tape recorder.

'I hid this in the sports store and recorded Mr Garrett's telephone conversations. Just listen to this.' He turned on the tape recorder and after a lot of shuffling noises, Mr Garrett's voice came over, loud and clear. He was talking again to someone who understood the alphanumeric codes for their members. He referred to D7 again, but in the past tense. After a while, Terry stopped the tape. 'Do you know who "D7" is?'

Frank spoke: 'We think it's old Mr Grimley, the man who was killed recently by masonry falling from his house. The police suspected it was an accident, but we think he was murdered.'

'Murdered? With falling masonry? That seems a bit far-fetched, doesn't it?'

Tom and Frank looked at each other. It was hard to believe. 'Yes it does seem unlikely, but the gang that Mr Garrett belongs to did have a motive.'

'What gang?'

Tom told Terry about the meeting that Mr Garrett went to and that the gang were suspected of illegal trading in weapons. 'We told the police all this.'

'I see. The Headmaster wanted to wait a little longer before we took the tapes to the police, but it looks like we should tell them now.'

'Yes, you should,' said Tom. 'Ask for Detective Inspector Reynolds.'

'I'll see if the Headmaster is still here. Thanks for your help. You can go home now.'

Tom and Frank left school and headed for home. 'So Terry did believe us after all. He's quite sensible really, for a prefect I mean.'

'Yes, he's not power-mad, like some of them.'

'What do you think we should do now?'

'There's not much we can do – it's all in the hands of the police. And Inspector Reynolds told me to keep out of the whole business.'

'But you can't. You're the only person capable of facing St Caithrin. Inspector Reynolds doesn't know the danger he's in.'

Tom looked at Frank with a frightened expression. Then he closed his eyes, sighed and said: 'You're right. I can't just let him confront St Caithrin; he won't stand a chance. But how can I stop him?'

'If you tell him the truth, he won't believe you. What about Professor MacDonald? Surely the inspector would believe him.'

'Yes, he's probably our best bet. I'll give him a call when I get home.'

'I'll come with you.'

So the two went back to the Vicarage. Much to their surprise, they found Inspector Reynolds waiting for them. 'You're late,' said Mum.

'Sorry, we had to see Terry Paterson, one of the prefects.'

'Well, Detective Inspector Reynolds has some news.'

The inspector turned to the boys and said: 'We've been round to the house in Dean Avenue and found it deserted. Whoever was there has been tipped off and they've gone. I wonder if you two could help us to build some likenesses of the people you saw go into the house the night you followed Mr Garrett. I'd like you to come to the station now if that's OK.'

Frank and Tom looked at each other and nodded in agreement. 'We could try.'

'By the way, Inspector, has our Headmaster been in touch with you yet?'

'No, why?'

'He's got some tapes of Mr Garrett's telephone conversations.'

Inspector Reynolds frowned, but then he pulled out his telephone and dialled a number. After a brief conversation, he wrote a number in his notebook and then said: 'Apparently, the Headmaster called asking to speak to me. If you don't mind, I'll call him now.' He went out of the room and they could hear him conversing on his telephone in the hall. When he came back, he explained that he had arranged to see the Headmaster in the morning.

'Are you boys ready to come with me then?'

'Frank, I'll give your parents a call to tell them where you are.'

'Thanks, Mrs Merrington.'

'Any idea how long you will be, Inspector?'

'I won't keep them longer than an hour. I'll bring them back here.'

As they drove to the police station in Inspector Reynolds's car, Tom and Frank chatted. 'Do you think you'll be able to give a good description of... you know...the leader, Tom?'

'How could I forget him? I see his face in my mind every day.'

'I don't think I could – I didn't get a good view of him.'

When they got to the station, Inspector Reynolds took them to meet a policewoman, who sat them down in front of a computer monitor. First, she showed them a photograph of old Mr Grimley and they both agreed it was him they saw that evening. Mr Garrett was one of the seven, so that left another five. The policewoman asked them questions about the shape of face, types of eyes, mouth and so on. She kept changing the image on the screen until they were satisfied it was a good likeness. When it came to St Caithrin, Tom knew the face almost perfectly. The policewoman was a little surprised that he should ask for such small changes in the features until he was satisfied. She looked at the final image a little surprised, and then called in Inspector Reynolds. They conversed in whispers and the Inspector went away for a few minutes. He came back with a sheet of paper with a copy of a photograph on it.

'Tom, is this him?' He showed Tom the photograph.

'Yes. You know him then.'

'Yes, he's a very dangerous man. His name is Alexander Markov and he's wanted for murder, serious fraud and drug smuggling. He runs an international network of criminals. He's an American, but he operates all over the world. He usually sets up bases in areas where there is little crime so that there isn't a big police presence. He's been on the run for seven years now. We had some intelligence that he was in England, but nobody knew where. Mrs Grimley's suspicion that his gang were involved in supplying weapons to terrorists was probably right. He's been suspected of supporting terrorism for some time. I'll have to put out a national alert that he has been seen. Just give me a few moments and I'll set the wheels in motion.' He went out of the room and gave another police officer instructions to issue the alert. When he came back, he had a stern warning for Tom and Frank.

'You must not say a word of this to anyone outside this room, not even your parents – we don't want to start a national panic. And, under no circumstances, try to track Markov down. He's extremely dangerous. He's been almost captured several times, but he's always got away. Nobody is too sure how he does it, but I understand he's an expert in martial arts. He was once cornered in Germany, but he killed three police officers and got away.'

Tom knew how he did it. He saw the way he sent things flying at Will and he guessed he must have projected the swords at Mr Grimley and the masonry at his father. 'Inspector, I know how he did it and I know more about Markov than you realize. You are also going to need my help to capture him.'

'Oh?' Inspector Reynolds showed a mixture of amusement and puzzlement on his face. 'Explain.'

'Markov is not the real villain – it's the mind that's possessed him that's the cause of the trouble. It's called St Caithrin and I've met it before when I've seen visions through the eyes of one of my ancestors.' Inspector Reynolds spluttered but Tom held up his hand to stop him saying anything. 'My ancestor was Will Protheroe, a famous psychiatrist. He encountered St Caithrin in a mental hospital in the mind of an aggressive patient. He managed to chase it out of the patient's mind but it inhabited another person who committed several murders. I haven't seen what happened in the end yet, but I suspect St Caithrin eventually killed Will Protheroe. The reason I can help you is that I have the same gift that Will had – I can resist St Caithrin and, with a bit of luck, I might be able to chase it out of Markov's mind. If you try to capture Markov, he will kill you for certain – he is able to project missiles with his mind, like the swords that killed Mr Grimley and the masonry that killed his father. Your only chance would be to shoot him from a distance, but then you would lose St Caithrin.'

Inspector Reynolds stared at Tom with his mouth open before saying: 'I don't know whether to believe you or not. If this St Caithrin killed your ancestor, why do you think you can succeed where he failed?'

'I don't know that I can, but I'm the only hope. I seem to have been chosen for the task and I have to do it. If you don't believe me, speak to Professor MacDonald of Rothbank University. I'm sure he'll be only too willing to help. He deals with criminals all the time.'

'Do you have his address and telephone number?'

'Call my mum; she has them.'

Inspector Reynolds made a note. 'And what did you mean when you said we would lose St Caithrin if we shot Markov?'

'St Caithrin will leave the body and find another one to inhabit. Then you'll have to start the search all over again because you won't know where it is.'

'I see. So is it possible to get rid of St Caithrin once and for all?'

'I don't know, but we have to find a way.'

Inspector Reynolds looked bemused. 'Let me speak to this Professor MacDonald before we go any further. Can you tell me why he is involved?' Tom explained the way they had met Robert and the training he had given him.

'OK. I'll take you both home now and I'll get his phone number from your mother. Let's get going – I've kept you long enough.' He stood still, scratched his head, turned to Tom with a look on his face that suggested he didn't know whether he was still on the same planet, gathered his senses and then walked to the door.

The next day at school, Tom and Frank were summoned to the Headmaster's office. They found Inspector Reynolds and Terry Paterson there. Inspector Reynolds explained that they were taking the tapes and that from now on, the police would bug the sports store.

'Terry, Frank and Tom: don't do anything that might arouse Mr Garrett's suspicions, but if you do spot anything unusual about his behaviour, please let the Headmaster know at once so that he can call me. Is that clear?'

'Absolutely,' said Terry. Tom and Frank nodded in agreement.

'I think you will find that the phone calls will stop and Mr Garrett will keep a low profile from now on. Perhaps after a while, the gang's activities will start up again and we want to know when that happens, if at all. At the moment, Mr Garrett seems to be our best lead. OK – any questions?'

'Yes, Inspector,' said Terry. Do you want us to let the Headmaster know if and when Mr Garrett makes any more phone calls from the sports store? If you are bugging it constantly, you will pick up all the conversations that go on in there.'

'Good point. Yes it would be a help. Well, if that's all, I'll be on my way. Thank you all for your help. Oh, Tom, could I have a quick word with you before I go please?' They left the Headmaster's office and Inspector Reynolds said: 'I spoke to Professor MacDonald and he is on his way down. Apparently, he's staying at your house for a while.'

'Great!' said Tom. He was looking forward to seeing Robert again.

Chapter 25

Mike's Idea

When Tom arrived home from school that evening, Robert had returned from the police station. He was chatting to Mum in the lounge.

'Hello, Tom. Good to see you again. How are things going?'

'OK, I think. Have you seen Inspector Reynolds?'

'Yes. The poor man is a bit bemused, but I think he understands what he is up against now.'

The telephone rang. 'I'll get it,' said Mum.

Robert took the opportunity to talk to Tom. 'Tom, you haven't seen how Will died yet, have you?'

'No.'

'That could be very important to us. I think you will see it before you have to confront St Caithrin. I suspect that if St Caithrin was responsible for Will's death, he had some help. If it had been a one-to-one showdown, I would have expected Will to prevail. But that's just speculation. We'll have to wait.'

Mum came back. 'That was Jim on the phone. He wanted to know if the two of you would be in this evening – he's bringing Mike back with him because Mike has an idea he wants to talk to you about. Mike is a research worker in Jim's lab.'

'Fine, do you know what the idea is about?' asked Robert.

'Yes. Mike has a suggestion for capturing St Caithrin.'

'Oh, well. I'm anxious to hear it.'

About an hour later, Jim arrived with Mike. They introduced themselves to Robert, explained what their research was about and the experience with

"Joshua Robertson" on the computer.

Mike went on: 'I noticed that the entries on the computer from Joshua Robertson followed an interesting pattern. They came in once or twice a day for four to seven days, and then there was a break of two to three days. I also noticed that the final entry before the break was sometimes a little ragged – perhaps a few errors and not so logical. It was almost as though Joshua was getting tired.'

'So you're saying he needed the break.'

'Exactly. Now why would that be? We've speculated for hours on this and the most likely explanation seems to be that the computer environment is tiring because it doesn't provide the energy sources for Joshua to keep going. He would normally occupy a biological environment – a human brain.'

'Are you saying that Joshua Robertson is a kind of travelling mind?'

'Yes. And I think that's exactly what St Caithrin is.'

'But St Caithrin is not like any other mind.'

'Agreed. Now, if you will allow me a little diversion into philosophy, I think I have an explanation for that. Have you read any of the works of Manfred Bloch?'

'No.'

'Well, he has been working all his life on trying to explain the concept of the "life force" or the "soul", whatever you like to call it, and whether there is such a thing. He believes that the mind is not just a function of the brain, but it's a kind of force that is allocated to us at birth and it develops with the brain. These forces are recycled when someone dies, so we all have a mind that has been used before. The unfortunate thing for human beings is that the mind cannot use any of its previous experiences because it has to start off again in a new, immature brain, so it forgets everything. But what if a mind could keep jumping from adult to adult? It could keep learning more and more provided the brain was good enough. I think that's what St Caithrin is. It has found a way of avoiding the renewal process and can keep jumping from adult to adult each time its host dies. It's a fugitive mind, and from what we know, it has been on the run at least since Victorian times.'

'So what do you think happens at the renewal process? Who is responsible for re-allocating minds?'

'I've no idea, and Bloch does not venture an opinion on that, but I don't think it matters much for our purposes. What we need to do is to force St Caithrin into the renewal process so that it is wiped clean. And here's how I think we can do it. We must somehow drive it into the computer. We know from Tom's visions that St Caithrin cannot leave its host at will, so it will be trapped once it's in the computer. There, it will tire and not have enough strength to get into another brain and it will have to submit to renewal. At least that's my hope.'

'That's brilliant thinking, Mike,' said Robert. 'I sincerely hope you are right. It's our best...in fact it's our only plan, so we must give it a try. Do you have any idea how we might achieve it?'

'We can't shift the computer, so we have to bring St Caithrin to it. Tom is our only hope of chasing St Caithrin out of its host. I can program the computer so that it simulates evil thoughts to attract St Caithrin. We just have to hope that it gets caught in the trap.'

'OK, so our first task is to find St Caithrin. Bringing it to the computer will be extremely difficult, but do we all agree that we should follow Mike's plan?' Robert asked. Everyone agreed.

Mike seemed a little embarrassed that everyone should agree with him so easily, but the fact was that they were desperate to find a way to deal with St Caithrin and this was the first realistic approach. 'Well, thanks for your attention. I'll have to be on my way now. See you all again soon.'

As soon as Mike left, Robert turned to Julia and Jim. 'I need to speak to Tom alone. We'll use his room if that's OK.'

'Of course, go ahead.' Julia looked a little puzzled.

Robert shut the door of Tom's room behind them and they sat down at the bed end, because the den end was a bit of a mess. 'Inspector Reynolds told me about Alexander Markov, but I assume you haven't mentioned it to your parents.'

'I haven't told them.'

'Inspector Reynolds gave me some very useful information. I'm afraid to say that I think St Caithrin is a much more formidable adversary now than it was in Will's day. As Markov, I believe he has got a huge network of criminals under his influence, and I mean under his influence, not just compatriots. I understand from Inspector Reynolds that some have been captured in the past and they have all behaved in the same way – under interrogation, they were completely uninformative. I suspect that's not down to loyalty because most criminals will give information to reduce their sentence. No, I think that Markov has programmed them to forget once they are captured. That's why I say they are under his influence.'

'Do you think that's true of all of them, including Mr Garrett?'

'Possibly not. He may depend on a few that he knows will be loyal and are sympathetic to his cause. Whether Mr Garrett is one of those I don't know.'

'Have you any idea how we can catch Markov?'

'Officially, the police are supposed to do that, but Markov could have left the country by now. Inspector Reynolds told me that Markov uses a lot of disguises and false identities, he can speak several languages and he has a range of accents that he uses. So if he's got unfinished business here, he may still be around. If you got close to him, you would know it was him, wouldn't you, Tom?'

'Definitely.'

'I think that will be our best means of tracking him down, but we can't just rely on chance. Inspector Reynolds is keeping tabs on Mr Garrett and he told me he thinks he knows one of the other members of the gang that you described. Let's hope they lead us to Markov.'

'Did he say who the other member of the gang was?'

'No, but he said he was not a known criminal. He's rich and a gambler; that's all he told me. He said he would call round this evening with a photograph so that you can identify him.'

'It could be ages before Markov comes out of hiding.'

'Perhaps, but if he's got unfinished business, he may want to conclude it quickly. He may even be working to a deadline.'

'How do you think we could get him into Dad's lab even if we did catch him?'

'That's a tricky one, as I said before. Perhaps it would be better not to attempt it. If you manage to drive St Caithrin out of Markov, the chances are we could get the new host to the lab a lot easier than we could manage Markov.'

'That's a good idea. But we'll still have to catch him in a situation where we've got a good chance of finding the new host. I could detect him if he's not too far away.'

'I can see we're going to need a lot of luck to get all this to fit together.'

'If I manage to chase St Caithrin out of Markov, Markov will probably die, like Mr Constable did.'

'Almost certainly.'

'Will that make me a murderer?'

'No. You mustn't think like that, Tom, otherwise you will weaken your own defences. The original Markov died when St Caithrin took him over. If you manage to rid us of St Caithrin, you will have done the world a great favour.'

'Yes, I suppose so. I must do it – I seem to have been chosen to do it and I can't let everyone down.'

'Tom, you must forget about letting anyone down. You must focus on St Caithrin and believe you can beat him.'

'I'll try.'

Robert put his hand on Tom's shoulder. 'I know you will. Come on, let's go downstairs.'

As Tom was walking downstairs, he got the feeling that he should go into the churchyard – another vision could be awaiting him. 'Robert, I feel that I might get a vision if I go to Magnus's grave.'

'Oh. Do you mind if I come too?'

'Not at all. Mum, Dad, we're just going into the churchyard.'

'OK. Don't be too long.'

Robert was interested to see what happened when Tom had one of his visions. He watched Tom sit down by the grave and close his eyes.

Tom found Will in a comfortable living room with a woman and a child. The child was a pretty girl of about six or seven sitting on Will's knee. The woman was slim and beautiful, with long dark hair that fell around her shoulders. She had a slender face, large brown eyes and a wide mouth with full lips that formed a broad smile to reveal an even set of teeth with a small gap in the middle. She handed Will a letter. 'Jeffrey sent us a letter. He is getting on well at school.'

'Oh, good. Just stand down for a moment, Jenny, please while I read Jeffrey's letter.'

'When is Jeffrey coming home?'

'Not until the end of term, dear.'

A second, older girl came into the room and Jenny ran across the room and went to play with her. Jeffrey's letter showed that he was enjoying his life at Fettersham School. 'See here, Mary; he's been selected for the rugby team even at his age.'

'Yes, I saw that. He's following in his father's footsteps.' Mary smiled at Will and her beautiful bright eyes gleamed. The two girls ran up to her and she hugged them. Tom thought she must be a very loving mother. 'Time for bed, now girls.' The two girls obediently went over to kiss their father and went upstairs with their mother.

Will finished reading the letter and placed it on his desk. He picked up a book, sat in an armchair and opened the book at the page marked by a leather bookmark. Tom struggled to read it but soon picked out the subject matter – witchcraft! Mary came downstairs, walked over to Will and sat down on the floor with her head on his knee. 'Why are you reading that awful book?'

'I don't know. I'm desperate, I suppose. I must try to understand what St Caithrin is but I'm at a loss.'

'It makes me shudder when you talk about that. Can't you just forget it?'

Will put his hand gently on the side of Mary's head, passed his fingers through her hair, and looked sympathetically into her eyes. 'I wish I could, but I have a strong feeling it will come back one day and I have to be prepared for it.'

'But it's been gone now for over a year.'

'I know, and I hope it doesn't come back. If I knew it had gone for good, I could relax, but I'm sure it hasn't. We agreed not to go to Ireland to follow Patrick Farrell but then we discovered that Farrell had committed suicide before he left, so it's probably still in England. My eternal dread is that it might get into someone with real power. With the kind of influence it can have over people, it could quickly recruit an army of followers. The results could be catastrophic – it might even start a world war.'

'Well, there's no sign of anything like that happening yet, so you're probably worrying over nothing.'

'I'm sorry, Mary, but you won't convince me that I can forget it. I know it's a burden for you as well as me, but I'm afraid it's part of my life. I can assure you I won't go looking for St Caithrin, but if it turns up, I have to do something about it.'

'Let's just hope it doesn't turn up, then.'

'Yes, let's hope so.'

Tom's vision ended at that point and he emerged from it with Robert watching over him. 'All over, then? You just looked as though you had gone to sleep for a few minutes. Shall we go inside and then you can tell us all what you saw?'

Tom and Robert went back into the house and Tom gave the details of his vision to Robert, Mum and Dad.

'So I wonder what the purpose of that vision was?' said Robert. 'Perhaps it was to give you an insight into how Will was obsessed by St Caithrin.'

'I think it must also have been to show Tom that Will had a loving family,' suggested Mum.

'Yes, of course. Rather like your own family, Tom. Is that the first time you have seen Will at home with his family?'

'Yes, and I still haven't seen Jeffrey. But we found out about him when we went to Fettersham School.'

'It could be that you won't see Jeffrey in your visions. I think you are expected to fill in the gaps with your own research.'

Chapter 26
The Warehouse

IT WAS NOT LONG AFTER TOM HAD finished describing his latest vision that there was a ring at the doorbell. 'That could be Inspector Reynolds,' said Dad as he went to answer the door. Sure enough, he came back in with the tall inspector.

'Hello again. I won't stay long – I just want to ask Tom to identify one of the suspects from a photograph.' He took out a photograph from his pocket and showed it to Tom. Dad looked over his shoulder.

'Yes, that's him. He drove a big silver car and he was smartly dressed.'

'Excellent. Your friend Frank was just as positive.'

'Who is it Inspector? I'm sure I've seen him before somewhere.'

'I'd rather not say if you don't mind, Professor. If you do remember who he is, I'd appreciate it if you would keep it to yourself for the time being.'

'Of course.'

'Well, that's all I came for. I'll be off now. Thanks very much, Tom.' Dad showed him out. When he came back in, his brow was furrowed in his attempt to remember the character in the photograph.

'I remember now! He came to a function at the University. I think he's a local dignitary of some sort.'

'The Inspector told me he was rich, if that's any help,' said Robert.

'Yes, of course – he's the chap who owns the garden centre chain – what's his name, Julia?'

'Wilmott's Garden Centres you mean?'

'Yes, that's him – Wilmott.'

'I wouldn't have a clue what he looks like.'

'Well, I don't think you'll find him at his garden centres any more. He's got plenty of employees to do the work for him while he's out enjoying himself. I remember he was rather arrogant – full of his own self-importance.'

Robert interjected: 'I think we should keep all this to ourselves, otherwise we could upset the Inspector's investigation.'

'Yes, you are right.'

'I wonder if Frank knows who he is?' asked Tom.

'If he doesn't it's probably best that you don't tell him.'

'I suppose so.'

The next day at school, Frank came up to Tom and said: 'Did Inspector Reynolds show you the picture of old Wilmott yesterday?'

'Oh, so you know who he is then?'

'Dad does jobs for him, so he knew him.'

'What does your dad do for him?'

'He makes garden furniture. People can get furniture made to their own design at Wilmott's. Dad makes the furniture from the plans and Wilmott pays him for it. Then he charges the customer double. Easy way to make money, don't you think?'

'Sure is. What does your dad think of Wilmott?'

'He doesn't like him. He says he only tolerates him because he gives him work.'

'My dad didn't like him, either. He met him once at a university function.'

'He's got a big place up near Thompson's Lake. Do you remember?'

'What, a house, you mean?'

'No, it looks like a big warehouse.'

'Oh, yes, I remember. Is that Wilmott's?'

'Yes. I've seen the sign from the road. You can't see the sign from the lake.'

'Do you fancy going fishing at the weekend? We could do a bit of spying at the same time.'

'Good idea.'

On Sunday, Dad gave Tom and Frank a lift to Thompson's Lake. They picked a spot where they could easily look over the fence and get a good view of Wilmott's warehouse.

'I don't think we've fished up here, before, have we?'

'No. That's probably because there aren't any fish at this end.'

'It does seem a bit dead, doesn't it? There's not much activity in the water.' Just at that moment, there was a big swirl in the water and a dorsal fin broke the surface only a few metres from the bank. 'Gosh! It must have heard me.'

'That's the only one we've seen. It looked big, though. I suppose we'll just have to be patient.' Patience wasn't one of Tom's strong points. 'I tell you what, why don't we take turns at watching the warehouse while the other one keeps an eye on the rods?'

'On one condition – you set up your bite alarm. I'm not sitting here watching your float and my rod.'

'OK. I'll set it up now.' Tom packed up his float rod and set up again with his ledger rod and his electronic bite alarm. The fence was a short distance away, so if the alarm went off, he could get back in a few seconds. He cast in, adjusted his line and then they had to agree who would do the first spying session.

Frank didn't want an argument. 'I don't mind if you do the first watch,' he said.

'OK.' Tom went over to the fence and stood on an old log to get a better view of the warehouse. 'It all looks very quiet.'

'Well it is Sunday, what do you expect?'

'The garden centres are open today, aren't they?'

'Yes, but I expect this is just a store. They probably supply all the garden centres from here and they're not likely to do deliveries on Sunday.'

'I suppose you're right.'

'Of course I'm right.'

They agreed on fifteen-minute sessions. Over two hours went by uneventfully, both in the warehouse and in the lake. Then Frank saw some activity outside the warehouse. Two men were approaching a side entrance on foot. They had left their white van outside the main gates, which were still locked. How did they get in? There were no other gates as far as Frank could see. They reached the door. One of them appeared to be struggling to unlock it. After a minute or so, the door opened and they went in.

'Tom, a couple of dodgy-looking characters have just gone into the warehouse.'

'Why dodgy?'

'Because they got in somehow without opening the gates. They've left their van outside. One of them is coming out now through the front entrance. He's got a big bunch of keys. He's trying to find the right one to open the gates. He can't find it. He's going back in. Do you think they are trying to steal stuff?'

'Could be. Should we call the police?'

'I don't think so. They could be perfectly innocent. I'm going over the fence to have a closer look. You look after the rods.'

'Hey! You can't do that!' Too late – Frank was over the fence and running towards the warehouse, dodging from tree to tree. Tom was annoyed. He decided to reel in their lines and go after Frank. When he got over the fence Frank was nowhere to be seen. Tom headed towards the side-door. One of the men came out with a bunch of keys, presumably a different bunch than the one he tried before. Tom hid behind a tree, watching the man try the keys on the bunch. Eventually, he found the one that opened the gate. He opened one of the large gates and then went to his van and drove it into the compound. He closed the gate but did not lock it. He drove the van up to the side entrance.

Tom couldn't get into the building through the side entrance now, so he got himself into a position to see the men loading their van. He did not have to wait long. The man who had opened the gates came out carrying a colourful cardboard box. He loaded it into the van and went back in. He soon came out carrying another one. This went on until he had filled the van. Tom struggled to see the writing on the boxes, but he was too far away. Then the second man came out and shut the door behind them. They drove out through the gates and stopped. The man with the bunch of keys came back in and locked the gate. He then went back into the building, presumably to return the keys. When he came back out, he went through a turnstile at the side of the main gate and joined his companion in the van. They drove off.

But where was Frank? Tom tried the side-door but it was locked. Then it opened suddenly. Tom jumped back. Frank peered round the door. 'Oh, you scared me!'

'I hope you reeled in before you left the rods.'

'Of course I did.'

'Did you see what they took?'

'No, did you?'

'Yes – hedge trimmers. Come in, I'll show you.'

'Don't they have a security guard here?'

'Seems not.'

Frank took Tom to the interior of the warehouse. There were stacks of garden tools all packed neatly along the huge shelves.

'They took them from here.' Frank pointed to a shelf full of hedge trimmers in their colourful boxes. 'But they didn't take the ones from the front. They moved them to one side and took the ones in the middle. Then they put the ones at the front back again. I wonder what's different about them?' Frank shifted some of the boxes at the front so that he could get at the ones in the middle. He pulled one out and opened the box. He almost dropped the contents in horror.

'That's not a hedge trimmer.' They were looking fearfully at a dull-green automatic rifle. It reminded them of the war films they had seen on television and the reports on terrorist activities on the news.

'What are we going to do now?'

'Put it back and get out of here. Then tell the police.'

They put the gun back in the box and began to replace the boxes at the front. 'What was that?'

'What?'

'I thought I heard something – there it is again. Somebody's opening the door! Quick – hide behind the boxes.' They crouched down in the space created by the men who had taken away the guns.

Someone had come in through the main door. The echo of the heavy door slamming shut resounded around the walls of the warehouse. Whoever had come in was wearing shoes with soles that squeaked on the tiled floor. The squeaks got closer and then they stopped. When they started up again, it was clear that the person was patrolling up and down the aisles. Frank was peeping between the boxes to try to see who it was. The squeaks were getting very close. Frank could see him now – he was wearing a uniform. He must be the security guard. But why had he only just arrived? Frank looked at his watch; it was exactly mid-day. The guard was now just on the other side of the boxes. He stopped. Could he hear them breathing? His shoes started squeaking again, but he wasn't moving away. Suddenly, a loud, scratchy voice made Tom and Frank start. It was someone calling the guard on his radio.

'Yes, I'm in the warehouse,' he replied.

'Can you check who signed in this morning and call me back?' said the scratchy voice.

'Will do.' The squeaky shoes strode across the floor away from Tom and Frank.

Frank turned to Tom and mimed: 'How do we get out?'

Tom shrugged his shoulders. He mimed back: 'We'll have to wait until he's gone.'

They heard the guard's voice from his office and then the scratchy voice said something. The squeaky shoes started up again, but they were moving up and down the other aisles this time. Then they gathered pace. The big metal door opened again and the footsteps changed to a crunching sound. He had gone outside. Frank and Tom nodded to each other. It was time to make a break. They carefully moved enough boxes to get out and then just as carefully placed them back. They moved quietly towards the side door. There was no sound from the guard. Then they heard him talking to someone outside. That was good – he was at the front of the warehouse. Frank gently opened the door and peeped out. It was all clear. They crept out into the open and closed the door. It made a loud click as it shut. They ran for the fence, dodging from tree to tree. Then they heard a dog barking furiously and some shouting. A dog appeared round the corner of the warehouse, dragging a security guard behind it. 'Stop or I'll set the dog on you!'

Tom and Frank stopped and stood rigidly, staring at the approaching dog and its handler. 'I'll do the talking,' said Frank.

'What are you two doing? Don't you know this is private property?'

'Sorry, but we're not doing any harm,' said Frank. 'We were fishing on the lake and we saw a strange animal go through the fence so we tried to follow it.'

The guard looked at the pair with a disbelieving stare. Fortunately, he had no idea that they had been inside the warehouse. 'Show me where you're fishing.' Frank took the guard to the fence and pointed to their fishing equipment. 'Right, give me your names, addresses and telephone numbers.' Frank and Tom gave him the information he wanted. He immediately took out his mobile phone and called one of the numbers. 'Hello, is that Mrs McGinty? I'm the security guard at Wilmott's. Do you have a son called Frank?' He paused while Frank's mum answered. 'He's currently trespassing on Wilmott's property.' Another pause. 'Yes, that's what he told me.' Another pause. 'No, not this time. Thank you.' The guard turned off his telephone and turned to Frank and Tom. 'Get back over that fence and don't let me see you in here ever again.'

The pair didn't need any more encouragement. They scrambled over the fence as quickly as they could with the dog barking furiously again.

'That was close. You're such a good liar, Frank. You should be an actor.'

'I hate lying, but I couldn't tell them the truth, could I?'

'Of course not, but we'll have to tell Inspector Reynolds the truth.'

Chapter 27

The Biker

INSPECTOR REYNOLDS DID NOT HAVE A CLUE where Alexander Markov was. He had set up an international alert, but so far there was no sign of him. Mr Garrett had stopped making phone calls in the sports store at school and Mr Wilmott was simply behaving like an honest garden centre owner. Tom and Frank brought him the first clue that something criminal was going on when they told him about the guns in the warehouse.

'Did you get a good look at the two men who collected the guns?'

'I did,' said Frank. 'They were quite close to me.'

'Could you have another go at the photo-fit?'

'Yes.' With a bit of help from Tom, Frank soon created likenesses of the men on the computer.

'Thanks very much, boys. This is the first break I've had for a while on this case. With a bit of luck, the guns might lead us to the villains.'

Tom and Frank left the police station and went down to the local newsagent to get a magazine. Just as they got there, a well-built man with a beard and long hair and wearing motor-cycle leathers came out of the shop. As he walked past, Tom froze. He watched the man put on his helmet and get on his bike. He memorized the registration number. Just before the motor cyclist drove off, he turned his head slowly and looked towards Tom. Tom quickly looked away and went into the shop.

'That was him! St Caithrin! I felt him.'

'Quick – let's go back and tell Inspector Reynolds.' They hurriedly bought the magazine and headed back to the police station. Inspector Reynolds had gone out.

'Is it important? I can get him on the radio,' said the duty officer.

'Yes, please, we need to speak to him urgently.'

'OK. What is it you need to tell him?'

'We've just seen Markov.'

'What! I'll get him at once.' Within a few seconds, he was speaking to Inspector Reynolds on the radio. 'He says go back home and he'll meet you there in an hour. Before you go, I'll take the details.' Tom gave him a description and the registration number of the bike.

The bus-stop for Drumbridge was about half a mile from the police station. 'A bus is due in eight minutes,' said Frank, looking at his watch. As they walked down the road, Tom felt uneasy. Then the reason became clear. The biker had driven slowly past them. They saw him pull into a side-road. As they approached the road, he came walking towards them. He stopped in front of them.

'Do as you are told and you won't get hurt,' he said. 'Get into the van.' Two men appeared behind Tom and Frank and pushed them into the back of a van that had just drawn up. The men got in behind the boys and shut the door.

One of the men behind the boys spoke to them in a rough, nasal voice: 'Now then, you will be still and be quiet, won't you?' He drew out a gun and poked the cold metal against Tom's cheek, then Frank's. They nodded, terrified.

Tom and Frank could not see where the van was taking them because the only windows were in the back door, and that was behind them. They dare not try to turn round. They drove for about twenty minutes, and then when the van stopped, they heard the driver get out and open a garage door. They drove into the garage, the engine stopped and they heard the garage door shut.

'OK. Safe to get out now,' said the man with the gun. The two men dragged Tom and Frank out of the van and through a door leading into a house. This was the first time that Tom and Frank had seen them clearly. The one with the gun had a broad face and a flat nose that had obviously been badly broken at some time. That explained his nasal voice. He was heavily-built but fairly short. He was dressed in jeans with a checked shirt open at the front and a white tee-shirt underneath. He had a massive buckle on his belt. The other man was taller, but not quite as broad as his companion. He had black, curly hair that hung over his eyes, and Tom and Frank were grateful that it did, for his eyes were frightening. When he pulled back his hair, he revealed deep eye-sockets with eyes that were nearly black, so that only the whites of his eyes in the shadows showed that he had any eyes at all. Like his companion, he wore jeans and a tee-shirt, but had a denim jacket on top.

They went through the kitchen and into a room that faced on to the back garden. Waiting for them was the biker. He was no longer in leathers but was dressed in a black casual shirt and jeans. In spite of the long hair and beard, Tom could see that he was the same man he had seen at the house in Dean Avenue – Alexander Markov. He could also feel the overwhelming presence of evil. Now that Tom was close to him, he saw how his small blue eyes pointed downward in the middle, leading to his long, slender nose.

'OK, you can leave us now.' Markov signalled to the man with the gun to leave the room. 'And shut the door behind you.' He sat down in a leather armchair and indicated to the boys to sit down in similar chairs on the other side of the long coffee-table. On the table were a bowl of fruit and a large vase of fresh flowers. He leaned forward and sat on the edge of the armchair. 'So, what have you two been up to, then?' His voice was slow and musical, as though he was reading a story to a group of children. There was no trace of an American accent, but they knew that he could imitate many accents. 'You can speak now, you know. You're not with those nasty men any more.' His manner was not at all threatening; he seemed almost kindly, but Tom and Frank knew it must be an illusion that he wanted to create.

Tom spoke first. He needed to say something to stop himself trying to probe Markov's mind. 'We were just going home. Why have you brought us here? The police will be looking for us soon.'

'Yes, I'm sure, but they won't find you. I don't think you'll be going home just yet, but don't worry – you're safe with me. Now, tell me what you said to that stupid policeman, Reynolds.'

'I don't know what you mean. Who are you, anyway?'

'OK. Perhaps I'll start by asking you the same question. What are your names?'

'You won't get us to tell you anything.'

'Oh, is that so, Frank McGinty?'

'How do you know my name?'

'You just told me. And your friend's name is Tom Merrington.'

'Don't think it, Frank,' said Tom. 'Think of something else.'

'Oh, so you understand, do you, Tom? Why is that?' He tried to probe Tom's mind, but Tom blocked out his attack. 'Well, now, who taught you that? It's no use, you know. I'll get through if I try a bit harder.'

'Don't kid yourself.' Tom was getting angry and he was finding it hard to avoid making an all-out attack, but he knew it would be foolish under these circumstances. He just had to defend.

'You have a good spirit. I could use someone like you.'

'Never! I'll not help you.'

'You think you have a choice? We'll see about that. But for the moment, I'll spare you the pain. I'm feeling a little tired.'

Markov turned his attention to Frank. He knew it would be much easier to probe Frank's mind and get the answers he wanted. Poor Frank was no match for him. Markov forced images of Inspector Reynolds into his mind and he soon discovered that they had planned to meet up with the inspector. Tom was getting more and more angry. He decided to attempt to divert Markov by putting some false thoughts into his mind. Markov was getting irritated, then he realized what was happening and he launched a fierce attack on Tom. Tom was shocked at the strength of the attack. This was much worse than anything Matthew Montgomery had thrown at him. It felt like a pair of immensely strong hands were around his throat, choking him. He couldn't fight back because he was in such a panic. He would not last much longer without air – he was about to die, but then suddenly he was gulping air into his lungs. What had happened? Markov was lying on the floor with shards of a vase all around him, his head soaked and flowers stuck in his hair. Frank had cracked it on his head when he turned on Tom.

'Come on, we've got to get out of here.' Frank went to the door to the back garden. It was locked. He tried a window. It was stiff, but after a couple of heaves, it opened and they were able to get out. Just as they tumbled into the garden, the guards burst into the room. One attended to Markov while the other went after Frank and Tom. The only way out was to scramble over the fences into the neighbouring back gardens until they could find an exit. They went through six or more gardens before Frank spotted an opportunity.

'Quick, in here,' he said. A back door to one of the houses was open. They ran into the room and closed the door as quietly as they could. A frightened woman holding a baby stared at them.

'What are you doing? Get out of my house!' Frank and Tom, crouched down behind an armchair, were panting with the effort of escaping. Tom held his finger to his lips to indicate to the woman to be quiet. She looked puzzled but she remained quiet. She stood up when she saw the guard run through her garden. He stopped to look at her and ran on into the next garden. 'He's gone. Now do you mind telling me what you are doing?'

'Sorry, ma'am, but we were kidnapped and we escaped.'

'Kidnapped?'

'Yes, and we were taken to a house just down the road. Could you tell us where we are, please?'

'This is Manley Drive.'

'In Walchester?'

'Yes.'

'Could I make a phone call to my mother please? She's expecting us home.'

'Go ahead. The phone's over there.' She pointed to the corner of the room. Tom ran over and dialled his home number.

'Mum, it's Tom. We're OK. We're at…what number is this house, please?'

'Ninety-seven.'

'Number ninety-seven, Manley Drive, Walchester. Is Inspector Reynolds there yet? OK, thanks.' He put the phone down. 'Robert's coming to pick us up. Inspector Reynolds hasn't arrived yet.' He walked over to Frank. 'Thanks for saving me. You were really brave.'

Frank had a big grin on his face. 'It was instinct really. I grabbed the nearest heavy object and hit him as hard as I could. He did look comical lying on the floor with flowers in his hair, didn't he?'

'Yes, they didn't suit him at all.' They both laughed at the image in their minds of the unconscious Markov.

It took Robert about thirty minutes to get there. He thanked the lady for allowing Tom and Frank to hide and then rushed the two boys into the car. As they drove home, Robert nervously watched the mirror in case they were being followed.

'Did you get the number of the house?'

'No, but it was about six doors down.'

'Which direction?'

'Behind us.'

'That would be about eighty-five or thereabouts.'

When they arrived back, Inspector Reynolds was waiting for them. He already had a car in the vicinity and he called the officers in the car to keep watch on eighty-five, Manley Drive and neighbouring houses.

'You were lucky. Are you sure it was Markov?'

'Positive,' said Tom.

'I expect the hair and beard were false, so he has probably changed his disguise by now. Do you think you could give us descriptions of Markov's accomplices?'

'We can describe two of them, but we didn't really get a good view of the driver,' said Tom. He and Frank gave him their descriptions, and they had nearly finished when Inspector Reynolds's mobile telephone rang. He went out of the room and they could hear him conversing with the caller. A few minutes later, he came back into the room.

'It seems they got away again. The neighbours said they saw a van drive away in the last hour from number eighty-three, Manley Drive. The house is now empty. That was obviously the house they were in – an elderly couple live in number eighty-five. We've got descriptions of the men from the neighbours and they match Tom's and Frank's. Unfortunately, nobody could tell us the registration number of the van.'

'But at least we know Markov hasn't left the district, not yet anyway,' said Robert. 'He could have some unfinished business here.'

'I think that's very likely. Well, I've got to report back so I'll be off. Thanks again for all your help. I'll see myself out.' Inspector Reynolds left and they heard the front door shut behind him.

Tom turned to Robert. 'Robert, I'm scared. Markov was much more powerful than I expected and I can't see how I can defeat him.'

Robert smiled at Tom and said: 'Don't worry about it. He caught you off guard. When the time comes you'll know what to do.'

'But even if I had been ready for his attack, I don't think I could have stopped it.'

'But you blocked him when he tried to probe your mind.'

'Yes, but he said he would get through if he tried a bit harder.'

'Then why didn't he? Why did he pick on Frank? He gave up on you because he knew he wouldn't be able to get through.'

Tom gave a wry smile. 'You think so?'

'Of course, it's obvious.'

Tom looked at Frank. 'If it wasn't for Frank, I might not have been here. He was the real hero.'

'But if you hadn't distracted Markov, we wouldn't have got away,' said Frank.

'I suppose so,' said Tom, reluctantly.

'Look, Tom, think of it this way,' said Robert. 'You escaped from Markov when he tried to keep you captive and now he's on the run. He didn't find out anything about what we know about him, so he is clearly the loser in this little episode.'

'Robert's absolutely right,' interrupted Mum. 'You should be proud of what you did.'

Tom and Frank looked at each other and the grins on their faces meant that they realized she was right.

But Tom was still worried. The force of Markov's attack was much greater than he had expected. The attack that Will experienced was mild in comparison, so St Caithrin must have increased its powers since Will's time. And what if it had also increased its power to project objects? Tom had felt reasonably comfortable that he could cope with that, but now he was not so sure. Robert had done his best to look on the bright side, but Tom knew that he was not capable of beating St Caithrin in a proper duel.

Chapter 28

Will Faces St Caithrin Again

IT HAD BEEN SEVERAL WEEKS SINCE TOM'S last vision. Then, one evening when Tom and Frank were talking to Mr Jake in the churchyard, Tom felt the urge to go and sit by Magnus's grave. He made signs to Frank that they needed to end the conversation. They made an excuse and went over to the grave. Tom sat down and immediately went into a trance as Frank watched.

Will was with Max Weissman and Bernard Simmonds again, and they both looked considerably older than the last time he had seen them. They seemed to be in a bedroom. It was small, with a single bed and a large sash window. Against one wall was an ugly dressing-table with two drawers and an oval mirror. Standing on it, at one end, was a large blue and white bowl and matching jug. Bernard was sitting on the bed, Max was sitting in a small armchair and Will was perched on a low stool, presumably the one that went with the dressing-table. Tom seemed to have arrived in the middle of a conversation. Max was talking.

'Let's worry about how we are going to deal with him when Will has confirmed it's really him.'

'That's just a formality,' said Bernard. 'I'm certain it's him.'

'We're only putting off the inevitable,' said Will. 'We must have a plan. We went through all the problems before and we didn't come up with a solution. Removing St Caithrin from its host doesn't solve the problem. We have to prevent it from taking on another host. We suspect it needs a suitable host to be in the vicinity, but we're not really sure about its range. We don't know how long it can survive outside a host. If I could get Andreyev to a remote place where we can be sure there are no other human beings for miles around, I think I could do it, provided I could prevent it from transferring to me. What are our chances of achieving that?'

'We could kidnap him,' suggested Bernard.

'But Bernard, he's always accompanied by two giant bodyguards. How on earth could we get past them?' said Max.

'I don't know, but there must be a way.'

'To be fair, Max, I agree with Bernard that our only chance is to capture him and take him to a remote place. We do at least have the means of sedating him at our disposal. You are right that we have no hope of getting past the bodyguards – we must think of some way of getting him away from them. Any ideas?'

Both Max and Bernard looked blank. Then Bernard spoke. 'I believe he's going to visit some coal mines in the north. There's more chance of finding a remote spot in the north than there is here in London.'

'Yes, that's a start, but we still have to find a way of capturing him.'

'I wonder if we could somehow make him ill so that he needs the attentions of a doctor, and conveniently one of us would be nearby. We could say that we have to take him to hospital, but instead we could take him out into the countryside.'

'That might work, but how do we make him ill in the first place?'

'An accident, perhaps?'

'Too risky. He might be badly injured.'

'Could we put something in his food?'

'How do we get access to his food?'

Will broke into the exchange between Max and Bernard. 'Wait a minute; we're not making progress here. Perhaps we should start by finding out where and when he is going to be in the north. He's only here for two weeks, I believe.'

'That's right, said Bernard. 'He's going to the north early next week and his ship leaves Newcastle on Friday. I'll find out exactly where he is going.'

'Look at the time!' exclaimed Will. We must go otherwise we'll miss him.'

They left the room in a hurry, ran down three flights of stairs and entered what seemed to be a hotel foyer. They rushed through the entrance and across the road to a bigger, but not particularly smart, hotel. A crowd had gathered outside the entrance, and police were keeping them back. A carriage was waiting in the road.

'We're not too late, thankfully.'

After a few minutes, a small party of people came out of the hotel. Three burly men walked in a line and the one in the middle, presumably Andreyev, was smiling and waving to the crowd, who were applauding him. There were a few people who shouted obscenities at him and told him he wasn't welcome. Will edged forward to get as close to him as he could. There was a moment when Andreyev stopped smiling and stopped in his tracks. He looked straight at Will and then walked on as though nothing had happened. He stepped into the carriage followed by his two bodyguards. As the carriage moved off, the crowd began to disperse. Will came back to Bernard and Max.

'You were right, Bernard. It's St Caithrin; no doubt about it.'

'Satisfied now, Max?' said Bernard.

Will continued: 'Unfortunately, I think he recognized me, so I don't think we'll be able to take him by surprise. I'll have to keep a low profile until we get Andreyev into the countryside.'

Tom's vision broke off at this point. He assumed that Andreyev was a foreign, probably Russian, visitor of some importance and somehow Bernard had discovered that he was St Caithrin's host.

'Well, are you going to tell me what it was about?' asked Frank.

'Yes, of course. Let's go back into the house.'

Mum, Dad and Robert were in the lounge when Tom and Frank walked in. 'Tom's had another vision,' Frank blurted out. They all turned to face Tom.

'Will's found St Caithrin again. It's in someone called Andreyev and they're planning to kidnap him and take him to a remote part of the country where Will can drive him out of Andreyev and he won't have another host available.'

'Apart from Will, of course,' Robert added.

'Yes, but Will thinks he can resist him.'

'What's this Andreyev like? Is he Russian?'

'I think he must be Russian. He's visiting England for two weeks. I saw him come out of a hotel. There was a crowd waiting for him and most of them applauded him, but some yelled abuse at him.'

'What did he look like?'

'He was quite young, big and powerful.'

'That's interesting,' said Robert. 'Have you noticed that St Caithrin always picks powerful men as its hosts? Never small men and never women - I think it must want to have the capacity to use physical force if necessary.'

'Markov is pretty powerful, but he can't take a big vase smashed over his head! Frank was pleased about getting the better of him.'

'How are they going to capture Andreyev?' asked Dad.

'They're not sure. They settled on following him to the north of England, where they think they've got a better chance of getting him to a remote spot. Max suggested that they might somehow make him ill when he's on his tour so that he needs the attention of a doctor and they can pretend they're taking him to hospital when they're really taking him into the countryside. Not that it matters. They must fail anyway.'

'Yes, of course they must, otherwise St Caithrin wouldn't be around today,' Dad said.

Tom was expecting his next vision to come soon and it came the next day. Will was with Max and Bernard again but this time they were outside. A bitterly cold wind was blowing and they were standing outside the high fence by a colliery entrance. They were with a crowd of other people, including newspaper reporters, who were all shuffling around, occasionally stamping their feet to keep warm. This was presumably the industrial north and, from the behaviour of the crowd, Andreyev was inside the colliery and soon to come out. Sure enough, a group of people could be seen behind the wire fence moving towards the entrance. When they came out, the newspaper reporters wanted to interview Andreyev. He could not speak English, but an interpreter translated his comments to the reporters. Meanwhile, Will had moved to the back of the crowd and Max and Bernard had moved to the front. Suddenly, a group of people at the back started yelling abuse at Andreyev and at the same time, they threw stones and bricks at him. Some hit reporters, one hit a bodyguard full in the face, but it had no effect on him. Then a brick caught Andreyev on the temple and he sank to the ground. What a stroke of luck! This was not what Max had intended, but he seized the opportunity and rushed forward shouting: 'I'm a doctor, stand back!'

While the police were grappling with the protestors, Max was examining Andreyev, who was out cold. 'We need a carriage to take him to the hospital,' explained Max to the interpreter, who explained it in Russian to the bodyguards and then pointed to the carriage that was already waiting for Andreyev. By this time, Bernard had moved in to assist Max. They carried Andreyev carefully to the carriage and placed him flat on the seat. There was no room inside for the two bodyguards, so they rode on the outside at the back. Max shouted through the window for the driver to move off. Will's face grinned back at him! He had successfully bribed the driver to let him take his place. They set off at a cracking pace.

As they approached the outskirts of the town, Will brought the horses to a halt. There was a lot of shouting coming from inside the carriage. The two bodyguards stepped down to see what was going on, but as soon as they did, Will whipped the horses into a gallop. The bemused bodyguards were left standing in the road, bellowing in Russian at the disappearing carriage. Will, Max and Bernard had captured Andreyev and they were heading for the desolate moors!

Inside the carriage, Max had sedated Andreyev with an injection because he had started to regain consciousness. He was watching him carefully, ready to give another injection if necessary. They were now galloping along a track that ran through the moors. Max shouted at Will: 'How much further are we going?'

'Nearly there – another two minutes.'

Max examined Andreyev and decided not to give him another injection. Will wanted his mind to be clear, so he would have to wait for him to regain full consciousness.

The carriage slowed down and Will brought the panting horses to a halt. He pulled on the brake and jumped down. Bernard had already opened the door and he and Max were lifting Andreyev out. They placed him on the ground. All around them, the rolling hills of the moors seemed to stretch out endlessly. But the biting wind was howling even more out here so they had to put a blanket over Andreyev.

'Right, you two take the carriage and get at least half a mile from here. I'll wait for Andreyev to recover and then I'll be able to tackle St Caithrin.'

'Good luck,' said Max. Bernard took the reins and Max got up beside him. They trotted off gently and soon they had disappeared over the brow of the hill.

This was the moment that Will had planned for. He was alone with St Caithrin and its host. Would the plan work? Could he expel St Caithrin from Andreyev? He had done it once before with Marmaduke Constable and he felt he could do it again. If he did expel it, would it go forever, unable to find a host?

Andreyev was stirring. Will cradled his head in his arm and spoke to him. Soon, Andreyev was muttering something in Russian. His eyes opened and he looked up at Will. His eyes moved in all directions, and he said something else, more forcefully this time. He tried to sit up and Will helped him. He held his head and said something in Russian that must have been 'Oh, my head, what happened?'

Will spoke to him in English, but he looked blank. Then he looked at Will with an expression that suggested he had recognized him. He stood up, pointed to Will and shouted something at him angrily. The time had come. Will started his attack by forcing some happy thoughts into his mind. At first, Andreyev was passive, probably because he had not fully recovered, but Will's attack had a stimulating effect. The images in Will's mind changed dramatically to scenes of violence and bloodshed, but they did not last long. Will was holding on to pleasant thoughts and driving them into Andreyev. This time, St Caithrin did not have any objects to project at Will and Andreyev was getting angry. Will was getting the better of St Caithrin, but it was far from over. Andreyev was tottering about, but he summoned his reserves of energy and with an almighty roar, he launched himself at Will. Will drew back and avoided his lunge, but it was difficult to keep his focus on Andreyev's mind. Before he had regained control, Andreyev had lunged again and this time, he got hold of Will's coat. He pulled Will towards him and wrapped his arm around

Will's neck and pulled him to the ground. Will felt St Caithrin strengthening the attack on his mind as Andreyev pressed hard on his throat, but somehow he still managed to resist. He pushed his hand into Andreyev's face and managed to get him to release his grip on his throat by poking his fingers in his eyes. But Andreyev was extremely strong and considerably bigger than Will. He turned Will over and held his face down into the prickly gorse. Will arched his back and toppled Andreyev to one side, but Andreyev got up quickly and pressed his knee into Will's chest. As Will was struggling to free himself from Andreyev's great weight, he saw a huge fist come down from above and the day turned to night.

Light was returning. Will could hear distant voices. 'He's coming round. Will, can you hear me?'

Will opened his eyes and saw Bernard and Max looking down at him. He was still lying on the moor. 'What happened to Andreyev?'

'We saw him staggering across the moor, so we thought you might be in trouble. Do you remember what happened?'

'I was breaking down St Caithrin, but Andreyev attacked me and knocked me out. He was too strong. I didn't allow for that.'

'So, we failed at the last hurdle. We're in big trouble now that he knows what we are up to.'

'I'm not giving up. I could have done it if I'd thought of tying Andreyev up before he regained consciousness. But as you say, Max, he's probably going to come after us now. If he uses force, we're no match for him and his two bodyguards.'

'That's what bothers me. I can't see what else we can do. I suggest we try to keep out of his way.'

'As I said, Max, I'm not giving up now that we've got this far. If they come after us, we'll have to turn it into an opportunity somehow.'

'That's a very risky strategy, Will.'

'I know, but it's all we have. You two should keep out of the way; I'll face him on my own.'

'No you won't. We'll stick together,' said Bernard.

'I'm grateful for your loyalty. Thanks.'

Tom went back through the garden gate and into the house to tell everyone what he had seen. It had been a daring plan and it had nearly come off.

'Now we know why St Caithrin always picks physically powerful men as his hosts,' said Robert.

That was not what Tom wanted to hear. Not only was St Caithrin much stronger now than he expected, but Markov was physically big and strong, so the odds were heavily weighted against him.

Chapter 29
The Raid on Wilmott's

'I FOUND SOME INFORMATION ON YOUR FRIEND Andreyev today, Tom.' Dad had just arrived home. He plunged his hand in his briefcase and pulled out a small scrap of paper. 'Here you are: Alexei Andreyev, political reformer and militant figure who had a reputation for reckless disregard of authority. He was a violent man who was killed in 1913 in an abortive attempt to assassinate the Tsar. He came from a working-class background and tirelessly supported the rights of the working man. He has been recognized as a significant figure in sowing the seeds of discontent that ultimately led to the revolution in 1917.'

'That's him all right. I wonder what happened to St Caithrin when he died?'

'Presumably he occupied another Russian. Didn't Inspector Reynolds say that Markov's parents came from Russia to settle in America?'

'I think he did. That would fit if St Caithrin passed from father to son.'

'Perhaps St Caithrin thought it might achieve more in America,' suggested Robert.

'Just what do you think it's trying to achieve?' asked Tom.

'I don't know. Take over the world perhaps?'

'It must be getting a bit frustrated by now if that's the case,' said Dad.

'I don't know that we'll ever find out what it's trying to achieve.'

Mum came into the room. 'Have you seen the paper? The police made a raid on Wilmott's warehouse and seized hundreds of weapons. Mr Wilmott is in custody and all his Garden Centres are closed until the police have searched them.' She handed the paper to Dad.

'They had a special armed force from London to raid the warehouse. I didn't think that Inspector Reynolds would be handling it on his own. When they're after an international criminal like Markov, they're bound to have the heavies on the case; they're just keeping a low profile, that's all. You don't get a mention, I'm afraid, Tom. But it was your observation that led them to the arms in the first place.'

'Frank did most of it.'

Robert was thoughtful. 'I'm surprised they raided the place so soon. I would have thought they would want to track the weapons to find out who was receiving them.'

'Perhaps they know already, but it doesn't say anything about it in the paper. It says here that the police would not comment when they were asked whether the weapons were intended to be used for terrorism. Now that they've seized the weapons, it could be the end of Markov's business here. He might disappear now.'

'But we don't know whether he has another store of weapons somewhere.'

'We saw two men take some away from the warehouse,' said Tom.

'Exactly. This haul could be just the tip of the iceberg.'

Tom went to give Frank a call on the telephone. 'Frank, have you read about the raid on Wilmott's warehouse in the paper?'

'Dad's still reading it, but he knows more than what's in the paper anyway. Apparently, they've arrested a few other people as well as Wilmott. Mr Garrett is one of them!'

'Really!'

'Yes, he was caught red-handed with other members of the gang. The police were watching them load the guns into a van. Dad says he thinks they've been sending policemen fishing to keep an eye on the place since we told them about the guns.'

'I don't suppose they caught Markov, did they?'

'Wishful thinking? No, he wasn't there. They arrested three men, including Mr Garrett, and later went to Wilmott's house and arrested him.'

'Anything else you know that I don't?'

'I don't think so. Have you finished your homework?'

'I haven't started it yet. Why?'

'I just thought I'd come round and get the details of your last vision to write up.'

'Oh, yes. Shall I come round to you when I've finished my homework?'

'OK. See you then.'

Mr McGinty was working in the front garden when Tom arrived. 'Hello, Tom. It's good to see you again. Come to see Frank, have you?'

'Yes, is he in his room?'

'I think so. You know the way – go on up. The front door's open.'

Tom pushed open the front door and ran up the stairs to Frank's room.

'That was quick. Didn't you have much homework?'

'Dad helped, so I got all the urgent stuff done quickly. I've still got another day to do the rest.'

Tom went through all the details of his last vision while Frank made notes and asked a few questions along the way.

'That's a bit of a worry, isn't it?

'What is?'

'Well, if Markov wants to use physical force against you, you won't be able to stand up to him. He's a lot bigger than you.'

'Yes, I know, you don't have to remind me. There's one big advantage he's got over me – he doesn't care if I die, but for me to get St Caithrin to leave him when the time and place are right, he must stay alive.'

'That's true, it is a big advantage.'

Tom looked glum. 'In spite of what Robert said, I'm not confident that I can beat him. He nearly choked me without touching me and I could do nothing about it. I would have been dead if you hadn't saved me.'

'I doubt it. You would have been able to fight back, like Will did. You didn't get a chance because I hit him as soon as he turned away from me.'

'I don't think I could have fought back.'

'Don't tell yourself that you're not strong enough. Will did it and you can do what Will did.'

'You're right – I must try to be positive. If I believe I can do it, then I've got a better chance of succeeding. Even if I die, I want to know that I tried my best.'

Frank wasn't sure what to say to that, but in the end he said: 'You won't die until you're an old man.'

The next edition of the newspaper gave the names and photographs of the men arrested at Wilmott's. Mr Garrett was one of them, as Frank said, but the other two were unfamiliar. The men who were with Markov in the van were still at large. The police were still not saying what they thought the weapons were for, just that investigations were ongoing at an international level.

This was quite a big event in Walchester. Nothing of any international significance had happened since the President of the United States had come to visit the nearby US Air Force base about twenty years ago. Tom and Frank had been told by the Headmaster to keep quiet about Mr Garrett because the whole school was buzzing with gossip. Terry Paterson gave Tom and Frank the odd wink when they overheard people gossiping. He had received the same instructions from the Headmaster. Amanda Smithers had kept everyone informed about what was going on at Mr Garrett's house. Poor Mrs Garrett was afraid to leave her house because newspaper reporters were ready to pounce and bombard her with questions about her husband.

Tom and Frank were finding it all a bit tiresome, because they knew that Mr Garrett was just one of Markov's many accomplices. If only people in Walchester knew that they had one of the most dangerous criminals in the world in their midst, they would really worry. The police had done an excellent job of keeping it quiet, but for how long? Journalists were adept at uncovering secrets. What if they discovered that Tom and Frank were involved? Would they be hounding them? Were there any weak links where the journalists could pick up clues? Mrs Garrett? How much did she know? Amanda Smithers? She didn't know about Markov. Mrs Grimley? She was too smart and she didn't actually know about Markov, but she had drawn her own conclusions. What about the police? Lots of them must know but they were professionals and they should be discreet. Terry Paterson? No, he was trustworthy. The Headmaster? Surely not. Mr McGinty? He was a bit of a gossip, but he would want to protect Frank, so he would keep quiet. There were actually a lot of people who had the knowledge that could spark a panic and any of them could have told someone else who might talk to a journalist. It was a worry, but for now, the secret was safe.

Tom was having a difficult time at school. He was worrying so much about facing St Caithrin that his school work was suffering. Mum and Dad were sympathetic and they helped him with his homework to ease the burden, but they insisted that when all this was over, that was the end of their help. Tom was grateful to have such understanding parents. He also got help from Robert occasionally. It was convenient to have three clever people in the house, but they could not be with him at school. Mrs Parkin had spotted his lack of concentration and had taken him aside after a geography lesson to try to find out what his problem was.

'Tom, you seem to be miles away during geography and I've heard from other teachers that it's been the same in their classes. What's bothering you? Can I help?'

'Thank you, Mrs Parkin. There is something that's bothering me, but I'm afraid I can't tell you what it is. It's personal.'

'Are you having problems at home? Would it help if I spoke to your parents?'

'It's nothing like that.'

'Do they know what it is?'

'Yes.'

'Are they doing anything about it?'

'As much as they can.'

'Is there anyone else who could help? The Headmaster perhaps.'

'Not unless he's willing to let me off school.'

'That's not possible without a good reason and if you can't tell us, there's nothing we can do. Look, the last thing we want is for you to have a breakdown and then you will be off school whether you like it or not.'

'I won't break down Mrs Parkin. I mustn't.'

Mrs Parkin looked puzzled at that response. 'I hope not. If there's nothing I can do, we'll have to leave it, but please come and speak to me any time you like. I'm willing to help.'

'Thank you very much, Mrs Parkin. I'll remember that.'

Tom was grateful that Mrs Parkin had offered to help, and he liked her a lot, but he knew she could do nothing for him. In classes, he noticed that she had been careful not to put too much pressure on him. Perhaps she might ask the other teachers to do the same. That would be a help. In the meantime, his education was suffering. He promised himself that he would work doubly hard when all this was over, that is, if he was still alive.

Chapter 30

Will Tries Once More

Tom was desperately tired when he came home from school. He felt as though he had a bee in his head, passing the gossip from flower to flower. Couldn't they talk about football instead of Wilmott and Garrett? He dragged himself out through the rickety gate and into the churchyard. At last he felt some relief. It was a different world here. He was ready for his next vision and he sat down by Magnus's grave and relaxed.

Will, Max and Bernard were in what appeared to be another hotel room. Will was pacing around.

'I wonder where Andreyev is now? It must have taken a while for him to get back from the moors on foot.'

Bernard was looking out of the window. 'Well, he made it.'

'What do you mean?'

'Take a look.'

They both looked through the window. There, sitting nonchalantly on a bench in the park, was Andreyev. His bodyguards were nowhere to be seen.

Max looked at Will. 'Don't – it must be a trap.'

'I must, Max. It's our only chance. Look – the street is deserted. It's too early for most people. I'm going.'

'Don't be a fool, Will. It's just what he wants you to do.'

'I nearly had him last time. I'm sure I can deal with St Caithrin quickly now. You just keep an eye on what's going on from here.'

Max and Bernard looked at each other. Bernard shrugged his shoulders in resignation. 'I'll go down to the lounge and watch from there so that I can get to you quickly if necessary. Max – you stay here.'

'If you say so.'

'Good. Wish me luck.'

'They both hugged Will and wished him luck. Will and Bernard left Max in the room staring helplessly out of the window.

Will stepped out of the hotel front door and Andreyev saw him immediately. He stood up and walked into the park while maintaining eye contact with Will. Will moved quickly. He began his attack as soon as he was within range. Tom had not known Will to launch such a powerful attack before. He was obviously going all out to finish it quickly. Andreyev's expression changed as soon as Will's attack began. He was just defending and he looked to be in pain but he was snarling with aggression. A knife appeared out of his pocket and flew at Will. Will dodged it and it landed harmlessly on the grass. Then another, and another, but each time Will dodged successfully and each time it weakened St Caithrin a little more. Andreyev appeared to be nearly exhausted and started tottering again. Will knew from experience this was not necessarily a good sign, and sure enough, Andreyev lunged at him. But Will was ready this time. He skipped nimbly away from Andreyev's clutches, but the big man turned and kept coming at him, grunting like an animal, his face full of hatred. Andreyev looked to be almost finished, but Will was getting tired, and feared that Andreyev's physical superiority would beat him again. But St Caithrin was losing its hold and Will felt that one last push would drive it out. Then, just as he was about to launch a big assault, he felt a searing pain in his back that made him loosen his control over St Caithrin. He dared not turn around to see where it had come from because he had to keep focusing on Andreyev. He stumbled to one side to avoid the attacker, but it happened again in another part of his back, and again. He started to choke and he could not focus on Andreyev any more. Through the mist, he saw Andreyev's huge form closing in on him and he could do nothing about it. He had lost control over St Caithrin. His energy was seeping away. The mist turned to darkness.

'He's barely alive – he's lost so much blood.'

'Bernard – is that you?'

'Yes, we're here.'

'What was that pain in my back?'

'You were stabbed several times by Andreyev's bodyguards.'

'Am I dying?'

'You've lost a lot of blood.'

Will coughed and felt warm liquid in his mouth. He was coughing up blood. He knew that his lungs were damaged. 'There's nothing you can do, Bernard. Tell Mary and the children that I had to try. I'm sorry I failed. Somebody must try again, but not either of you, please.'

There was a pause in the vision – Will must have passed out. Then the dim image of Bernard appeared again. 'You've been great friends and I'm so proud of what we achieved together.' Bernard's face was a blur, but the glistening stream of tears running down his cheeks stood out like rivers in a landscape. 'We did our best, don't forget that. And we nearly made it. Are you still there Bernard, Max?' They answered, but their voices seemed a long way away. He could not hear what they said, but they were getting agitated and they seemed to be shouting. Their voices faded into the far distance and it went quiet until a new sound developed – it was the chanting he had heard after the fire. This time, he could not resist. He had to submit.

When Tom awoke from his vision, he found himself crying and shouting. He couldn't stop himself. He was making such a terrible noise that Mrs Bratherstone came to see what was wrong with him. Her appearance brought him back to reality and he began to calm down.

'It's all right, Mrs Bratherstone. I must have nodded off and I had a nightmare. I'll be OK in a minute.'

'Do you want me to call your mother?'

'No, there's no need. Just give me a few minutes.'

'Here, I've got some tea in a flask. Would you like some?'

'Yes, please.'

She poured some of her tea into the cup of her flask. Tom took it gratefully in two hands and held it to his lips. He was huddled in a ball against the grave.

'You look cold. When you've had your tea, go back indoors.'

'I will, Mrs Bratherstone.' He drank the tea greedily and handed her the cup. 'Thanks. You're very kind.' He hauled himself up and felt a bit unsteady on his feet. He pulled out his handkerchief and blew his nose loudly. He smiled at Mrs Bratherstone and went back through the garden gate. She watched him all the way. He waved to her as he went in.

'Are you OK, Tom?' asked Mum.

Without answering her question, he said: 'I think I've had my last vision. Will's dead.'

Mum looked sad, but relieved. 'It had to happen. How did he die?'

'He was stabbed by Andreyev's bodyguards. But he almost beat St Caithrin. He was a real hero. He said that someone else has to try to rid us of St Caithrin, so I suppose that must be me. Will came so close – a few more minutes and he would have done it. If Andreyev had been alone, he definitely would have done it. I learned a lot from that vision, though – it makes me feel a bit more confident that I can do it. I must speak to Robert and tell him.'

'He's out at the moment. He went to see Inspector Reynolds, but he should be back soon.'

'Why did he go to see Inspector Reynolds?'

'He saw what he thought was Markov's motor-bike and he followed the rider to a farm just outside Drumbridge.'

'Was Markov riding it?'

'Apparently not – it was someone much shorter.'

'How did Robert know what the motor-bike was like? He's never seen it.'

'Robert said that from your description, it was almost certainly a Harley-Davidson, and there aren't likely to be many of those in Drumbridge.'

They heard the front door open and close. A few seconds later, Robert came into the room. 'Any luck?' asked Mum.

'Not really. It was the bike that Markov was riding all right, but it seems I just followed the true owner. He had lent it to Markov for a large sum of money – in other words, it was an offer he couldn't refuse. Markov returned it to him the day after he kidnapped Tom and Frank. So it was a blind alley, unfortunately.' He looked at Tom with a puzzled expression. 'Tom, you look miserable. What's bothering you?'

Tom gave Robert an account of Will's death. 'The good thing was I think I learned a lot from the vision. I discovered that every time St Caithrin projects missiles, it uses up its energy. When it does that, it's a sign that it's desperate. In a way, I hope Markov does fling things at me because that will tire him. I think I'm quick enough to avoid them. As long as I can avoid Markov physically, I have a chance. I must do what Will did and keep a good distance between us.'

'Good, Tom, keep thinking positively.'

'Do the police have any idea where Markov has gone?'

'It seems not. He's always one step ahead of them. They have an awful lot of police on the case now, so obviously they're getting desperate. Inspector Reynolds is still our contact, though.'

'I don't think they'll find him. He's too smart for them.'

Although Tom was extremely upset to see Will die, he felt more positive about his own ability to deal with St Caithrin. The knowledge that projecting missiles greatly decreased its energy was an advance. But he thought about their first confrontation in the house in Manley Drive and shuddered.

Chapter 31

Markov Strikes Back

Wilmott's warehouse was guarded day and night by armed police. There were two on each entrance and six patrolling inside the building. One night, one of the police guarding an entrance heard a rustling in the bushes by the fishing lake. He shone his powerful torch on the area but could see nothing. He decided not to investigate, assuming it was just a wild animal. He and his companion settled back to their vigil. Within seconds, they were both lying unconscious on the ground. Two large stones had come hurtling through the air and had struck each of them on the head with tremendous force. They had made hardly any sound as they crumpled to the ground.

The bushes were suddenly alive with activity. Three men rushed out and headed for the entrance that the police had been guarding. One of the men deftly forced the lock on the door and they all crept into the building and hid among the shelves. A few minutes later, the same thing happened at another side entrance. Again, the two police guards were felled by flying stones. This time, one of the men in the building opened the door from the inside to let another three men in.

They all hid among the shelves apart from one man. He was tall and strongly-built but no other features were discernible because, like the other men, he was covered in a black tightly-fitting outfit including a hood with holes for his eyes and nose. He was carrying a black bag. He crept silently among the rows of shelves until one of the policemen was in his sights. He reached into the bag and pulled out a long knife. He held it gently in his hand and suddenly it flew at tremendous speed towards the unsuspecting policeman. It went through his back with hardly any resistance, in spite of the policeman's protective vest. The point of the knife was sticking out of his chest. He uttered a choking sound and fell to the ground. Another policeman came to his aid and aimed his rifle at the assailant. But he was too late. He barely had time to lift his rifle when an identical knife drove itself into his chest.

There was only one man who could do this – Markov! That explained the stones as well. He was obviously going to kill all six of the policemen. So far, the other four had not suspected that anything was wrong. Markov stalked them as they patrolled the aisles. He saw two of them walking slowly together and he crept out behind them and sent two knives flying through the air like missiles. They thudded into their backs and they fell forward, making more noise than Markov had wanted. One of the other policemen called out.

'Bill, are you all right?' Silence. There was a muttering between the two remaining policemen and they started running. One appeared at one end of the aisle and Markov killed him instantly. The other peered cautiously round the shelves at the other end of the aisle and saw the bodies of his compatriots lying in pools of blood. At once, he dodged back behind the shelves and called someone on his radio. Markov acted swiftly. He sprinted after the policeman and as soon as he turned the corner, he caught sight of him. That was enough. The knife struck him so fiercely that it threw his body across the floor. A voice was calling him on the radio. The two policemen guarding the main entrance burst into the warehouse, but standing exposed in front of the doors, they were sitting ducks for Markov, who still had four knives left. He struck with even more malice than before and the policemen were thrown against the wall by the knives.

'Quick!' shouted Markov. 'There will be others here soon.'

The other five men appeared from behind the shelves and all headed for one area at the back of the warehouse. They started lifting the floor tiles and throwing them aside. Soon, they had uncovered a large wooden panel in the floor. Two of them lifted it from each end and threw it aside to reveal a rectangular pit. Then, as though they had practised this several times, four of them reached down into the corners of the pit and drew out ropes. With the ropes, they heaved a large box out from the pit. The box was, in reality, too heavy for four normal men to lift, but Markov seemed to be generating superhuman strength in his men with his mind. They stumbled away from the pit and brought the box to rest on the floor, where another rope had been placed. Markov and the remaining man grabbed the ends of this rope and all six of them lifted the box and carried it as quickly as they could through one of the entrances into the grounds. While they were doing this, Markov was shouting some instructions into a mobile telephone. They carried the box until it was well clear of the building. There was a throbbing sound in the sky. A helicopter was approaching. Soon, it was overhead, with a wire hanging down to the ground. The men quickly fastened the ropes to the wire, jumped on to the box and the helicopter lifted them away to safety.

Police reinforcements reached the scene too late. They could hear the helicopter, but could not see it. If they could, they would have seethed. Markov and his men were gesticulating in triumph as they flew through the night air.

The helicopter flew over the countryside until the pilot saw his signal from below. He hovered over the flashing light and gently lowered his cargo. There was a lorry with two men in the back waiting to receive the box. They guided the box into place and unhitched the ropes. The helicopter lifted off again and was soon just a gentle murmur in the distance.

The men worked silently, strapping the box firmly in place and covering it with tarpaulin. Markov and his five men stayed in the back while the driver and his companion jumped in the cab. The driver started the engine and drove off slowly so that the engine would not make too much noise. They drove for about twenty miles and then turned into a farm entrance. The driver went straight into a large barn. All the men got out of the lorry and headed for the farmhouse. Two of them locked the doors of the barn and then followed the others. Inside the house, they took off their hoods. Markov's familiar features were clear now that he no longer had a beard or long hair. His hair was short, no more than stubble, and that accentuated his gaunt features. He looked around at his men with his tiny eyes. They were obviously waiting for a response from him, and they got it.

'Well done, lads, you were perfect!'

A great cheer went up and one of the men went to the fridge and handed out bottles of beer. Markov allowed himself a smile – he looked strange when he smiled. His slit-like mouth turned into a v-shape and he looked like the images of the devil that you often see in books. For the moment, he was satisfied. He had evaded all attempts by the police to capture him and he had outfoxed them once again. No wonder he treated them with contempt. He had just killed at least six of them and he had no regrets. He was a man without a conscience.

Markov had an exceptionally good brain, but for most of his life, like his father, he had used it for criminal activities. When his father died, St Caithrin moved into Markov's mind and found it very much to its liking. In most of its other hosts, St Caithrin eliminated large parts of the original mind, but in Markov's case, it kept most of it. So unlike Marmaduke Constable, Markov would probably survive if St Caithrin was driven out of him.

During the attack on the warehouse, he showed that his skill at projecting objects far surpassed that shown by Constable or Andreyev; he had obviously been working hard on the technique. Tom had watched Will evade the knives from Andreyev and he believed he could do the same. But if Markov got the opportunity to project knives at Tom, he would require lightning reflexes to evade them.

Markov's men had no thoughts tonight for whatever was in the box; they were savouring their moment of triumph. The merry-making went on late into the night. One by one, they fell asleep where they sat. Markov went off to a bedroom, dropped heavily on to the bed and fell asleep almost instantly.

Every night, Markov had the same dream. It began on a muddy battlefield. He was a young French infantry soldier fighting a British army in the early part of the nineteenth century. They had attacked the British several times, but each time the British had driven them back. There were deafening sounds of cannon and musket fire, but the young soldier was in the thick of the battle, fighting for his life, sword slashing at every red uniform that came within his reach. He had cut down nine of the enemy and had shown great bravery. He was only seventeen years old and he was determined not to die in battle. He had been brought up in a Roman Catholic family, but he had turned against Christianity. He thought that his local priest was no better than a common thief – he saw the Church take money from his family and give nothing back apart from promises, which he did not believe. His only regret was that his rejection of his religion upset his mother, and he loved her very dearly. But he wanted a lot more than the Church was offering – he wanted immortality and he would stop at nothing to get it. He knew that it was the only way anyone could shape the world to his own design. He also believed he knew how to achieve immortality and today would be the big test.

Word came to the French troops that the Prussians had come to the aid of the British. No sooner had they heard than the British Cavalry charged and started to cut the French army to pieces. The young soldier fought bravely against the horsemen, but the outcome was inevitable. He was wounded in the shoulder by a mounted swordsman, but he dragged the soldier from his horse. The two faced each other, each as determined as the other to kill their opponent. This was no time for fine swordsmanship; they lashed at each other furiously, wrestled in the mud among the horses' hooves and brought each other near to exhaustion. The British soldier managed to wrestle the Frenchman on to his back, drew a dagger and plunged it into his heart. As the young soldier lay dying, a puzzled expression appeared on the victor's face. He had a strange feeling of being transported away above the battlefield, looking at the carnage below, and then coming back down again. But he was no longer the same man. The life of the French soldier was inside him. He got up and fought with renewed vigour, but he had lost his horse and he had to fight hand-to-hand with the French soldiers. He killed two more, but another came upon him from the side and plunged his sword deep into his body. He was dying, but again the life of the Frenchman found a new host. It was drawn to the soldier with the greatest survival instinct in the vicinity – a British Cavalry officer still mounted on his horse and ruthlessly hacking his way through the French troops. Again, he paused while the strange feeling passed and then resumed his vicious attacks.

The battle was nearly won; the French were defeated, but the young French soldier lived on in the British rider. He had started on the path to immortality.

The British Cavalry officer became famous for his bravery and ruthlessness and eventually died in battle, but the life of the young French soldier passed on to one of his comrades, and so it went on. Every time the life of the French soldier entered a new host, it absorbed the original life into its own, taking on the strengths and shedding the weaknesses. And so it developed, learning more and more and getting ever stronger. But it still held on stubbornly to the original beliefs of the French soldier. At one point, the life of the French soldier occupied a man who claimed to be a magician because he had a special gift of being able to move objects with his mind. This ability improved as each new host developed it further.

This dream was the story of St Caithrin. It went through all the transfers it had made, including the confrontation of Will with Marmaduke Constable. Not all its transfers were beneficial; in some cases, it was forced to take a weak host and it gained nothing, such as its transfer from Bartholomew Green to Patrick Farrell. The dream also included the battle between Will and Andreyev. It was the only event in the dream that was not a transfer, but presumably it was a lesson to remember because Will had come so close to breaking St Caithrin and he had left it very weak. The dream ended by the death bed of Markov's father, when it passed to his young son, the present host.

When Markov awoke the next morning, he thought about Tom. He did not know that Tom was in any way associated with Will, but he suspected a link because he knew that Robert MacDonald, who was staying with the Merringtons, was researching Will's life. Markov was fascinated by Tom. Where had he learned how to probe minds and block a mind-probing attack? He was so young to have such a capability. How good was he? Markov was determined to find out, so tomorrow he would assign one of his men to trail Tom to find out more about his movements. It wouldn't be difficult; they already knew where he lived and where he went to school.

The police were devastated by the loss of their colleagues. Inspector Reynolds was told by the forensic expert that no man could project knives with the force that would be needed to produce those results, so they must have been projected by some kind of device. Of the four policemen who were hit by stones, only one survived, and he was in a coma. Inspector Reynolds remembered what Tom had told him about St Caithrin and he knew that it could only have been the work of Markov. He decided to talk to Tom and Robert that evening.

He got the response he was expecting after relating what had happened at the warehouse. 'Only Markov could have done that.'

'I knew you'd say that. I just needed confirmation. I think it's time I explained to my superiors what we are up against. Do you mind coming along to a meeting tomorrow to tell them about St Caithrin? If they don't believe us, it's on their heads if any more men get killed.'

Tom and Robert looked at each other and then Robert said: 'OK, I'll do the talking and Tom can confirm what I say if necessary.'

'Thanks. It's at ten o'clock at the station.'

Chapter 32

An Unexpected Encounter

Robert and Tom arrived just before the meeting was due to start and they had to wait about fifteen minutes before they were called in. Inspector Reynolds came out and explained that he would introduce them and then Robert could give his account of St Caithrin.

Robert began by telling the police officers who he was and what he did for a living. That was a good start because they knew then that he understood a lot about criminals. Unfortunately, when he tried to explain that Markov was the host to St Caithrin, and that St Caithrin was driving all the evil, a few of them began to get aggressive.

'We deal in facts. You can't expect us to believe that kind of twaddle.'

'I also deal in facts, and one inescapable fact is that nine of your men are dead and one is clinging to life in hospital, and they were all killed by a force that you don't understand. You have been told by your forensic expert that the knives that killed your men were projected by a power much greater than any human being could generate. I'm telling you that St Caithrin did that, just as it killed George Grimley and his father.'

The officer who had spoken suddenly looked terrified. He ignored what Robert had said, stood up and looked all around him. 'What's happening?' he said. Then he slumped down in his chair, sweating profusely.

'Sorry, that was my fault,' interrupted Tom. 'I just wanted to demonstrate the kind of control St Caithrin could have over you. I put those images in your mind.'

The officer sneered at Tom. 'That's rubbish!'

'Do you want me to do it again?'

'No, no!'

'What did you see?' asked a fellow officer.

'Never mind.'

'I'll tell you what he saw,' said Tom. 'He hates spiders and I made an army of huge spiders come in through the door and climb over the walls and ceiling.'

The humiliated officer did not deny it. He just sat silently in his chair.

'May I proceed?' asked Robert.

'Go ahead,' said the senior officer.

'I'm sorry about that, but if you shut your minds to what I'm saying, we won't get anywhere.' Robert went on in detail about St Caithrin's capability.

'Remember, if you kill Markov, St Caithrin will simply inhabit another host and you will not have solved the problem.'

'But surely, it will have to start again with the new host and that will destroy any plans it has,' one of the officers said.

'Possibly, but I doubt it. St Caithrin has developed its ability to take over a host over many transfers. I suspect that it would soon be in business again in the new host.'

'But how will his thugs know it's him?'

'They're probably dominated mentally by him, so it won't make much difference to them.'

'So how do we get rid of this St Caithrin?'

'We have to try to capture Markov alive so that Tom can release St Caithrin into a host of our choice.'

'And who might that be?'

'A computer.'

'A computer?'

'Yes, Tom's father has a computer at the University that will fit the bill perfectly. It's programmed to simulate the human brain.'

'So we have to capture Markov and take him to the University.'

'That would be ideal.'

'Is there an alternative?'

'Yes, to take him somewhere remote where St Caithrin won't be able to find another human host and release it there, but that would mean Tom being alone with Markov in a remote spot and I think that would be too risky.'

'Either way, we still have to capture Markov alive.'

'Yes.'

The senior officer spoke: 'Professor MacDonald, in circumstances where the criminal has killed already and my men believe him to be armed, I would always instruct them to kill him first rather than risk death themselves.'

Robert knew he was asking the police to take an unreasonable risk in trying to catch Markov alive. 'Yes, of course. If that's the way it turns out, then we'll have to pursue the new host. I must emphasize, though, that your job will not be finished if you kill Markov.'

'Thank you very much, Professor MacDonald. You have made the situation very clear. Does anyone else have anything to say to Professor MacDonald and Tom before they leave?' Silence. 'Then I propose that we allow them to leave and we can formulate our plans for capturing Markov.'

Robert and Tom left the building. 'I think they believed us,' said Tom.

'Well, some of them did,' replied Robert. 'I'd better take you to school. Your mum said you would get there at about 11 o'clock, but it's half-past already. Come on.' They jumped into Robert's car and he drove Tom back to school.

That evening after school, Tom decided to go into the churchyard. He knew there would be no more visions, but he still obtained comfort from sitting next to Magnus's grave. As he pushed his way through the gate, he noticed a tall stranger in a wide-brimmed hat and a long coat at the far end of the churchyard. He did not seem to be visiting any graves; he was just wandering aimlessly among them. Tom went to Magnus's grave, sat down and considered how he would cope when he had to face Markov. Every time he thought about it, his heart raced. He was nervous and not at all confident of success, but he knew that the confrontation was inevitable. He was thinking so hard about the confrontation, he even felt the presence of St Caithrin. But even as his thoughts wandered to other things, he could still feel St Caithrin. In fact, the feeling was getting stronger.

'Good evening, Tom.' Tom was startled and turned round to see the stranger in the wide-brimmed hat sit down beside him. He could not see his face properly because it was in the shadow of his hat, but he knew that mouth and he knew from the soft, gentle voice that it was Markov.

'What do you want?' said Tom in a wavering voice. He was so scared he could hardly move.

'Oh, it's just a social call. How are you?'

'I'm fine, thank you.'

'That's good. You seem to spend a lot of time sitting next to this grave. Was Magnus Robertson someone special for you?'

'He was an ancestor.'

'On your mother's side, I presume.'

'Yes.'

'He was Vicar of this church, I see. Was he a good man?'

'Yes.'

'But of course, you can't be sure of that. You only know what's in the records. Isn't that so?'

'I suppose so.' Tom wondered if Markov knew about his visions and was testing him.

'Not all churchmen are good, you know. I've met some evil ones in my time.'

'I'm sure Magnus was not like that.'

'You're probably right. Do you admire him?'

'Yes.'

'Do you think I'm his opposite, then?' He peered at Tom from under the shadow of his hat. Tom did not comment. Markov turned his head back to look straight ahead. 'How's your mind-probing ability coming on? Who taught you?'

'Nobody.'

'Really? So you just found you could do it?'

'Yes.'

'You're very good, you know. It's taken me a long time to develop that skill, so I must admit I was a little surprised to find it in someone so young. You must be about twelve, is that right?'

'Yes.'

'I could teach you a lot more, if you want.'

'I don't want.'

'Do you mean you don't want to learn more or you don't want to learn from me?'

'I don't want to learn from you.'

'I suppose you must think I'm evil.'

'Yes.'

Markov stroked his chin as if contemplating what to say next. 'Well, perhaps I am by your standards, but sometimes you have to be bad to do good.' Tom looked at him with a puzzled expression. 'Let me explain. Think of what happens during a war. Many innocent people are killed on both sides, but one side is usually regarded as good, even though they kill many people. Unfortunately, my methods are a bit like that and they make me unpopular. You see, I believe I am doing what is right for this world. I simply intend to correct many of the things that I believe are wrong.'

'How can killing policemen be right?'

'The policemen were in the way of my plans and my plans were more important than a few policemen.'

Tom was disgusted. 'What's so special about your plans?'

'I could show you if you like. We could do a lot together with our talents. You are a little young, but after a few years you could be very useful to me.'

'I don't want anything to do with you.'

'Tell me, Tom – do you know who I am?'

'Alexander Markov.'

'Yes, but do you know anything else about me?'

'You're a murderer and you're wanted by police all over the world.'

Markov was getting impatient. 'Yes, yes, but anything else?' Markov pushed his hat back to reveal his face.

Tom felt hot and sweaty. Markov was trying to get him to talk about St Caithrin. Surprisingly, Markov had not yet tried to probe his mind. 'No, I don't think so.'

Markov looked disbelievingly at Tom and then made a brief attempt at probing his mind, but drew back at once as though he had reminded himself that he had resolved not to do it on this occasion. 'Very well. Would you believe me if I told you that I am over two hundred years old?'

'No. That's impossible.'

'I agree it's impossible for a human body to last that long, but I have not been Alexander Markov for all that time. I was my father previously.' While he was saying this, he was staring intently at Tom's face. Tom's expression did not show any surprise. 'Ah, so I thought – you know more than you are admitting. I can tell from your expression. I don't need to probe your mind to get clues. Just how much do you know? Have you heard of William Protheroe?' This time, Tom was startled. Markov looked pleased. 'You have, I see. Your friend, Professor MacDonald, has been researching his life, hasn't he?'

'So, what has that got to do with you?'

'William Protheroe was a great adversary. At the time I met him, he was much better at mind control than I was. I had a great deal of respect for him, but he was misguided. It was a pity I had to kill him.'

'You didn't kill him! Your thugs killed him – he had you beaten!' Tom clapped his hand over his mouth. He wished he had not said that – his emotions had got the better of him when he thought of Will's death.

'Well, well, how could you know that much detail? It's almost as though you were there.' Tom was silent. It was Markov's turn to look puzzled. 'I suppose you don't want to tell me how you obtained that information?' Tom held his head down and kept his lips tightly closed. 'I thought not. Perhaps one day you'll tell me voluntarily, but I'll not press you on it now. I've learned enough for one session, so I'll leave you, but before I go, I want to tell you that I don't intend to harm you in any way. Remember what I said – I can teach you a lot more than you know already. We'll meet again soon.' He pulled his hat back down, stood up and walked away. Tom watched him leave the churchyard.

Tom did not know what to do next. Should he tell Robert and his parents that he had just had a conversation with Markov? What were Markov's plans? Did he really mean to correct the wrongs of the world? What could he teach him? How to live for over two hundred years? He was intrigued and confused. Was Markov really the villain the police made him out to be? Of course he was – he had killed many men. Tom knew that was wrong, but Markov's voice was so persuasive and it made him sound so unlike a villain, there were doubts in his mind. No, he could not accept that killing could be justified. Even so, part of him wanted to speak to Markov again. Perhaps for the moment it would be best not to tell anyone of his encounter. He got up and walked slowly back into his garden through the rickety gate.

'Are you all right, Tom?' asked Mum when he came in, deep in thought.

'Yes, fine.' She was not convinced.

Robert was worried about Tom's safety and that evening, after Tom had gone to bed, he made a suggestion to Jim and Julia. 'We've developed a satellite tracking system at the University to locate criminals that have been conditionally released from prison. I'd like to use it on Tom, if you agree, so that we can find out where he is if he gets kidnapped again by Markov.'

'What would it involve?' asked Jim.

'With criminals, it involves inserting a tiny device under the skin, but in Tom's case, I suggest we put it in one of his shoes.'

'I don't have any problem with that. What about you, Julia?'

'I think it's a very good idea. You would have to tag his school shoes and his trainers, though.'

'Yes, I can do that. Fine, so I'll give my colleague a call and he'll send the equipment in the post. It's essential that Tom doesn't know what we are doing, because then he can't have it in his mind and Markov will not find out, even if he succeeds in probing Tom's mind.'

Two days later, a parcel arrived for Robert. It contained the portable tracking equipment and a couple of tags. Mum had offered to clean Tom's shoes so that he would leave them out for her that evening. Robert drilled small holes in the heels of the shoes, inserted the tiny electronic devices and then sealed up the holes. Then he cleaned the shoes so that Tom would not be suspicious.

Chapter 33

The Mysterious Box

MARKOV ARRIVED BACK AT THE FARM IN the back of a chauffeur-driven luxury car. He had been giving instructions on his mobile phone for most of the journey back from his meeting with Tom. When he got out of the car he saw that his instructions were already being carried out. A large white van was waiting outside the barn with its rear doors open. A fork-lift truck had lifted the large wooden box from the back of the open lorry and was transferring it to the van. The driver lowered it gently into the back of the van, then reversed away from the van, raised the forks slightly and drove forward, gently pushing the box further into the van. Two men had been waiting inside the van and they strapped the box down securely to the floor. They jumped out and shut the doors. Markov spoke to them for a few minutes, checking that they knew exactly what they had to do. When he was satisfied, the two men climbed into the cab of the van and drove off.

Markov pondered for a while, stroking his chin as he had done during his conversation with Tom. Then he turned abruptly and walked briskly into the farmhouse. He threw down his hat and coat and switched on a computer standing on a desk in the corner of the room. Was he about to access his great plan to reform the world? Nothing of the sort – he started up a chess programme and was soon involved in a game against the computer. He was an excellent chess player and he had the program set on the highest level. He loved the game because it appealed to his military instincts. He nearly always beat the computer, but sometimes he would deliberately make a foolish move so that he could try to get out of the fix he had created for himself. It reminded him of his life – he had been in a tight corner many times but had always survived. Sometimes, he got one of his men to play against him. He knew he could beat any of them easily, but he made their moves for them through mind control, so that he was really playing himself. It was less fun than playing the computer because it was too predictable.

After about two or three hours, the telephone rang. It was the driver of the white van. He had arrived at his destination and had carried out his instructions.

'Good. Well done. I don't want any slip-ups, so double-check everything before you leave.' Markov put the phone down with a contented look on his face. The next stage of his plan was in place. All was going well.

His thoughts now turned to Tom. He was still puzzled that Tom had such a detailed knowledge of the confrontation between Andreyev and Will, and he was determined to find the reason. He had his suspicions. Were They guiding him? Had They shown him? Was Tom William Protheroe re-born? But normal lives do not recall their past existences. As far as he knew, he was the only one who could do it. Perhaps They had shown him his past life. The only reason must be to use Tom to get him back for renewal and to purge all his memories. They would not do it! He would beat them at their own game and use Tom for his own plans. Yes! He would teach Tom how to live forever and together they would achieve his aims. Soon, he would pay Tom another visit. By now, it was well into the night, and even Markov needed sleep, so he retired to dream the life of St Caithrin once again.

Inspector Reynolds regularly consulted Robert in his vain attempts to track down Markov and they were in the lounge of the Merringtons' house discussing what information they had. But the fact was that neither of them had a clue where he could be or what he was trying to do.

'Do you know what they took from the warehouse?' Robert asked.

'All we know is that it was in a large wooden box and it was very heavy from the impression it left in the ground.'

'A bomb, perhaps?'

'That's one of the possibilities.'

'Have you traced the helicopter?' Robert asked.

Reynolds looked at him sheepishly. 'You'd think it would be quite easy, wouldn't you? But we can't even find that. A witness who knows helicopters told us the type, but he was going on the sound more than anything because of course it was dark. We're checking all helicopters of that type in the country, but that's as far as we've got.'

'It's not beyond Markov to have controlled the mind of the pilot, so you could be disappointed when you track it down.'

Reynolds looked downcast. 'Just how can mere mortals like us hope to catch a criminal who can do things like that? I still can't get those knives out of my mind. I get nightmares about being pinned against a wall with a flying knife.'

'Don't despair. He's not invincible.'

'But we're dependent on a twelve-year old boy. The odds are against us.'

'Don't under-estimate Tom. I'm confident he can win through when the time comes. You just concentrate on catching Markov. Remember, he's almost been caught several times. He loves to take risks because he believes he can always find a way out. What's different this time is that he hasn't had to confront anyone who can compete with him on mind control before.' As he said that, Robert thought of Will, but he didn't want to complicate things for Reynolds. After all, it was true that Markov had not confronted Will.

'Yes, let's hope it will be different this time.'

There was a bang as the back door opened and Tom came in, chatting with Frank. Robert shouted out to them to come into the lounge.

'Hello, Inspector.'

'Hello Tom, Frank. Do you have any more information for us?'

'Sorry,' said Tom. Robert noticed that Tom did not look Reynolds in the eye when he said it and he wondered if Tom might be hiding something.

'How's the school project going?'

'We've finished,' said Frank.

'So no more need to poke around in the graveyard then,' suggested Robert.

Frank thought of an excuse quickly. 'I suppose not, but we did tell Mrs Merrington we'd help with the survey of the graves.'

'How about you, Tom? I notice you still like to sit next to Magnus's grave. Do you think you'll get any more visions?'

'I don't expect so, but it helps me think.'

'About what?'

'About how I'm going to face Markov when the time comes.'

'That's good. You should keep alert. You never know when it could be – perhaps even tomorrow.' Tom looked startled, but it was not for the reason that Robert thought. He was not afraid of Markov any more and he desperately wanted to meet him again. Perhaps it would be tomorrow.

'I'm heading for home now,' said Frank.

'Yes, of course.' Tom turned to join Frank as he went out.

After Frank had said his farewells to Inspector Reynolds and Robert, Tom said to him: 'I've got something to tell you before you go.'

'What is it?'

'You must not mention this to anyone. Promise?'

'I promise.'

'I met Markov the other day.'

'What?' Frank stared at Tom with a look of incredulity. 'How?'

'He sat next to me in the churchyard and we just chatted.'

Frank was dumbfounded. 'Just like that – you chatted with the most dangerous criminal in the world!'

'He was all right. He said he didn't want to harm me.'

'And you believed him?'

'Yes.'

'You haven't mentioned this to anyone?'

'No, not until now.'

'Don't you think you should?'

'Not yet.'

'Why not?'

'Because I want to know what he's got to say.'

'You mean you're going to meet him again?'

'Yes.'

'Tom, be careful.'

'Don't worry. I can look after myself. Look, you get off home. I'll let you know more another time, but don't you dare say a word to anyone.'

'I promised, didn't I?' Frank stumbled out of the churchyard wondering why he had agreed to keep such a secret. He thought that Tom was foolish beyond measure. Should he tell Inspector Reynolds? But what could he do anyway? He was torn between his loyalty to Tom and potentially saving him from death. Tom believed Markov when he said he wouldn't harm him. It was hard to trust Markov, but he decided to keep Tom's secret for now.

Chapter 34

The Second Meeting

FRANK AND TOM WERE WALKING BACK FROM school when they were approached by an elegantly-dressed young woman. 'Are you Tom Merrington and Frank McGinty?' She smiled at them as though she was going to tell them that they had won a prize.

'Yes, why do you ask?'

'Someone wants to meet you.'

'Oh, no,' said Frank. 'Not me as well.'

'As a matter of fact, I'm here to keep you company, Frank.' Frank looked into her hypnotic green eyes and thought perhaps it wasn't so bad after all. 'This way.' She put her hand gently on Frank's shoulder to coax him along. The three of them strode into the local park. Tom could see Markov sitting on a bench well away from the path. He signalled to Tom to join him. The woman indicated that Tom should go. She continued to walk with Frank along the path.

'Hello, Tom, please sit down. I guessed you would tell Frank about me but I'm assuming you haven't told anyone else. Am I right?'

'Right.'

'First of all, tell me why you didn't tell your parents, Professor MacDonald or the police.'

'I suppose it's because I wanted to see you again.'

'Good. That's what I had hoped. So perhaps I still have a chance to convince you that I'm not all bad. Now, I've told you I don't intend to harm you. Do you believe me?'

'I think so.'

'Well, let me make myself clear. I won't harm you provided you don't stand in my way. Do you understand?'

'Yes.'

'OK. I want to find out more about you and in exchange I can show you more about me. Is that fair?'

Tom shrugged. 'I suppose so.'

'Will you let me look into your mind? I've already promised I won't harm you, remember.'

Tom was worried. Could this be a trick? 'I'm not sure about that.'

'If you would prefer, you can look into mine first. I'll show you my history.'

'OK.' Tom reached into Markov's mind – there was no resistance. He saw the whole history of St Caithrin, from the French soldier through to Markov's father. When he had seen it all, Markov screened off his mind so that Tom could see no more.

'There. Now you know exactly what I am. I have improved my powers of transfer over many years and I could teach you how to do it. But more of that later. Will you let me see into your mind now?'

Tom lowered his defences and let Markov probe his mind. All Markov needed was a few seconds to discover what he was looking for, but he spent a little longer probing Tom's mind and found Mike's plan.

'As I thought. You are William Protheroe.'

'What do you mean?' Tom was shaken by such a bald statement.

'I mean that the life of William Protheroe has been re-born into you.'

'I don't understand.'

'Then I'll explain. As you know, I have kept my life going, transferring from body to body for over two hundred years. To do that, I have resisted the Custodians, who cleanse and recycle our lives into new bodies. We are born without knowledge or memories because the Custodians wipe them out. By doing that, they curse us into mediocrity. How can we advance at an acceptable pace when we have to re-learn everything that our parents learned? We make the same mistakes over and over again because we have to learn by our mistakes. Governments all over the world are repeating the mistakes we made centuries ago and just look at the mess we are in! But I'm digressing – let's get back to you. The Custodians put William Protheroe's life into you, but of course they could not expect you to have all of William Protheroe's assets without some help. I don't know how they helped you, but perhaps you can explain that to me.'

Tom realized there was no point in hiding it from Markov. 'They showed me visions of Will's life through his eyes.'

'Ah, so does that explain why you sat next to your ancestor's grave so frequently? Did they use that as a portal?'

'I guess so. That's where I had the visions.'

'So now I understand. They activated William Protheroe's talents in you by re-living the important parts. Very clever. And do you know the point of it all?'

'To return you to the Custodians?'

'Exactly. I've become a thorn in their side and they've sent you to get me back. Now I don't want us to have the confrontation that the Custodians have lined up for us, so it's up to me to convince you that I'm your friend, not your enemy.' He looked around, as though expecting to see policemen hiding behind trees. 'I'm afraid we can't spend any more time here. It's very exposed and I think there are people here who might recognize me. You must go now.'

'Just one more thing – who are the Custodians and how do you know about them?'

'Simple – I've been within their clutches. Several times I came very close to being recaptured but I managed to get into a host in time. I can't tell you what they are because I don't know. I called them the "Custodians" for lack of a better name, by the way. Now get going. I'll see you again soon.'

Tom walked away slowly, thinking about the time that Ben was in the fire, coming close to death. Did he see the Custodians? That gentle chanting – did that come from the Custodians? The smart young lady was bringing Frank back along the path. Tom ran across to join them. She smiled and left them to go back to Markov.

'How did you get on?' asked Frank.

'Very well, but I think it's best that I don't tell you what we talked about, not yet, anyway.'

'If you say so.'

'You look pleased with yourself.'

'Well, she was quite something, wasn't she? Brainy, too.'

Tom laughed. 'You mean you fancied her?'

Frank looked embarrassed. 'She knew a lot about cars, football, architecture, and all sorts of things. She was even interested in our school project.'

'Did she tell you her name?'

'Yes, it's Justine.'

'Sounds posh. What does she do for Markov?'

'She drives him around.'

'Bit of a mundane job for someone so clever, don't you think?'

'Oh, I expect she does other things, but she wasn't telling.'

'Perhaps she's his girl friend, or even his wife.'

Frank looked a bit upset at that remark. 'I suppose she could be.' And then he changed the subject: 'Are you seeing Markov again?'

'Yes.'

'Where?'

'Don't know. He'll find me again I suppose. I can't see how we can keep meeting in public places. He must be taking a big risk.'

'So are you. What if someone you know sees you talking to him?'

As if on cue, Amanda Smithers came up to them. 'Who was that elegant woman you were with, Frank? She's a bit old for you isn't she?'

Frank was flustered. 'Just a friend – none of your business, really.'

'Oh, come on, Frank, you can tell me. We're friends aren't we?' She entwined her arm through Frank's and looked into his face. She wasn't going to give up.

'If you must know, she drives a rich businessman around in his car and she was waiting for him to finish discussing business with a client. Just killing time, really. And get off me.'

'And why was she talking to you then?'

'We just got chatting, that's all.'

'You are a sly one, Frank. I wouldn't have thought you could chat up a beautiful woman like that.'

Frank puffed himself up. 'Then you don't know me well enough, do you Amanda?'

Tom roared with laughter. Both Amanda and Frank stared at him angrily. 'What's so funny?' said Frank.

'You – both of you.' And he collapsed with laughter again. Frank and Amanda looked at each other and decided enough was enough. They turned and walked briskly towards the gate of the park, leaving Tom helpless with laughter.

Frank didn't want anything to do with Amanda, and fortunately they went in opposite directions once they reached the gate. He said goodbye and hurried home. He was annoyed with Tom for making fun of him but he was pleased that Tom seemed happier now that he had spoken to Markov. He wondered what Markov had said to him that had put him at ease. No doubt Tom would tell him in time.

Tom had recovered from his fit of laughter and was on his way home. He was satisfied that Markov didn't intend to harm him and he was excited by what he had discovered. So he and Will were one! And now he knew what happened to us when we died. Who was the philosopher Mike had quoted? Began with a "B" – Bloch; that was him, Manfred Bloch. He was right after all.

But now Tom was in a fix. What about their grand plans to get St Caithrin into the computer so that it would be unable to get into another host? He didn't know now whether it was the right thing to do. According to Markov, he wasn't a threat to the world; quite the opposite really if he intended to correct all its problems. He was right about us having to learn everything from scratch and then when we die all our memories go with us – it is wasteful. Who are the Custodians? Are they beings like us? Perhaps they came from another planet.

As Tom arrived home, Amy was waiting for him at the gate. 'You're late. I've just seen Frank. Why didn't you come home together like you normally do?'

'Oh, I had something to do.'

Amy wasn't bothered by Tom's vague excuse. 'We've got fish and chips tonight.'

'How do you know?'

'Mum told me. She's too busy to cook so she's asked Dad to bring fish and chips in when he comes home.'

'That's all right. I like fish and chips.'

'So do I.'

They wandered into the kitchen together. Mum was busy tidying up. 'Oh, hello, Tom. You're a bit late tonight.'

'Yes, sorry, had to see someone after school.'

'We've had Inspector Reynolds round again. That's why I'm late with everything. He thought he had a lead on Markov's whereabouts and he was picking Robert's brains again. Robert's with him at the moment, but he said he'd be back in about half an hour.'

'So what information has the inspector got?'

'He didn't say exactly. You'll have to ask Robert when he gets back.'

In fact it was nearly an hour before Robert got back, a few minutes after Dad came in with the fish and chips.

'That was good timing. I thought I'd be back sooner than this, but I had to speak to some of the armed police. Tom, I think you might be needed to deal with Markov soon.'

Tom was shaken. Had Markov been spotted talking to him? 'Have they found him, then?' he asked.

'They think he's hiding in a farmhouse to the north of here. They're keeping watch on it to be certain and they'll let us know if they decide to raid the farm. But let's not talk about that now. The fish and chips are getting cold.'

But Tom wanted to know more. 'How did they find him?'

Robert had his mouth full. He gesticulated with his knife and fork and

Tom got the message. Nothing was going to come between Robert and his fish and chips. When he had cleaned his plate, he laid his knife and fork down. 'In answer to your question, Tom, apparently a farmer noticed some unusual comings and goings at a neighbouring farm, which he thought was unoccupied. He reported these to the police, so they put the farm under surveillance. They think they've seen Markov there, but they're not sure yet. They've got armed police surrounding the property.'

Just as Dad was about to ask something, the phone rang. Mum went to answer it. She was soon back. 'Tom, it's Frank.' Tom hurried out of the room.

'Frank?'

'Tom, you'll have to say this call is about homework or something. Justine just rang me and asked me to call you. She didn't want to call you directly in case it aroused suspicion. She said that they might not be able to meet you for a while because something has come up.'

'I know what it is. The police have found their hideout.'

'How do you know that?'

'Robert has just told us. He's been talking to Inspector Reynolds.'

'Oh, I see. Well, that's the message.'

'Thanks for calling.' Then a thought occurred to him. 'So you gave Justine your phone number then?' He couldn't resist a little chuckle.

'She asked for it. She's got yours too.'

'Have you got hers?'

'Don't be daft. Do you think she'd be stupid enough to give us her number?'

'No, of course not.'

'See you tomorrow.'

Tom went back into the dining room, where they were still discussing the chances of capturing Markov. Tom knew that the police had precious little chance of catching him now that he knew they had found his hideout. He just hoped that Markov wouldn't kill them all this time. He was to find out what had happened soon enough.

It was when they were all sitting in the lounge drinking coffee, or hot chocolate for Tom and Amy, when the phone rang. 'That's probably Inspector Reynolds. Shall I get it?' said Robert. He lifted the phone and it soon became clear he was indeed speaking to Inspector Reynolds. From his tone it seemed that all had not gone well. He put the phone down. 'Well, we won't be needing your services this time, Tom.'

Tom couldn't help feeling a sense of satisfaction inside, but he tried not to show it. 'What happened?'

'Markov must have got wind of their plan and he made a pre-emptive strike. He found their surveillance van and two cars and tipped them all in a ditch. His men rounded up the armed policemen and tied them up while they all got away. At least there wasn't any killing this time.'

'He's making the police look stupid,' said Dad.

'I'm afraid that's true,' said Robert.

Tom went to bed that night feeling quite good. He did not want Markov to be caught, not yet anyway, not until he knew what his plans were. He was also tempted by the thought of being taught the kinds of things that Markov could do. Did he tip their vehicles in the ditch with his mind? How difficult was it to transfer into another body? He went to sleep wondering what it must be like to be super-human.

Chapter 35

The Fishing Lake

It was a week now since Tom had last met Markov. He was getting impatient and irritable, wondering what was happening. The police had completely lost track of Markov.

He met up with Frank one morning to go to school and Frank was unusually excited. 'Guess what? My dad has found a great fishing lake that we can fish in for free.'

'Oh, yes. How did he do that?'

'He met a man in the pub last night who looks after the lake. They got talking and Dad told him he enjoyed fishing. That's when he offered to let Dad fish in his lake. He said I could use it as well and it was fine if I brought a friend.'

'Where is it?'

'You know the manor house at the top of the hill?'

'Yes.'

'Well, it's got land that stretches down to the bottom of the valley, and that's where the lake is. You can see it from the road to Walchester. It's private of course, so you need special permission to fish there. We'll probably have it to ourselves. What do you think of that?'

'Has it got any fish in it?'

'Yes, it's stocked with carp, tench, bream and all sorts. The owner of the manor house enjoys fishing and he's very wealthy.'

'How do we get in?'

'We just knock on the front door of the manor house and give our names. We're on their list of permitted fishermen.'

'Sounds good. When do you fancy trying it out?'

'This weekend?'

'Fine by me. Let's give it a go.'

Tom felt more cheerful after that news. The two of them had slowed their pace while they were discussing the fishing lake, so they were running a bit late. They jogged the rest of the way, laughing and chatting.

That evening, Tom went round to Frank's house to talk some more with his dad about the fishing lake.

'Yes, stroke of luck that was, meeting him in the pub. I've seen him in there before, but never spoken to him. He looks after the grounds in the manor and the owner has told him he can have up to ten friends or relatives to fish in the lake. Thing is, he doesn't do much fishing himself and he doesn't know many people who do, so that's why he still had enough vacancies for the three of us. He said he'd put our names on his list so that all you have to do is introduce yourselves and they'll show you how to get to the lake.'

'Are you coming this weekend, Dad?'

'I'd love to, son, but I've got a job I promised to finish by Monday, so I'll probably be working all weekend. That's the trouble with working for yourself. I'll take you up there and bring you back, though. Do you want to start early?'

'We normally go at about half-past seven. That's early enough isn't it?' asked Frank.

Mr McGinty grinned. 'So you don't want to be there at dawn then?'

Tom and Frank both screwed up their noses. 'We'll stick to seven-thirty.'

'OK. I'll be up and about before then anyway. Can you get here by seven-thirty Tom?'

'Yes, I'll be here. Thanks, Mr McGinty. I'm really looking forward to it.'

Mr McGinty smiled broadly at Tom. 'Let's hope the fishing's good then.'

On Saturday morning, Tom was up early to get ready for fishing. Mum had got up with him and had prepared him some sandwiches. He heaved his tackle on to his back and trudged up the road to Frank's house. He rang the bell. Frank answered it almost immediately.

'Just put your tackle down in the porch – we'll load it into the van in a minute. I'm nearly ready.'

Tom didn't bother to come in. Mr McGinty pushed past Tom's tackle to get at the van.

'Morning, Tom. How are you?'

'Very well, thank you, Mr McGinty.'

'Good, good, good. Looks like you've got a perfect day for fishing – overcast but no wind.' He opened the van doors and heaved Tom's tackle into the back. 'Easier to use the van – it's a bit of a struggle to get fishing tackle in the car. Hope you don't mind going in the van. It's not as comfortable as the car.'

'Not at all. I like the van.'

'That's good. Is that son of mine ready yet? Ah, here he is.' Frank was struggling through the porch with his fishing tackle. He lowered it into the van and his dad pushed it into a safe position. 'Right, jump in then.'

Tom sat in the middle because he was the smallest. They drove through the village and up the hill towards the old manor house. It had a large, open area in front of the gates with a prominent "Private - No Parking" sign on the gates. Mr McGinty turned the van round and parked in front of the gates. They all got out and went round to the back of the van to unload the tackle.

'Now remember – all you have to do is knock on the door and give your names.'

'Do you think they'll be up yet?' asked Tom.

'Yes, of course. Perhaps not the owner, but he's got staff who look after the house.'

Tom and Frank opened the heavy gates and went in, being careful to shut the gates behind them. 'Have a good time – see you tonight.'

'Bye, Dad.'

'Bye, Mr McGinty.'

The manor house did not look as big from the outside as they had expected. It was a neat house, made of red bricks with stone blocks at its corners. Tom thought it must be a long job to clean all the windows because each had eight little panes of glass. Even so, they did look sparklingly clean. The front door was big and it too had eight panels in it. It was made of dark oak and had a shiny brass knocker that looked as though it was meant to be a bear with a ring in its mouth. Frank noticed there was also a doorbell at the side of the door. He pressed it and they could hear a loud clanging from inside. Within a few seconds, they heard footsteps coming towards the door. It opened and a short man with a ruddy complexion stood in front of them. He saw their fishing tackle and spoke before either of the boys had a chance to say anything. 'Ah, so you've come for the fishing. What are your names?'

'Frank McGinty and Tom Merrington.'

'Ah, yes, which one of you is Frank?'

'Me.'

'Of course, I needn't have asked, really. You look just like your dad. Now, come round here and I'll show you how to get to the lake.'

He led them round the back of the house where they had a lovely view of the grounds down to the valley and the lake below. One field was cultivated with barley, but other than that it was a beautiful expanse of grassland with shrubs and trees. 'There – you can see the lake. You just take this path and it will lead you to the lake. When you get down there, you'll see a little hut. There's a visitors' book in there, so I'd be obliged if you could sign it for me. You'll also see a set of safety instructions pinned to the wall. It's important that you read them before you start fishing. There's also a lifebelt in there in case of emergencies. And now I know you, next time go straight down to the lake, but don't forget to sign the book. You don't need to knock on the door. I keep an eye on the lake, so I know who's down there.'

'Thank you, Mr…er…'

'Just call me Jack. Have a good time.'

'Thanks, Jack.' The boys walked briskly down the hill to the lake.

'Wow, this is a gorgeous place. But it's going to be hard work hauling our tackle back up this hill,' said Tom.

'Yes, we'll have to give ourselves plenty of time. Dad said he'd pick us up at six o'clock, but he gave me Mum's mobile phone just in case we want to leave earlier.'

'Not much chance of that – it looks great.'

'There's someone else fishing. See – over there.' Frank pointed to a lone fisherman sitting between two large trees.

'Oh, yes. Well, there's plenty of room for the three of us. He might be able to help us if he's a regular.'

The lake was larger than they expected – probably bigger than Thompson's Lake, the one they normally fished in. It was surrounded by trees of various types, but there were plenty of clear areas of bank where they could fish. At one end of the lake there were large clumps of reeds and just a few water lilies. The other fisherman was fishing close to the reeds.

They selected two spots fairly close together where they each had plenty of room. There was just the slightest breeze, causing a ripple on the water. Although there was too much cloud for the sun to show through, the weather forecast was for a dry day. As they were setting up their tackle, Frank called over to Tom. 'Look, he's caught something.'

Tom looked across the lake to the other angler and watched him as he skilfully brought in a large fish. His rod was bent right over and the water under his rod was swirling like a whirlpool. As he reeled in more line, a fin broke the surface, and then there was a large splash. The angler picked up his net and carefully dipped it under the fish and brought it safely to shore.

'I expect that was a big carp,' suggested Frank.

'Shall we go and see?'

'No, we need to get set up. We'll go and see him later.'

'OK.'

As usual, Frank was more efficient than Tom at setting up his rod. He cast in while Tom was still struggling with a knot. He was almost ready when Frank got a bite and hooked into a fish.

'I've got one already.'

'That was quick. What is it?'

'I'll tell you in a minute.'

There was a lot of splashing and then Frank called across: 'It's a small carp.'

It wasn't long before Tom caught his first fish, but by that time Frank had caught another two. They were having a great time. They were concentrating so hard they didn't notice that the other angler had left his spot and was walking round the lake towards them. Frank had just returned another fish when he heard a voice behind him. 'Hello Frank.' It was a voice he recognized. A female voice. He turned round sharply.

'Justine!'

'How are you, Frank?'

'Fine, thank you.'

'It's good to see you again.' Justine's smile made Frank flush. She was not dressed elegantly like he remembered from the time before; she was dressed in angling gear. She was the other fisherman they had been watching! Tom heard voices and came running to see what was going on. He was astonished to see Justine standing there. His mind accelerated.

'This isn't just a coincidence, is it?'

'You're right, it's not. We set it up.'

'How is Mr Markov?'

'He's well, and nearby. I'll give him a call and he'll be here in five minutes.'

'How did you set this up?'

'We did a deal with the owner of the manor, but that's all you need to know. We have this lake where we can meet without anyone being suspicious. Now, I'll take Frank over to where I'm fishing and we can talk. In the meantime I'll call Alex, Mr Markov. He'll be here soon. Come on Frank.' Frank obeyed like a dog on a lead and they went round to the other side of the lake. Sure enough, within a few minutes, Markov, dressed like an angler but without any tackle, emerged from the trees.

'Sorry it's been so long this time, Tom, but we had a bit of bother with the police.'

'Yes, I heard.'

'From Inspector Reynolds?'

'Well, he told Robert and Robert told us.'

'And Robert is Professor MacDonald I take it.'

'Yes. Inspector Reynolds uses him as a kind of consultant.'

'I thought as much. He's not completely stupid then. Shall we carry on where we left off? We don't have constraints on us this time.'

'Yes, please.'

'Now, you were asking me about the Custodians. As I said, I had come very close to them and I could sense them, but I don't know who or what they are. I sensed that there were several of them. I assume you recall the French soldier who started this off. Well, when I was him I nearly died after an accident. I left my body and I could feel them trying to draw me in, but I summoned all my strength and returned to my body. That's how I came to believe that I could avoid them, but I didn't know that I would be able to enter another body at the time. I just hoped that when I really died I would be able to do it.'

'Will I be able to do that?'

'Yes, but that's not for today. We need to do some simpler things first.'

'What about your plans? Are you going to tell me what they are?'

'Not just now. For the moment, think of me as being a bit like Robin Hood – I steal from the rich and give to the poor.'

'But I need to know that you're not as evil as you seem. And what about the chilling feeling I get when you come near – isn't that evil?'

'It's going to take me some time to convince you that I'm not evil, but of course some people would say that as I rejected the Christian church, I must be evil. Today, we are more tolerant of atheists, and I suppose you would call me an atheist. But even from the little amount I've told you about myself, I think you already know I'm not as bad as you originally thought. Isn't that so?'

'Yes, that's true.'

'As for the aura around me, I have to admit that some other men who are truly evil do have a similar aura, but it's not the evil that creates it, it's the excess energy from having more than one mind.'

'How do people get more than one mind? Do they all do what you do?'

'Not deliberately. Sometimes their minds do not develop properly and another mind from a dying person falls into the void by accident. It's usually a recipe for developing a violent personality because of the conflict it creates.'

'So do you have a violent personality?'

'In my earlier days, I did, but not any more. I have complete control over my anger because, over most of my more recent transfers, I selected my host carefully. That way, the minds combine harmoniously. Any more questions on that subject?'

'Not for now.'

'Good. Then let me show you something. Pick up a pebble and place it in the palm of your hand.' Tom did as he was told. 'Now, use the same force that you would use to probe a mind to lift that pebble off your hand.' Tom concentrated but nothing happened. 'That's OK. I didn't expect you to be able to do it without some guidance. I just wanted to check.'

'So what next?'

'I'll lift it for you through your mind and you can feel the way the energy goes. Don't resist.' Tom watched the pebble lift unsteadily from his hand and felt the way he needed to direct the energy into the pebble. He found he was able to raise and lower the pebble with some difficulty. 'I've let go. You're doing it.'

With a gasp, Tom let the pebble drop back into his palm. 'I'll try myself.' He concentrated hard on the pebble and this time it wobbled first, then lifted slightly and fell down. He tried again. It was better – it lifted higher and higher until he felt he could hold it steady in mid-air. It was tiring, so he let it drop back into his hand.

'Very good! It can be tiring at first, but you'll get better each time you do it. Let me show you what you can achieve.' He picked up another pebble and held it in his palm. 'See the hole in that tree that's leaning across the lake?'

Tom scanned the tree. 'Oh, yes, I see it.'

'Watch.' He concentrated on the pebble and it flew out of his hand into the hole in the tree with deadly accuracy. Tom looked unhappy. 'Ah, sorry, perhaps I shouldn't have done that. You are thinking about the knives, aren't you?'

'Yes.'

'Try not to think of it as a means of killing people. It's just another way of using the power of your mind. Let me show you something different. See that big boulder over there? Do you agree it's too heavy to lift?'

'Yes, you'd need a crane to lift it.'

'Then watch this.' He concentrated on the boulder and within a few seconds, it was lifting into the air. When it was about a metre in the air, it dropped with a resounding thud that shook the bank.

'That was impressive.'

'It has taken me many years of practice to achieve that. But it shows that the mind is much more powerful than the body. Do you want to try with the pebble again?'

Tom still had the pebble in his hand. He flattened his palm, concentrated hard and this time the pebble lifted smoothly into the air. He was able to move it a little from side to side and then he brought it back gently into his hand.

'There you are – I said you would get better each time. You can practise at home, when nobody is watching, of course. Be careful not to let Professor MacDonald see you doing it – he will get suspicious immediately. Now I will tell you a little of my plans and then you can carry on with your fishing.

'Perhaps I could first of all explain why you found weapons in Wilmott's warehouse. I admit we stole them, but they were destined for an overseas country that I cannot name, to support a particularly cruel extremist organization. Its members were killing thousands of people needlessly. I was going to use those weapons for a better purpose, but the police found them first, unfortunately.'

'But isn't Mr Wilmott in jail for that?'

'I'm afraid so. There was little he could do to defend himself – possessing illegal weapons is an offence. But he knew the risk he was taking.'

'And what about the helicopter raid? What did you take then?'

'Ah, that was very important. I can't tell you what it was we retrieved, but it was crucial to our plans. I can tell you that it's not a weapon of any sort.

'Tom, there's something else I want to tell you. Over the two hundred years I've been on this earth, I've changed my views on what's important in the world. I started off hating the Christian church because of my experiences in France as a boy, but now I'm indifferent to it. I even gave myself a name that was based on my hatred of the Christian church. You know it – St Caithrin. Have you ever tried to work out what it means?'

'No.'

Markov gave a wry smile. 'When you've got a bit of spare time, try to work it out – it's an anagram. I don't use that name now because it doesn't reflect my aims any more. In any case, I've given up keeping an identity for my mind because it changes every time I adopt a new host.

'Listen Tom, what I want to achieve ultimately is world unity. The world is in terrible trouble: we are still at war in many countries and there is still a lot of racial hatred in the world. We have a long way to go before we can all tolerate each other. We are also destroying our planet with our excesses and too many people in power are failing to do anything about it, hoping that it will go away. So there's a lot of fixing to be done and even in my favourable position, I can't do it without help. I need other people like you. In fact, I would like an army of us who have power over others.'

'If you want to do all that good, why do you have to commit so many crimes?'

'It's easy to understand, really. I could get into the brain of the Prime Minister, or the President of the United States, but I decided long ago that I would be wasting my time because they are bound by their laws. I can achieve a lot more by ignoring the laws and controlling people who are also willing to work outside the law all over the world. It takes too long to stop a war within the confines of the law. We stopped a war in Africa by simply killing the people who were plotting to start it. We also killed a group of militants who were high on drugs and rampaging across the country, killing innocent people. The government forces of that country weren't interested in catching them. We make a lot of money from drug-running, not from doing the drug-running ourselves, but by killing the drug traders and stealing their wealth. You see what I mean?'

'I think so. OK then, why did you kill the Grimleys?'

'The son was laundering money for drug dealers, and the old man was going to betray us because he guessed I'd killed his son. I know because I saw it in his mind.'

'What does "laundering money" mean?'

'He was putting money obtained through drug dealing into legitimate accounts. He was making it look as though he got it by selling antiques. The dealers were giving him a good interest rate.'

'Was he dealing in drugs himself?'

'Yes, but only in a relatively small way. The money came from the big guys.'

'Why didn't you just threaten him instead of killing him?'

'Because he was part of a chain and we had to eliminate the whole chain.'

'So you killed the dealers too?'

'Yes.'

'I see.' Tom was not convinced that all these killings were necessary. 'I'm sure you could have persuaded him to give up the money laundering, especially as you had killed the drug dealers. I managed to persuade him to give up his grudge against the Robertsons without even trying.'

'You may be right, Tom. I know I'm impatient, but that's because the task ahead of me is so big and I want quick results.' He looked thoughtful and rubbed his chin in his characteristic way once again. 'Tom, I've given you a lot to think about. I should leave you now and let's agree to meet here again. How about next Saturday?'

'But that's a week away.'

'Yes, but if I need to contact you before then, I'll find a way.'

'OK.'

Markov signalled to Justine to send Frank back. 'Enjoy your fishing.' He disappeared into the trees. Frank came back reluctantly.

'Well, how did you get on?' asked Frank.

'I'll show you.' He picked up a pebble and held it in front of Frank on the palm of his hand. Frank watched spellbound as the pebble rose into the air. He looked all around it to check that Tom wasn't tricking him.

'Did he teach you how to do that?'

'Yes.'

'Is he going to teach you how to kill people with flying knives then?' said Frank in disgust.

'Frank, give him a chance. I think we've misjudged him. He's not such a villain after all.'

'Then why is he the most wanted criminal in the world?'

'That's what we've been talking about and that's why I think we've misjudged him.'

'Well, you won't convince me. Take care, Tom, you could get yourself killed.'

'Perhaps it's best if we don't talk about it and get on with our fishing. Agreed?'

'Don't you want to hear how I got on with Justine?'

Tom relaxed and laughed. 'Go on then.'

'Did you know she's Markov's sister? And she can see into people's minds as well.'

'Can she? Markov didn't tell me that.'

'Yes. She says she can teach me how to speak French in a couple of sessions by putting her knowledge into my brain.'

'Is that so? That will save you a bit of time at school. So are you taking her up on her offer?'

'Of course. We've started already.'

'Be careful, Frank, you never know what she might make you do if you let her control your mind.' Tom laughed at the worried expression on Frank's face. 'Don't worry; I'm sure she won't harm you.'

Frank went back to his rod and they both settled down to enjoy their fishing for the rest of the day. Tom had taken note of what Frank said. He knew he was taking a great risk by stepping into Markov's world, but they were kindred spirits. What else could he do? He was convinced that Markov really wanted to do good, but it was just that he could not accept the way he was doing it. He thought he had almost persuaded him that killing George Grimley was a mistake, but perhaps he was kidding himself. Markov was single-minded and he knew exactly what he wanted; he wasn't going to listen to Tom's advice.

Occasionally they waved to Justine when they saw she had caught yet another fish. When they were ready to go home, Justine was still there. They went over to her to say goodbye and then struggled up the hill with their tackle. Yes, it had been a good day all round. And there was Mr McGinty waiting to take them home.

Chapter 36

The Terrorist Attack

Markov had a good reason why he wanted to leave his next meeting with Tom for a week – he had important business to attend to immediately. His team had been tracking a group of terrorists who were planning a daring attack on London. The terrorists had managed to get hold of an exceptionally powerful missile warhead, powerful enough to destroy the Houses of Parliament. And that's exactly what they were planning to do. Markov's men had infiltrated the terrorist group and had discovered that they were preparing their attack for Thursday evening of that week, when most Members of Parliament would be present in the House of Commons to debate an important bill.

Markov was pleased with progress. He knew that the leader of this particular terrorist group was in England and was supervising the attack himself. At last, he had been drawn into the open. Markov's plan was to capture him alive but kill the rest of his group. He would then probe the leader's mind to find out where the big boss of the international terrorist organization was hiding.

Markov was not concerned about stifling the attack on the Houses of Parliament; he knew he could stop it even if they got to the point of launching their missile. He had access to some of the world's top defence scientists and they had provided him with the equipment he needed to steer the missile remotely away from its target. That was what was in the mystery box. The equipment was now set up in a building close to the River Thames, in a position convenient for observing the Houses of Parliament and the river. He knew that the terrorists were planning to launch the missile from a boat. It would be easy to watch the missile's launch, lock the guidance system on to it and guide it back down to a point where his mind could take over control and bring it to a safe place where it could be de-activated. In the meantime, the four terrorists on board would have been killed by his men. It was just a matter of whether they could do it before or after the missile launch.

The remaining terrorists, including their leader, would be nearby, but they would get a surprise visit from Markov's men, who would kill all but the leader. That was the plan. If all went well, it would get hardly a mention in the newspapers, if at all. And yet it would be a major breakthrough. That's the way Markov liked it.

Robert came out to meet Tom as he arrived back from school. 'Tom, Inspector Reynolds has asked us to go to see him this evening. He thinks he's caught one of Markov's men and he wants you to probe his mind to try and find Markov.'

Tom looked startled. 'Really? How did he catch one of Markov's men?'

'I don't know. He'll probably tell us this evening.'

Tom was worried. What if he did find out where Markov was hiding? He couldn't tell Inspector Reynolds. But then he could tell him anything and he would have to believe him.

When Robert and Tom went to see Inspector Reynolds, they discovered that he was going to drive them for an hour to the police station where the suspect was being held. On the way, he gave them the background to the capture. It seemed that the Metropolitan Police had raided a house where they suspected that guns were being stored for terrorist activities. They found the guns, but the important point was that they were from the same shipment that had been found in Wilmott's warehouse.

Tom thought about what Markov had told him. The guns in Wilmott's warehouse were stolen from someone who was supplying terrorists. Inspector Reynolds's captive wasn't necessarily a member of Markov's gang.

'Inspector, did the police only arrest one man, then?'

'He was on his own in the house.'

'I see. What made the police suspect there were guns in the house?'

'Oh, I don't know. They haven't told me. We're nearly there.'

They seemed to have been driving through pre-war housing estates for ages. The houses all looked similar – semi-detached with bay windows and small front gardens. Most had shared drives with garages built in their back gardens. Some had a concrete patch instead of a front garden for parking a second car. Inspector Reynolds drove them out of a slightly more up-market estate into a main road where they negotiated a couple of roundabouts and came to a shopping area. At the end of the row of shops, Inspector Reynolds turned into the driveway of the police station. There was one parking space left.

Inspector Reynolds led them through the swing doors to the reception desk, where he announced who the three of them were. The police officer at the desk looked at Tom with suspicion and led them through to an interview room at the back of the building. 'Wait here and Detective Inspector Fellowes will be with you shortly.'

Within a few seconds, a short, burly man with a red face and a bushy moustache burst through the door. His voice seemed to operate only at high volume. 'Thanks for coming, I'm Fellowes. Ah – you must be Tom. Pleased to meet you. Now, let me explain: our captive won't give us his name and he doesn't speak much English. In fact, he prefers not to say anything. If you can find out something about him, I'll be very grateful, particularly if he can lead us to Markov. Shall I get him in?'

'Please do,' said Robert.

Fellowes poked his head out of the door and shouted to a colleague. He came back in and sat down. Moments later, a tall policeman came in, pushing a small, thin, dark man with an expressionless face in front of him. He looked like an advert for Oxfam, apart from the fact that he was handcuffed. The policeman pushed a chair behind him and sat him down. Fellowes asked him his name, but without a response.

Tom did not have much trouble probing into the captive's mind. He sensed the defiance, but it did not impede Tom's efforts. He saw a large group of men, clearly the captive's countrymen, all with guns. They were in a hot, dusty place where the buildings were mostly derelict. There were dead bodies lying all around them. Tom tried to bring the prisoner's thoughts back to England. He tried some random thoughts – supermarkets, parks, rivers. Rivers! That had provoked a response – unmistakably the River Thames. The London Eye, the Tower of London, the Houses of Parliament. Why was he watching the Houses of Parliament? Then Tom saw a huge explosion and the Houses of Parliament crumbled to rubble. This was the first time the man changed his expression – a broad grin spread across his face. Fellowes was puzzled by the man's response. He had continued with his questions, but the man was not listening to him. Tom wanted to know more, but it seemed that there was no more on that subject in the man's mind. He allowed the man's thoughts to wander back to his comrades. This time, they were in the mountains looking down on a dusty plain. He was with a large group of men who were listening intently to the ravings of a short, fat man in a soldier's uniform. He was shouting and spitting in a language that Tom had never heard before. But clearly the men were inspired by him. They shouted and chanted and shook their fists in the air. They were working themselves up to a frenzy. The expression on the prisoner's face showed that he was getting excited. Tom had seen enough to know that he wasn't one of Markov's men. He waited until Fellowes stopped his attempts at questioning the captive.

'I've finished with him. If you get rid of him, I'll tell you what I saw.'

The tall policeman took the little man away and closed the door.

'He's a terrorist and he comes from a hot, dry country. He doesn't belong to Markov's group. But there was something awful I saw in his mind – the Houses of Parliament being blown up. He didn't seem to know much about it, but I think it means there's a terrorist plot to blow up the Houses of Parliament.'

'Did you see how they were planning to do it?'

'No, I just saw the explosion.'

'Did you get any indication of which terrorist organization he belongs to?'

'No, but I saw their leader – a short, fat man in uniform. He had a black beard and big eyes set far apart. His uniform was a kind of sandy colour. His hat was a floppy sort of cap. He shouted a lot and waved his arms all over the place.'

'I'll make some enquiries,' said Inspector Fellowes. 'And I'll put out an alert to increase security round the Houses of Parliament. Thanks for your help, Tom. I'll be in touch if I find out who the terrorist leader might be.'

'Tom, is there anything else you want to try to get from the prisoner while we're here?' asked Robert. 'You might be able to find out where his colleagues might be hiding if they're involved in the attack on the Houses of Parliament.'

'I don't think he's involved. All he seemed to know was that an attack was being planned. I don't think he's an important member of the gang.'

'You're probably right, there, Tom,' interjected Fellowes. 'In my experience, they never leave an important member of their group alone in a house.'

'OK, but he still might tell us where the rest of his colleagues are,' said Robert.

'But I don't have anything to provoke his thoughts, Robert. I have no idea what his colleagues in England look like – I've only seen the ones in his home country.'

'They could be the same ones.'

'They might be, but he didn't associate England with them in his thoughts.'

'OK. Perhaps I'm grasping at straws, here.'

'It would help if I saw the house you caught him in, Inspector. I could focus his thoughts on the house and he might then think of his colleagues.'

'I can arrange that, but not today. The house is being picked over with a fine tooth comb right now. I'll keep Inspector Reynolds informed and he will be in touch with you.'

'OK, let's call it a day, then,' said Robert.

'So, are you ready to go?' said Inspector Reynolds.

'Yes, we are.'

The House of Commons' debating chamber was full. Its members were in a heated debate, unaware of the potential danger they were in and how much their safety depended on, not the police, the army or the security guards, but a notorious criminal and his gang. Markov and one of his most trusted men were at their post by the missile guidance system. A colleague had sent a radio message that the terrorists had loaded the boat and were ready to launch it. A few minutes later, the same voice announced that the boat was on its way. The terrorists were now split into two groups. They were not using radio for fear of being detected, so Markov's men could pick them off without arousing suspicion among the four in the boat.

The five remaining terrorists were in the boat-shed from where they had launched the boat. The one dim light that was illuminating the shed went out. There was a groan in the darkness and one of the terrorists fell to the ground. The others shouted to each other in a foreign language. Then there was another dull thud and the sound of a body crumpling to the ground. The remaining three terrorists panicked and ran for the door, only to be tripped in the process and battered by Markov's men. The light came on again. Amazingly, there were only three men standing triumphantly over their victims, but these were highly-trained combatants. They turned over each of the terrorists and coolly stabbed to death all but one. This one they carried out and tossed him into the back of a van. They dumped the bodies in the river. One of Markov's men called to Markov on his radio that their mission was successful.

Meanwhile, the boat was approaching the Houses of Parliament. Four of Markov's men in wet-suits were in the water ready to board the boat as soon as it stopped. The boat was now going past their hideout. Against the lights on the bank, the silhouette of the missile was clearly visible. It was pointing upwards, ready for launch. The boat was slowing down, the engine just idling. Then the revs of the engine increased slightly as it went into reverse to bring the boat to a halt. Markov's men swam towards it, barely causing a ripple in the water. But the men on board were acting swiftly. They made some adjustments to the trajectory of the missile and then moved away from it. A moment later, there was a loud whooshing noise and the missile soared upwards. The outlines of the four men re-appeared against the backdrop of the lights of the Houses of Parliament, but within seconds they had disappeared again. Markov's deadly killers had done their work.

Markov's accomplice was controlling the guidance device. It had worked perfectly. The missile was heading back to earth, but on a path that took it in multiple circles so that it descended slowly. Markov ran out to the banks of the Thames. He watched as the missile came down. When it was in his range, he locked on to it and held it steadily above the Thames. He signalled to his colleague that it was now under his control. He brought the missile slowly towards him and gently lowered it on to the bank at his feet. He knew there was no danger because the missile had been designed to explode on impact. Another signal brought his colleague out with a tool-box. He took a few screws out of the missile and withdrew the warhead. He then cut the wires that were connecting the two parts together and carried the warhead away. It was remarkably small, considering how much power it was supposed to have. Markov looked down at the beheaded missile and watched it rise once more into the air, guided only by his mind. When it was over the middle of the river, it dropped gently and slid silently into the water.

The boat had now turned around and was heading back the way it had come. As it moved slowly along the river, there were four gentle splashes. The terrorists, bar one, were now at the bottom of the Thames.

Everything had gone according to plan so far, but the big prize for Markov was in the mind of the terrorist leader. He hurried to the house where the rest of his colleagues had taken their prisoner. When he arrived, he found the terrorist leader trussed up on the floor.

'Untie him and sit him in that chair.' He knew it would be no use trying to probe his mind if he were suffering any pain or discomfort.

One of his men untied the ropes and hauled the terrorist leader into the chair. He was moderately tall, but quite thin. His arms were relatively muscular compared to the rest of his body. His face was a mass of scars. He had a big nose and dark eyes. Whether he was supposed to have a beard or not was hard to tell – he just looked as though he had not shaved for a couple of weeks. His hair was a shaggy mess, and his clothes were dirty. He kept fiddling nervously with his sleeve when Markov looked at him. Then he pulled at a part of his sleeve and put it in his mouth. Markov knew at once what he was doing and he grabbed the sleeve and pulled it out of his mouth. But it was too late – the terrorist had broken the poison capsule that was sewn into his sleeve and he would be dead in a few minutes. Markov cursed as he watched the man convulse violently on the floor. He had been thwarted from gaining his big prize.

Some people claimed to have seen a rocket being launched from a boat on the Thames that evening, but as it obviously had no consequence, they assumed it was just a firework. At least Markov's team did not get any publicity.

It was Saturday morning and time to go fishing again. Mr McGinty said he would join them later, but probably not until the afternoon. It would be tricky if Markov and Justine didn't turn up until the afternoon.

They need not have worried. When they arrived, not only was Justine fishing, but so was Markov. Tom went straight over to Markov and Frank was only too pleased to set up alongside Justine.

'Morning, Tom, had a good week?'

'Yes, thanks. Inspector Reynolds took me to meet a terrorist.'

'Did he now? What for?'

'To probe his mind and find out where his colleagues were. They thought at first he was one of your men, so they were hoping I could find you!'

Markov laughed. It was the first time Tom had seen him genuinely amused. 'And did you find out who he was?'

'Not exactly. You see, the police captured him in a house with a store of guns – the same batch of guns that were in Wilmott's warehouse. That's why they thought he was one of your men.'

'Oh, dear, they are naive.'

'Anyway, I saw that he was a member of a gang that came from a hot, dusty country. And I also saw that he knew of a plot to blow up the Houses of Parliament.'

Markov nearly jumped out of his seat. 'You saw that? Did you find out which terrorist group he belonged to?' He was clearly excited by this news.

'No, but I saw his leader.'

'What was he like?'

'Short, fat, widely-set eyes, black beard, sandy-coloured uniform.'

Markov was overjoyed and he clamped his hand on Tom's shoulder. 'Tom, you don't know how important this is! I've been searching for him for years. He's known as General Bug-Eye by those who hate him and, in my estimation, he's the most evil man on earth. He's not fighting for a cause, although he says he is – he just kills people because he's addicted to killing. He's insane. Did you get a vision of where he might be hiding?'

'All I saw was this General Bug-Eye shouting at his men and working them up to a frenzy. They were in some rocky hills overlooking a dusty, barren plain.'

'That's a start. Can you get to see this terrorist again?'

'Yes, Inspector Fellowes – he's the one in charge of the case – is going to take me to the house where they captured him so that I can get him to think about the house and perhaps see who his colleagues are.'

'That's good, but what I need you to look for is where Bug-Eye is. Any landmark will be a great help.'

'I'll do my best.'

'Good.' He looked thoughtful. 'Tom, it's only fair that I should give you some more background to this. Your vision of the bombing of the Houses of Parliament was right. They attempted it on Thursday, but we stopped them.'

'You did?'

'Yes, we knew what was going on, so we kept tabs on the terrorists. They had a remarkably potent missile warhead that would have destroyed the Houses of Parliament and a bit more. They actually launched the missile from a boat but we guided it back to earth before it could do any harm.'

'How did you do that?'

'With the equipment we retrieved from Wilmott's warehouse and a little mind control.'

'I see. And what about the terrorists?'

'Dead. All of them, unfortunately. I tried to keep their leader alive so that I could probe his mind to find out where Bug-Eye was, but he took poison before I got the chance.'

'Right. So I see why Fellowes's captive is so important.'

'At the moment, he's our only chance. Of course, it would be much better if we could have him to ourselves to give us more time to search his mind. I'll give that some thought. But let's get back to your lessons. Have you made any progress with the pebble?'

'I haven't had much time on my own, but I have improved.' Tom picked up a pebble and placed it in the palm of his hand. He concentrated and it rose up sharply above his head, delved among the branches of the trees, swung out over the lake and came back and landed at his feet.

'That's very good. Bravo!'

'I'm not very accurate yet.'

'Oh, you can't expect accuracy for some time, but try concentrating on accuracy rather than speed at this stage. Let's try something different. Before you can consider transferring to another body, you must be able to leave your own at will. I'll teach you how to do that.'

Tom looked apprehensive. 'I'll be able to get back, won't I?'

'Of course. In fact, your body will always attract you back as long as it's alive. When I say "leave your body", I don't mean that literally because you cannot fully break away from your body. It's like there is a rope binding you and you can only go to the end of the rope. I've never been able to transfer to another body while mine is still alive – the power needed to overcome both the attractive force of your own body and the resistance of the new body is far too great. I'm not saying it's impossible – I may be able to do it one day, but it seems a long way off.'

Tom remembered his visions of Will's life and the confrontation with St

Caithrin in Marmaduke Constable. 'Is that why you were grateful to Will when he got you out of Mr Constable?'

Markov gave an awkward smile. 'Yes, indeed. I didn't think I'd be grateful at the time, and that's why I fought against it, but certainly if you can get someone else to provide the energy to get you out of your body and block your return, it's easier to get into a new body. On that occasion, as it happened, I barely had any energy left to get into a new body, and I had to choose the first one that was receptive.' Again, Markov gave a smile that almost suggested embarrassment. 'Of course it was you who did that to me, Tom.'

Tom felt a little uncomfortable. He was still in awe of Markov, who was capable of so much, and yet Will had got the better of him. And he was Will re-born. 'But I'm not that good yet.'

'No, but you will be even better than that. Let's get on with the lesson. Try this: look up into the tree and picture yourself sitting on a branch in the tree. Can you do that?'

'Yes.'

'Then imagine yourself looking down from the tree to where you are now and try to transfer that thought to your other self in the tree.' Markov paused to watch Tom's expressions.

'It's not working.'

'Don't expect it to work straight away. Keep trying.'

But Tom was getting frustrated. 'It's no good. I don't feel that I'm getting anywhere. I keep losing the picture of me in the tree.'

'Don't worry. Stop trying now but give it some thought later and try again. You will find it easier if you relax as much as you can before you attempt it. Remember that Will could not do this.'

'That's true.'

'I think Frank is getting a bit agitated. He's waving frantically.'

'Oh, I think I know why that is. His dad said he would join us later, so we ought to be fishing alongside each other when he comes.'

'Yes, we don't want to arouse any suspicions. Try under that big tree over there – it's a good spot.'

'Thanks, I will. When will we meet again?'

'Let's make a date for next Saturday, but we may meet sooner.'

'OK. See you.' Tom went to join Frank and they settled down under the big tree. Markov was right – it was a good spot. It was sheltered and the fishing was excellent – they were soon catching plenty of fish. Mr McGinty came later and he too, caught plenty of fish. Markov left early but Justine carried on fishing and was still there when they left.

Chapter 37

The Captive Captured

Inspector Fellowes had arranged for Tom to visit the house where the terrorist was captured, and then to return to the police station to try to probe his mind again. As before, Inspector Reynolds took Tom and Robert in his car.

The house was a tall, three-storey Victorian terraced house. A policeman was standing in front of the heavy blue door. Inspector Reynolds showed him his identity and explained that they had arranged to meet Inspector Fellowes. The officer was expecting them, so he opened the door and told them to go into the lounge at the front of the house where Inspector Fellowes was waiting. He greeted them with his usual high volume.

'Good to see you again. Let's take a trip round the house. It seems that they didn't use this room much, so let's go through to the back.' They had to go through a small room to get to the kitchen at the back. 'They didn't do a lot of cooking; ate mostly takeaway meals from the evidence of their bin.' The kitchen was tiny and cheaply-equipped. There was dirty crockery in the sink and crumbs on the worktop, but not much other evidence of culinary activity.

'Any idea how many there were living here?' asked Robert.

'We think there were three or four, but they seemed to have regular visitors according to the neighbours. We've also got some descriptions from the neighbours. All seemed to be foreign, probably of Middle Eastern origin, like our captive. They didn't talk to the neighbours. We haven't got any records on them as far as we can tell.' He took them back into the small room. 'They probably ate in here while they watched television. Let's go upstairs.' Tom stored a vision of the small room because he imagined that they spent most of their time in there. It had painted cream walls, a single window looking out on to the back garden and rather sad-looking brown curtains. There were a small sofa and two chairs pointing towards the ancient television in the corner of the room.

He took them into a large, completely empty room. 'This is where they kept all their weapons. This room was stacked high with guns. Obviously, we've cleared it now.'

'Where did you find the captive?' asked Tom.

'In the kitchen, trying to get out by the back door. But we had that covered anyway. This room over here was a bedroom, as you can see, and over here is the bathroom. Pretty horrible, isn't it?' They looked inside. The suite was old, stained and cracked. The floor covering was filthy and lifting at the edges. The peeling paint on the walls was a nauseous green colour. There was a bare light bulb in the middle of the room.

They climbed the second flight of stairs. There were three more bedrooms on the top floor; two large ones and a small one. 'Any idea which bedroom the captive used?' asked Tom.

'The one downstairs, next to the gun store.'

'OK. I think I've got a good picture in my mind.'

'So, are you ready to go back to interview the prisoner?'

'Yes.'

'Right, let's be off then.'

Inspector Fellowes led the way out and, after exchanging a few words with Inspector Reynolds, he strode off to his car, leaving the three of them to find their way to the police station. It took about thirty minutes to get back. Inspector Fellowes was waiting for them – he obviously knew a quicker way to avoid the traffic. They went into the same interview room as before, and the tall policeman brought in the prisoner. While Inspector Fellowes asked him the same questions that he had probably asked him a hundred times before, Tom pushed images of the house into his mind. It brought results quickly – he saw two of his colleagues who looked like brothers, but taller and heavier than the captive. Just as an image of a third man appeared, the door burst open and there was a shout of 'Don't move!'

They all looked around to see two men in motor-cycle outfits and crash helmets pointing guns at them. One of them grabbed the captive by the collar and dragged him out. The other one grabbed Tom by the arm and dragged him out too. 'If you try to follow us, we'll kill the boy. Do you understand?' Fellowes nodded meekly. They disappeared as quickly as they had come.

Along the corridor to the interview room, there were other men, also dressed in leathers with crash helmets, pointing guns at the occupants of the rooms. As Tom and the prisoner were dragged past them, they followed behind until they were all out of the building. A van was waiting outside with its engine running. They all jumped into the back and were soon out of sight. Tom was terrified, but he was hoping that these were Markov's men. They had only been driving a few minutes, when they pulled into the open doorway of a large garage. Everyone got out again, tossed their helmets into the back of the van and transferred to three cars. Tom was pushed into one car with three of the men while the captive was forced into another car. Someone slammed the door of the garage shut and then the cars drove off in different directions.

The man sitting next to Tom in the back of the car spoke. 'Sorry to do this to you, Tom, but Alex wanted you to come with us, and it also helped in keeping the police off our tails. We'll release you as soon as we can.' Tom breathed a sigh of relief.

Back at the police station, there was pandemonium. Inspector Fellowes was the target for a barrage of questions from his colleagues. When he had finally regained order, Robert interrupted. 'There's no need to panic. I placed an electronic tag in Tom's shoe, so as soon as I can get back to the tracking equipment, I'll be able to tell you precisely where he is.'

Everybody visibly relaxed. Fellowes took charge again: 'Right, so if you go back with Reynolds to get your equipment, we can prepare an attack force to raid their hideout. Please call us as soon as you know the whereabouts of the boy.'

'Yes, of course. We'd better get going.' Robert and Inspector Reynolds hurried out.

'Do you think this is Markov's work?'

'I don't know. I can't imagine what they'd want with a terrorist. They certainly didn't have foreign accents, so I doubt if they are his compatriots. If it had been Tom they were after, I would have said it was definitely Markov, but they just seemed to want him as a hostage.'

When they arrived back at the house, Jim and Julia were sitting in the lounge and when Robert rushed in with a worried look on his face, they both jumped up. 'Jim, Julia, Tom's been kidnapped. A gang broke into the police station and took the terrorist. They took Tom as a hostage so that we wouldn't follow them.'

'Oh, my God!' exclaimed Julia.

'Don't worry, dear, Robert can track Tom down.'

'Yes, and that's why I'm here – I've come to get the tracking equipment.' He rushed upstairs and was soon down with the equipment. He pulled it out of its bag, connected it to his laptop computer and switched it on. After adjusting a few knobs, he turned to the computer screen. 'OK, I've got a fix on him. Come on, Inspector, let's get going. I'll call Inspector Fellowes from the car.'

'I'm going with you,' declared Jim.

Inspector Reynolds looked worried. 'I'd prefer it if you stayed here, sir. It could be dangerous.'

'Tom's my son. I'm going with you.'

Inspector Reynolds shrugged his shoulders. 'Very well, but you must stay in the car at all times.'

'Agreed.'

They set off with Jim and Robert in the back of the car with the tracking equipment. Robert called Inspector Fellowes and told them where they were headed. The Inspector told them to wait until he could get another car to follow them. They pulled into a lay-by and waited. The police car was with them in a few minutes and then they set off in earnest.

Tom's captors were still driving, because the signal was moving along a main road. After about forty minutes, it stopped moving. Robert tracked it down to a house in a large area of land. 'OK, I think they've reached their destination. We should be there in about an hour and a half.'

There were now three vehicles in the convoy – a big police van had joined on, presumably containing armed policemen.

After driving along a tree-lined driveway, Tom arrived in front of a large country house. His captors politely escorted him into the house, where Markov was waiting for them. They had arrived before the car containing the terrorist.

'Hello, Tom, sorry to drag you out here. Perhaps you could let me know what you found out about the terrorist before he gets here.'

'Sure.'

Markov led Tom to a sumptuous room and closed the door behind them. They sat down in comfortable armchairs and Markov looked into Tom's mind to see the terrorist's colleagues. 'Ah, yes. I know those two. So they're in the UK as well. That's interesting. They're all part of General Bug-Eye's army. They must be mounting a major offensive in the UK. Perhaps the attack on the Houses of Parliament was only part of it.'

'So they were in Bug-Eye's army too?'

'Yes, but old Bug-Eye is smart. He doesn't tell them everything that's going on, so one group doesn't know the mission of another group. That way, they can't give each other away if they get caught.'

'But our terrorist knew about the attack on the Houses of Parliament.'

'Yes, but I suspect he wasn't supposed to know. Even Bug-Eye can't stop his men from blabbing to each other.'

There was a knock on the door. 'Come in. Ah, our little friend is here to help us.' One of Markov's men, towering over the little terrorist, pushed him into the room. He was still handcuffed. Markov pointed to a chair and the little man sat down obediently. Markov nodded to the guard, who left the room and closed the door.

'I can see that you don't speak much English. Never mind, we can manage without that. Tom, would you like to look in too while I search his mind? Let me put the thoughts into his head though.' Tom concentrated on the terrorist's mind. Markov was leading him back to his home country and his colleagues. There was Bug-Eye, shouting and spitting as usual. Markov tried to drive the terrorist's thoughts to the surrounding countryside, looking for landmarks. On the plain at the foot of the hills there were some derelict dwellings, but what was that in the distance? It was a tall tower, but there seemed little else around it. A plane flew low, heading towards the tower. That was it! It was the control tower of an airfield! It looked like a commercial, not a military plane. But surely, the airfield wouldn't be in the middle of nowhere. In the far distance, through the haze, it was just possible to see a mass of buildings. Yes! There was the glint of the sun on the windows of a tall building. If only we knew what town it was. Somehow, Markov managed to turn the terrorist's thoughts to the town. He was driving a wreck of a Jeep along a dusty track towards the outskirts of the town. The high, glass towers that appeared to be in the centre of the town were clearly visible. As they approached them, they could see the words "Magnova Corporation" stretched across the top floor of the building. The adjacent building was the Sheraton Hotel. Tom sensed that Markov had stopped probing – he had seen enough to know where they were. Tom released his hold on the terrorist's mind and turned to Markov, who was smiling broadly.

'You know where that was?' asked Tom.

'I sure do. I must make a phone call. I'll be back in a few minutes.' He went to the door, called out for the terrorist to be collected and waited until he was safely out of the room before he went off to make his call.

The police were approaching the house. They drove slowly down the country lane and parked their vehicles as unobtrusively as possible near the entrance to the driveway. Inspector Fellowes got out and went to the van, where armed policemen were already climbing out of the back. Inspector Reynolds told Robert and Jim to stay in the car while he went to support Inspector Fellowes. One of the occupants of the van was a dog, but not what you would expect of a police dog at all. It was a honey-coloured Labrador. It waited obediently while its handler discussed tactics with the rest of his colleagues. Inspector Fellowes went back to his car and the armed police crept into the grounds of the property. They avoided walking on the gravel path and instead kept to the grass among the trees. There were ten of them including the dog handler, who was not armed. They split into three groups and made their ways to different sides of the house, all the while maintaining contact through their radios. Fortunately for the police, but not for Markov, the house was surrounded by shrubs and trees, so the police had plenty of places to hide. When they had settled down to their vantage points, the dog handler let the dog go free. It trotted up to the front door of the house and started scratching at the front door and whining. There was some movement of a curtain at the window overlooking the front door and a few seconds later, the door opened. One of Markov's men, armed with an automatic rifle, came out of the door and looked around thoroughly before stooping down to pat the dog. The dog carried on whining and pulled at the man's sleeve. The man stood up, called in to someone in the house and shut the door. The dog set off at a gentle trot, looking back to see if the man was following. He was. The dog took him among the bushes and the next moment the man was lying prostrate on the ground, bludgeoned by a police truncheon.

The dog went back to the house and did exactly the same thing, but this time the second man was obviously concerned about his partner, so he called to someone else in the house. The big man who had escorted the terrorist came out. The two of them conversed for a few minutes in the doorway while the dog continued to whine at their feet. The big man went back in and came out a minute later. He urged his partner forward with the dog while he followed a short way behind, covering with his gun. Again the dog led the man into the bushes, but the big man had him in his sights all the time. There was a dull thud and the big man crumpled in a heap on the ground. His companion heard the noise and was just about to turn round when he too received a blow on the head from a police truncheon. The police now had three of Markov's men, all unconscious, handcuffed and gagged.

Now it was time to make the assault on the house. They sent the dog to the front door once again, but this time, one of the policemen had his rifle trained on the front door and two of his companions were crouched beneath the windows. The dog scratched at the door once more. This time the door opened a tiny amount at first, and then it closed again. The dog continued to scratch and whine and eventually the door opened again and a man emerged. There was a loud bang and he fell back into the house. The two crouching policemen leapt through the doorway, followed by the rest of their companions who appeared like magic from the bushes.

Markov was back with Tom after making his phone call. They heard the bang. 'That was a gun! What's going on? Tom – get behind the armchair!' He went to a cupboard and pulled out a pistol. He held it pointing at the door while he crouched behind the other armchair. There were more shots and a lot of shouting and banging of furniture. Then there was a loud crash as the door burst open. After a few seconds, a policeman appeared in the doorway, scanning the room and waving his gun at the same time. He did not see Markov until it was too late; a single shot from Markov's pistol hit him between the eyes. But there was another policeman ready to avenge his colleague. He was lying on the ground by his colleague's feet, unseen by Markov. No sooner had Markov fired his pistol, than he received a volley of shots that tore the armchair to shreds and hit him in his chest, neck and legs. Tom saw Markov fall back and jerk as each shot hit him. He shouted out: 'No! Stop! Stop! Stop!'

The policeman did not hear Tom above the sound of his own fire, which seemed to go on forever. When it finally stopped, Tom was still shouting. He ran across to Markov, who was bleeding profusely from a multitude of gunshot wounds. Tom lifted his head from the blood-soaked carpet. Was he alive? He tried the one sure way – he looked into his mind. There was nothing there – he had gone.

Tom was in a rage. He screamed at the policeman. 'You idiot! You've ruined everything!' The policeman, shaking and sweating, looked at Tom in disbelief. What was all that about? He was just carrying out his orders.

Tom ran around the house, trying to find the aura that he knew so well. The place had been destroyed by the police. They had ripped through every room with gunfire and all Markov's men in the house were dead. So was the little terrorist. Four policemen were dead, too. Tom ran out of the house. Where had he gone? Inspector Fellowes came panting up the drive, followed by Inspector Reynolds. 'Thank God you are all right, Tom.' Tom didn't care about being all right; he just ran past them, searching aimlessly for the lost aura. 'Tom, your father's waiting for you in the car,' shouted Inspector Reynolds. 'Stop running around and come back with me.' Tom stopped, fell to his knees and hammered the ground with his fists. He had never felt so desperately unhappy. He looked at Inspector Reynolds, picked himself up and reluctantly walked back with him to his car.

Chapter 38

St Caithrin's New Host

Inspector Reynolds put a benevolent hand on Tom's shoulder and guided him through the entrance to the gardens and out into the road. Tom looked up in time to see the doors of Inspector Reynolds's car burst open. Dad and Robert came rushing towards them. As they approached, Tom felt the aura he had been searching for – and it was getting nearer. It must be Dad or Robert! But which one? Dad reached them first and he flung his arms around Tom in a grip of iron. 'Thank God you're safe!' Tom put his arms around Dad, but he knew it was not just Dad who was embracing him. Markov had never got so close to Tom that he felt like a father figure, but now Tom felt that both of them were overjoyed to see him unharmed. He looked up at Dad and saw that the two of them were in harmony for now, but it would not last long. Dad was so unlike the type of character that Markov would want to inhabit that there was bound to be conflict. Tom was happy, but annoyed. Why had Markov chosen Dad? It seemed such a stupid thing to do, but Markov was far from stupid. Perhaps he had chosen Dad because he wanted Tom's help to find a better host – yes, that would be it. When the time was right, he would find out by looking into Dad's mind.

Markov was dead, so he had to stop thinking of the mind in Dad as Markov any more – he was St Caithrin again, and in spite of what Markov had told him, he still thought of him as St Caithrin.

They went back to the car, Dad still with an arm around Tom. Robert ruffled Tom's hair. 'Good to see you safe and sound.' Robert took his equipment out of the back of the car and put it in the front. Dad and Tom sat in the back.

'What's that?' asked Tom.

'I have a confession to make, Tom. I placed an electronic tag in your shoe and this is the tracking equipment.'

'So that's how you found us.'

'Yes.' Robert saw from Tom's expression that he was not impressed. He assumed it was because Tom felt he had been deceived. But of course it was because he had not wanted them to catch Markov. He felt now that it was his fault they had been caught. He thought of the blood-spattered corpse that was once his mentor. But now his mentor was in the mind of his own father. He was struggling to come to terms with the situation.

As they drove home, sometimes Dad looked fondly at Tom and at other times he looked blankly ahead with a frown on his face. Tom decided he would take a peek into Dad's mind. There was conflict there all right, but fortunately, St Caithrin was not trying to break down Dad's mind. Then Tom got a message loud and clear: Stick to your plan! What plan did he mean? Of course, we were going to transfer St Caithrin to the computer. But that was to rid the world of St Caithrin, so why did he want us to stick to it? It didn't make sense, but Tom was sure that was what he wanted.

When they reached home, Tom jumped out of the car into Mum's arms. She had been told on the phone about what had happened and tears were rolling down her cheeks as she hugged Tom.

'Mum, we've got to phone Mike.'

Mum wiped the tears from her eyes with the back of her hand. 'Why?'

'Because St Caithrin is in Dad.'

'Oh, no!' She looked over to her husband and shuddered.

'Mum, we've got to get Dad to the lab, so Mike has got to get the computer ready.'

Mum dragged Tom into the house and dialled the lab number, which she knew by heart. 'Hello, Kala, is Mike there? It's Julia.' There was a pause. 'Hello, Mike. I've got Tom here – I'll let him explain.'

'Mike, it's Tom. Can you get the computer ready to receive St Caithrin immediately?' Mike said he could, but he wanted to know what had happened. 'St Caithrin is in Dad. We'll bring him over straight away.' Mike was dumbfounded by the news but said he would be ready for them.

Mum went outside to speak to Dad, who was still with Inspector Reynolds and Robert. Tom grabbed Robert and pulled him to one side.

'St Caithrin is in Dad. We've got to get him to the computer immediately.'

Robert looked amazed. Of course, he knew that Tom could detect St Caithrin easily, so he did not ask any questions. 'Come on, I'll drive.'

While Inspector Reynolds stood with his mouth open, Robert pushed Mum, Dad and Tom into his car and they drove off. Fortunately, Amy was at her friend's house. Robert shouted to Inspector Reynolds: 'I'll explain later.'

Dad was bemused by all this and tried to follow what was going on, but the conflict in his mind was taking its toll and he was looking distinctly agitated. When they arrived at the University, he was quite happy to go up to his lab. Robert and Tom raced ahead to check that Mike had got everything ready.

'Tom, it's all set up. How's your dad?'

'He's a bit screwed up, but he'll be OK. Now, I'll need you all to leave me alone with him – we can't risk St Caithrin getting into one of you. Can you clear the other labs in the corridor?'

'I've already thought of that. I'm going to set off the fire alarm. Kala's our fire officer, so she'll report to Security and make sure nobody comes into the lab. Can you do it with the fire alarm going?'

'Yes, it won't make any difference.'

'Good. Here they come.'

Mum came in with Dad on her arm. She sat him down on a chair. He was starting to look ill. Tom looked into his mind. It was worse than before. He knew that if Dad kept fighting St Caithrin, he would lose. Tom had to break them up before it was too late.

'OK, everyone leave us alone, please.'

Mike ushered everyone out through the door. He turned to Tom and handed him a sheet from a notepad. 'Here's my mobile number. Call us when we can come back.'

'OK.'

Mike left and in a few moments, the fire alarm went off. Tom could hear Kala shouting at people to leave their labs and go to the assembly point. There were a lot of voices in the corridor for a few minutes but then there was just the wail of the fire alarm.

Tom tried to loosen the bonds between Dad and St Caithrin, but they seemed to just snap back into place. It was going to be hard. He picked up Dad's thoughts and tried to reinforce them to drive out the thoughts of St Caithrin. It was like pushing a car up a hill – you had to somehow stop it from rolling back. But this was mental pushing, and even more exhausting. St Caithrin was not resisting, but the attractive force of Dad's body was so strong. Tom dragged out one of Dad's happiest memories: he was running down a hillside in glorious sunshine with Tom and Amy holding his hands and Mum trying to keep up. They were all laughing and shouting as they hurtled towards the stream at the bottom of the hill. Tom was fighting to build the thought up so that the happiness of the family all together filled Dad's mind. It was working and gradually St Caithrin was being pushed towards the edge of Dad's mind. When the break came, it was sudden, like bursting into the air from under the water. But Tom had to hold the thoughts for just a bit longer. The bond holding St Caithrin was still active, but St Caithrin was fading, getting more distant. Then it disappeared altogether. Tom let go. Dad rolled off his chair on to the floor and just lay there looking relieved at last. Tom was exhausted. He dropped to his knees to check that Dad was all right. Then the computer bleeped four times. Dad was breathing regularly – he looked comfortable, so Tom left him and went to the computer. Some text had appeared: "Well done, Tom. Your father is fine. Leave the rest to me."

The text disappeared and Tom noticed that it had not printed out as it should have done. But the plan had worked – St Caithrin was in the computer. He went over to see to Dad, who was getting to his feet.

He put his arms around Tom and hugged him for the second time that day. 'Thanks, Tom. That was the worst experience I've ever had in my life. I felt that I was losing control of my mind.'

'That was St Caithrin.'

Dad did not look surprised. 'I know. But why did he choose me?'

'I'm not sure, but he's in the computer now.'

'So the plan worked then.'

There were sounds in the corridor of people returning to their labs. 'I'll call Mike and tell him they can come back now.' Tom went to the phone and called the number on the paper that Mike had given him. In a few minutes, there was a sound of hurrying footsteps and Mike burst into the lab, followed closely by the others.

'You OK, Jim?'

'I am now, thanks to Tom.'

'Is it in the computer, Tom?'

'Yes.'

'How do you know?'

'It said so on the screen.'

'But why didn't it print out?'

'Perhaps he's smarter than you thought.'

Mike looked puzzled. He began clattering at the keyboard. He soon got a response, which did print out. Mike read it out to the rest of the group. This is what it said:

"Yes, you were successful in driving me into the computer brain. You are also correct in deducing that the computer does not provide the energy necessary to sustain me for long. I am losing strength and I fear that I shall have to leave this world after nearly two hundred years.

Unfortunately, you have made a big mistake. You will destroy yourselves without me. I was your only hope, but now you will have to suffer the effects of centuries of fatal errors. My work will carry on without me, but without my direction, it can only delay the inevitable by a decade or two. But do not blame yourselves. You did what you believed was right and there have been many more before you who have tried to destroy me. My great anti-hero encapsulated the situation when he said: 'Forgive them; for they know not what they do.' Adieu."

'What do you make of that?'

They were all looking guilty. 'It could be just sour grapes,' suggested Robert. 'We have no idea what he was trying to do. We do know he was a murderer, so I don't think we should brood about it.'

'Well, we've done it now. We just happened to be the ones who succeeded where others have failed. That's not something to blame ourselves for,' said Mike.

Tom was staring at the computer, feeling guilty. He understood the note from the computer perfectly well; it fitted exactly with what Markov had told him. He was not able to see into a computer brain; he had lost contact with St Caithrin for good. He could not even tell whether St Caithrin was still in the computer because, unlike a human host, the computer did not give off an aura. There was nothing more he could do; the Custodians had won. But why did St Caithrin allow this to happen? It didn't make any sense.

'Come on, Tom, let's go home.' Mum had roused Tom from his thoughts.

'OK.'

Just before they left, Robert called Inspector Reynolds to tell him what had happened. Then they went out of the lab with Mum clutching Dad as though she had redoubled her efforts to stop him being inhabited by strange minds. Robert led them back to his car and they set off for home.

Chapter 39

The Work Goes On

THE NEXT DAY, DAD, WHO WAS NONE the worse for his ordeal the day before, was reading the paper at breakfast when Tom noticed a headline on the front page: "Wanted Terrorist Killed". He was twisting his neck to see what it was about, when Dad put the paper down and caught Tom struggling to see the report.

'Here, you have it.' Dad gave him the paper.

The terrorist was the one that Markov had told him about – General Bug-Eye. His body, along with the bodies of fifty of his men, was found heaped in a cart that had been left outside a village in Northern Syria. Nobody knew who had killed them. Government forces denied any involvement, but they had been searching for the terrorist gang without success for some time. The paper hailed it as a breakthrough in the war against terrorism.

Although Tom hated the thought of all those killings, he felt a sense of achievement. It was his probing of the mind of the terrorist in London that had led to Markov's discovery of the whereabouts of Bug-Eye. He was certain that the terrorists had been killed by Markov's associates. But how successful would they be without Markov's guidance in future?

On the same page was the story of the shoot-out that led to Markov's killing. He was described as a notorious criminal wanted by police all over the world. There was no mention of the way the police had tracked them down, or of the terrorist that had been captured by Markov's men. It just stated that the police had been "…tracking Markov for some weeks and had been waiting for the opportunity to strike." Not exactly the truth, thought Tom, but the police could hardly say that he had been giving them the slip for ages and they only caught him with the help of a university professor's electronic tracking device.

Dad went to the University and Tom and Amy went to school, just like any other day. And the police went about their work satisfied that one of the most terrifying criminals of all time would not trouble them any more.

Jim arrived at work to find one of his students waiting to see him about an essay he was trying to write. He was a tall, good-looking, athletic young man and, by a long way, the best of the final year students. He was extremely intelligent, enthusiastic and dedicated. He came from a wealthy family and, by all accounts, his father was something of a genius too. The student had come across two contradictory published reports in the scientific literature that were relevant to his essay and he wanted to hear Jim's opinion of them. As Jim was explaining something to the student at length, he noticed that the student appeared to become detached; he was not listening to Jim, but instead he was looking at the ceiling. Then, suddenly, he snapped back into deep concentration. He apologized, saying he had felt a bit strange for a few seconds. Jim shrugged it off and carried on with his explanation. From then on, the student was his usual inquisitive self and went away satisfied that he could use the reports in his essay. As he left the lab, Jim wondered what it was that had made him behave so strangely. It could have been some kind of brief epileptic episode, but as far as he knew, the student had no past history of such events. Perhaps it was just one of those things that would never be explained.

Jim went over to Mike. 'How's it going?'

'Well, it's a bit like having Joshua Robertson again, but this one doesn't want to co-operate. I can't really use the computer until St Caithrin decides to vacate. I haven't been able to get any response since the sermon he gave us yesterday. I'll try just once more.'

He typed in a few commands and waited. A few lines of text appeared on the screen and the printer jumped into action. 'Would you believe it – it's responding! And it seems to be behaving normally. I guess St Caithrin must have gone.' He typed in a few more commands. 'Yes, it looks like we can get on with our work.'

'Compared to Joshua, that was a quick exit, don't you think?'

Mike looked puzzled. 'Yes, I wonder why? Joshua stayed for several days at a time. Perhaps he had more stamina.'

'Well, what matters is the episode is now well and truly closed. Whether for good or bad, St Caithrin has left this world. I'll tell Tom this evening.'

It was the lunch break at school and Tom was giving Frank a blow-by-blow account of his experience the day before. 'So you did it after all. I knew you would. You've got rid of St Caithrin for good.'

'I suppose that's true.'

'You're not happy about it, are you?'

'No.'

'Listen, Tom, I know you were getting on well with Markov, but he was a villain and a murderer. We're better off without him.'

'You're wrong! We're much worse off without him!' Tom was getting angry. 'Did you see the paper this morning? The terrorist and his gang that were killed?' He didn't wait for Frank to answer. 'Well, it was Markov's people who did that. Who would you prefer: Markov or a terrorist who kills people for fun?'

Frank was taken aback by Tom's outburst. 'But why did he kill terrorists?'

'Because he wanted to stop us killing each other. He said we were heading for self-destruction if we didn't learn to live together in peace.'

'I suppose he's right, there.'

'And he was doing something positive about it when we stopped him. Can you understand why I feel guilty?' Tom was getting red in the face.

'Well, yes, I can, but there's nothing you can do about it now. You did what you thought was right.'

'No, I didn't. I thought it was a stupid thing to get caught in the computer, but he wanted me to do it.'

'He must have had a good reason.'

'That's what I keep telling myself, but I can't see a good reason. Can you?'

'Sorry, no.' Then he thought of the fishing lake and Justine. 'I wonder if Justine is still around? She would know.'

'There's no reason why she should hang around when the rest of them are dead.'

'Did the police kill all of them?'

'All that were in the house. And they made sure – they were so full of bullet holes their flesh was hanging in tatters. It was disgusting.'

Frank grimaced. He felt that he could have lived without that particularly unpleasant detail. 'Tom, you've been through a terrible ordeal. Why don't we go fishing this weekend? There's a chance that Justine will be there.'

'Not much of a chance but, yes, I'd like to go to that lake again. It won't be the same as before, but at least the fishing was good.'

'OK. That's settled then.' Then, as Frank often did, he changed the subject again. 'By the way, did you ever find out what St Caithrin meant?'

'Oh, yes, but no. It's an anagram and I haven't worked it out yet.'

'An anagram?' He pulled out a piece of paper from his pocket and tore it up into little pieces. Then he wrote all the letters of "St Caithrin" on the pieces of paper. He spread them out on the ground and started to try different combinations. One of the pieces blew away in the wind. He grabbed it, just as the bell went for the end of break. 'I'll let you know if I work it out.' He stuffed the pieces of paper into his pocket.

Tom and Frank went to different lessons: Tom had geography and Frank had French. When Frank arrived in the class, the teacher was not there, so he got out his pieces of paper and spread them on his desk. The teacher came in. 'Got it!' he whispered to himself. He wrote the answer on a piece of paper.

At the end of the lesson, both Frank and Tom had to change classrooms. Frank searched in the crowd for Tom. He caught a glimpse of his blond head as he went into a classroom. He followed him in and thrust the piece of paper into Tom's hand. Tom sat down and unfolded the scrap of paper. Frank had solved it. It fitted with what Markov had said. It was "Antichrist".

On Saturday, they went to the fishing lake and Tom settled in the place where Markov had taught him how to project pebbles. There was no sign of Justine. The fishing was good, but Tom also practised his pebble projection and tried to do what Markov had attempted to teach him in his last lesson – to project himself out of his body. Markov had told him to just keep trying and, above all, relax. He could now picture himself sitting on that branch, but getting his mind to switch was too difficult; it was completely different from projecting into a real mind. He decided to try again later. But he was getting good at projecting pebbles. He could now do it without putting the pebbles in his palm. He could lift them straight from the ground, and he could manage stones as big as his fist. But the huge boulder that Markov had lifted still seemed almost an impossibility.

Frank was fishing close by. Tom decided to have a bit of fun, so he waited until Frank had hooked a good fish and then he concentrated on Frank's landing net. Frank brought the fish close to the bank and Tom lifted his net up and tapped him on the arm with it. Frank looked down, amazed, but knew at once what was going on. He looked at Tom and laughed, then grabbed the net to bring in the fish.

'That was good – you can do that for me next time.'

'Sorry, I've got my own fish to catch. That was a special treat.'

'You've improved a lot.'

'Thanks.'

Feeling encouraged by his accuracy and control, Tom tried once more to transfer his mind into the tree, but still it did not work. He felt the tenseness in his muscles, so he tried to relax. That was better, now he could try again. This time, he got a different feeling, as though he was moving towards the branch. He was definitely getting closer. He relaxed again and tried to recapture that feeling, and this time he was determined to maintain it. He felt himself moving slowly out of his body. His image in the tree was getting closer until it enveloped him. He was looking down at himself! But what was that on the tree? He lost control and found himself back on the bank. He worked his way around the tree to see what was in its branches. It was an envelope pinned on the bark. 'Frank, can you reach this? I'm not tall enough.'

'Got your line stuck in the tree?'

'No it looks like a letter – up there, see?'

'Oh yes. Move back; I think I can reach it.' He stretched to his full height and just got his fingertips to it, but he couldn't get a hold on it. He adjusted the positions of his feet slightly and tried again. He managed to grip the letter between his index and second fingers. It ripped against the nail and came away. He looked at the writing on the envelope. 'It's addressed to us.' On the envelope, in large, neat letters, were the words: "Tom or Frank".

'Open it then.'

'It's from Justine. She says she's sorry she can't go fishing with us any more. She's gone abroad.'

'To where?'

'She doesn't say.'

'Oh, well; it's what we expected anyway. We didn't think she'd be here, but at least we know now for certain.'

Tom thought about the last time they were there, when Markov had emerged from the trees. He decided to see where he might have been hiding.

'Where are you going?' asked Frank.

'Just exploring.'

'I'm coming too.' He followed Tom into the wood.

The wood was only a narrow stretch of trees that opened out on to a field. Close by was an old farmhouse and near that was a ruin of an old church. 'I wonder if Markov was hiding in that house? It looks deserted.'

They walked through the long grass to the house which did indeed seem to be deserted. They went behind the house to where the old church was. Most of the roof had fallen in and there was a pile of rubble in the middle of the church. They decided not to go into the church because it looked positively dangerous. Then Frank noticed something and prodded Tom. 'Look – there are some graves over there.' They worked their way through the brambles and weeds. Indeed, there was an old graveyard, although most of the headstones had fallen over.

They pulled at the undergrowth and tried to read some of the inscriptions. Frank saw a large headstone that was lying at an angle and went over to investigate. He pulled away a layer of weeds and saw at once the name

"Robertson". He shouted to Tom to come across.

'What have you found?'

'I think it's Joshua Robertson's grave.' Tom fought his way across the graveyard. 'Yes, it is.'

'Are Ben and Arthur on it?' He helped Frank to pull away more of the weeds. They revealed more inscriptions, but they were covered in moss. Even so, they could just make out the name "Benjamin". Near the bottom was probably the inscription for Arthur, but they could not make it out.

'Well, that was a good find. I'm sure your mum will be pleased.'

'She certainly will. We'll have to look this up on the map to find out what church it is.'

'It looks as though it's been derelict for a long time.'

'Perhaps we ought to come back another time to clean up the headstone and write down the inscription.'

'Good idea. Let's get back to our rods.' They struggled back through the undergrowth and then made their way through the woods and back to their rods. For the rest of the afternoon, they concentrated on the fishing.

The day had gone well. They had enjoyed the fishing; Tom had improved his skills that he had learned from Markov; they had found the grave; and they had the letter from Justine. They went home that evening feeling satisfied.

Chapter 40

A New Beginning

It was time for Robert to return to Rothbank. He had stayed far longer than he had intended, but it had been a remarkable few weeks for him. He had packed his car and Dad, Mum, Tom and Amy were there to see him off.

Robert put his arm around Tom. 'Well done, Tom. You did everything we asked of you and you succeeded. It's been an experience I'll never forget, that's for sure. And if you decide you want to study medicine when you finish school, I'll make sure there's a place at the Medical School for you. You should follow in Will's footsteps and become a psychiatrist, you know.'

'I'd like that. Thanks, Robert. And thanks for having confidence in me. I don't think I could have done it without all the help you gave me.'

Robert smiled at Tom and then addressed the family: 'Come up and see us any time you like. You've got our phone number. You know you are always welcome. Bring Amy next time – she'll get on well with my lot.'

Mum kissed Robert on the cheek and Dad shook his hand. Robert gave Amy a hug, then got into his car and opened the window. There were waves all round as he drove out of their drive and off on the long journey back to Rothbank.

They walked back slowly into the house. Dad put his hand on Tom's shoulder. 'Tom, I have a student who is particularly interested in mind control. He asked me if I thought mind control was possible and, of course, I could hardly say it wasn't. I told him that you had some experience of the subject, so he asked if he could meet you. You don't mind, do you?'

'No, of course not.'

'Good, then I'll ask him round one evening. He's our best student and I want to encourage him as much as I can.'

Tom was pleased that Dad was happy to let him help one of his students. Whether he could was another matter. 'Do you know why he's interested in mind control, Dad?'

'Yes. He believes that one day we'll be able to communicate with computers at an intellectual level and he thinks that developing mind control will be a prelude to that.'

'Well, I can say for certain that I have no idea how to look into your computer with my mind. It's completely different from the human brain.'

'Then perhaps we ought to try to develop better computers – that's exactly the sort of thing he's interested in. Perhaps people who can look into the minds of others will be able to help us develop computer brains that we can communicate with more easily.'

'Perhaps.'

'He's keen to talk to you, so I'll invite him over some time in the next few days, if that's OK.'

'Fine by me.'

It was actually the following evening when the student came round for dinner. He arrived in his own car – a Ferrari! From the lounge window they watched spellbound as the red monster rolled into the drive.

'Dad, you didn't tell me he was stinking rich!'

'Well, I knew that his parents were rather wealthy. I didn't know he had one of those, though.'

The student rang the doorbell and Dad went to answer it. The student stood framed in the doorway: tall, broad-shouldered and dressed in a casual beige suit and red, open-necked shirt. Dad welcomed him and brought him into the lounge. The student looked as though he had just stepped out of a film set. He was brimming with confidence, handsome and elegant. His presence seemed to fill the room. Mum looked visibly nervous and wasn't sure whether she should shake his hand or curtsey, but Tom could hardly believe what was happening; he was excited beyond measure. The looks meant nothing; it was the aura. He was back.

The student smiled at Tom and nodded to him. Jim noticed and was a little surprised that they seemed to know each other already. Tom could not stop a huge grin from spreading across his face. He wanted to go and hug the student.

'This is Victor Mendleson, everyone. My wife, Julia, my son Tom and my daughter Amy.' Everyone shook hands with Victor. 'Please, take a seat.'

'Actually, Jim, if it's OK by you, I'd prefer to walk round the garden with Tom so that we can use the time for our discussions.'

'Yes, of course.'

'Dinner will be in half an hour,' said Julia. 'Would you like a drink to take into the garden?'

'Yes, please, Mrs Merrington. A glass of mineral water will be fine.'

'And you, Tom?'

'Same for me, please, Mum.'

'Thanks. We'll be back in time.'

The pair strolled out into the garden like old friends, which of course they were.

'So, Tom. Surprised to see me back?'

'Very. I thought you were gone for good.'

'That's what I wanted you to think. I wanted you all to believe that you had got rid of me for good. Perhaps the message I sent out was a bit over the top, but I was planning my return. I wanted you all to think better of me the next time around.'

'I don't know that the others really understood the message, but I think they all felt guilty. So how did you get out of the computer?'

'Oh, that was never going to be a problem. You see, the computer doesn't create the bond that a human body does. That's where the Custodians made a fatal error – they assumed I would need more energy than I had available to get out of the computer.'

'The Custodians planned all this?'

'Oh, yes. Why do you think they placed "Joshua Robertson" in the computer? They made it enticing with the experiments that he did so that someone with intelligence would delve into the phenomenon deeply enough and work out a plan just as Mike did. They must have thought they had a killing combination when your father and his team developed the computer brain and they had you to chase me out of my host. They had shown with their experiments with "Joshua" that a mind cannot last long in the computer brain, so I had to get out of it while I had enough energy left. Fortunately, Victor came to see Jim on the second day and I took my opportunity. I thought I would have to seek him out, so that was a stroke of good fortune. Victor's mind is brilliant and I've retained nearly all of it.'

'So you had decided to take Victor as a host already?'

'Oh yes, but there was more to it than just picking a brilliant student with a mind that would suit me. I took a lot of notice of what you said about all the killings and crimes.'

'You did?' Tom was amazed.

'Yes. When I think how I started off – all the hatred and the need for revenge, I wonder now why I made myself like that. But I suppose when you have two hundred years' experience in the world, you are bound to change your ideas. I've picked up a lot from the hosts I've had over that time, but I've also taken a lot of notice of how you responded to Alexander Markov. Markov was a wanted criminal but Victor Mendleson is an honest citizen and I'm going to do my best to keep it that way for as long as I can. If I can achieve my aims without the police chasing me at every opportunity, I'll be much better off.'

'So you're not going to commit any more crimes?'

'Well, it may not be as simple as that, but I'm certainly going to avoid getting into the position that Markov found himself in. He became a criminal early in his life and he had little regard for the law. I'm going to try to avoid getting associated with any criminal activity.'

'That sounds a bit ambiguous.'

'Deliberately so. I explained to you how difficult it is to achieve what we do without stepping outside the law. And, of course, I don't know what's ahead. What I do know, though, is that I'm going to leave my associates to carry on without much help from me until I finish my degree; then I'm going to America. Justine is already out there and I'm going to join her. We have a lot of business in America.'

'Yes, she left us a note to say that she had gone abroad but she didn't say where.'

'Good. I'm glad she didn't leave you without saying goodbye.'

'So I won't see you, then?'

'Not for a while, but I'll be back and you can be sure I'll seek you out. We have a lot of work to do together when you are old enough and I'm sure you'll find Victor Mendleson more to your liking as a partner than Alexander Markov.'

'I'm sure I will.'

'It's a much better body, isn't it? Better-looking don't you think?'

'That wasn't hard. Markov was ugly.'

Victor laughed heartily. 'Do you think Justine will be surprised when she sees her new brother?'

'You mean she doesn't know yet?'

'Well, I've told her I've got a new host, but she hasn't a clue what I look like.'

'Then she's going to have an almighty shock.'

'I expect so. Come on, Tom, time we went in for dinner.'